DAYBREAK

BY AJ NAVAB

This book is a work of fiction. Names, characters, places and incidents either are the product of the author's imagination or are used fictitiously, and any resemblance to actual persons, living or dead, events, or locales is entirely coincidental.

Printed in the United States of America
Print ISBN: 978-1-951490-67-6
eBook ISBN: 978-1-951490-68-3

Library of Congress Control Number: 2020919183

Publisher Information:
DartFrog Books
4697 Main Street
Manchester, VT 05255

www.DartFrogBooks.com

To my dad,
who believes in me and supports my dreams as if they were his own.

To my mom,
who introduced me to the world of magic through
Disney, Hogwarts, and Middle Earth.

To Ms. Georgina (my high school biology teacher):
thank you for letting me write my novel in
your class instead of taking notes.

To Ibrahim, my late grandfather:
you were an amazing grandfather, a better human
being, and you will always remain my inspiration.
Cheers to you in heaven, Grandpa!

And last, but never least,
to my two dear childhood friends who shared my world of magic
and encouraged me to publish it for everyone else to enjoy.

CONTENTS

PROLOGUE

They appear without a word or warning, without being seen or heard, and without a single soul knowing. When someone finally does notice the unnatural happenings that hint at their presence, the damage would have already been done. Ordinary people, those that fear the things they cannot understand, called them *demons*.

But don't misunderstand. They weren't the unrealistic, ridiculous sort of monsters that rose from hell in so many myths and horror movies. No, these were just different creatures, those not found in a typical science book. People who did understand them called them Rev'ers. Some were animalistic, others ghostly, and then there were some—the most dangerous of them all, in fact— that couldn't be told apart from humans.

And it was on a night like this, when the full moon shone at its brightest, when the most dangerous one of them all, raced through a pitch black forest, leading a group of men into a trap that they never saw coming.

"Don't lose sight of him!"

"Bring him back at all costs!"

"Keep your eyes open! He's a tough one!"

Warnings and commands rang out as the assassins ran to catch up with their quarry. They moved with the sort of stealth that took years to master. In the otherwise silent forest, their footsteps echoed like those of stampedes crushing wild grass under their feet. In the lack of light, the green trees stood black. Their chase came to a halt when the target suddenly disappeared from view. And in a dense forest like this, there were a hundred places to hide; their eyes were not like *his*, able to take in everything almost at once.

"He's gone," one of them finally said.

They had to remain calm and show no signs of weakness; he could sense it, would smell their fear a mile away.

"Weapons," the commander said in a hushed tone. The echoes of swords being removed from their sheaths rang around them. They listened silently for *his* movements.

"There!" One of them spotted *him* quickly moving between the eerie shadows of the forest. With raised swords they chased their enemy, and the darkness deepened as the clouds shifted to hide the moon, dimming their only source of light. They didn't know that they had walked into the trap of a deadly beast.

One by one, the men were taken. *He* effortlessly pulled them into the pitch black abyss, never to be seen again. The sounds of their shrill, pained cries frightened the remaining assassins. They cowered as if they were the prey. They gave in to their fear, lost the will to fight back, and soon almost all of them had vanished. Only the commander was left standing.

He stood still and eyed every corner of the surrounding wilderness as he listened to its nighttime sounds: the distant howl of wild animals, the slight whistling of the wind, the chirping of a thousand crickets. The fallen leaves crunched as a figure dropped from the branches above and landed on the ground, just a few feet away.

The commander spun around. "I see you haven't forgotten your ways."

Two silver blades shone in the darkness. In a matter of seconds, the Rev'er had crossed the space between them.

But the commander's reflexes were quick. He raised his sword just in time to block the Rev'er's first swing. Sword clashed against sword repeatedly as both avoided each other's attacks and struck back without pause. It was a game of death, and neither wanted to be the one to wind up dead.

Finally, the commander's blade sliced through his enemy's skin and the Rev'er disappeared into the darkness again. Thinking that he had inflicted a mortal wound, the commander let his guard down. All it took was that single moment of overconfidence and he found himself pinned to a tree with the Rev'er's hand on his throat and a sword in his gut.

He gritted his teeth against the pain and looked into his killer's familiar face. "Bezaleel," the commander whispered *his* name. "This isn't...over. The clan...will...find you." Blood stained his lips and dripped down his chin.

The Rev'er, who possessed all the features of a human save for his wings and the color of his eyes and hair, leaned in to hiss back, "If they value their lives, they will not."

Before his life could leave him, the commander took one last look at Bezaleel. He mercilessly stared back. The clouds parted and the moonlight fell on Bezaleel to reveal his shining, snow-white hair and a face that was partially covered by the black mask pulled up to the bridge of his nose. His eyes showed no hint of regret, but plenty of anger as they stared back at the commander's dying ones: a pair of eyes with the same gradient red and orange colors of daybreak.

CHAPTER ONE

MAFUYU

Mafuyu examined the sleeping girl. Her cheeks were flushed red, and sweat stuck to her forehead; a few beads had gathered at the bridge of her nose. Her lips parted for air and she breathed heavily.

He touched her forehead with the back of his palm. No temperature. In fact, her skin was cold to the touch. This was not some ordinary fever. Nevertheless, he turned toward her parents to make sure of the situation before drawing any conclusions of his own.

"Have you taken her to the doctor?" Mafuyu asked.

The mother exchanged worried glances with her husband, who looked equally troubled. "We took her to several doctors. None of them could figure out what was wrong."

"That was when we thought maybe we should call for your kind of professional," the father added.

"Have you noticed anything else lately? Something out of the ordinary perhaps?" Mafuyu questioned softly, trying not to sound too brusque.

Her mother moved closer to the futon her daughter slept on. She took off the blankets covering her sick child and gently turned her on her side. There was a dark bruise on the juncture between her shoulder and neck.

"She came home with this about three weeks back. It was very tiny then, and we thought she got it from playing in the field so we didn't bother looking more closely. Later, when her health started getting worse, this thing also started to get bigger." Her mother's voice trembled, likely stricken by the unfamiliar and frightening situation.

Mafuyu bent forward to get a better look. The ugly bruise had an irregular shape that couldn't have been made by a human hand, neither was it an animal's scratch. He wondered if it was even a bruise at all, or something else entirely.

As if in answer to his internal questions, the bluish-purple mark pulsated and, right in front of their eyes, grew in length like it was alive, inching its way to rest just under the girl's chin.

Her parents let out shocked gasps while Mafuyu simply pressed his lips together. This definitely wasn't an illness. "We need to hurry, before your daughter gets worse." Mafuyu rose from the floor and straightened his clothes. "Please show me where in the field she went the day she returned with this."

The girl's parents nodded, still shell-shocked by the odd development in their daughter's condition. After draping the blanket back on their daughter, they led Mafuyu to the back door. Their backyard consisted of a huge garden—or, what was left of it. All the leaves were a toxic, dark green and most of the vegetables had gone dry or appeared ruined from the roots.

"Was your garden always in this condition?" he asked as he raked his eyes across the small field surrounding them.

The father shook his head. "No. A couple days before our daughter got sick, all the plants started dying. The ones we tried to replant also got sick with some kind of fungus or virus." He paused before continuing in a subdued tone. "We are farmers. This is our main source of income. If our plants keep dying like this...."

"I understand," Mafuyu sympathized. "Please return back to your house and stay indoors until I come back."

"Is this really a demon?" The father was clearly struck with fear, his eyes wide and his frame tense with it.

"You could call it that if you like, though they aren't exactly demons." Mafuyu tried to calm them down, but he could tell his explanation wasn't having the desired effect. "The creature that's doing this, that made the mark on your daughter, is more beast than spirit."

"Are we in danger?"

"I'll know more once I have a look around. But if you are, it won't stay that way any longer." Mafuyu pulled out a gun from the holster secured around his waist. "Please wait inside."

The parents didn't need to be told a third time. They hurried back into the house while Mafuyu kept watch—just in case.

"Now then, let's see what we are dealing with, shall we?" he muttered as he clicked the safety off of his gun and inched further into the wilderness.

The two acres of land were dark despite it being midday. The rows of trees lining one after the other blocked out all sunlight. If there were any monsters around, they would definitely hide out here.

After four years of finding himself in countless situations similar to this one, hunting Rev'ers had become second nature to him. His job, his life, was anything but normal. People like him were different. They weren't the sort that everyone else would categorize as normal. He hunted down monsters that everybody else feared, beings that ordinary people could not see and were not even aware existed. But for as long as he could remember, Mafuyu saw them. He'd always thought that was common in this world until he found out, in the worst way possible, that that wasn't the case at all.

When Mafuyu was in primary school he would often claim to see things other people couldn't. As a result, everyone around him would either be wary of or ridicule him. Kids his age would bully him for constantly lying or playing make-believe. Their parents made sure he was excluded, be it at school or from things going on in their neighborhood. They all thought that he was strange and wanted nothing to do with him. Their ruthless gazes would follow him, and their unkind whispers would assault his ears wherever he went.

His own parents started seeing him as an obligation and less as their son. It wasn't like he didn't understand their reaction. Any parent would think it strange when their child constantly said that he saw little unusual creatures running around, or a girl ghost crying in the park, or snarling beasts roaming around in the shadows.

But not once did they ever try to understand him, never asked him to explain or to show them where the monsters hid. And as Mafuyu got older, his parents got angrier—to the point that they called him a liar. A fake. A child that they regretted having. A shame to their family.

So, at the tender age of nine, he did the only thing his broken and outraged heart could think of. He left home on a cold winter's night and walked for miles, until his little feet could no longer hold him up. With no place to go and no one to turn to, he sat in the corner of an old rundown shop in Kyoto.

As hours passed, the falling snow had piled on his shoulders, hair and lap, until he was half covered in it. He would have probably frozen to death that night if a kind young man hadn't seen a small figure shivering in the cold and stopped to help. He asked little Mafuyu if he was lost, but all Mafuyu could register was a three-tailed fox whizzing past them. Given his past experiences, Mafuyu expected the young man to stare, to call him strange and walk away. But his eyes were also fixed on the three-tailed fox running in the direction of the closest village. The young man had turned to him and smiled. It was so sincere that Mafuyu thought it as beautiful as the cherry blossoms blooming in spring, and for a minute it warmed his heart.

The man's long fingers then brushed the snow off Mafuyu's hair and shoulders as he said, "So you see them, too. Do you want to learn more about them?"

That night, Mafuyu witnessed a group of people just like him banish a monster—which he then learned was called a Rev'er, just like the beings he'd been seeing for years—to rescue others. They were trained fighters, with weapons that moved in ways that made Mafuyu's heart beat faster. It changed his life forever and placed him on the path to becoming who he was meant to be: the man who could swing a weapon in the midst of dense trees while hunting unworldly beasts, risking his life without a second thought. Not a profession that everyone would consider, but Mafuyu never regretted it. It was his way of using his abilities to the fullest, even though part of him still resented people for their close-minded tendencies and shunning people for being a little different. He probably always would.

"Where are you hiding?" Mafuyu mumbled. The eerie silence was broken when a low growl rumbled behind him. He stopped in his tracks and slowly swiveled around. He made a face. "You're as ugly as your reputation."

The beast that stood before him couldn't be explained by science. A yellow, toadlike face with huge bulging eyes towered at least ten feet above the ground. Its dark green legs were about as thick and muscular as a rhino's. It growled again and Mafuyu got a glimpse of its sharp teeth.

This kind of beast was called a Third-Level in Mafuyu's circles. They were nasty creatures, but they possessed almost no intelligence. Third-Levels could get aggressive if provoked, but otherwise they were easy to banish.

Saliva oozed out from the monsters mouth, a sort of sticky serum that burned the grass below. Mafuyu cocked his head to the side. That explained all the dead plants.

"Okay, I promise this won't hurt, so stay still for me." Mafuyu pointed the gun at the Rev'er. The bullets were specially made with inscriptions to banish supernatural beings from this world.

Mafuyu pulled the trigger, and that should have been the end of it. This was, after all, a lower level beast; they were the easiest to banish. But as the shot echoed through the forest, the Rev'er did the unthinkable—it ducked its head. The bullet whizzed past it and pierced a thick tree branch instead.

Mafuyu only had time to widen his eyes before the Rev'er jumped into the air and flung itself at him. Mafuyu's reflexes were quicker; he immediately dropped to the ground, tucking and rolling out of its way. The ugly Third-Level crashed down, right where Mafuyu had been standing. Its thunderous impact created cracks in the ground and sent dust flying everywhere.

Mafuyu grimaced. His gun had slipped from his hand while he got himself out of the way, and now it lay at the monster's feet.

But the Rev'er wasn't through surprising Mafuyu. With an awareness that Third-Levels didn't usually display, it looked at the gun, raised its leg, and stomped down on it. There was a hideous cracking noise and Mafuyu knew that the bullets inside had been smashed to smithereens.

He couldn't believe his eyes. A Third-Level Rev'er understood that the gun was intended to harm it and had crushed it. He clicked his tongue in irritation. This wasn't how Third-Levels usually were. They weren't so tough or predatory, hence why they were the easiest to take down under normal circumstances.

Puzzling as it was, Mafuyu didn't have much time to think before the Third-Level whipped out its tongue to lash at him. He ducked as the tongue flicked at him again and again, doing his best to dodge and jump out of its way so that its venom didn't touch and burn him as badly as it had the family's crops. Mafuyu only had time to stand up as the Rev'er grew tired of the chase after a few tries and decided to charge at him instead.

"So persistent." Mafuyu whispered to himself.

As the Third-Level got closer, Mafuyu reached back and drew out a bo staff he'd strapped onto his back. . He spun it between his fingers, getting a decent grip before holding it in his palms. He widened his stance, legs firm on the ground as the monster lurched at him. Mafuyu took the opportunity to swing his weapon with all his strength.

The bo staff struck the Rev'er's skull, and a golden light brightened their surroundings for a fraction of a second before the Third-Level vanished into thin air.

Absolute silence. No growl of monsters. No stampede of a wild beast. No Rev'er or violent Third-Level. It was just Mafuyu, with his bo staff still poised to strike. The only trace left of the monster was the damaged grass in the field.

Mafuyu relaxed his stance and strapped the bo staff onto his back again.

Banishing Rev'ers could only be done using weapons that had special inscriptions on them. Mafuyu always opted for either his gun or the metal bo staff, which was about two meters long and covered in the inscriptions necessary to banish any supernatural being. Both were light and easy to carry, but the bo staff could easily break a skull.

Mafuyu had started walking back to the house of his client when the pocket of his jeans started vibrating. He pulled out his cell phone and found a familiar name lighting up the screen: Kaoru Nagisa.

He swiped the screen with his thumb and brought the phone to his ear. "Yes, Captain?"

"Mafuyu, are you done?" Nagisa's voice came through loud and clear.

"You could say that."

"Zen wants you back at headquarters as soon as possible."

Mafuyu thought he sensed urgency in her voice, or maybe he was reading too much into it. But for his captain to call him out of the blue was rare. If they had a mission, the entire team would be informed. An individual call hinted that there was something more serious at hand.

"Understood," he replied, "I'll be there soon."

The elevator stopped and dinged loudly. The steel doors opened and Mafuyu stepped out.

The team's headquarters were based in a tall skyscraper that stood in the quieter part of Yokohama. As part of the Rev'er Hunter

Corps, an organization that focused on solving crimes or defusing situations that were too violent or impossible for the Military Police to handle, Mayufu and his colleagues—known as Hunters—were called in to deal with the supernatural on a regular basis.

But they didn't go around exorcising angry ghosts in haunted houses. Their work was different and much more complicated. Hunters were the only ones that could see and study the existence of Rev'ers, or animalistic beasts that were not of this world. They learned all about their different origins and whether they were harmful or not, then trained so they could banish them to a world called the Jihan. It was the same world these beasts originally came from, a world that no human could enter.

The Rev'er Hunter Corps was always buzzing with people continuously on the job, coming or going with some task or another. Just because the majority of the population couldn't see Rev'ers didn't mean there were any less of them out in the world. There was always a case that needed sorting out, though sometimes clients came with personal requests. Then it was up to the head of the organization to assign a Hunter to the specific task.

Mafuyu yawned as he walked down the hallway. He had intended to stay a day in Kyoto and rest, then take the train back to Yokohama the next day. Instead, he'd spent that eight hours traveling, and it was rather tiring.

The moon was already out by the time he came back. Mafuyu knocked twice on Zen's office door. There was no answer, but he could faintly hear Zen's voice coming from inside the room. Mafuyu pushed open the door and peaked in.

Zen stood facing the far wall, which was one large window, his cell phone pressed against his ear.

"I know, that's why I'm asking for this as a personal favor." At the sound of the door creaking when Mafuyu opened it further, Zen turned, smiled, and motioned for him to come inside. "Great! Hanamatsuri, it is then." There was a pause and then Zen smiled. "Of course. Wouldn't have it any other way." With that, he cut the call and placed his phone on the table before he addressed Mafuyu. "You're back earlier than I expected."

"Ha! Like you had nothing to do with it." Mafuyu retorted as he made his way toward him.

Zen was a man in his mid-thirties, but his years had yet to physically catch up with him. He stood tall, with a slim build, calculating eyes, and a perpetual smile playing at his lips. He was the man who found Mafuyu ten years ago, nearly frozen on the street. He'd taught the younger boy a lot more than just fighting monsters; he taught him to hope, to do the right thing, to stand for good. Most important of all, he gave him a new name, and along with it a new life. When the boy refused to say his birth name, Zen had lovingly called him Mafuyu, a name meaning "midwinter" that he chose for the snowy season during which he had found him.

"How was Kyoto?" Zen asked.

Mafuyu gave a casual shrug and replied with borderline sarcasm. "Fun. I almost got killed by a Third-Level."

"What do you mean?" Zen's playful tone immediately changed into a serious one.

"A Third-Level actually interpreted my moves and *thought*. As in, a lower level Rev'er displayed significant intelligence. That's never ever happened before. *It shouldn't happen.*"

Zen placed his thumb and forefinger under his chin. His eyes fell on the floor as he pondered what he'd just heard. "Nagisa ran into a similar problem." He looked up at Mafuyu again. "I've readied a team to sort out the case. We will know what's going on soon."

Mafuyu bit back everything else he was prepared to throw at the man regarding the seriousness of the situation. He knew he shouldn't have worried as much as he had on the journey back. Zen was competent and far more capable than anybody else he knew. That's why he stood at the top of the organization. He should have known that the man had already put a plan in motion.

"Were you able to wrap up the assignment even with that complication?"

"Yes, and I made sure that the girl and her family were okay before heading back here."

Zen smiled, "Give me all the details about the rogue Third-Level in your report. It will help going forward if we know what kind of Rev'ers are being affected by whatever this is."

Mafuyu nodded before moving on to the next topic on his mind. "So, why did you rush me back here?"

"Do you know a man called Mirai?"

"I've heard Nagisa mention him before. He worked as a Hunter for a short time before resigning, right?"

Zen nodded and walked around the table to stand directly in front of him. "I'm assigning you to him as his bodyguard."

"Bodyguard?" Mafuyu raised an eyebrow. To an outsider, it might not have sounded like an unusual task, but given their type of work and the kind of requests they got, run-of-the-mill bodyguard duty seemed out of the ordinary. And if Zen was personally requesting it of him, Mafuyu knew that there was something bigger at play. "That's not exactly my area of expertise."

"I'll explain things on the way tomorrow. Will you do it?"

Mafuyu nodded in earnest, "You know I will." It seemed like there was more than met the eye.

CHAPTER TWO

MIRAI

Tokyo was a vibrant city that was always buzzing with energy. Time seemed to pass faster here than any other part of the country. By day, the citizens were rushing to work. At night, the city came alive in hues of orange and yellow: bright streetlights, flashing neon signs, shops and bars lit up to attract customers. A colorful world indeed.

A cool spring breeze ruffled Mirai's jet black hair as he stood on the balcony of his apartment, taking in the sight of the city below him and thinking he would never tire of the view. He folded his arm over the railing and leaned further out. It was beautiful, but then again, if he had a choice he would have perhaps chosen to live on the quieter side of Japan. A countryside, somewhere peaceful. A place where he wouldn't always have to keep an eye out for the otherworldly.

His cell phone vibrated on the living room table. Thanks to the deafening silence of his apartment, it only took two buzzes for him to hear it. He went back inside, picked it up, and checked the screen before answering. Mirai's lips twitched into a smile when the caller ID flashed Zen's details back at him. He swiped at the screen and brought it to his ear. "Hello."

"Mirai. Are you busy now?"

"Not at all. What's the matter?"

Zen and Mirai kept in constant communication in case help was needed on either side. They had a good relationship while Mirai worked as a Rev'er Hunter, and Zen made sure it remained that way even when Mirai quit the organization. Rather than keeping a typical superior-subordinate relationship, over the years theirs had grown into something resembling a trusting friendship.

"I have a favor to ask." Zen's voice sounded urgent.

"Favor?" Mirai echoed. That was enough to get his attention. Zen hardly asked for favors.

"Yes, I need you on the job...temporarily."

Mirai frowned, "Even though I don't work as a Hunter anymore?"

"I know, that's why I'm asking for this as a personal favor."

Mirai sighed. He couldn't say no to much when it came to this man. Not only was he impossible to argue with, but he had helped Mirai in a time when he needed it the most and he still hadn't repaid that debt. He wasn't in a position to reject him outright and Zen knew that.

Mirai gently pinched the skin between his eyebrows. *Of all the things he could ask for.*

"It doesn't seem like you'll let me off the hook," Mirai joked. "Let's meet up at my shop tomorrow morning so we can discuss this properly."

"Great!" Zen's voice perked up. "Hanamatsuri it is, then."

"Just so you know, I wouldn't do this if it was anyone else."

"Of course. Wouldn't have it any other way."

"Then I'll see you later." As soon as Mirai cut the call he slumped onto the couch, dropping his cell on the cushion beside him. Troublesome things always had a way of finding their way back to his life, and they never seemed to unfold according to his calculations. Such was life.

Hanamatsuri was cleverly tucked front and center under a three-floor building just one block away from where Mirai lived. Its location made it easy for anyone walking down the street to spot.

The keys jingled as Mirai pulled them out of his pocket and unlocked the door with a quiet click. As he stepped in, the fresh scent of gardenias, peonies and jasmine filled his nose. Mirai dropped his bag on the counter and went to check on the new flowers growing in the small plant nursery at the back of the store. He went about his routine on autopilot, checking the plants, watering them, and adding in the fertilizers. Every so often he brought a pot or two to the front and added it to the abundant flowers and greens lining the shelves.

He heard the sound of the bell hung up on top of the doorframe to alert him when a new customer dropped in. He emerged from the nursery and dusted his hands off on his apron. "*Ohayou*, Kana-san." He greeted one of his regulars with a smile so charming it rivaled the blooming roses that surrounded them. "What can I get for you today?"

"*Ohayou*, Mirai." She cheerily returned his good morning wish, then pursed her lips and tapped her chin as her eyes traveled to all the various flowers around the shop. "Can you make a simple bouquet? It's for a dear friend of mine."

"Of course," he nodded and turned around to pick a pair of scissors from the shelf. "Birthday?"

"More of a 'congratulations', actually. Mind if I come pick it up early this afternoon?"

"No problem. I'll have the perfect bouquet ready," he said in a voice as smooth as velvet. The woman couldn't help but blush a little, then she thanked him, patted him on the back with a grin, and rushed out of the door. Mirai figured she must have stopped by on her way to work.

Mirai mused, looking around the shop for the perfect flowers: something that spoke of happiness and good luck. Before he could decide on anything, the bell chimed again, alerting him of yet another visitor. Except this time, it was a person that had never been his customer but with whom he was quite familiar.

"All your physical features are still frozen in time, Zen-san," Mirai teased as Zen walked in through the door.

"Like you're any better," Zen returned. Mirai's responding laugh was sweet and echoed like bells. "How have you been?"

"Same as usual."

"I see the shop is going well." Zen looked around the room. "There are more flowers in here than the last time I visited."

"Yeah, business has been picking up. Once the festival seasons come in I won't have time to sit still."

"I'm glad." There was softness in Zen's eyes as he took in the blooming beauties. These flowers told a story, one that only Zen and Mirai knew.

Mirai left Zen's remark alone as his eyes shifted to the young man that stood next to Zen: a teenager with bleached brunette hair and a tall, lean frame. "Who's the delinquent?" he teased.

"Wha—" The boy started like he was offended, but Zen quickly cut him off.

"I'd like you to meet Mafuyu," he motioned towards the young man, who gave a slight bow and dropped Mirai's comment. Good manners. Mirai mimicked his action with a court bow of his own. Zen didn't dawdle any further and turned toward Mafuyu. "Do you mind waiting outside?"

Mafuyu nodded and exited to stand to the side of the shop, unaware that Mirai could see him through the glass walls. Mirai walked over to the door and flipped the sign from "OPEN" to "CLOSED."

"What about your customers?" Zen gestured to the door.

"This isn't usually a busy time of day," he reassured him as he pulled a chair from behind the counter for Zen to sit. Mirai made himself comfortable by leaning against the countertop, arms folded across his chest and eyes fixed on his guest. "So, Mafuyu, huh? He is definitely questioning my personality right about now."

Zen snorted. "You've just met him and you can already tell?"

"It's just a guess."

"Do those eyes of yours see everything?"

Mirai gave him a small smile. "They obviously have their limits."

Zen leaned back on the chair. "But there is no denying that you were always the smartest Hunter at the Corps."

Mirai was quick to change the subject from his service record. "Why exactly did you want to see me? I'm pretty sure it wasn't to reminisce about the past."

"I need you to guard Mafuyu for some time."

"Guard?" Mirai arched an eyebrow. "Guard him from what?"

"Something dangerous," Zen replied vaguely.

Mirai tilted his head, as if he was trying to find the right angle from which to study his every move. Part of him just didn't want to believe what he was hearing. "Why didn't you just hand this over to the cops? Or hire a professional bodyguard?"

"You know the stuff we deal with isn't something that normal people can handle," Zen reasoned. "He is being hunted by something terrible, of that I'm sure. But I don't have enough evidence to prove it. His parents were massacred; the police can't find a link and they hired us. So, I was hoping you could watch over him while I sort things out. I can't keep an eye on him *and* deal with the organization." When Mirai showed no sign of giving in, Zen resorted to pleading. "Please? If he's with you, I can trust that no harm will come to him."

Mirai sighed, "Even if I say no now, you're probably going to sweet-talk me into agreeing eventually."

"Do you not trust me to convince you fair and square?"

"If I didn't trust you, Zen-san, I wouldn't be standing here next to you." Mirai smiled. He could have just rejected the whole thing outright and gone home, but that would be utterly rude. He would cause a rift in their friendship if he did that. He trusted Zen more than anybody else, and he knew that Zen would rather die than cause him harm. Besides, he did owe the man. "Fine. I'll do it. I'll guard him from this...thing."

Zen opened his mouth to speak, but stopped almost immediately when his attention was redirected to the side of Mirai's face. Mirai's eyebrows furrowed in question when Zen stood up and closed the gap between them. He raised his hand and twirled a couple of strands of Mirai's hair around his forefinger. "It's going white."

"What?"

"Your hair."

Mirai jerked away from him and tucked the strand behind his ear while casually brushing some darker strands above them.

Zen laughed at that while Mirai rolled his eyes. "You're so vain! Relax, your hair isn't going to go totally white for another ten years."

"Ten? I'm only in my late twenties. Aren't you the one who should be worrying about grey hair?"

Zen snorted and waved his hand as if shooing away something invisible in the air. "Please. I'm only thirty-five."

"Seems old enough to me." Mirai noticed that Mafuyu had undoubtedly gotten bored while they bantered, if the look on his face was anything to go by, and jerked his head in his general direction to indicate that they'd kept him waiting long enough.

This time it was Zen who reversed the sign on the glass door. He pulled it open and spoke to Mirai over his shoulder. "I'll see you later, but feel free to drop by sometime. Nagisa often asks about you."

Mirai nodded. "I will."

With that, Zen smiled and walked out. From the inside of the shop, Mirai watched Zen briefly speak to Mafuyu. The boy then nodded and headed back into the store.

"Um," he said, shuffling awkwardly.

Mirai decided to put him out of his misery. "Are you good with your hands?"

"Huh?"

"Another pair of hands around the store would help me out. I have a few orders I want to take care of, but I need more manpower to finish it."

"S-sure. But why?"

"You got anything better to do?"

"No...not really."

"Good. I can't leave the store midday, so you might as well start now. Consider it an exchange for a free place to stay."

As Mafuyu trotted behind the older man, Mirai couldn't help but think this situation was a little strange. This boy's eyes were not haunted like one would expect after a person just lost his parents in a massacre. They weren't weak or confused; they were brave and determined.

CHAPTER THREE

LIE

After a grueling day working at Mirai's flower shop, Mafuyu dragged himself to Mirai's apartment. He felt like his body was about to just stop moving and drop where he stood. Talk about no mercy. Mirai had worked him to the bone hauling heavy bags of fertilizer, helping load a truck full of plants, watering said plants... The list went on.

Just thinking about it made him angry. He had mud under his nails and felt like a kid who had rolled around in the sand all day. Mafuyu bore holes into the man's back with his narrowed eyes. To think he had to live with him for God knew how long.

The golden rays of the setting sun streamed in through the apartment's windows and bathed Mirai's home in a warm, golden light. There wasn't much in the way of decoration except for some pieces of furniture: two couches, a coffee table, a TV stand, a dining table, and a bookshelf, all neatly arranged around the apartment. It spoke to how Mirai didn't often latch onto material things.

There was a single bedroom, a kitchen, and a dining area. Although it was enough for Mirai alone, but with a sudden guest it was a tad inconvenient.

"I don't have another room, so is a futon okay with you?" Mirai asked as he dropped his jacket on the back of the nearest couch.

"I'm fine with anything." Mafuyu replied.

"You can lay it out in my room or the living room. Your choice."

"I'll take the living room."

"Alright."

Mirai turned to retreat to his room, but was stopped short when Mafuyu spoke up. "No rules or anything? Nothing about what I should and shouldn't do?"

Mirai tilted his head to side-eye the boy. "No. Make yourself comfortable. Just don't leave the house. It will be easier for me to watch you."

The evening passed in either silence or stilted chitchat that more closely resembled Q&A sessions than actual conversation. It mostly came from Mirai's side, asking Mafuyu about things he liked and disliked when it came to food and anything else that would help make their temporary arrangement more comfortable.

The hours ticked by faster than Mirai expected. After finishing up a delicious dinner that he had cooked, both men retired to bed.

Mafuyu spread the blanket over his legs. His phone screen glowed in the darkness of the living room. He glanced towards the bedroom. Mirai had already gone to sleep; at least, that's what it looked like since there was no sound of him moving around behind his closed door. Then again, one doesn't have to be asleep to be quiet.

Mafuyu turned back to his phone as he scrawled over the texts he was exchanging with Zen. The conversation from earlier played over and over in Mafuyu's head: everything that Zen told him and warned him about before they met with Mirai.

"Remember that I said I was assigning you to be his bodyguard?" Zen asked. His eyes were fixed on the road ahead as he sat behind the steering wheel of his black Camry.

"Yeah."

"And you are aware of First-Levels, aren't you?"

Mafuyu nodded. Of course he was aware of First-Levels. They were the only Rev'ers that all humans could see. Only a handful of them actually had spotted them, and they claimed that they were close to humans in appearance, though with a higher intellect and far superior physical strength. First-Levels were said to have huge wings sprouting from their back, and unusual hair and eye colors. Every Hunter had to study what little information was available on First-Levels because they were the most dangerous and deadly of the three types of Rev'ers out there. They were elusive, mysterious, and their origins remained unknown. If anybody came across one, it was wiser to run than stand and fight.

"What about them?" Mafuyu questioned.

"Mirai has a past with one. A brief but explosive past, and I'm afraid that, because of that, he is in danger."

"What?" Mafuyu tried unsuccessfully to suppress his shock. "Are they hunting him?"

"It seems very likely, but I need concrete proof. Meanwhile, I need you to protect him. He can be reckless sometimes and I'm afraid he is more at risk than even I think. I just want you to watch over him and keep him safe until then."

"Got it."

When they stopped at a red light, Zen took a hand off the steering wheel and leaned toward Mafuyu's side of the car. He opened the dashboard, still keeping his eyes on the road, and pulled out a brown leather book that he then handed to him.

"What's this?" Mafuyu asked as he turned it over in his hand. The word "Zalek" was etched onto the front cover.

"It's a language," Zen replied. The light turned green and he changed the gear. "As far as I know, it's a language that only First-Levels speak."

Mafuyu furrowed his eyebrows. "How did you get this?"

"That's a long story." He turned right. "Anyway, it might be of use to you."

Mafuyu flipped through the pages, trying to absorb words that had been translated into a language he had never seen or heard spoken before. He looked at Zen. So many questions formed in his mind, but he pushed them all away to simply thank him for the opportunity instead. Zen was placing tremendous trust on Mafuyu by handing over something so confidential. "I'll do my best."

"By the way, Mirai is unaware of the situation. He won't take it well if he knows First-Levels are after him. So no matter what, don't let him find out why you're really staying with him." Zen gave the gas a light push. They drove past buildings, their facades whipping by until they blurred together. "I don't want him to worry unless he absolutely needs to."

"You plan to lie to him?"

A second of silence passed before Zen heaved a sigh. "Yes."

Mafuyu's head hit the pillow as he lay back down.

The first glimpse Mafuyu got of Mirai in the shop was branded into his memory. He was a well-kept man and his eyes seemed to be trying to take in everything about his surroundings at once. But nothing else about him stood out. He doubted if Mirai was even that strong a Hunter in his time. It was more likely that it was his knowledge of First-Levels that made Mirai valuable to the Corps. Mafuyu couldn't help wondering what caused him to leave the job behind in the first place.

The cell phone in his hand vibrated again with a new text. **Keep me updated on everything.**

Mafuyu's thumbs tapped the keypad. **Of course. He doesn't suspect anything.**

A couple of seconds passed before the phone vibrated again. **Good. Keep it that way.**

Mafuyu didn't bother to reply and immediately deleted all the messages, getting rid of the evidence before he placed his cell beside the futon. He pulled the blanket up over him and closed his eyes as the day's events replayed in his mind like a record.

And in absolutely no time, he fell into an undisturbed slumber.

CHAPTER FOUR

FIGURED

The first words Mafuyu had exchanged with Mirai made him believe that Mirai was the type of person he disliked most: sharp-tongued and uncaring of others. But in the days that followed, he realized he had been too quick to judge the man.

Mirai was a warm person, and easy to talk to. He was sincere with Mafuyu and stuck to his role as bodyguard as Zen had asked him to—Mafuyu wondered how he'd react if he ever found out that it was a facade.

It was easy to adjust with Mirai and the man wasn't tough to handle. The only downside was that he was a workaholic of sorts, and he made Mafuyu work the same hours with him in his flower shop. He would have liked to keep an eye on Mirai without also having to lift heavy pots, fertilize the plants, water them, and anything else that came to Mirai's mind. It felt like a side hustle he wasn't getting paid for. But the other side to that was it gave both men a chance to quickly get accustomed to each other. The rigidity they both had during the first couple of days lessened as the day eight wore on. Mafuyu even found himself thinking that this was the first time he'd ever felt so at ease with someone else.

The bells on the doorframe rang as yet another customer stepped in. Mafuyu let out a heavy breath. This was more exhausting than he had expected. Who knew owning a flower shop was so much work? He always believed it was all sitting at the counter and reading a book until someone waltzed in and bought a bouquet. Easy.

"Oh my." The customer put her index finger to her lip as she scanned Mafuyu from head to toe. Maybe she found his apron funny. "Did you hire a new part-timer, Mirai-san?"

"Something like that." Mirai smiled at the lady like they were old friends. Her knees nearly melted at the sight of Mirai's friendly grin. All the ladies did. They would turn to putty and gush over him until the second they left the shop. The regulars were somewhat used to his pretty face, but the new ones couldn't stop blushing when they made eye contact.

And why wouldn't they? Even Mafuyu would admit that the bastard had an undeniably pretty face. He wasn't just handsome; he was gorgeous.

There was the strong jawline, full lips, thin nose, and features that looked like they were sculpted with precise measurements and utmost care. His eyes were grey with the transparent beauty of glass. He had black hair that fell in graceful waves to the base of his neck. And then there was his physique: broad shoulders and lean muscles. Add in the surrounding flowers and the man was practically a fairy-tale prince.

Mirai was aware of all of it. He would even use it to coax customers into buying things. A gentle smile and some sweet words would make any woman happy enough to spend a little more. But, he never stepped out of line; he was a decent man.

The lady giggled at Mirai's words as she picked out a bouquet, and Mafuyu couldn't help rolling his eyes. *This* was the guy that Zen wanted him to protect? Who on earth would hunt him down? Except for maybe jealous, angry boyfriends or husbands. Mafuyu had seen and dealt with enough hunters and Rev'ers that he couldn't even imagine someone like Mirai knowing what a First-Level even *was*, let alone take one on all by himself. He was too passive to deliberately put himself in one's path. He probably played the role of a strategist in a team back in the day. After all, would someone who knew a First-Level be so carefree? Mafuyu could only guess.

Then again, Mirai seemed meticulous, and he did have his own weird habits. He was restless at night; most of the time he didn't asleep. Mafuyu often heard him padding through the apartment in the wee hours to head out onto the balcony and observe the vibrant streets. Sometimes he caught Mirai simply staring at the flowers in the shop's nursery with a distant look in his grey eyes. But Mafuyu never asked him about it.

"Something on your mind?" Mirai's voice broke Mafuyu from his train of thought. The customer had already left and it was just the two of them again.

"I was just thinking about some stuff," Mafuyu answered, hoping he didn't sound suspicious.

"Such as..?"

"Such as how you have your customers wrapped around your finger."

Mirai blankly stared at Mafuyu for a good few seconds and then burst into full, booming laughter. "I didn't know you were capable of thinking like that!"

"Do you want me to pour the fertilizer over your head?"

"Do that and *you* will end up as the fertilizer for my plants."

Mafuyu made a face and looked Mirai up and down in mock disgust. "You are so creepy."

Mirai scoffed and pulled his apron over his head. "We're done for today. Let's head out."

"Great! I couldn't stand seeing another blushing girl drool over you." Mafuyu removed his apron and wiped his muddy hands on a damp towel on the counter.

"Don't be jealous. You're popular with the girls, too. A couple of them even asked me for your name," Mirai teased.

"Somehow that's just infuriating coming from you."

Mirai laughed as he locked the shop and slipped the key into the pocket of his jeans. The sky was painted orange, yellow and pink as the sun started to set between the tall skyscrapers. The streets were busier than in the morning, with workers from all industries trying to make their way back home. People flooded the streets as they exited buildings, trains and cars.

Mafuyu watched Mirai from the corner of his eye as the two walked, lagging a foot or two behind him. This man was so mysterious even though he really wasn't hiding anything. He'd been lied to and told to protect Mafuyu, yet he hadn't asked him a single question about the circumstances: not even what kind of trouble Mafuyu was in or how he ended up needing a bodyguard. Perhaps he was just being considerate.

Whatever it was, Mafuyu didn't want to garner any suspicion.

It had been ten days since Mafuyu and Mirai began cohabiting, and so far there were no real issues with the arrangement. Nor had they come across any First-Levels, though Mafuyu couldn't exactly ask Mirai if he'd noticed anything out of the ordinary. Mafuyu was beginning to believe that Zen had just gotten some kind of false alarm, and he really hoped that's all it was. It would be better for all of them if things played out that way.

On a lazy Saturday afternoon, Mirai walked out of his room dressed in a simple black shirt and jeans. As he crossed the living room on his way to the door, he called, "I'm heading to the convenience store to buy some stuff. Do you want anything?"

"No, thanks," Mafuyu replied from the couch, where he lay with a book in his hand.

"Okay." Mirai slipped on his shoes. "Lock the door and don't step out until I get back."

As soon as Mafuyu heard the door close and the click of the lock falling into place, he pulled out his phone and opened an app. A map popped up, and a green dot blinked on the screen. Mafuyu had slipped a tiny tracking device into Mirai's shoes—small enough not to feel, yet good enough to emit a strong signal—soon after he started crashing with Mirai. He waited until Mirai got into the elevator before grabbing a hoodie from his bag and making his way out of the apartment. He rushed down the stairs in time to observe Mirai walk out of the elevator and out of the building. Mafuyu quietly and hurriedly followed behind him.

The streets weren't as crowded as he had guessed they would be, but there was still enough foot traffic to provide the cover he needed to stay hidden from Mirai's sight. Mafuyu pulled the hood over his head and slipped into the growing crowd, maintaining enough distance to remain unnoticed, yet keep an eye on Mirai at the same time. He stealthily maneuvered through the crowd, following him around every curve and turn, stopping when Mirai did.

The strategy worked splendidly until Mirai suddenly turned around. Out of reflex and shock, Mafuyu jumped into an empty alley and out of Mirai's line of sight. He froze there for a few seconds, hoping that he hadn't been spotted. While he waited what he hoped would be enough time to convince Mirai to move on, he furrowed his eyebrows. Did Mirai sense him? Impossible. He was too far away to have noticed. No, Mirai must have looked back for another reason. Maybe someone called out to him. Or, he turned around to look at something else.

Mafuyu carefully poke his head around the side of the wall, checking to see if Mirai had double backed or gone ahead. Mirai's tall frame was getting smaller as he kept on, his momentary distraction evidently forgotten.

"Damn it," Mafuyu cursed under his breath and hurried to catch up before he lost him. But, on the upside, it looked like Mirai was indeed unaware of Mafuyu's presence. Just as he thought.

He took a step forward only to be yanked back by his shoulder and shoved against the side of the closest building. A muscular forearm pressed tightly against his throat. Great. This was the last thing he needed.

"What do we have here?" his assailant scoffed.

"Don't be...stupid," Mafuyu wheezed, trying to get as much air into his lungs as the man's hold would allow. "It's the middle....of the...day." He tried to wiggle away from the wall and free himself, but it was turning out to be easier said than done.

"I don't give a damn," the brute hissed.

Mafuyu choked on a sarcastic laugh. Of course he didn't. To do something like this in broad daylight meant he was either as stupid as he looked or just desperate. Plus, Mafuyu was standing in a twisted alley and not immediately visible to his fellow pedestrians on the sidewalk. If the man managed to keep him quiet, he doubted anyone would notice what was going on and come to his aid.

But Mafuyu didn't have the time or the inclination to play the victim anyway. His cover be damned; he had a job to do. If he had to knock this thug out of his way and risk drawing attention to himself to do it, then so be it.

Mafuyu grabbed the man by his collar roughly, tugged him forward, and drove his knee hard into the man's stomach. He loosened his hold and bent over in pain. Mafuyu used that split second to quickly drive his elbow into his back. The impact was hard enough for the other to fall flat on his front.

Mafuyu didn't have time to let out a breath before a second thug came at him. Almost on a reflex, he swung his leg out in a roundhouse kick and sent the man flying backwards.

Mafuyu was about to flee the scene when he heard a click behind his head. A cold, round metal edge touched his scalp: a gun. Mafuyu raised his hands in the air to show that he was surrendering and waited. The shooter hesitated, and it wasn't hard to figure out why. If a gunshot was heard at this time of the day, the cops would definitely come running.

Mafuyu was about to give the finishing blow when a deep and stern voice said, "Enough."

There was no mistaking that voice. Mafuyu tilted his head and saw that, sure enough, it belonged to Mirai, who stood there with a deadly glare aimed right at him. He looked furious, and the thugs, who were apparently only pretending to be unconscious, stood up.

Mafuyu's eyes widened to the size of saucers.

They dusted off the dirt from their clothes and turned towards Mirai. "There you have it," one of them said. "Just as you asked."

Mirai didn't utter a word as he took a small bag out his pocket—probably their compensation for playing along—and threw it toward them. The man standing closest to him caught it and they scurried away, not even once turning back to look at Mafuyu.

Mafuyu stood there in an absolute daze. He couldn't believe it. He'd fallen right into Mirai's trap. Mirai had waited until he let his guard down around him so he could read him more clearly. This entire time he was aware that he was being followed. More precisely, he *knew* he would be followed before he even walked out the door that morning. He must have realized that Zen hadn't told him the truth.

But when did he figure it out? More importantly, *how*? He'd been so sure of his theory that he'd even hired goons to attack Mafuyu, just to test it. And Mafuyu was dumb enough to have played right into Mirai's hands.

He cursed at himself. He'd underestimated Mirai. The man was far cleverer than he let on. Mafuyu should have listened when Zen told him to be cautious.

Mirai took a slow, predatory step toward him.

Mafuyu gulped. Oh boy.

CHAPTER FIVE

PRETEND

Mirai threw open the door to his apartment and flung Mafuyu into the living room, ignoring how he almost tripped on his own feet with a light yelp as he slammed the door shut.

"Furious" was an understatement. It was taking everything in his power to resist tossing Mafuyu off the balcony.

"Why are you here?" Mirai demanded. The fact that Zen would lie to his face pissed him off even more than the kid following him. "I knew something was off from the beginning. You were never here to protect me."

"How did you know?" Even as shocked as he was, Mafuyu's voice didn't betray him.

At any other time, Mirai's good humor would kick in and he'd scoff playfully at the situation, but not now. Instead, he barely controlled his voice as he barked out, "The first day we met you looked at me like you were sizing me up. I was told that I needed to protect you because you didn't know what was going on, yet you never showed a hint of confusion or fear. You were way too at ease." He didn't know why he was explaining himself to this brat. But words were pouring out his mouth and this seemed like a better method than holding the boy down and breaking his jaw. "Exchanging texts with someone at the exact same time every night, quietly observing everything I do, following me everywhere. You thought I wouldn't notice?" He grabbed Mafuyu by the collar and slammed him against the wall. "Now talk. Who are you reporting to?"

Mafuyu's eyes traveled all over the room before finally settling on Mirai's grey ones. "I'm here as part of an assignment," he finally answered.

Mirai stared hard into Mafuyu's dark eyes. There wasn't a flicker of lie in there. He was telling the truth. "What assignment?"

"To protect you."

"What?" Whatever Mirai thought he was about to hear, that certainly wasn't it. Protect him? Why would he need protection? There wasn't anything that he couldn't handle. *Unless...* "Why would I need a bodyguard?" When he was met with stubborn silence, Mirai tightened his jaw, the last bit of his control crumbling. "This is why I hate people like you."

"Hate? So were you were just pretending to be friends?" Something in Mafuyu's eyes changed. The apathetic expression he usually wore turned into dejection, and an icy coldness crept into his eyes. Strangely, it appeared it was Mafuyu who had been more affected by this ordeal, even though he hadn't seemed to enjoy Mirai's company much at all in their short time together.

"Who was the one that was actually pretending?" Mirai asked pointedly. Mafuyu clenched his jaw and remained silent, unable to deny it. Mirai paused for a second before letting go off his collar and dragging the younger man along by the arm. "Come with me."

Mafuyu tried to break Mirai's grip, but it was stronger than he expected. "Where are we going?"

"To your boss," Mirai replied in a voice that held the deadly calm of a tiger about to tear apart its prey.

Zen stood at his desk, desperately trying to figure out the puzzle spread out in front of him. Documents and illustrations were scattered messily amidst a few photographs of Rev'ers here and there. He plucked a few papers from the pile and placed them in a file before opening a drawer and dropping it inside, out of sight for the time being.

His concentration was broken when the door to his office banged open and he was greeted by a ticked off Mirai dragging an equally irritated Mafuyu by his arm.

He flung the younger man inside ahead of him like a rag doll.

"Mirai? What are you doing here?" Zen asked even though he could guess the answer already. The fury glinting in Mirai's eyes, coupled with the way Mafuyu stood off to the side with a frown and failure written all over his face said it all.

"You lied to me," Mirai started.

Zen looked at Mafuyu and raised his eyebrows, silently conveying that they'd discuss the importance of *not* blowing one's cover later.

Meanwhile, Mirai stepped in between them, demanding Zen's full attention. "Why?"

"I don't think this is the right time to tell you," Zen replied.

Mirai narrowed his eyes, his sharp, unrelenting gaze daring Zen to lie or give him any more lame excuses. Zen rubbed the back of his neck and let out a defeated sigh. He wanted Mirai to be safe and unburdened with the details, but from the looks of it, Mirai wouldn't rest until Zen spilled everything. And after knowing him for a while now, he knew Mirai could be quite stubborn when he wanted to be.

Zen walked around the desk, picking up a photograph from the center of the pile along the way. He handed it to Mirai and instantly regretted it when Mirai's face was drained of all its color.

"What is this?" he asked, even though he knew what he was staring at.

Mafuyu peeked over Mirai's shoulder. The photograph was blurry and dark; it was probably taken at night. The figure in the photograph appeared to be a human man, except that his silhouette featured what looked like large feathery wings protruding from his back. From the angle at which the picture was taken, the figure was perched somewhere higher than the photographer's location.

"Is that a First-Level?" Mafuyu asked in disbelief.

"Nagisa saw it during one of her missions."

"Does this have anything to do with…" Mirai paused before continuing. "Bezaleel?"

Zen scratched his cheek, searching for the words that would make it sound less dire than it looked. Knowing Mirai, he needed to be careful with how he presented the situation. "I don't know. I'm not going to come to any conclusions without proper proof, though. It could have nothing to do with you. This is just a blurred photograph," Zen explained. He walked to Mirai and put a hand on his shoulder. "But if they *are* looking for Bezaleel, you'll be the first one they'll come after. So I wanted to put you under protection. Just in case."

"Wait, hold on!" Mafuyu interjected, causing both men to turn their heads in his direction. "Bezaleel? As in, the Frist-Level Rev'er with red eyes and black wings that destroyed an entire town in Iwami four years ago? The Rev'er that could kill as easily as plucking a flower? The Rev'er everybody is scared to death of—and for good reason? *That* Bezaleel? And *that's* the First-Level you wanted me to look out for?"

"We're not sure who or what the one in the picture is," Zen calmly interrupted.

"So there's more than one First-Level to look out for?"

Zen raised his hands, palms facing towards Mafuyu as he tried to calm him down. "That's not what I meant. It could be a Second-Level."

" I'd like to believe it's some crazy idiot in a costume!" Mafuyu cut in.

"Or it really could be another First-Level." Mirai handed the photo back to Zen. "Not that this world needs any more of them."

Mafuyu clutched the fabric of his shirt over his chest. "You people are going to give me a heart attack."

"Zen-san, take Mafuyu off this bodyguard assignment. You're putting him in more danger than he needs to be by keeping him near me."

"Mirai, I don't think that you should be overly worried about this."

"You think that way even after everything I told you about Bezaleel?"

"We are experts at dealing with things like this." Mirai rubbed his forehead, and Zen took his silence as an invitation to continue. "Besides, didn't you tell me you took—"

"I don't want to talk about that," Mirai snapped.

"Sorry," Zen apologized.

"First-Levels can't be dealt with. You of all people should know that."

"That's only because we haven't yet figured out how."

"Because you can't!" Mirai gestured wildly, unable to control his frustration any longer.

"*You* can." As soon as Zen muttered that, he knew he had stepped out of line.

Mirai glared at his friend. "I don't want to."

Mafuyu's gaze darted to and fro between the two men, confused by the context of their argument. He wasn't even sure what they were talking about anymore.

Zen pinched the skin between his eyebrows and sighed again. "Look, let Mafuyu do this. At least for my peace of mind." Mirai kept his silence. He could be quite rebellious when he wanted to be, much to Zen's dismay. Arguing with logic was clearly not working, so he tried appealing to Mirai's emotions. "Will it make you feel better to know that Mafuyu is part of Nagisa's team?"

At that, Mirai's creased forehead smoothed back over. Nagisa always had that effect on him. "Fine but I want to be alone for a while. Mafuyu, you can come back later." Mirai didn't give Zen a chance to say anything else and left, shutting the door with a loud, angry thud on his way out. Mafuyu flinched at the sound.

Zen understood why Mirai was being so stubborn and cautious. He didn't blame him in the slightest. Bezaleel caused the deaths of hundreds of innocent people, burned and destroyed a whole town, and almost tore the world apart. If events from the past were coming back to bite them, then the future seemed bleak and dark indeed.

Like so many others who witnessed all that destruction, Mirai was a man who had lost his peace, and this would threaten the only sanity he had left.

CHAPTER SIX

BANISHING OR GUARDING

Mafuyu pulled the trigger five times and watched every single bullet hit the target right in the middle as the gunshots echoed off the soundproof walls in the training room. The cardboard target fell back, and the machine automatically replaced it with another.

Ejecting the empty magazine, he quickly swapped it with a loaded one. He was in the middle of firing his next rounds when the automatic door to the side slid open. The woman who walked in had short dark hair tied neatly into a ponytail. Her toned arms were on display in her short-sleeve training shirt, her eyes held the strength and authority of a natural commander, and she exuded an aura that intimidated everyone in her presence. She made her way toward Mafuyu, a bo staff in each hand.

"Captain Nagisa," Mafuyu greeted. It was rare to see her around at this time of day. She was usually busy sorting out reports from previous missions.

Instead of greeting him back, she threw one of the bo staffs at him.

Mafuyu caught it in midair with practiced ease. He looked at the wooden stick before raising his eyes back to Nagisa. "So you're throwing things at me now? I'm don't think I've done anything to piss you off lately."

"You're wasting your bullets," Nagisa replied.

"Huh?"

"You're already a good shot. Firing bullets at an idle target isn't going to help you."

"Captain, I would only spar with you if I *wanted* to get my ass kicked."

Nagisa was a strong fighter, a deadly combination of power, skill and brains. But if there was anybody who could go up against her with a prayer of coming out on top, it was Mafuyu. She pointed her bo staff at Mafuyu's forehead. The end of the stick hovered an inch away from his skin. "Mafuyu, are you backing off from a challenge?" she provoked.

Mafuyu knew better than to reject Nagisa's invitation to spar. She would never let him live it down. If there was one thing she was terrifyingly good at it, it was psychological torture. And Mafuyu didn't want to be at the wrong end of the stick: figuratively and literally.

Above all he knew his captain wasn't someone to simply walk in and demand to spar for fun. Mafuyu sighed. It would be better to just go along with her rather than against her. Nagisa had her reasons and it was better to trust them.

He took a few steps away from Nagisa without breaking eye contact. Finding a decent grip on the weapon, he dropped his hips and raised the staff in a defensive position. A second of silence passed before Mafuyu and Nagisa rushed at each other. The battle had begun.

Mafuyu was the first to strike, swinging the bo staff high at Nagisa's head. She raised her own staff in retaliation and blocked it in one perfect move. Mafuyu repeated his attack, striking Nagisa with the other end of the staff only to be blocked again with as much as speed and accuracy as before. This went on for two more rounds. Strike and block. Strike and block.

Then Nagisa switched from defense to offence. She crouched down, swiping the bo staff at Mafuyu's feet.

Mafuyu jumped, avoiding the blow, then swung the back end of his staff at Nagisa's head when she straightened back up. But

Nagisa was quicker. She bent backward to avoid the blow, came up, spun her bo staff around, and struck at his hips.

Mafuyu blocked her attack; he'd always been swift and keen. He pushed her back with the momentum he gained by spinning on his heel and went for a low strike at her stomach. Nagisa caught his staff against the middle of hers and immediately went for Mafuyu's chin with the lower end.

For several minutes, he kept blocking Nagisa's barrage of strikes from all directions. She was quick and light on her feet, and struck with impeccable precision. Each blow was powerful, and Mafuyu didn't want this to go on longer than it had to. If Nagisa kept gaining momentum, he would soon lose to her.

So he upped his game. He spun the bo staff in a continuous, rapid figure-eight motion and pointed it at Nagisa. They charged at each other, both going for an upward strike at the same time. Their wooden staffs clashed loudly as they almost immediately went for a low strike on both sides of their opponent's leg. Their staffs clashed again, but this time Nagisa twirled around to Mafuyu's back and tried to strike him from behind. Mafuyu swung his staff back and blocked Nagisa from hammering his spinal cord.

He twisted on his heel to face with Nagisa again. Their bo staffs rose and collided midair before he slung his right at Nagisa's jaw, but she dodged it at the last second. They simultaneously revolved around each other and swung with full force. Both bo staffs had halted an inch away from the side of each other's neck.

"A draw...again," Mafuyu huffed between heavy breaths. "I think I preferred the still statue."

"Are you over your anger now?"

Mafuyu's lowered his weapon. "Captain, did you come here because you thought something was bothering me?"

Nagisa gave him a lopsided smile and drew back her staff. "Now that you've calmed down, you can tell me what's on your mind."

Mafuyu flopped onto the floor, still catching his breath. Nagisa followed suit and made herself comfortable opposite to him.

"When did you come back from your mission?" Mafuyu decided to ease in with small talk.

"Last night. Zen told me about your bodyguard assignment. I was surprised when I heard about Mirai."

"You've worked with him before," Mafuyu said.

"For a while." Nagisa shrugged. "He came here in kind of the same way you did. Zen-san found him wandering the streets one day and that was that."

Mafuyu placed his hands on top of his knees and leaned in. "What was he like?"

"He was friendly, easy to talk to," Nagisa recalled. "Despite being quite young and a newbie he knew a lot about war strategies and tactics. He was quick to come up with a plan and he was very level-headed. Nothing seemed to faze him. Even in the most dangerous situations he was calm and focused, which was strange because even the bravest of newbies will cower in front of a Second-Level the first time. But Mirai was strangely grounded. It seemed like he'd already seen much worse, so the Rev'ers didn't shake his confidence."

Mafuyu quirked an eyebrow, surprised that the man he'd written off as soft came with such a reputation for the opposite. "Then why did he quit?"

Nagisa shrugged again, even more indifferent than before. "I don't really know. I think it was a deal between him and Zen. He was good, but he never did seem comfortable working as a Hunter."

"Did he hate it?"

"Not that I know of."

"Could I ask you something else?"

"If it's relevant."

"Earlier today, he mentioned Bezaleel. Do you know how he met a First-Level like that?"

"Mirai is from Iwami. The same town Bezaleel destroyed." Nagisa gazed down at him carefully. "Being curious and questioning your circumstances are good, but we can't afford distractions in our line of work. It could cost you your life, or the lives of your teammates. So get a hold of yourself and do your job properly, whether it's banishing a Rev'er or guarding a man from one."

Mafuyu let out a deep breath. He felt like he was drowning in a sea of confusion and doubt.

Nagisa must have sensed this. "Hey," she called softly, and Mafuyu tilted his head up towards her. "I know that you mostly hate people, and that you have a hard time getting along with and trusting them. I don't blame you for it. You grew up in circumstances that no child should have to. But that's in the past. You can't use that as an excuse to act like that stubborn child from here on out. Mirai was someone we trusted with our lives. Give him a chance to prove your assumptions wrong. If you want to know more about Bezaleel, he is the only one that can give you answers."

Mafuyu relaxed. Nagisa always made her points clear, with facts that no one could use against her. She never failed to make perfect sense. He stood up from the floor and dusted off his pants. "I apologize. As one of your teammates, I should have known better than to doubt his capabilities," he said earnestly.

"It's alright. I'm your captain. It's my job to make sure my teammates are in top form."

Mafuyu's nearly constant frown broke into a small smile. "Thank you, Nagisa-san," he whispered, as if he didn't want anyone but the two of them to hear him and his vulnerability.

Nagisa acknowledged his sentiment with the same kind of smile and a subtle twinkle in her eye, then walked out the door without another word.

Mafuyu stretched out his limbs. He couldn't just ignore the fact that he had an assignment to guard Mirai. He would have been happy to be dismissed from the task, but he knew that was just wishful thinking.

He forced himself to get up from the floor and dragged his feet toward the door.

CHAPTER SEVEN

MISSING

Mirai could see it clearly, could feel the heat of the roaring flames. The house was on fire, crumbling all around them. Pieces of wood cracked and fell from the ceiling. Ash and smoke thickened the air around them, swallowing the oxygen and leaving them to choke on what was left.

She wrapped her seven-year-old son in a blanket and pressed him close to her chest as she coughed. His little arms held on for dear life. The father's larger hands wrapped around them, as if they could keep the fire at bay.

They kept frantically glancing around for an opening as the furious flames inched closer and closer, devouring anything and everything in their path. They had to get away before they were consumed, too.

The parents ran for the door, dodging falling debris and sparks, taking care not to step on the part of the floor that was breaking underfoot. The flames only grew, and the family started to suffocate in the thick smoke as they desperately made their way to the door.

The exit was within reach. The mother extended her hand toward the doorknob, just a couple of feet away. But as she did, the roof above them reached its limit and collapsed. As it tumbled down in a heap, the father pulled the mother and child back to keep them from getting crushed. Still cradling her son to her chest, she looked up at the figure that now stood before them, having crash-landed through the ceiling: a demon dressed in black with, wings as large as a vulture's.

"...irai..."

His eyes reflected the color of the burning flames and he held a long blade in his fist, making his murderous intentions crystal clear.

"Mirai..."

The mother let out a bloodcurdling scream as he swung his weapon above his head, then brought it down with unyielding force.

⎯⎯⎯◈⎯⎯⎯

"MIRAI!"

Mirai jolted awake, sweating and panting. Mafuyu stood over him, his hands pinning Mirai's shoulders onto the bed and a faintly worried expression pinching his face. Mirai tried to focus on the boy's furrowed brow instead of his own racing heartbeat.

"You were having a nightmare." Mafuyu spoke just above a whisper.

After a few more seconds, he eased his grip and Mirai slowly sat up straight, rubbing his temple. It felt like his brain was hammering against his skull.

"Yeah, happens sometimes," he brushed it off. "How did you get in?"

"I...uh...copied your keys." Mafuyu chuckled nervously.

He copied his keys? When did he even manage to pull that off? *Some nerve this boy has.* Mirai blankly stared at Mafuyu, too exhausted to even react. At any other time, he would have probably given him the lecture of his life and forced him to give them up, but right now he was not in the right state of mind. He decided to let it slide. There was no need to add to his headache. Besides, after hearing Zen's explanation, he was sure that Mafuyu just did it as part of his job to guard him. Getting unnecessarily angry over it wasn't going to solve anything.

"Are you alright?" Mafuyu's concerned eyes dispelled whatever irritation was left in Mirai's mind.

"I'm fine." He really was. It was just a nightmare that kept recurring every time he closed his eyes. He knew why. This wasn't just a dream. The events in this dream were connected to the memories of his past. A past he wished to forget, to undo completely if he only had the chance.

"Is this why you can't sleep at night?" Mafuyu's voice was like cool, soothing water on a sunburn. In the dead silence of his room, where Mirai had suffered alone for years, it was comforting to have someone by his side, checking up on him when he needed it. Though, he would never admit that out loud. It was a privilege he felt he didn't deserve.

"You noticed?"

"Yeah. I'm a light sleeper, so I always hear you when you walk around and go out on the balcony."

"Aren't you full of surprises?" Mirai shot him a toothy grin despite the weight on his heart, trying to make light of the situation.

Mafuyu picked up the jug from Mirai's bedside table, poured a glass of water, and handed it to him. He then tentatively lowered himself to sit on the edge of the bed near Mirai's legs. "Listen... about before. It wasn't my intention to lie to you and I didn't want you to find out what's really happening in such an ugly way, either. I know that made it even more difficult for you to trust me."

Mirai was grateful for the glass of water. It refreshed his dehydrated lips, and he managed to finish it in just a few big gulps before setting it back down on his bedside table. "It's not your fault," he said and reached out to ruffle Mafuyu's hair. For a moment, Mafuyu's eyes widened and Mirai thought he'd stepped out of bounds. But when he didn't pull away or shrug him off, Mirai figured that his reaction was prompted more by surprise than dislike. "You were just following your orders and doing your job."

Mafuyu relaxed. "I'm still sorry for lying to you in the beginning." He extended his hand as if they'd just been introduced. "Nice to meet you. I'm Mafuyu, and I'll be acting as your bodyguard until Zen requests otherwise."

Mirai smiled and took his hand. "I'll be in your care." But instead of loosening his grip on Mafuyu's hand after they shook, he tightened it and added, "No more secrets." It was more of a warning than a question, but Mafuyu didn't seem to take offense.

"No more secrets." Mafuyu let a ghost of a smile lift his lips. "So what kind of dream shook you up like that?"

He was trying smooth things over, but the innocent inquiry still made Mirai shift uncomfortably.

"It was about my family." When Mafuyu's lips curved into a frown, Mirai waved it off and said, "Don't make that face. It happened a long time ago."

But the answering silence still sat heavily in the air between them. Mafuyu must have heard about what happened to his hometown years ago and then put two and two together when the First-Level was brought up in Zen's office. Otherwise, Mirai couldn't fathom why a simple mention of his folks would make him so uncomfortable.

Mirai pulled back the sheets and started to get up. It wasn't like he'd be able to go back to sleep anyway. "Did you have dinner?"

"No."

"Come on, then." Mirai led Mafuyu into the kitchen. The scent of Mirai's dinner was still present, filling their nostrils with a delicious aroma of spices and herbs the moment they set foot in the room. Light flooded the kitchen as Mirai flipped the switch, and Mafuyu took in the meal with wide eyes: white steamed rice, chicken stew, and seasoned vegetables.

"These...you cooked my favorites." He stared at Mirai as if the man had done something much more extraordinary than saving him some leftovers that he happened to like.

Mirai cocked his eyebrows. "Well, I thought you might come back in the evening and you're picky with your food. Better this than having you throw it away." He grabbed a plate from the dish rack and put a generous helping of everything on it before handing it to Mafuyu.

"I didn't think you had a soft spot for me," Mafuyu mumbled as he took the plate. He probably meant to speak the words in jest, but it sounded more sincere than most of what he'd said to Mirai thus far.

"I don't," Mirai said with a toothy grin, not wanting to make the kid more uncomfortable than he likely already was. "If you do anything that annoys me, I'll just give Zen a call and kick you back over to headquarters."

Mafuyu made a disapproving face. "Then I'm afraid you'll have to wait for the next two days."

"And why is that?"

"Because Zen-san went to Aokigahara. A client requested a team to find their missing daughter and friends. Some twisted sense of adventure sent them off exploring the Suicide Forest."

Mirai's playful smile vanished. "Zen-san hardly goes on any team missions these days."

Mafuyu pursed his lips and looked away for a moment before bringing his eyes back to Mirai. "I don't know if I'm supposed to tell you this, but there have been instances lately of Third-Levels showing intelligence."

"Intelligence?"

Mafuyu nodded. "The last one I fought was able to anticipate my movements and understand my intentions. It even smashed my gun. Zen-san went to Aokigahara to see if he could get any clues as to what was going on. That place is a haven for monsters, after all. If something is wrong, there will definitely be some kind of traces of it left there."

Listening to the update on the Third-Levels, Mirai couldn't help but wonder if somehow all of these recent developments were connected. First the news about Bezaleel, and now the Third-Levels. Mirai wasn't a person that drew conclusions from mere guesses, but all of this felt like more than just mere coincidence. And he hoped to God above that he was wrong in believing that things were taking a bad turn.

⬦

Mafuyu sighed in contentment as the water hit his bare skin, soaking his muscles in its gentle warmth. It had been two days since he patched things up with Mirai and resumed his duties as a bodyguard properly this time. No lies.

Mirai was more accepting of him now, but there were still times where things still felt a little rigid between them. Mafuyu knew that most of that had to do with him. Like Nagisa had said, he typically liked to keep his interactions with humans as minimal as possible. But for a reason he couldn't put his finger on, he was more relaxed with Mirai. He would talk to him more than he did with anyone else, even with Zen. He chalked it up to Mirai's easygoing personality. It was impossible to be angry at him and his good nature for too long. He couldn't imagine anyone holding a grudge against that man.

As Mafuyu rinsed off the soap he'd scrubbed himself with, he heard his cellphone ring. He ignored it. Whoever it was could just leave a message and he'd call them back when he was done.

Except the person on the other line wasn't very patient. The phone rang again. And again.

"Oh, for God's sake!" Mafuyu turned off the shower tap and carefully stepped out of the slippery tub. The bathroom had completely fogged up with steam.

He crossed his way to the shelf where he had left his phone. He took the towel next to it and wrapped it around his waist. Water droplets slid down from his soaked hair to his neck and chest, and he could smell the fresh scent of the shower gel on his skin. He dried his hands on another towel before reaching for his phone, then swiped the screen without looking at the caller ID. "What?" he hissed.

"Where the hell are you?" If voices could kill, Mafuyu would have died a thousand deaths already.

He gulped. He knew that hardcore, pissed off tone. Nagisa.

"I was in the shower. What's the matter?" he asked, much calmer this time around.

The next words Nagisa spoke made Mafuyu's eyes pop open in shock. He didn't think twice about racing out of the bathroom in his towel and finding Mirai, who was reclining on the living room couch. Mirai's head snapped around and his eyes darkened as soon as Mafuyu breathlessly delivered the news.

"Zen-san is missing."

CHAPTER EIGHT

UNFORESEEN

Mirai eyed the sharp, dangerous weaponry decorating the walls of the spacious room. Different kinds of swords, bows and arrows, and bo staffs—made in all shapes and sizes to suit all types of fighters—were separated into sections. All of them had been forged with special inscriptions for banishing Rev'ers.

But what he was drawn to was the table that stood in the middle of the room. His eyes trailed over the silver guns laid out in a perfect line, one after the other, on the tabletop. He reached out and picked up a Beretta 92. These were once his favorites. They made a satisfying *bang* when he pulled the trigger, but didn't draw too much unwanted attention: smooth, with a powerful pitch.

He checked its magazine. Sure enough, it was loaded. He placed it in the holster fastened at his hip, then picked up its twin and secured it in the holster strapped around his chest.

His attention shifted from the guns when the door of the weapons hold slid open. Nagisa strode in and made her way toward him. Although her face was blank, unemotional, the grimness in her eyes spoke volumes. She was apologetic and Mirai knew exactly why.

"Hey." Her voice didn't carry its usual authority as it broke the silent air. This wasn't the kind of reunion expected or wanted to have.

"Hey," Mirai greeted back, albeit a bit more enthusiastically.

"I'm sorry to drag you into this mess when all you want to do is stay out."

"Before we get into all that, aren't you missing something?" Mirai extended his arms to his sides and Nagisa smiled before closing the gap between them to wrap her arms around him in a brief hug.

"It's good to see you," she said.

"It's good to see you, too." When they parted, Mirai continued, "Please don't apologize to me for any of this. You need my help to find Zen-san and I'm more than happy to offer it."

Nagisa nodded. "I heard about Bezaleel."

"Looks like nothing gets by you."

"Especially things related to you."

"If it's anything like what happened before, the ones hunting Bezaleel can easily harm all of you if they want to. I won't let that happen."

Nagisa put a steadying hand on Mirai's shoulder. "I know that what you went through is something we can't even begin to imagine, but... Sometimes, fear can be more detrimental than the danger itself."

"You don't understand." He leaned in closer and spoke just above a whisper. "The ones coming after me might be—"

The door opened again and Mirai abruptly cut himself off as several people marched in: four ladies and three men, all armed to the teeth.

"Captain," one of the men addressed Nagisa. "Tsubasa is ready with the chopper. We can leave now."

Nagisa nodded to Mirai and he returned it. It was obvious they were on the same page; their discussion would wait until they got back.

"Since we're heading into Aokigahara, we have to round everything up before sunset," Nagisa said, making eye contact with each of her teammates. "You all know that place is crawling with Rev'ers, so things can get really ugly when darkness falls. That means we have roughly six hours to find them: Zen-san and whoever is still left standing. Am I clear?"

"Yes, ma'am!" all of them answered at once.

"Our team formation is simple for this one. We stick together no matter what."

"Yes ma'am!"

"Good. Let's go." Without wasting another second, Nagisa led the troops out.

The first time Mirai and the Hunters laid eyes on Aokigahara, it was from within the safety of the helicopter. The aerial visual of the land below was packed with dense green treetops. Nothing but a stretch of thick woodlands for miles and miles. The sight filled their minds with a sense of unease. It was not because of the kind of vicious creatures they would encounter down there, but the thought of whether Zen was even alive amidst all that foreboding wilderness.

But that feeling was nothing compared to when they landed on the ground and began navigating through those very same eerie trees. Even then, despite their obvious fear, they steeled themselves for whatever was to come. If there was one thing Nagisa's team was known for, it was their unwavering courage.

"Man, this place is as creepy as its name," Hiro, one of the boys in the team, said as he stole across the muddy ground littered with leaves. He was the last one to climb down from the helicopter. As soon as his feet touched the mud, the ladder was pulled up back into the chopper hovering fifty feet above them.

"Nagisa, I'll keep circling around. Give me the signal when you've wrapped up," the pilot spoke through the earpiece. When she replied in the affirmative, the blades of the helicopter slashed through the air above them and grew more and more distant, until they couldn't hear it anymore.

"Stay close, guys," Nagisa warned her teammates. "And remember, don't split up for any reason," she called over her shoulder as they inched forward, careful and steady.

Aokigahara was a forest that Rev'ers thrived in. Its lack of human presence made it the perfect place for all sorts to gather. Its broad trees threw long shadows, and their dark leaves provided impeccable camouflage that made it next to impossible to spot anything hidden in the woods. Between the heavy leaves and thick branches, even the bright midday sun wasn't enough to light up the dark and gloomy forest.

Mafuyu pulled his phone out from his pocket and checked the screen. The signal bar showed red with an X on it, as expected. That explained why Zen couldn't contact any Hunters for help. Nagisa had told her team how she received nothing but a scratchy call from him hours ago, and now it was clear why he couldn't give them more information about what he'd gotten himself into.

But, she clearly heard him yell, "Too many Rev'ers...team injured." She was clever enough to fill in the blanks. Something had obviously gone wrong. Their experts traced the signal and Nagisa decided to take initiative and round up the team to find him.

Dried leaves and thin twigs snapped and crunched under the Hunters' feet, breaking the stillness around them. All of them needed to keep their senses sharp if they wanted to survive the Suicide Forest. The myths surrounding it usually kept every human away, but the ones that did wander into the forest were unfortunate enough to come across all of its Second- and Third-Level inhabitants.

If they were to survive there, they needed to hear things that they otherwise wouldn't hear, and see things their eyes couldn't normally pick. In short, they had to be as close to superhuman as they could manage.

Leaves rustled nearby. Mirai was sure that wasn't caused by any wind.

He and Nagisa stopped and exchanged knowing glances. The rest of the team came to halt behind them, their fingers on their triggers and their ears open. Without a word, Mirai gestured to the side with his gun. The team turned their heads just as a Third-Level sprang out from the branches between the trees, its four limbs and long, sharp talons outstretched.

Mirai didn't think; he just pulled the trigger. The bullet whizzed through the air and hit the beast square in its forehead.

In the gunshot's echo, chaos ensued.

They didn't have a moment to blink as several Rev'ers lunged at them, one after another. They came from beneath the tree roots, from within hidden shadows, and from between the dark branches. Nagisa's team didn't bat an eye. They pointed their guns at their targets and let loose a barrage of bullets. They engaged in a furious, rapid fight and moved with precision, ducking, swinging and hitting anything that wasn't human.

Repeated gunshots and loud, animalistic growls and shrieks rang through the forest. They banished Rev'er after Rev'er without staggering or flinching.

Mafuyu constantly spun his bo staff at the horde. The encryptions on his weapon glowed as he swung it into a Third-Level's skull. The Rev'er evaporated in a puff of smoke.

"Mafuyu, watch out!" Mirai yelled. Shoving him out of the way, Mirai shot the Second-Level that had lunged for the younger man.

"There is no end to these things!" a female Hunter shouted above the din.

"We need to keep moving!" Nagisa yelled over her shoulder. She didn't need to tell them twice. The team immediately fell in step with her.

While the rest jumped overgrown roots and shot at anything that bared its fangs, Mirai abruptly spun on his heel and charged in the opposite direction the team was heading, sprinting with all his might.

"Mirai?" Mafuyu called out, utterly confused. The team came to a complete stop and turned back to try and find out where on earth Mirai was heading.

Unbeknown to any of them, he had spotted Zen a few meters away, running for his life. A boy followed closely behind him. With the way the gun drooped from Zen's fingers, Mirai figured that they were out of bullets.

"Mirai, wait!" a Hunter named Azumi shouted, but he didn't heed her. Mirai evaded all the Rev'ers that tried to jump at him like they weren't even there, and he shot at them with deadly accuracy.

"Come on!" Nagisa shouted, having realized what was going on, and led them all after Mirai.

"How did he know where Zen was?" Hiro spoke in between his pants. "He was too far away, and running the other way, with us!"

"Probably luck," Nagisa replied shortly as she pushed herself to move even faster.

Mirai checked over his shoulder to find Nagisa and her team following behind him. When he saw reinforcements were on the way, he carried on without hesitation. He saw a Second-Level hidden among the leaves on one of the higher branches, its eyes fixed on Zen.

But Mirai was quick on his legs. His feet pounded into the ground under his feet as he ran almost impossibly fast.

As soon as the Rev'er leapt out of its hiding spot, Mirai lunged for Zen, pushing the man down and out of harm's way. The boy Zen was holding onto fell with them, shielded by the Hunter's larger frame.

Mirai turned over on his back, raised his gun, and fired at the Second-Level. Once it was gone, he jumped back on his feet, hastily grabbed Zen, and helped him and the boy up.

Zen drew in a sharp breath, shock and worry etched on his face. "Mirai! You're—"

"I know," Mirai interrupted. He shut his eyes for a moment and released a slow breath.

"Are you alright?"

"I'm fine." Mirai brushed away Zen's concern and glanced at the boy standing next to his friend. This must be one of those damned brats who wondered off into this place and started all of this trouble to begin with. But there was no time for him to be irritated or to lecture the kid. Not yet, anyway. "Hurry!"

Mirai started running again, pulling the older man and the boy along without another word. Nagisa had reached them by then and shot two Rev'ers in pursuit to cover their escape.

"Zen-san! Where are the others?"

Zen shook his head. His grim silence said all that Nagisa needed to know. Her footsteps faltered and stilled just long enough that for a moment, it felt like the whole forest had, too.

In the midst of all the chaos during the team's fight for survival, none were aware of two pairs of eyes watching them, hidden between the branches.

CHAPTER NINE

FOUND

So *predictable.* Rahel smirked. *Yes, so very predictable. Gullible, too.* To have followed seven dead people into a godforsaken place just to save two of them... It was beyond stupidity. They'd behaved just as he had guessed they would.

Well, except that Rahel would have thought that at least *he* would have known better. But he walked into the trap just like the others did. Foolishness. But, he had to admit that these people were formidable...for weaklings. They held their ground much better than he would have assumed. Rev'er after Rev'er attacked them and they remained strong. *That* was commendable, if nothing else.

"My, my! Such ferocity. They are tough!" Rahel commented with amusement as his eyes traveled from one human to the other.

"Indeed they are," the man crouching beside him agreed.

"Perk up, Zephyr. It doesn't hurt to have a little fun," Rahel said as he watched the group of Hunters from their high tree branch. It had taken him two years to find Mirai, and there he was. So close.

"Say, these Hunters—what do they call us again?"

"First-Levels," Zephyr replied.

"First-Levels? Not very interesting," he snorted. "I wonder what terrified faces they would make if they saw us now."

Zephyr glanced at his master from the corner of his eye. A dark smirk spread his thin lips from cheek to cheek. "Would you like to see?"

"Do you need to ask? Oh, and when you do, make sure *he* sees you."

Understanding Rahel's implied command perfectly, Zephyr leapt from the branch, spread his dark brown wings, and flew toward his prey.

<hr>

Mirai switched his empty magazine for a loaded one in a few lightning fast movements as

Nagisa pressed the button on her earpiece. "Tsubasa! We found them!"

"Roger. Light it up," Tsubasa answered.

Nagisa removed the flare gun from the holster around her thigh, raised it above her head, and pulled the trigger. The flare flew into the sky and burst into a striking color of red, a sign for the pilot to follow.

"I see you. I'm coming down. There is a clearing to your north. Head there now."

"Copy." Nagisa turned to her team. "Mafuyu and Azumi, you're in the rear. Make sure nothing follows us too closely. Hiro and Riko, you're at the center with Zen and the boy. Chiyo, stand guard between Azumi and Hiro. Jun, between me and Riko. Mirai and I will guard the front."

"Understood!" all of them yelled in unison. They swiftly got into the formation and started moving forward.

As they retreated, several Second- and Third-Levels tried picking them off.

Mafuyu took out a spray bottle from the bag at his hip. He lifted his hand into the air and sprayed all around him, unleashing a white smoke-like substance that banished all the Rev'ers nearby, giving them a momentary reprieve.

As the clearing came closer, so did the roar of the helicopter.

They could see their ride out of that awful forest. Only a few more feet and they would be safe.

But just when they were only seconds away from escaping that hell, Mirai detected a flash of metal in his peripheral vision. He grabbed Nagisa by her collar and jumped back just before a glistening blade pierced the ground where Mirai previously stood. A dark figure blurred across the sky and dropped to the ground with a loud thud. When Mirai saw the figure, his eyes widened. He could hear shocked and scared gasps coming from the team behind him, but he didn't dare take his eyes off the monster crouched dead ahead.

The first thing he noticed was a pair of huge brown wings, stretched out and intimidating—like an eagle cornering its prey. The next was the glint of a shining silver sword clutched in the beast's hands.

There was no doubt about it. Mirai was looking at a First-Level Rev'er.

"Run! Now!" Mirai bellowed to the others. No one waited around for a second warning. They all ran for the helicopter as fast as their legs could carry them.

Mirai glowered at the First-Level, who simply stared back. He didn't know this one. Why was he there, and why was he not attacking them? He took a step to the side, and yet the First-Level stood still.

Mirai was about to lunge forward and deal the first blow when the Rev'er taunted him in a low, dangerous tone. "Found you."

When he heard that, Mirai felt his heart stop. His legs froze and he couldn't move. It was only then that he registered the emblem marked into the hilt of the sword and on the sleeve of the Rev'er's robe. The sight of it drained the blood from Mirai's face.

"Mirai! Come on!" Nagisa's holler jolted him back to their current predicament. The First-Level still stood there, unmoving, with eyes that baited and teased him.

Mirai understood then that the Rev'er was there for something else. And that was not to kill him...yet. And if Mirai stood there any longer, he might be putting the lives of the whole team in danger.

So he decided to cut his losses and sped toward the others and the waiting helicopter.

He turned his head for one more glimpse of the First-Level, but the Rev'er was nowhere to be found. He'd vanished just as he'd appeared—without a trace.

Tsubasa brought the helicopter down and as soon as all of them climbed back into the cabin, he spirited them away from that hideous land. They were all safe...for now.

Some of the Hunters simply dropped to the floor of the helicopter when their knees gave out, their adrenaline rushes having run their course. Everyone had fresh scratches and bruises marring their bodies. Their grey uniforms were dirtied with brown forest mud. Azumi even had a twig or two stuck in her tresses.

Nagisa gently guided a fatigued Zen and the boy he'd rescued to a seat. She gave them each a bottle of water, and Zen gulped his down without a word. Water droplets dripped down his chin, making tracks in the dirt he had smudged there. "What happened?"

"You were right. The Third-Levels have gotten smarter on us." Zen paused as everyone's attention turned to him. "But not all of them. Only some, it looks like." He took out his phone and handed it to Nagisa, but the battery was dead. "I took some pictures. The changed Third-Levels all had similar markings on them. They hunted us down like wolves and led us deeper into the forest. Then that First-Level you saw attacked the rest of us. I was able to fend them off for a while, but if you guys had taken longer to arrive..."

Nagisa patted his shoulder. "It's alright. We're glad you are okay."

"Thanks to all of you." He managed to send a weak smile around the helicopter.

"Do you have any idea why the First-Level targeted you?"

"I don't have a clue." Zen shook his head. "Actually, I don't think it was *me* it targeted. They are probably plotting something bigger." He looked at everyone gathered around him. "We need to prepare ourselves for potential threats."

The team was silent. Nagisa clutched the phone in her hand and locked eyes with Mirai.

But Mirai's mind was trailing somewhere else, somewhere his own eyes couldn't actually see at the moment. He knew a First-Level planned this. But why? And why didn't it attack him when it had the chance? It just stood there, staring at him. If he wanted to kill Mirai, he had the perfect shot. So why didn't he take it?

Mirai leaned back and rested his head against the seat. His clothes were stained with sweat and dirt. He closed his eyes and let out a desperate sigh. His heart thumped so wildly in his chest that, for a moment, he thought his veins would explode. The words the Rev'er said rang through his head on a constant loop.

Found you...

CHAPTER TEN

DOWNPOUR

The mission to Aokigahara was more mentally draining than anybody would have predicted. Mirai leaned his shoulder against the large window in Zen's immaculate office, arms crossed over his chest. The day's earlier events kept coming back to him, as unavoidable as a river rushing over a broken dam.

He looked out to the city below, hoping that the bright colors would distract him from the unsettling images of the past circling his mind—images of burning houses and bloodied bodies.

Mirai's eyes followed the skyline. Dark grey rain clouds were rolling in, looking like they were ready to burst any minute. A storm was coming.

He let out a long, loud breath and wondered why trouble always seemed to find him one way or the other, no matter how hard he tried to stay away from it. He looked over at Mafuyu, who was curled up on the couch, fast asleep. Mirai walked over to him and draped his coat over the boy. Mafuyu reflexively dragged it closer to keep himself warm. He looked exhausted, more tired than anyone his age should be, and Mirai hated that they'd dragged an innocent boy like him into this whole mess.

Though he probably could have used the rest, Mafuyu didn't stay asleep for long. His eyes fluttered open when he heard the creak of the door opening and the subdued clacks of Zen's shoes crossing the marbled floor. The door swung shut just as Mafuyu sat up straight. Weariness still weighed on his face, causing his eyelids to droop, but he rubbed it off and tried to appear alert and focused.

"We're holding a funeral to honor the other team members the day after tomorrow," Zen informed them both.

Silence. Neither Mirai nor Mafuyu had anything to say.

Perhaps noticing the grim atmosphere, Zen changed the topic. "Mirai—that First-Level we saw. Do you know who he was?"

Mirai shook his head. "I've never seen him before."

"Could it have been Bezaleel?" Mafuyu's groggy voice chimed in. He hadn't gotten up from the couch yet.

"No," Mirai answered. "Bezaleel has white hair, orangish-red eyes, and black wings that are longer and bigger than the ones on the First-Level we saw today."

"He seemed to know you," Mafuyu pressed. "I mean, he could have gone for any of us. But it seemed like he targeted you right from the beginning and then didn't even try anything. It's almost like he wanted—"

"—to scare me."

"Yeah."

"But why?"

"I don't know."

Mafuyu looked pensive as he asked, "Can First-Levels disguise themselves as humans?"

"If they could hide their wings, sure, but that's impossible. They can't retract them back into their body." Mirai ran his fingers through his thick tresses. First-Level this. Bezaleel that. He thought he was past all this.

Zen placed a hand on Mirai's shoulder in an effort to soothe him. Mirai's weary eyes softened at the comforting gesture, and Zen said, "Maybe you should head home and freshen up. Try to rest for a while."

Mirai nodded. "Yeah I think I'll do that."

But before Mirai could leave, the older man caught him by his elbow, stopping him for a short second to whisper, "No matter who you saw in that forest—"

"I know. Don't worry. I won't act on impulse," Mirai replied with a tired smile.

Believing the sincerity in his voice, Zen let go off his arm.

As Mirai walked out of the room and hurried across the long hallway, a sudden flash of lightning stopped him in his tracks. He looked through the closest window in time to see a second bolt of lightning zip across the sky, illuminating the darker side of the space. A bellowing clap of thunder followed seconds later—a sound loud enough that it seemed to shake the earth to its very core.

The sun had completely set by then, and the clouds were heavy and dark as steel against the inky black sky. A few doves hurriedly flew over the neighboring buildings, seeking shelter from the impending downpour.

It had been an hour since Mirai left for his apartment. Mafuyu stayed at Zen's office and was told not to follow him for now. Mirai looked like he wanted to be left alone, and Zen had decided that it was better to give him some breathing space that night. Besides, Mafuyu knew better by now than to tag along with an irritated Mirai. Though the man was hardly ever moody, it was still unsettling to be around him when he did get annoyed. He would be passive-aggressive and his aura would make Mafuyu want to stay as far away as possible from him. Being the loner he was, Mafuyu never knew how to rightfully deal with such situations anyway.

But, Mirai was the first person that Mafuyu was starting to understand with just actions alone. He could tell when the other man was annoyed, upset, or just plain angry. Even though they've only known each other for a couple weeks, Mafuyu thought he had seen all the expressions Mirai could make. Until now.

Mafuyu never knew that someone who normally looked like they couldn't be bothered by anything at all could wear such a distressed face.

Mafuyu flipped through the pages in the book Zen had given him before he met Mirai. He had never thought much of his own abilities as a Hunter, even though he was called skillful many times. But one thing that did come in handy and set him apart from his peers was his photographic memory and his ability to learn things, even languages, by merely flipping the pages in a book a couple of times. Zen said once that it was similar to hyperthymesia. All Mafuyu knew was that it had helped his team multiples times on countless missions.

"How's that going?" Zen's voice broke into Mafuyu silent musings about the book.

"I'm almost done," Mafuyu replied as he went back to skimming the pages. "It was actually challenging for a change, but I think I have almost nailed the language."

Silence followed once again, and Mafuyu took the opportunity to study Zen. The older man was sitting on his chair, eyeing some paperwork. That was so like him. He was already trying to figure out what the hell went on in Aokigahara, not stopping to give himself some rest first. Mafuyu knew that Zen was trying to do his best to honor those that had lost their lives fighting to protect him and themselves.

"Hey, old man," Mafuyu addressed Zen, much to the other man's amusement. "Was it really okay to leave him alone? Mirai, I mean."

Zen lifted his head from the mountain of papers on his desk. "He needs some time to think."

"Of what?" Mafuyu's irritation leaked out in his voice. "What aren't you telling me?"

"What do you mean?"

"You know what I mean." Mafuyu gritted out between his clenched teeth. "Isn't it kind of weird that I'm on guard duty without knowing what exactly it is I'm guarding against? I think it's time you give me just a tad more information. Why is Mirai really so scared of this First-Level?"

"He isn't scared of First-Levels. He is cautious about them." Zen answered. Mafuyu quirked an eyebrow, urging him to go on. "Everybody in Rev'er Hunter Corps is aware of the incident that happened seven years ago in Iwami—including you."

"Yes, the town that Bezaleel destroyed."

"That was Mirai's home. The whole town was burned down, and a lot of people with it. Some of them were brutally murdered. And some of them happened to be the few people that Mirai dearly loved."

When Nagisa mentioned Mirai and his hometown, Mafuyu had predicted that that might have had been the case, but it still chilled him to hear it confirmed. "Bezaleel killed his family?" Mafuyu echoed.

"I believe he was one of the reasons they were killed."

"One of them?"

"Yes. The incident in Iwami wasn't ever resolved. Police couldn't find any leads. Then they hired us and even we met with nothing but dead ends. Mirai helped us figure out that Bezaleel had a hand in destroying that town, but everything else is still murky. How did it happen, why did it happen...nobody knows."

"So the First-Level we saw in the forest—"

"—could be related to that, yes. He is also a potential indicator as to why First-Levels are appearing in our world again and why they are causing so much havoc. We need to put an end to it before more people lose their lives. If we can get to the First-Levels before they get to Mirai, we will be able to connect the dots. Otherwise, they'll find Bezaleel, and then I fear all hell will break loose."

"Is Bezaleel really that dangerous?"

"He could single-handedly kill everyone in this building with both eyes closed, even if we all attack him at the same time."

Considering the building they were in had around or more than three hundred active Hunters, Mafuyu really didn't like those odds. "That strong, huh?" He sighed, "I shouldn't have stayed back here. Mirai could be in danger this very minute."

Zen nodded, but let a small smile curve up his lips. "You've never cared about someone so much before."

"Every other person I have saved from a Rev'er looks at me like a hero or some crazy guy they can't understand. But when Mirai looks at me, he is looking at *me*. He doesn't see a Hunter. He sees Mafuyu." He paused to gather his thoughts, slightly embarrassed that he'd said so much already. "He is different. I feel like he understands me more than anyone else ever has." Clearing his throat, he stood and walked to the corner where a spare umbrella rested. "Anyhow, I'll get going. Thanks for telling me about the First-Levels, Zen-san," he said as he grabbed it and headed for the door.

"It's pouring outside. Be careful on your way back."

When he stepped out of the building the only thing he could see was the outline of the street that had become hazy amidst the heavy rain continuously falling from the sky. There was no sign of it stopping anytime soon. The orange glow of the streetlights blurred in the thick sheets coming down, and the roads looked wet and slippery, reflecting the silhouette of the vehicles that dared to travel on it in this weather.

Puddles started forming on the sidewalks. Splashing wet footsteps echoed as someone ran for cover from the deluge. The entire street was almost empty. People had fled inside shops and buildings to seek shelter.

Mafuyu opened his umbrella and stepped out onto the wet pavement. He tried to avoid walking on as many puddles as he could; he hated the feel of waterlogged shoes and socks. But avoiding the puddles didn't help him much either way. Even walking under his own little shelter, the occasional gust of wind would blow droplets his way and drench his sides entirely. He had to hold the edge of the umbrella's canopy to make sure it didn't bend inside out in the sudden strong winds that threatened to expose him to the wet weather.

So *ridiculous*. He figured he might as well just walk without one.

After a few minutes, Mafuyu took a turn around a corner that led towards the back alley behind the rows of various buildings, away from the main streets.

He'd never really liked alleyways. They were dark and always seemed to be shady, seedy places—especially in a rainstorm like this one. But this particular one provided a shortcut to the nearest train station. If it wasn't for the heavy rain, he probably would have stuck to the main streets, even if some of them did take him on a longer route.

As he quickened his pace, an uneasy feeling started to bubble up inside of him. Maybe it was the lonely surroundings and the eerie atmosphere. But he wasn't normally someone who would get carried away with something so circumstantial. His eyes darted around as he kept walking and told himself that it was just his imagination.

But then he heard them. Quiet splashes coming from a couple of meters behind him—the sound of someone's shoes treading carefully through shallow puddles.

He didn't have to turn around and look to know that he was being followed. *Damn it.*

Whoever, or *whatever* it was, running away wouldn't help him at this point. They would obviously chase him down, or maybe even shoot at him if they had a gun. Not that Mafuyu didn't have a gun of his own that he felt perfectly comfortable using. His potential assailant didn't know that, though, and he didn't want to give away his hand too soon.

So he did the one thing no one else in this situation would do. He slowed down his pace until he came to a complete halt. Then he whipped around and stared into the darkness around him, squinting his eyes against the falling rain.

"Who's there?" he called out.

No response. Mafuyu furrowed his eyebrows as he concentrated on his surroundings. He could sense a presence. A very *strong* presence.

Just as he started to demand that his stalker show himself, a figure walked out of the shadows to stand before him.

It was a tall, lean young man with sharp features. His long, unnaturally silver hair was tied in a low ponytail and draped across his shoulder. It wasn't the kind of silver that came from age; this was the kind of glinting silver one would find on jewelry, or even a blade. His equally silver eyes practically sparkled in the scarce amount of light coming from beyond the alley.

For a good, long minute, the only sound was that of the raindrops pelting the asphalt.

"Who are you?" Mafuyu finally asked.

"I thought you had already figured that by now." The man's voice was like the weather that soaked them: cool like the rain, but tinged with flashes of lightning.

With any other being, Mafuyu wouldn't have taken that line seriously. But there was something different and very unnerving about this man. He appeared to be the same age as Mirai. But, unlike Mirai, the unnatural color of his hair and eyes screamed that this man wasn't human, and Mafuyu dealt with inhuman monsters almost every day

With one swift move, Mafuyu let go off his umbrella and drew his gun from its holster, firing twice. Maybe Mafuyu had actually believed the bullets would pierce his skin, banish him from this world, and that would have been the end of this strange encounter. His confidence curdled into shock and horror as he watched the man raise his arm, catch the whizzing bullets with his bare hand, and crush them as easily as if they were soft grapes. They didn't even scratch him, let alone hurt him. He simply opened his palm and the crushed bullets fell with a dull *clink* against the wet ground.

A sinister smirk quirked up his lips, and the cold twinkle in his eyes made the hairs on the back of Mafuyu's neck stand on edge. He should have done what they trained him to do in situations like this one: run. And yet, Mafuyu found himself unable to do so. It was as if he was literally rooted to the spot.

The man stepped forward and Mafuyu's fear got the better of him for the first time in ages, freezing the very blood in his veins.

CHAPTER ELEVEN

RAHEL

Nagisa reveled in the comfort of her favorite cafe. It was just a five-minute walk from headquarters, which made it the perfect place to take a break after a long day's work.

It had only been a few hours since they returned from their rescue mission. She swiped through the pictures on her phone. Zen had managed to take some of the Third-Levels and had shared them with her to see if they were similar to the intelligent ones she'd encountered on other missions.

Nagisa zoomed in one of the images and squinted. Her eyes hadn't deceived her; there was the sixth Third-Level that had the same mark as all the others. She pressed her lips together. This was not some strange phenomenon. Someone was doing this on purpose. Someone was placing the mark on the Rev'ers and controlling them.

She had to find out as soon as possible who was behind this, or these intelligent Third-Levels could really start to do some damage in this world. She shoved the phone back into her pocket and took a sip out of her hot tea as she stared outside through the café's glass wall.

The rain outside was getting pretty heavy. She decided to wait there for a few minutes to see if it would calm down before heading back to headquarters.

As she took another sip, a familiar figure on the other side of the street caught her attention. Nagisa's lip twitched up into a half-smile at the sight of Mafuyu striding hurriedly through the heavy rain.

She would have sat there, quietly sipping her cup as he went about his business, if she hadn't seen the suspicious figure that followed him just before he disappeared from her line of sight. To make matters worse, Mafuyu didn't seem to be aware that he was being tailed.

Nagisa immediately shot up, dropped some money on the table, and rushed out of the café. She didn't even pause to wait when the waitress called out to remind her to take her umbrella.

The sound of Nagisa's rushing footsteps was lost in the rain's racket, providing her a safe cover to pick up the pace and shorten the distance between her and the unknown following Mafuyu. She wasn't yet close enough to stop him but she kept a sharp eye on the decidedly male figure trailing Mafuyu. As she got closer, she slowed her steps so as not to make so much noise; it was easier to see the man, but the question of who he was and what he was up to remained.

What was even more odd was that Mafuyu hadn't noticed his stalker—surprising for someone of his caliber. His senses were usually strong and sharp.

Something was terribly off.

Mafuyu turned another corner, and so did the man. She followed suit and stuck to the shadows as they walked a few more steps into the alley. Mafuyu suddenly stopped in his tracks, spun around, and voiced out, "Who's there?"

So Mafuyu *did* sense him. Nagisa kept herself hidden, standing with her back against a jagged wall. She poked her head around the corner just as the man stepped out from the shadows to reveal himself to Mafuyu.

The only visual she had of him was the back of his white trench coat. He offered something in return to Mafuyu's question, and Nagisa strained her ears, hoping to find out if there was anything familiar about his voice. But the rain's din turned his words into an incoherent mumble.

She slowly drew her gun from her hip holster and kept her finger on the trigger.

The conversation between Mafuyu and the other person might not have been clear, but what Nagisa saw next spoke volumes.

Mafuyu pulled out a gun. There were two shots, and then those very same bullets were crushed by the assailant's hand.

Using her free hand, she grabbed her cell phone from her pocket and dialed Mirai's number. The second the call connected, she pushed the phone back into her jeans without telling him who was on the other end.

Not wasting another second, Nagisa rushed forward, aimed the gun at the assailant and fired five consecutive shots. But even before she was done, she knew it was of no use. The assailant didn't even turn around as he caught three of them in his hand and dodged the other two by simply stepping out of the way. He made it seem as easy as playing a schoolyard game of kickball.

But it gave Nagisa what she wanted—an opening. She darted toward him, jets of water splashing up around her as her feet thudded on the ground. Within seconds she'd reached Mafuyu, grabbed him by the arm, and pushed him behind her back.

"N-Nagisa-san!" Mafuyu sputtered in disbelief. Nagisa pointed the gun at the assailant, but Mafuyu grabbed her by the shoulder. "It's no use Nagisa-san! The bullets don't—"

"I know." Nagisa's voice remained calm and steady, and she didn't take her eyes off their attacker as she whispered, "Mafuyu, stay as far back as possible."

The air around them grew cold, and she knew, all too well, that she was staring into the eyes of a First-Level.

The assailant snorted, taking the situation as if it were mere child's play. "Such a strong look in your eyes." He spoke their language so fluently that it was difficult to believe he was a First-Level. He took a measured step in their direction. "So tell me; *where* is he?"

It was a demand, though the Rev'er had thinly disguised it as a question. Nagisa had no doubt that if she didn't give him what he wanted—whoever *he* was— he had the means to make her wish she had.

"Who the hell are you?" Nagisa countered. Not a single flicker of fear in her eyes.

He smiled sweetly in response. "Oh, my apologies. Allow me to introduce myself." With a gentlemanly bow, he said, "My name is Rahel."

It was like hearing death speak its own name.

Against her will, Nagisa's eyes widened. Rahel? Impossible. There was no way he could have made it to their world. She grit her teeth, steeling herself for a fight. There was no way she was going to let this First-Level lay a hand on Mafuyu or get to Mirai.

Nagisa pulled the trigger and shot another several times but none of the bullets even came within an inch of Rahel. He evaded them like they were moving at a snail's speed, side-stepping and ducking every bullet aimed at him.

Still, Nagisa kept firing even though she knew it wouldn't be enough to keep Rahel away. All she saw was a blur as he approached them at lightning speed.

An uncontrollable chill ran up her spine as she fired her last bullet. But before it could get to him, Rahel jumped and cartwheeled into the air. As he did, the tip of his index finger touched Nagisa's gun's front sight and a purple light engulfed the two Hunters, glowing brightly enough that it would have blinded any curious onlooker caught in the wrong place at the wrong time.

Two seconds later, all of them, including Rahel, had vanished into thin air.

There were no of traces of them left, and no witnesses. All that remained were the bullets that had fallen on the ground and the umbrella Mafuyu had been holding, drenched through on the wet asphalt.

⸎

Mirai glanced at the clock on his wall. Five minutes past ten. It was getting late.

Where was Mafuyu? This wasn't like him. He was very punctual and organized, not the type to stay out late for the fun of it.

Did the exhaustion get to him? Did he faint on the way back? Mirai frowned to himself. That wasn't something to joke about, not even in his own thoughts.

Mirai looked at the dinner laid out on the dining table. He had eaten his share, but the plate and its delicious contents for Mafuyu were growing cold.

He had made dinner with Mafuyu in mind before he even realized what he was doing. Perhaps he was getting too used to having that boy around. He really should get rid of that habit of his, the one where he got attached to people a bit too easily. He could only blame his childhood for that.

Mirai glanced at the clock once again. This was getting ridiculous.

He got up from the dining table and walked into his room to fetch his phone from his bedside table. Just as he reached out for it, it buzzed.

Mirai eagerly picked it up and checked the caller ID.

Nagisa? She almost never called him, and certainly never so late.

"Yes?" Silence. Mirai pulled the phone away from his ear and made sure they were still connected. "Nagisa? Are you—"

He was interrupted by the deafening echo of gunshots.

"Nagisa!" Mirai yelled, hoping that he'd misheard and that Nagisa would confirm that if he could just get her attention.

Instead he heard muffled sounds on her end. Voices? Was that Mafuyu?

He strained his ears, trying to pick up the gist of the conversation, but the rain subdued everything to the point that he was starting to think—to hope—that someone was playing a joke on him. Until he heard more gunshots.

This time, he didn't wait for an explanation. Still clutching his cell, he threw open his wardrobe and roughly pushed aside the clothes on the hangers. Two swords in black and red sheaths rested at the bottom of the cupboard.

Despite the urgency of the situation, Mirai took a moment and gazed at the weapons he'd promised himself he'd never use again. But he found himself reaching for them anyway, because at this very moment there was something much more greater at stake than some vow from his past—the lives of his friends depended on him.

He clutched the swords tightly in his hands.

A loud beep brought his attention back to his phone, and Mirai hurried to check the screen. A small yellow dot showed Nagisa's location on a digital map. She must have switched on her tracking system to leave breadcrumbs behind for Mirai to follow.

Mirai secured the dual blades at his hips before bolting out of his apartment, pointing himself in the right direction and taking off as soon as his feet hit the pavement outside.

Just as he thought, a deadly storm had rolled in.

CHAPTER TWELVE

BEZALEEL

"Mafuyu..."

He heard a faint voice, like the chime of a bell ringing in the distance.

"Mafuyu..."

The soft whisper called out only to him.

"Mafuyu! Wake up!"

As soon as he snapped open his eyes, he was greeted by darkness. For a moment, Mafuyu thought that he had gone blind. Then, as his vision started to focus, he realized that it was simply a lack of light disorienting him, not any problem with his eyes.

He groaned. His body felt like someone had used him as a punching bag before tossing him into the corner of a room. His clothes were still damp from the rain, and he felt nauseous. The musty smell in the air only added to his misery.

His temples throbbed; he wanted to clutch his head and soothe it, but found that he couldn't bring his hands around to do so. They were tightly bound behind his back. Mafuyu mumbled a few curses under his breath.

"About time you woke up," Nagisa said from the other corner of the makeshift cell. At least he hadn't been hearing things after all; it was her voice that had called to him and jolted him awake.

From where he sat, Mafuyu could see Nagisa sitting at a tilted angle. Before he could read too much into the strange vantage point, the cold hard floor started to numb his body, and Mafuyu realized that he was lying on his side. He looked around.

They were in a small, dark room. Cobwebs dangled in the ceiling. There were no light bulbs and no electrical outlets as far as he could tell. The paint on the walls was cracked and there was a moldy smell in the atmosphere. It was the kind of space he'd expect to find in an abandoned building.

How unoriginal. Someone really lacked creativity.

"What happened?" Mafuyu mumbled. The last thing he remembered was standing in an alley with a blinding purple light surrounding them.

Nagisa glanced at the bolted door. "We got teleported here—wherever *here* is. As soon as the purple light was gone, someone clubbed you in the back of the head. Rahel wanted to know where Mirai was, and when I refused to speak he knocked me out as well." Nagisa gestured around with her head. "And that brings us here."

"Teleported?"

"Are you really that surprised after everything you've seen?"

"Yes! None of the Rev'ers we fought teleported us anywhere!" He remembered the First-Level that they had encountered earlier. "Where is he? Rahel?" he whispered his name as if saying it out loud would burn his tongue.

"I don't know."

"Why didn't he kill us?"

"He's saving that for later. There are other First-Levels with him, so maybe they want in on the action."

Mafuyu's face paled and he hissed out a few words that he normally wouldn't dare utter in front of his captain while he struggled against his confinements. "These don't feel like ropes or handcuffs."

Nagisa lifted her hands from her lap to show him what he was working with. A thin violet line coiled around her wrists like a transparent rope, except it shimmered with a soft glow in the dimness. "It's called a Nahm. It works the same way a spell would," she explained.

"Spell? What do you mean a *spell*?" Mafuyu blinked twice. Nahm. The phonology sounded familiar. "Is that Zalek?"

There were only a handful of things that ever took Nagisa by surprise, and judging by the sudden stiffness of her posture, this was one of those instances. "How do you know Zalek?"

"How do *you*?" Mafuyu countered.

"Let's save that topic for later," Nagisa answered. "We need to get out of here first."

He watched Nagisa use the wall to push herself into a standing position. She walked over to Mafuyu, grabbed him by the shoulder with her bound hands, and helped him sit up. "There is a dagger strapped to my back, under my shirt. Take it out," Nagisa ordered as she turned around.

Mafuyu lifted the hem of her shirt and saw the dagger, its sheath tied to her waist. He pulled it out by its brown hilt and paused to skim the inscriptions etched into the surface of the blade, guessing from the looks of them that they were written in Zalek.

Nagisa turned again and took the dagger from him before balancing the butt of it on the tip of her fingers and then tossing it precisely into the air. As it came spinning down, it sliced the Nahm right off, freeing her hands.

Nagisa grabbed the dagger and sliced off Mafuyu's restraints as well. As soon as his hands were free, Mafuyu rubbed his wrists. Usually, such a tight binding would leave red marks on his white skin, but these didn't. Although he definitely felt the magical rope while it was still intact, the minute Nagisa cut it off, it was as if it never existed. The binds had disappeared completely.

His gaze fell to the weapon Nagisa held. It was a strange dagger, and Mafuyu knew for a fact that no one else in the Corps had one like it. No Hunters used weapons with those of kinds of inscriptions. He couldn't help but wonder how Nagisa got her hands on it.

Mafuyu ripped his stare away from the dagger when he felt Nagisa drop something into his pants pocket. "Was that your phone?"

"Yes. Keep it with you. If we get split up, it will help get you to safety. I've switched on its tracking system."

"You alerted Zen?"

"I alerted Mirai."

"Mirai? You're pulling him into the one situation he should stay away from?"

Anything else he had to say on the matter got stuck in his throat when he met her glare.

"Out of all of us, Mirai is the one who knows First-Levels the best. He is our only chance to get away from here—*alive.*"

"But what if they kill him?"

"They won't," Nagisa countered. "They need him for Bezaleel. And we need to get all of us out of here alive. If we die here, the information we got on Rahel would go to waste. The Corps would go back to square one."

"Alright," Mafuyu agreed, although deep down he was against bringing in Mirai. But at the moment, he didn't have a lot of other options.

Nagisa walked around the room a few times, looking for a weak spot to exploit. She needn't really have bothered; as soon as she tried the door, she was able to push it open with almost no noise.

Mafuyu couldn't quite suppress the doubts brewing in his gut. Why would they leave the door unlocked with two prisoners inside?

"Wait." He grabbed Nagisa's shoulder before she could take another step. "What if this is a trap? They want us to get out. There is no reason why they would leave the door unlocked otherwise."

"Either way, we can't stay here," Nagisa replied. "We need to find a way out."

Mafuyu could only choke out a hum as he realized that he really could get killed at any minute. In all his years as a Hunter, Mafuyu had known about the First-Levels, but they were so rare he never thought that he would have anything to do with them. His stomach did a violent flip and Mafuyu felt sick. He was starting to doubt that he would live to see the next sunrise.

Nagisa and Mafuyu took timid steps outside. The entire place reflected the atmosphere of the room they were held in—dark and eerie. A flight of stairs leading to the floors above and below came into view. He felt like he was standing in the middle of a road that had been split into two foreboding looking paths, both of which were marked with signs indicating terrible danger. Nagisa took the stairs to the floor below while he followed. Trapping themselves upstairs certainly wasn't going to help.

With each careful and silent step they inched down, Mafuyu could feel his heart beating even harder—to the point that he wondered if Nagisa could hear it. This was the first time he was so anxious about a Rev'er; more importantly, he feared they were walking into a horrifying trap, and that that might have been Rahel plan all along.

And as Mafuyu's unfortunate luck would have it, his assumption was proven correct. At the bottom of the stairs, four First-Levels stood as if they were just waiting for them to arrive.

One of them smirked. "*Akhir ni ethi.*"

Mafuyu tensed as he interpreted their words. *Caught in the trap.*

The *swish* of Nagisa's dagger spinning in her controlled grip echoed through the air. As brave as Nagisa was, even a fool would know that there was no way she could fight them all off.

"Mafuyu," Nagisa whispered. "Run."

Happy to follow her command without question this time, he spun on his heel and bolted back up the stairs. He was positive that Nagisa was right behind him, but when he glanced back and realized that she wasn't, he stopped just in time to watch her race sideways and jump out the broken glass window.

He didn't know which floor they were on but he hoped to God that she was unharmed and could still fight for her life. But while he was crushed that she could so easily choose to put herself in danger just to save him, he knew he had to keep going. Otherwise her sacrifice would be for nothing.

Mafuyu's lungs burned as he kept running. He'd almost reached the topmost floor. He glanced behind and instantly regretted it when he saw the First-Levels closing the distance in no time flat. Mafuyu quickened his pace and in a few short seconds, he slammed open the metal door and sprinted out onto the broad, flat rooftop: a dead end.

There was nowhere left to run. But the roof didn't have any barriers or railings to box him in. He peered off the edge and guessed that he was about eleven stories from the ground. He couldn't jump unless he wanted to kill himself, and he didn't even have weapons to protect himself. Panting, Mafuyu whipped around, looking for a way out, but there weren't any.

He was trapped.

Cold sweat broke out on his back when he heard rapid footsteps approach the rooftop door. He inched backward until his feet were dangerously close to the edge of the roof. One more step and he would fall to his death.

The pounding footfalls grew closer until they echoed as loud as thunder. As the door flung open, Mafuyu thought that this was it—the end of his life. Until Mirai came into view.

⎯⎯◈⎯⎯

"Mafuyu!" Mirai sped towards him, "Are you okay?"

He grabbed Mafuyu by the shoulder and pulled him away from the edge. His eyes darted all over his body, inspecting the boy for even the slightest injury.

"Mirai," Mafuyu whispered his name dazedly. He couldn't believe his eyes, and he had never felt so much relief at the sight of another person. What impeccable timing!

But something didn't add up. Mafuyu saw Mirai come up using the stairwell. Did that mean he was able to outrun the First-Levels? Impossible.

"How did you get here so quickly?" Mafuyu asked.

"I'll explain later. Where is Nagisa?"

"I don't know. She... She jumped out and we got separated."

Mirai seized him by the wrist and pulled him along. "We need to get out of here and find her."

"Wait!" Mafuyu pulled back to get Mirai's attention. "We can't go that way! There were—"

Just as Mafuyu tried to explain, two First-Levels burst through the door and onto the roof. They stood in between the Hunters and their only way out.

Mafuyu sucked in a breath—trapped again. How were they going to get out of this one? Mafuyu didn't have a weapon, and Mirai wasn't strong enough to handle a First-Level. No one was—not even the best Hunters.

Or so Mafuyu thought. All he registered was utter disbelief when Mirai took a step *toward* the First-Levels instead of retreating back. This time Mafuyu was the one to grab him.

"You can't fight them!" he warned desperately. By then, Mafuyu had realized that Mirai wasn't carrying any guns, but two swords he'd strapped to his sides.

"I can," Mirai replied unwaveringly. Mafuyu let go of his arm; there was something different about the way he answered. Those two words held depth and power, but what was even more unsettling was that Mirai appeared as calm as a predator moving in for a sure kill. Mafuyu couldn't help but shiver at this other side to the gentle Mirai he knew. *This* Mirai had chaos, danger and violence written all over his face.

Mirai clutched the hilt of each of his dual swords. The sharp blades cut through the air with a metallic *shwing* as he pulled them out of their black and red sheaths.

When the Rev'ers' eyes fell on the emblem embedded on the swords' handles, their smug expressions twisted with something like fear. In unison, they gasped, "Raathri!"

Mafuyu didn't have time to wonder what that word meant as he saw them dash forward, their murderous eyes leaving no room for doubt; they fully intended to kill Mirai. And no matter how brave Mirai was, Mafuyu knew there was no way that he could hold off two First-Levels, much less defeat them. He was sure that this was the end of Mirai *and* him.

But much to his shock, Mirai stood his ground. The First-Levels raised their swords and closed in on Mirai. In one lightning-fast swivel, Mirai blocked both First-Levels' advances with his swords. The sound of steel meeting steel rang out. He evaded all their strikes: twisting, turning and blocking with rapid motions Mafuyu could barely follow with his eyes. It was like Mirai had practiced for this moment a hundred times before.

Mirai was so swift that none of their strikes even managed to land an inch near his skin. He was more monstrous than them, faster, more accurate. Mafuyu could only stand and watch, feeling utterly useless as one of the Rev'ers closed in on Mirai, raised his sword, and brought it down in a horizontal strike.

But Mirai had sensed it and raised the sword in his right hand to block the attack. The Rev'er's body was left open and Mirai used that opportunity to slash across his abdomen in one swift flick of his wrist. The First-Level let out a choked whimper as blood oozed from his body. All he could do was stare at Mirai, flabbergasted, before crumpling to the granite floor, lifeless.

But that wasn't the end. The other First-Level used Mirai's distraction to sneak up behind him and swing his sword straight into Mirai's back.

Mafuyu gasped in horror. He didn't even have time to warn Mirai, but he needn't have bothered anyway.

As the First-Level moved to drive his sword into him, Mirai spun one of his around his back and blocked the oncoming attack. He didn't even turn around to face the First-Level. Mirai tilted his head to take in the Rev'er's scowl.

At that moment, Mafuyu saw a red spark flash across Mirai's eyes, and his grey irises took on a vibrant reddish-orange shade. He whirled around on his heel and drove his sword straight into the Rev'er's gut. Bloodlust was painted all over Mirai's features, sending a chill up Mafuyu's spine.

When the Rev'er collapsed, Mirai's gaze fell on Mafuyu, but it was like he was seeing a version of Mirai that he didn't know. It just proved that Mafuyu hadn't been seeing things. Mirai's eyes really had turned a different color in the heat of the moment.

"Mirai, your eyes...they—"

His words were cut off by someone's slow applause. Clap. Clap. Clap.

A figure came through the door and onto the roof.

"Rahel," Mirai said. Mafuyu whipped his head around to stare at Mirai. He knew this Rev'er?

"How splendid. You were always wonderful with swords. You wield them as if they were extensions of your hands," he said in Zalek. "But I'm sure you found more fun toys to play with in Yalim." He pulled out a gun from the inside pocket of his trench coat. Mafuyu's gun. "Like this one." Mirai stiffened, as did Mafuyu, who was then more focused on the other man than he was on Rahel. "You're so good at playing hide-and-seek that even the boy standing next to you doesn't know. Allow me to enlighten him."

Rahel clicked off the gun's safety, and the sound drew Mafuyu's attention back to him just in time to watch the First-Level point the gun at him. There was a loud bang with the pull of the trigger. The bullet whizzed through the air, headed straight for Mafuyu's forehead.

There was no time to move, to evade it. Mafuyu did the only thing he could. He squeezed his eyes shut and waited for death, waited for the moment when his life would be cut short.

But instead of pain, or nothing at all, Mafuyu heard the bullet ricochet off of hard metal. He cracked open one eye and the sight before him was something he would never have expected, even if he were to live another ten lives.

Mirai stood in front of him. Black, feathery wings as huge as a vulture's protruded from his back. They were big enough to cover Mirai entirely from head to toe, preventing the bullet from hitting either of them. Mirai stretched his wings sideways so that Mafuyu could see that his black hair had turned snow white. His eyes shone brightly with different shades of vermillion.

"After living in this world, I thought that you would have become weak. I couldn't have been more wrong," Rahel said, his eyes never leaving Mirai's. "You're as strong as ever...Bezaleel."

When Mirai heard Rahel utter his real name he realized there was no going back. His secret had been revealed, much to his chagrin. This was what he'd tried so hard to prevent from happening all these years.

"What are you doing here, Rahel?" Mirai demanded.

"I take it that you're not very happy to see me."

Mirai's eyes bore into Rahel's silver ones, trying to understand the thoughts swirling in the other's godforsaken mind.

"Are you angry because I revealed who you are to your friend?"

"How did you lift the Veyil?"

Rahel sighed, seemingly put out with Mirai's demands. "That part was fairly easy." As he muttered those words, a pair of grey wings sprouted from his back. They were just as big as Mirai's, and looked just as strong.

Mirai wasn't someone that was easily taken aback, but even he couldn't suppress his surprise and disbelief when he realized what Rahel had done. "You stole the Scrolls again?"

Rahel brought his hand level with his face. A black, poisonous smoke emitted from the tip of his fingers until it covered his entire palm. He swung his hand forward and the smoke raced through the air, heading directly towards Mirai and Mafuyu.

Mirai extended his own hand. A blue light glowed and a striking symbol appeared in midair. The symbol was made of circles in various sizes interlocking with each other, with letters forming in between as well as around them. It stopped Rahel's poisonous smoke from reaching them or spreading out any further.

Rahel's lips twitched into a smirk, "So did you," he chuckled darkly. "You think that just because you betrayed us and got your own people killed that everything stopped there?" Rahel shook his head at his own words. "You were careless. You burned most of it but a part of it survived—the part with the revival Nahms. I used them to get the spells back."

Mirai gritted his teeth, trying to keep his anger bottled up as he mentally cursed himself for his stupid mistakes yet again.

Rahel only managed to add to his fury as he continued. "Because of you, our clan was captured. Most of us were executed and the rest of us were forced into exile. But you see, Bezaleel, fate has a way of working in ways we least expect. I used the Scrolls to get here. It took me a couple of years to find you. You had changed your appearance; there was no trace of you."

"So how did you find me?"

"You came to me."

Mirai started connecting the dots, his mind racing. "You're the one behind the changes in those creatures. You put spells on them so I would have to notice."

"Indeed."

"And the incident in Aokigahara." Rahel's canines showed as he shot Mirai a sinister grin, confirming his suspicions without a word. "Why have you brought us here?"

Rahel snorted. "I would have thought you'd work that one out by now."

And on some level, Mirai had. He had known Rahel since they were toddlers. He could usually figure out what Rahel had planned simply by reading between his lines. Mirai turned his head and glanced at Mafuyu from the corner of his eye. Sure enough, the boy was frozen, disturbed by what he was seeing and hearing.

They had wasted enough time here. The longer they stayed, the more dangerous it was—for the both of them, not to mention

Nagisa if she'd survived her own battle. Rahel had become a terrifying entity that Mirai couldn't even begin to fathom.

Mirai took a step back, still keeping his gaze trained on Rahel as he grabbed Mafuyu by the collar and jumped from the edge of the building.

Mafuyu screamed loudly enough to strain his own lungs and threaten to burst Mirai's eardrums.

As Mirai fell with Mafuyu held tightly in his arms, he spread his wings and let the air lift him high above the trees.

"Mafuyu, wrap your arms and legs around me."

"What?" That was all the boy managed to say before Mirai wrapped his wings around the both of them and spun like a spinning top. That was all it took for Mafuyu to clutch on to Mirai's back and waist for dear life.

Mirai twisted and turned, flying between trees and avoiding their sharp, narrow branches, looping around their thick trunks. Leaves were ripped from their stems as Mirai whizzed by. It wasn't long before he spotted Nagisa only a few miles away with five First-Levels closing in on her from all sides.

CHAPTER THIRTEEN

LIFE & DEATH

Nagisa sealed her lips tightly so that even the faintest of sighs wouldn't escape her mouth. She took in long, deep breaths through her nose to calm down her thundering heartbeat. Poking her head around the tree she was using as cover, she quickly assessed the situation.

Five. There were five First-Levels. And they were searching for her.

Just as one of them turned to look in her direction, Nagisa pulled back behind her hiding spot. The sudden jerk caused a jolt of pain in the side of her abdomen. She grit her teeth and tried not to wince, then slowly pushed the hem of her jacket aside. There was a red stain spreading across her waist, drenching her shirt. She touched it, and a thick wetness coated her fingers. Blood. Her blood. She was wounded, probably from when she jumped and broke through that window earlier. The jagged edge of the glass must have ripped her skin.

Nagisa leaned her head back against the tree and huffed inaudibly. She listened to the rustling that was going on behind her, trying to formulate a plan.

If this had happened before she met Mirai, she would have believed that it was only by a miracle that she was even alive at this point. But these First-Levels were different. They weren't anything like how Mirai had described them to her. They weren't anything like Mirai.

If they were, she would have already been dead by now. They wouldn't aimlessly search for her like this, and she wouldn't have been able to hide from them, let alone fight them off.

Where are you, Mirai? Hopefully he had found Mafuyu and both were safe.

Just as she was starting to plan out an escape route, she heard a heavy crunch. A twig breaking in half. Then there was a whisper by her ear. "You can't run."

Nagisa jerked away from the voice and the tree she was leaning on only to expose herself to the Rev'ers. Now she was wide open for them to hunt as they pleased.

"Damn it," she cursed under her breath. How careless. She doubted that her single dagger could help her now. To make matters worse, she was losing more blood as she moved around.

But even with odds stacked against her, Nagisa wasn't the type to give up as long as she was still breathing. So she stared into the eyes of the First-Level that had startled her. It was then that she recognized him. This was the same bastard from Aokigahara. The one that tried to hurt Mirai.

Oh.

This was all part of his plan, or someone else that was pulling his strings. They must have figured out who Mirai really was.

Nagisa rotated her blade between her fingers and clutched the hilt tightly in the palm of her hand. The Rev'er snorted as the rest closed in on her.

She was going to die here, but she didn't fear it. If she was going to go down, then she was going down with a fight to remember. Her eyes raked across every single one of her enemies, calculating their distances, their stances, and the best way to counter their inevitable advances.

The first Rev'er to attack came from her right. He lunged forward with a raised sword and an angry growl. Nagisa blocked his blade with her own and used that to distract him so she could throw a punch at his gut.

The Rev'er on her left wasted no time and rushed at her before she could regain her stance. Nagisa swung her leg in a roundhouse kick to his jaw, but he dodged it. She recovered by dropping to the ground and swiping his feet out from under him with her leg. The Rev'er fell to the ground with a resounding thud.

As soon as Nagisa stood up, the next one swung his sword at her. She dodged it, and in one swift move, she got behind him, grabbed his hand, twisted his wrist, and made him drop the sword.

But these Rev'ers were stronger than her, even if she wasn't injured. No matter how many times she tried to lay them out, they wouldn't stay down. Soon, Nagisa found it difficult to keep up. She was getting exhausted, and it was that exhaustion that made her careless, blind to the First-Level who pulled out his blade and crept up behind her.

By the time Nagisa realized what was happening, it was already too late. The First-Level had closed the space between them and thrust the sword toward her. But even as she knew the end of her life was fast approaching, Nagisa watched fearlessly as the sharp blade inched towards her gut.

In a flash, the First-Level was violently yanked back and thrown several feet away from her. His back crashed against the ragged bark of a tree, and he dropped to the ground, still.

Nagisa's eyes widened in shock when Mirai landed in front of her, his back facing her with his wings sprawled sideways and his white hair shining in the darkness.

The shocked gasps didn't go unnoticed by Mirai's sharp ears. Each of the Rev'ers uttered his true name in absolute fright, and one hard stare from him was all it took for their legs to tremble. He was, after all, *the* Bezaleel. The assassin that single-handedly stood against an entire clan and had killed more people than he could count.

Mirai didn't need to look around to see how many First-Levels surrounded them, but he

tilted his head to look at Nagisa. Mafuyu had already run to her side as soon as he let the boy down.

"Are you alright?" Mirai asked her.

"Given the circumstances, I think I'm doing alright."

But she wasn't. Nagisa's sagging shoulders and slightly hunched posture indicated that she was hurt. Blood seeped from her side. They needed to get out of there. He doubted that Nagisa could hold on much longer.

While Mirai seemed distracted, one of the Rev'ers took the opportunity to fling himself at him and brought his long sword down towards his head. Mirai didn't even need to look as he intercepted the attack. His arm automatically rose up and blocked the assailant with his own blade. He turned his head and his colored orbs landed on each of the First-Levels in turn. Bezaleel's eyes were feared, and for all the right reasons. Nothing and no one could escape his fiery gaze.

As his sword was still locked with the Rev'er's blade, Mirai used his other hand to draw the second sword from its scabbard. In a flash, he slashed the blade across the Rev'er's gut. Blood stained the tip of Mirai's silver blade as the First-Level fell to the ground lifeless.

From there on, Mirai was an unstoppable killing machine.

Two First-Levels attacked him from both sides. Mirai ducked and the enemy swords clashed against each other above his head. In that split second, Mirai spun his sword between his fingers and stabbed the leg of the Rev'er on his right. He wailed in pain, stumbled, and fell on his back. Mirai wasted no time and sliced at the Rev'er on his left while he was still distracted by his fallen cohort. The latter managed to back away and swung his sword at Mirai. But Mirai was far more skilled than all of them combined and dodged the First-Level's attack by mere merely stepping to the side. In another swift move, he closed in and drove his sword through the challenger.

All of this happened so quickly that Mafuyu and Nagisa couldn't keep up with their eyes. Mirai moved with such speed that he was almost blurry to them.

He didn't need their help. What they could do was just stand still and stay out of his way.

But this fight was far from over.

In his peripheral vision, Mirai spotted the final lackey trying to sneak up on him. What a depressing last resort.

Just as the other neared him to strike, Mirai turned on his heel and grabbed the lackey by the wrist. With his other hand, he grabbed him by the neck. The First-Level choked as Mirai easily lifted him off the ground, his feet dangling in the air. He flung the Rev'er away like he was a softball. The First-Level skidded across the forest floor like a pebble before coming to a stop under the foot of a tree. His body was covered in dirt as he lay there, perfectly still.

Finally, Mirai turned toward Zephyr. He had come back to his consciousness, much to Mirai's displeasure. If he had stayed down, he could have finished this off quickly. The longer Zephyr and Rahel existed, the greater the threat they posed to humans as well as to Ashkhaar.

Mirai took a couple of unhurried steps toward Zephyr as the later shakily stood up. He narrowed his eyes in an unforgiving glare. This was the end for him, but he was far from accepting of his fate. Mirai was seconds away from finishing him off when a bright blue light emitted from beneath his feet. His gaze flew down and around, searching for the source of the light, and his eyes widened when he recognized the symbol that had formed right beneath his shoes.

Mirai's body reacted on instinct. He flapped his wings and lifted himself up off the ground, but he wasn't quick enough. Several metal chains sprung from the dirt as if they had been resting below the earth this whole time. They coiled around Mirai's legs like snakes and, with a painful grip, pulled him back down. The force of it knocked the air from Mirai's lungs and his swords slipped from between his fingers, falling to the forest floor.

Mirai's knees crashed to the ground and more chains sprang up. These wrapped around Mirai's wrists, crawled up his forearms, and tightly fastened to his body. He was completely bound and trapped.

Nagisa and Mafuyu couldn't stand still and watch anymore. They rushed forward to help, but stopped just as abruptly when Mirai yelled, "Stay back!"

Rahel came swooping in like a hawk, but he didn't attack Mirai. Instead, he descended in front of him before slowly, gracefully lowering himself to the ground. He looked around and clicked his tongue at the sight of the lifeless bodies.

"You're as violent as ever." He crouched down to Mirai's eye level. "And here I thought Yalim might have softened your heart."

Mirai gritted his teeth. The very sight of Rahel irked him to no end. "To think you stooped so low as to believe a couple of weaklings could hurt me. Pathetic," he mocked.

Rahel remained silent as he held Mirai's gaze without uttering so much as a hum. His face was eerily calm. Mirai had never felt such uneasiness in someone's silence, but he wouldn't let anything give away his discomfort.

Finally, Rahel said, "You're right about that. Especially since those wings of yours are so invincible."

Mirai only got a glimpse of the black smoke forming at the tips of Rahel's fingers before an excruciating pain seared his wings. It felt as if someone was burning him alive. He tried to keep the agonizing pain to himself, but after only a few seconds it was too much, and he let out a bloodcurdling scream.

"MIRAI!" Mafuyu couldn't stand idly by any longer.

"Mafuyu, wait!" Nagisa tried to get a hold of him, but he slipped past her and ran toward Mirai in a futile attempt to save him.

He was only able to get within five feet of him when Zephyr stepped in front of Mafuyu and whacked him right across his face. Mafuyu stumbled, lost his footing, and fell with a heavy thud. He hit his temple on the edge of a small jagged rock and lost consciousness.

Mirai could hardly keep his eyes open due to the torment

spreading across his back, but as his ears picked up the sound of Mafuyu's body hitting the ground, he gave Rahel a glare that would have sent the demons of hell scurrying.

"Rahel." Mirai's voice was but a whisper, but it conveyed danger that even Rahel couldn't ignore. "If anything happens to that boy, I will kill you."

It was not a threat. It was a promise.

But Rahel snorted and cupped Mirai's chin gently, keeping their gazes locked. "Kill me? With your broken wings, you can't even catch me." A scowl came over his face. "I would like to see you in agony while you think of a *futile* attempt to stop me, Bezaleel." Mirai knew he wasn't referring to the chains. He meant something far worse. "I'm looking forward to your misery."

With that, Rahel lifted himself off the ground, Zephyr by his side, and flew off into the distance.

A few minutes later, the Nahm undid itself and Mirai's chains broke. As soon as his arms and legs were free, he crawled to Mafuyu's side. Nagisa was already crouched beside him, checking his vital signs. She released a breath. Mafuyu was still alive.

Mirai silently thanked the heavens above. If anything had happened to Mafuyu, he would never have forgiven himself.

His colored orbs fell to Nagisa and met her worried gaze.

Rahel was planning something much worse than what they'd gone through that night: something that could likely turn two worlds upside down. Innocent human lives could get tangled in a mess that would only result in death and chaos on all sides.

And Mirai would do everything in his power to stop it from happening.

CHAPTER FOURTEEN

WORLDS

The first thing Mafuyu saw when he opened his eyes was darkness. Again. The first thing he felt was the dull ache persisting at the back of his head and the soft mattress he was laying on. His mouth was dry and his limbs felt heavy.

He lay still and let his eyes adjust to the blackness that surrounded him until he could trace the four corners of the ceiling. The walls. The window. The curtains that covered the windows and blocked out the sunlight.

He knew this room. It was Mirai's.

He shot up straight. The unexpected movement made his temples throb, and nausea rumbled up his throat. This almost felt like déjà vu.

The last thing he remembered was fighting a First-Level at some godforsaken place. Rahel. And Mirai...

Had it all been a dream?

The soft clinking of metal brought him back to his senses. That was when he realized he wasn't alone in the room. Mirai stood before a small table by the window, his back to Mafuyu. He was putting a few cotton swabs onto a metallic plate. The room smelled like antiseptic.

Mirai's hair was back to its original black and he was shirtless. Mafuyu eyed his bare skin, from the back of his neck to the middle of his back, where a black tattoo in the shape of wings stretched from one of his shoulder blades to the other.

A pricking pain throbbed in Mafuyu's temple. He groaned and covered his eyes with his palms, as if blocking his vision would somehow lessen the hammering inside his brain. His fingertips brushed the soft wool tied around his forehead. Mafuyu felt around before realizing that it was a bandage.

"Are you awake?" Mirai's voice carried across the room, and Mafuyu could tell that the man was in anything but a good mood by its hostility.

"What happened?" Mafuyu asked. He *needed* to know. He was sure he didn't die because there was no way that heaven or hell looked like Mirai's bedroom.

Mirai pulled on a white silk shirt to cover his bare skin. "You don't remember?"

"The last thing I remember was getting whacked on the head by that First-Level. Then everything went black."

Mirai wasn't very quick to fill in the gaps. He stood still for a couple of seconds before turning around to face him. Mafuyu's breath hitched. Mirai's eyes were like the sky at dawn, painted with striking oranges and reds.

The dimness of the room made them appear even brighter than Mafuyu remembered them being on that rooftop, and he found himself unabashedly staring for so long that it could be considered offensive. He didn't know that the color of a First-Level's eyes could be so beautiful.

Mirai was indeed the one and only Bezaleel.

"Why didn't you tell me?" Mafuyu asked before he thought better of it.

"There was no reason to tell you."

The cold reply irked Mafuyu, perhaps more than it should have. "What are you talking about? I—"

"You what?" Mirai interrupted. "Look at me properly, Mafuyu. I'm not human. Why would I trust you with a secret like that when I barely even knew you?"

"But—"

"From the very beginning, I didn't want you here. I pretended to tolerate you, but now you've become a burden that I don't want to bear. You've disrupted my life enough, and I want nothing more to do with you." Mirai briefly closed his eyes. When he opened them again, they were his normal grey orbs, except they were much colder than Mafuyu had ever seen them. "I've packed your things. Get out. I don't want to see your face again." His fingers curled into fists as he turned away from Mafuyu.

With each word Mirai uttered, Mafuyu's heart broke. All these years, he never cared what other people thought about him. But this cut him deeper than knives ever could. He pressed his lips together and swallowed down the emotions that wanted to burst out of him.

"Is that really how you felt all along?" he asked, his voice trembling despite his best efforts to control it.

"Yes," Mirai replied without a second's hesitation. No lies, no pretenses.

So Mafuyu did the only thing left to do. He shakily stood up, grabbed his duffel bag from where it sat at the foot of the bed, and walked towards the door.

Before turning the doorknob, he paused and murmured, "I thought that, with you, I finally knew how it felt to have a family."

"You were the only one who felt that way." Mirai's words were like gusts of wind blowing on a midwinter's night. They left him feeling cold and hollow.

Mafuyu said nothing more as he put on his shoes and walked out of the apartment, never once turning back.

A deep sense of sadness and anger gnawed at him. So this was what it all boiled down to?

If he'd known that this was how it was all going to end, he wouldn't have gotten involved in the first place. He would have refused Zen's assignment. Now he just felt cornered and lost.

With a heart full of anger, his feet gained strength and picked up the pace, carrying him to the one person who, he was sure, knew about Mirai's identity all along.

It was about time Zen gave him a proper explanation.

* * *

Zen sat at Nagisa's bedside in the medical room and watched as she slept peacefully. Her chest rose and fell with every breath she took, but it had been a close call.

Last night... Zen didn't even know how to explain what went down last night. He had been sleeping soundly in his apartment when he received the call from Mirai. He had urged Zen to meet him halfway in the village of Hinohara as soon as possible. Everything else after that seemed like a blur.

Zen had never driven faster in his life. It helped that the streets were almost empty at that time of night, or else he would have crashed his car for sure.

As he drew near Hinohara, he saw Mirai carrying a motionless Mafuyu and supporting a pale and stumbling Nagisa—all in the form of Bezaleel. The headlights of the car shone on them and made them look even worse for wear.

Zen had rushed to help them get situated in the car. Once he started the engine again, Mirai explained what had happened while they made their way back to headquarters.

The organization's doctors had been fast and efficient. They told him that Nagisa's wound wasn't that deep, and that even though she had lost a lot of blood, she'd make a full recovery once it healed.

Mafuyu's injury hadn't been serious, either. He had been knocked out by a blow to the temple, but was likely to wake up soon.

Zen leaned forward and brushed a lock of Nagisa's hair away from her sleeping face. He stood up, walked out, and got into the elevator. On the way to the third floor, he wondered how things were with Mirai and Mafuyu. Mirai had reverted back to his human form while in the car, and he'd stayed with them until he heard that Mafuyu would be alright. After that, he had insisted that he took the boy with him while he was still unconscious. A normal person would have found it difficult to carry a person's dead weight, but for a First-Level, it was an easy task.

Zen couldn't decipher the reason behind such an odd request, but he ultimately let Mirai do as he pleased. All that was left was making sure that Mirai hadn't been spotted by anyone outside or inside the organization. Which, considering how well the man normally flew under the radar, Zen was sure would be straightforward enough.

The elevator stopped and Zen stepped out. As he walked towards his office, he couldn't help but wonder if Mafuyu had seen Mirai in his true form before he was knocked out. Either way, things were much darker than he had predicted when he first assigned Mafuyu to his friend.

He heaved a sigh and pushed open the door to his office. He almost startled when he saw Mafuyu sitting on the sofa, waiting patiently for Zen. When Mafuyu saw the older man, his face twisted into an angry scowl.

He stood up, seething. "How could you?"

Zen shut the door, knowing that this was going to get ugly. At times like these, he was thankful that the office was soundproof.

"How could you lie like that, over and over and right to my face?"

"Mafuyu," Zen murmured, trying to calm him down.

But the boy showed no signs of backing down. "Even after asking you several times, you still kept the truth about Mirai hidden from me."

"And what if I had told you? Would you have accepted him and treated him the same way?"

"Of course I would have!"

"Really? You wouldn't have been afraid of Mirai for even a second if I told you that he was Bezaleel?"

"Not after I got to know him. First-Level or not, he is still Mirai. He's not a bad person. You know that better than anybody else."

Zen leaned back and his shoulders relaxed. "That's also one of the reasons I put you with him."

"What do you mean?"

"You should know by now that Mirai never needed any protection. I asked you to stay with him to keep him under control. I knew he would come to trust a person like you and that it would stop him from doing anything rash and foolish—like chase after Rahel on his own."

Mafuyu's eyes widened to the size of saucers. "You know about Rahel, too?"

Zen nodded. "Mirai told me everything last night."

Mafuyu shook his head, his eyes never leaving Zen's face. "Unbelievable. I thought we were keeping secrets from Mirai, but the one who was being kept in the dark was me. I was the idiot all along."

"Mirai kept dropping clues about who he was from the beginning. You just didn't see it."

"And how did you expect me to see it?"

"You were trained better than that. Think back. How did you think he found me in the forest so quickly at Aokigahara? I was nowhere near him and no one should have spotted me, but Mirai did. Unlike humans, he has three-sixty-degree vision. He can see everything around him, even in pitch darkness."

Mafuyu stiffened. Zen guessed that it was because he was sorting through a range of emotions, from disappointment in his own carelessness to betrayal and anger. Finally, he said, "He was able to control it."

"Control what?"

"His eyes and his wings. Even the color of his hair. He said that First-Levels couldn't hide them, but *he* did."

Zen sighed. There was no point in hiding the truth from him anymore. It was time he knew everything. If anything, it could help Mirai to have someone like Mafuyu in the know. He walked toward the door, turned the key, and clicked it shut. "Sit down, Mafuyu."

"Why? So you can tell me more lies?"

"So I can tell you the truth about who Mirai—" He paused before correcting himself. "About who Bezaleel really is, the First-Levels, and the destruction that we need to prevent from happening."

Mafuyu didn't argue, and although he hesitated for a couple of seconds, he eventually swallowed his pride and sat back down with a huff. Zen dragged a chair over to sit across from him.

"What I'm about to tell you is a secret that can't leave these four walls. Do you understand?"

Mafuyu nodded cautiously.

"First-Levels are not Rev'ers at all. They come from another world called Ashkaar. It's a world that couldn't be more different from ours; things we can't even imagine exist there. And protecting that world are four main guardians called Devas, or 'protectors.' We call them 'First-Levels.' We saw them as mysterious creatures who could easily wreak havoc, but the reality couldn't be more different."

Mafuyu listened intensely as Zen continued. "Ashkaar and our world are hidden from each other. Everyone living in Ashkaar is a normal human being, just like you and me. They don't know about our world, and for the most part, we are unaware of them. They live as if in a different time, with magic and things that we have never seen and will never see here. The only ones who do know about our world are the Devas, and it is their job to keep both worlds hidden from each other. They do this by guarding a portal they refer to as the Veyil. It's like a gate that lets a being cross between both worlds. The Devas are the only ones that can open it. Do you follow what I'm saying?"

When Mafuyu nodded, Zen went on. "Ashkaar has four main nations. Well, they call nations what we'd call continents. Each is ruled and protected by gifted Devas born of a certain bloodline. Jabilsa is guarded by a Deva called Mikael, Varos is guarded by Leka, Seylon is guarded by Ismat, and Alayl is guarded by Eiwa. These privileged Devas guard and rule the nations because they are born of a certain bloodline from their specific clans and exhibit a number of gifts even as children. 'Deva' means protector; they're similar to what we call kings, but are only given this title and status when they prove themselves worthy to rule a nation. When they are born, they are called Teiyyans.

"Teiyyans have wings and differently colored eyes and hair, but that's not all. They are intelligent and skilled fighters that wield specific powers. As they grow up, they are trained to become the most powerful warrior of their land, and eventually become a Deva. Their first duty is to keep the peace in the nations.

"Apart from the four main Deva clans, there was one more: a clan called Raathri. It produces unbeatable warriors with intelligence and deadly combat skills that are second to none. They were powerful, but no Deva was ever born into their clan. Because of their infallible war strategies and strength on the battlefield, the Endhra clan—Eiwa's clan—appointed them as the Devas' own warriors. They became assassins: loyal, powerful fighters who carried out their duty in the dark and were feared by all.

"But one day, for the first time in Ashkaar's history, a Teiyyan was born to the Raathri clan: a child that would be raised as the clan's strongest assassin yet. They named him Bezaleel."

CHAPTER FIFTEEN

PLAYED

ezaleel's controversial birth sparked a nationwide argument, from the common people to the higher-ups. Was Bezaleel a curse? Why had fate chosen a member of the Raathri to become a Deva after all this time? Was the land damned? A multitude of theories arose from all corners of Alayl.

Eiwa's father, Rasa, was the one to dispel the rumors and bring down the uproar. As the nation's leader, he had to make a decision regarding Bezaleel that would ease the minds of the people, but he couldn't upset the Raathri clan in the process.

So he made a deal with Marvak, the leader of the Raathri.

Bezaleel was born to the Raathri and so he would remain with them, train under them. When he came of age, Rasa, along with the three other Devas, would decide if Bezaleel was fit to claim the position of a Deva, and if he was, Rasa himself vowed to take the boy under his own wing and train him to become who he was destined to be alongside his own daughter, Eiwa.

And so, Bezaleel trained under the Raathri day in and day out from the age of five. He was gifted at both the pen and the sword—much more than Marvak had first perceived. By the age of seven, Bezaleel had already surpassed half of the Raathri's assassins as the strongest fighter. At thirteen years old, Bezaleel was capable enough to lead an entire unit on missions. In him, Marvak saw a future.

But a single mission changed the fate of the Raathri and Alayl in ways they could never have expected. One mission was all it took to uncover a horrible truth.

On a winter's night, Bezaleel was summoned to the Raathri clan's Ancestral Hall. The hall was an ancient dome-shaped building built from white stones. Five pillars supported the front archway. Bezaleel climbed the stairs and looked around. Inside, the décor was simpler than the hall's grand exterior. There was only one floor, with a couple of rooms sectioned off. The space was decorated with antiques and subtle, yet intricate designs that reflected the Raathri themselves. The walls showcased paintings of the clan's leaders over the generations. The upper part of the dome was made out of glass panes that let in natural light during the day. Once the sun set, wall lamps came to life and brightened the place.

Bezaleel made his way across the entryway until he stood in front of a double mahogany door. He knocked twice.

"Enter." With Marvak's permission, Bezaleel let himself in. The room was as subtle as the rest of the interior. Lamps lined the walls, giving the room light even on the darkest of nights. A thick rug carpeted the floor. In the middle of the room was a big, round wooden table with chairs positioned all around it.

"You summoned me?" Bezaleel asked.

"Yes." Marvak sat behind the desk, his face scrunched up in a constant frown. Creases were etched around his temples, and his eyes held little compassion—and even less mercy. He was a stern man who didn't tolerate disobedience and disloyalty. The Raathri respected him out of fear.

He handed Bezaleel a small white scroll with an aqua blue ribbon tied around it.

Bezaleel untied the ribbon and saw the seal of the Endhra clan on the topmost corner of the page. It was a message from Lord Rasa. After he'd read it, Bezaleel spread the page out on the table, as if the weight of its contents was too much to hold in his hands. He looked up at Marvak. "This is impossible."

"That's what we all thought. Yet here is proof to the contrary," Marvak replied.

"Are you sure you want me to lead this mission?"

"Yes." Marvak jabbed the note with his index finger. "I think your abilities will be a great asset. I'll let you choose the three members you would want as teammates. You know the importance of this mission. Whatever you do, *don't fail.*"

Bezaleel nodded; he didn't need Marvak to remind him that this mission would be a grievous one. Someone had stolen Ashkaar's Forbidden Scroll, which was supposed to be safely guarded at the Deva's palace in Alayl. It was a grand feat to swipe it from under the nose of a Deva, which meant the traitor was likely someone they'd all truly trusted.

While the contents of the Forbidden Scroll were unknown to Bezaleel, or anyone except the four Devas, one thing was for sure. It was of utmost importance that no one see it, touch it, or read it without the Deva's permission.

And now he was entrusted to retrieve it from whoever had stolen it. Like Marvak had said, failure was not an option.

Bezaleel had gone on countless missions where failure was equal to death, but none more important than this one. One wrong decision and the Scroll could fall into the wrong hands, bringing chaos to all of Ashkaar.

With that in mind, Bezaleel stuffed the note under his robe. He bowed to Marvak and left to get his team ready. He already knew who he'd choose, and one of them was the second best warrior the Raathri clan had, another prodigy and a potential future leader of the clan: Rahel.

As soon as he was assigned the mission, Bezaleel contacted his selected teammates and waited for them outside the gates of the Raathri estate.

"Bezaleel!" Rahel waved as he arrived with the two other members, Abel and Kaniel.

That was Rahel: punctual without a fault.

Once they gathered around Bezaleel, he explained what it was that they needed to do.

"Our mission states only one spy, but we know better. A feat like stealing the Forbidden Scroll requires help. There will be more of them, and they will be extremely skilled," Bezaleel explained. "We need to proceed with caution and retrieve it before sunrise. If word gets out that the Scroll can be stolen, Alayl's enemies won't rest. The public will panic. We need to settle this quickly and effectively. Eliminate whoever is involved, and leave no traces behind."

"Understood!" the trio shouted in unison.

"Let's move." Bezaleel signaled and they headed east, toward the gate that sealed off Alayl's land. If a spy had to flee, he would have to get out of town first.

Bezaleel launched himself into the clouds while his teammates covered the land. His black wings provided the best cover when he was surrounded by the darkness of night. They were as hard as diamond, impenetrable: a perfect shield. No one could sense or see him coming, but with his eyes, he could see everything around him. His eyes were far from those that were normal. Three-hundred-sixty-degree vision that could pick up the heat and life force of any humans up to three miles away: no one could escape him. No one could sneak up on him. No one stood a chance against him.

As he flew over the trees, his gaze fell to his teammates running below. They were just as swift with their legs as he was with his wings. He kept an eye on them as they covered the ground at warp speed, all while treading with the stealth and accuracy of a pack of wolves.

As they silently surveyed the area, Bezaleel spotted movement a few feet away from his teammates, but they charged ahead, completely unaware of the danger that awaited them.

Bezaleel changed his course and dove, coming down as fast as an arrow from its bow. He landed in front of his teammates, crouched, with his wings spread out like a glider. The others stopped at the sight of him. They didn't need words to understand that Bezaleel had sensed something.

He could see the figures partially hidden between the trees and the tall, wild grass. One…two…five…seven. Seven men waited in silence to ambush them.

Bezaleel had no time to signal his teammates before a chain scythe slashed out toward his side. A normal person wouldn't have seen it until it was too late, but Bezaleel summersaulted into the air and the weapon pierced the trunk of a tree that was behind him. He landed on the wide, blunt surface of the blade, grabbed the weapon's chain, and yanked on it. A man came stumbling toward him, still clinging to the other end.

Once he was close enough, Bezaleel grabbed him by the neck and tightened his fingers around the man's throat. "Tell them to surrender," Bezaleel demanded. The enemy wheezed in his grip, but otherwise remained silent as he raised his hand and made a sign. The six other men leapt from their hiding places, ready to attack. But it did not faze Bezaleel or his teammates. They were assassins for a reason.

The Raathris fought back with more vigor and skill than the men could hope to match. Weapons clashed loudly in the night. Silver blades sliced through skin and spilled blood.

Although most of them targeted Bezaleel, the rest of the Raathris weren't ignored in the skirmish. They defended, attacked, dodged and slashed at anyone who got in their way. They countered their enemy's moves like they had rehearsed them ahead of time. Their reflexes were sharp; they were agile and fast.

Amidst the bloody battle, Bezaleel's eyes picked up on movement in the distance. A man, roughly a mile away, ran on foot.

"Rahel," Bezaleel called out and Rahel turned, throwing a man over his shoulder and twisting his arm as he did. The sound of a bone cracking punctuated his movement. "Take care of things here."

"Leave it to me," the boy assured.

Bezaleel flapped his wings and he took off, speeding across the dark sky. When he spotted the spy, he swooped down like an eagle and tackled him. The man fell forward and they both tumbled to the muddied ground. The Scroll flew from the man's hand on the impact and landed several yards away from them.

Bezaleel rose to his feet first, but got pulled down just as quickly when the man grabbed his leg and pulled. As he fell on his back he managed to kick out at his opponent. The spy dodged him and scrambled to his knees before he drew out five sharp daggers from his pouch. He threw one at Bezaleel, who jumped up and cocooned himself in his wings just in time. Feathers became as hard as steel, and the daggers graced their surfaces with a dull thud, then fell into the mud.

The spy rushed forward, thinking that Bezaleel hiding in his wings would have blocked his vision, but he was sadly mistaken. Bezaleel's eyes could see through objects, and he knew the man was dashing right by him.

The man drew out a sword at the same time that Bezaleel opened his wings. The spy swung at his head, but he ducked and punched the spy's ribs, then hooked his hand under his shoulder and tossed him to the side like he was made out of rubber. The spy let out a groan as he landed flat on his back. Bezaleel drew his sword from his sheath, launched himself at his prey, and hovered over him with the blade positioned at his throat.

Bezaleel would have finished him off right then if the spy hadn't stopped him with a question. "Who are you fighting for?"

Bezaleel stayed his hand and furrowed his brow.

"You think you are serving the right people, but you are just being played, Bezaleel," the spy continued. "A Deva that is also an assassin is unheard of. No one will accept you as one. You are born to a clan of darkness, and that's where you belong. You will be the reason that Ashkaar will fall."

"You should have chosen your words more wisely," Bezaleel muttered before he raised his sword and drove it into the spy's chest.

Blood poured out of his body and blended with the mud beneath them. Bezaleel stayed and watched the light leave his eyes. As soon as it did, he ran his fingers over the man's eyelids, closing them.

Bezaleel stood up, picked up the scroll, and returned to his team. All the while, the spy's warning echoed in his head, but he soothed himself by remembering that they were just words of a vengeful man whose plans were spoiled right before he met his end at the hands of an assassin.

As he made his way back, night came to an end and the first hints of daybreak filled the sky.

"Bezaleel!" Rahel sounded satisfied to see him unharmed. "You retrieved the Scroll."

"I did," Bezaleel answered as he glided down. His wings created a wave of wind across the grass as he landed. His eyes fell on the now bound intruders, each of them looking bloody and broken.

In Bezaleel's eyes, it served them right for going against the Raathris, who had no history of holding back against their enemies. His team only had a few minor scratches between them; Rahel stood completely unharmed except for a torn sleeve. *This guy. If Rahel was born a Deva, he would surpass Lord Rasa.*

But Bezaleel's attention was immediately wrenched away from the warriors when he saw two children, not much younger than he, tied up separately from the rest. Tears stained their cheeks, and fear and helplessness was apparent in their eyes.

A peculiar irritation prickling in Bezaleel's chest; he didn't like what he was seeing.

"What's this?" he gestured towards the children. Hearing his voice, the young captives raised their heads toward him.

The sun had now started to show itself, and the golden light fell on Bezaleel, illuminating his dawn colored eyes and his long white hair, tied back as it usually was. Even his jet black wings seemed to shimmer under the warm rays.

"We found them wandering in the forest. They must have been with the spies."

"No we are not!" the boy defended himself and his sister. "We don't know what spies you are talking about!"

Bezaleel briefly glanced at the real spies, but none of them seemed to care, much less recognize the two.

"We were just looking around for the Night Flowers. We wanted to pick some for our mother. She is sick and these flowers will help her, but they only grow around here, after nightfall. That's why we were looking for them in the dark," the girl tried to reason.

Bezaleel stared at the two and saw in their eyes that they were speaking the truth. They'd just stumbled upon the wrong place at the wrong time.

But one of Bezaleel's teammates didn't seem convinced. Abel stalked toward them and raised his sword. The children screamed in despair as the man aimed for their heads, but

Bezaleel managed to wedge himself between them and impending doom. There was a loud, ear-shattering clang as Bezaleel's sword met Abel's.

"What do you think you're doing?" Bezaleel snarled, his eyes narrowed at his teammate.

Abel stood his ground and glared back. The fact that he was older and more experienced made him stubborn and arrogant. Rahel calmly watched to see where this would lead, who would come out on top.

"No loose ends. They might be spies, and we ought to finish them off before they can use whatever they've learned against us. It's our responsibility as assassins," Abel argued.

"Our responsibility is to protect Alayl," Bezaleel retorted. "That doesn't give us the right to spill innocent blood based on false assumptions." He pushed Abel back hard enough that he stumbled. Bezaleel turned towards the two children and sliced through the ropes that bound their hands. The boy got up first and helped his sister. "Get out of here."

They needed no more prompting and bolted in the other direction. In that moment, the assassins had witnessed Bezaleel display a characteristic that the rest of the clan lacked. He showed kindness, and a reluctance to needlessly take someone's life. Little did they know that for one born from the darkness, he had a heart that was anything but. Soon, that paradox would throw all of Alayl into mayhem.

CHAPTER SIXTEEN

ENDHRA & RAATHRI

Bezaleel kneeled, the Scroll safely held in both hands and above his head as he presented it to Rasa.

The long white cloak fluttered around Rasa's ankles as he moved forward. He took the scroll with both hands, and when his palms were empty, Bezaleel tilted his head and glanced at the Deva who ruled Alayl.

Rasa was dressed in the traditional Deva's robes. Beneath his cloak was a long blue shirt with golden toggle buttons, paired with white tunic pants and knee-length light blue boots. His cloak was held in place at his right shoulder by a pin with the Endhra clan's emblem. The back of the cloak proudly showed off his status as Alayl's Deva with a traditional symbol. His waist-length, aqua-colored hair was tied loosely at the base of his neck with a golden hairpin that had the same design as his shirt buttons.

"I heard that you handled the mission well," Rasa said. "As expected of a prodigy from the Raathri clan."

"Your words are kind," Bezaleel replied. "But it was also because I could count on my teammates."

"Speaking of, I also hear that you have another gifted member among the Raathri. Rahel, was it?"

Bezaleel nodded. "There is no doubt that he will lead the Raathri clan in due time."

"Indeed. Is it true that you ruthlessly killed the spy who stole the scroll? For a child your age, you showed no remorse. You may be an assassin, but should I be concerned, Bezaleel?"

Bezaleel's orange-red eyes bore into Rasa's white ones, both of their gazes unflinching.

Rasa was clearly testing him.

"I'd rather not spill any blood, my lord. But had I hesitated, all the secrets that Ashkaar's Devas have tried to protect for generations would have been revealed. I'm not happy taking someone's life, but sometimes the right decisions are the hardest ones to follow through with."

Rasa's lips twitched into a smile. "I see a great future for you, Bezaleel. Sometimes it's hard to remember you are but a child." Rasa rested the scroll vertically on the ground, his fingers still holding onto the top as if it would disappear the minute he let go. "You may leave. Don't hesitate to come to me if you ever need help."

"You're very kind, Lord Rasa." Bezaleel got up and approached the door. After two knocks, it opened from the other side by two guards. At the sight of both Bezaleel and Rasa, they bowed. Bezaleel felt their eyes lingering on him when he walked by. He could almost hear what they were thinking.

This boy of the Raathri clan is to become a Deva? What will be the fate of Alayl? Maybe that's why young Lady Eiwa will also be in a position to rule—it's so she can keep an eye on him.

As much as Bezaleel wanted to dispel their doubts, he was in no position to do so. It would be like adding wind to a wildfire; it would inevitably blaze even more fiercely. All he could do was pay the naysayers no mind and do his duty.

Once Bezaleel was out of the Devas' residence, he spread his wings and took flight, observing the town below. The town was called Marim, and it was the capital of Alayl. From his position in the sky, just beneath the clouds, Bezaleel had a spectacular aerial view of Marim's landscape: flat land abundant in green and all other sorts of colors and patterns. Cobblestone pathways zigzagged through it, making proper roads for travelers and merchants. The humble town had been built without disturbing nature, speaking to the folks' respect for Alayl's fertile soil and all living things.

Marim's center had a thriving marketplace, with tons of shops, stalls and inns that were always crowded. The streets curved and split like a spider web in all directions. The cluster of buildings started to spread out more from one another the further they got from the center of the capital.

Away from the central town, scattered cottages indicated where farmers and the poorer population lived. Inns popped up every now and then for passing travelers that needed a hot meal and a warm bed on the road.

As he watched the land below, the image of the siblings from earlier in the forest came to mind. They had said that they were looking for the Night Flowers to cure their mother's illness, which meant that they couldn't afford proper medicine, likely because they were peasants.

Bezaleel changed course and flew towards the modest houses further away from the city center. He silently landed on roof of one. He wanted to make sure the siblings hadn't lied. If they really were spies, Bezaleel promised himself that he would kill them with his own hands.

It would be easy to spot them since Bezaleel now knew their energy signatures. A red spark whizzed across his eyes as he activated them, and then he saw the world in different shades of blue; white energy signs denoted people, and everyone had their own unique sign. He looked around, tilting his face and rolling his eyes in every direction until he spotted the children he was looking for. Bezaleel swooped down to a small cottage quietly, gracefully—like a kite that let the wind guide it.

"I'm sorry. But the situation hasn't changed. She is still the same as before."

Bezaleel heard voices and crept quietly across the roof until he neared the window from which he could hear them better. He hung from the top of the window like a bat, but stayed hidden with just the top of his hair, forehead, and his eyes peeking through the windowpane.

The siblings sat on chairs beside a lady lying on a worn-out mattress. A man stood by, and a much older man sat by the bed. He checked the woman's eyes, took the wrist of the lady's arm and sat still for a few seconds before responding, "There is nothing more I can do. Her health is deteriorating and you need to get the medicine as soon as possible." He stood up and the younger man walked him out the door after thanking him.

The boy spoke up. "If only we could get the Night Flowers." The sister pressed her lips together into a tight frown, but said nothing.

"Dan, it's okay," the lady, their mother, said. She ruffled his hair with weak fingers. "The Night Flowers only grow in the Newara Forest, on the side that belongs to the Raathri clan. We are not allowed to go into their territory." She lay her hand back down, as if even that small movement tired her out. "Don't worry. I'll survive."

"For how long?" the girl choked out.

The mother smiled softly. "For as long as I can"

Their father returned to the room a moment later, breaking the stillness with an overly bright voice. "What's this grim atmosphere? You two just wait. I'll get your mother's medicine in no time!"

The mother made a playful comment and they laughed, but Bezaleel could tell it was only to cover the sadness they were feeling. As he watched the little family struggle, something tugged at the strings of his heart. The siblings were telling the truth. Their mother was dying, and the only way they could save her was to risk breaking in to the clan's part of the forest to retrieve the nectar of the Night Flowers. Bezaleel quietly flew away.

Later that day, the family heard a knock on their door. A basket full of Night Flowers awaited them, some with their roots still attached. There was enough to cure a dying lady's sickness and more.

Outside of Marim's central town and a few miles away from the cluster of houses where the family lived, the entire Raathri clan lived on a stretch of land that belonged only to them. Bezaleel passed rows of low-roofed houses and made his way to the Ancestral Hall.

He climbed the stairs and made his way to the main room, where Marvak awaited him.

Bezaleel knocked twice on the door and entered once he heard Marvak's raspy voice bid him do so from the other side.

"I take it that you returned the Scroll to Rasa," Marvak said, a quill in his hand. The ink dripped onto the paper below it as Bezaleel nodded. "Rahel told me that you defended two suspected spies."

That snitch. Was he trying to get Bezaleel in trouble?

"I was defending our clan's honor. They were just children: nothing to be suspicious of. I made sure of it," he explained, choosing his words carefully.

Marvak hummed and went back to scribbling on his paper. "You may leave."

Bezaleel executed a quick bow before returning to his modest house. Marvak was hard to please, and did not often give away what he was thinking.

It was unsettling to stay in his presence for long.

As he walked, the daunting words of the spy echoed inside his head. "*You think you are serving the right people, but you are just being played, Bezaleel.*"

The problem was that Bezaleel didn't know if it was the truth or not.

BLACK FEATHER

A warm breeze made its way through the forest, gently stirring and waking everything it touched, including a Teiyyan who was resting high among the trees. Bezaleel leaned his back against a thick branch, his eyes closed, hands behind his head, and one knee propped up. His grey cloak was splayed across his lap.

It was one of those days where he was free, with no missions or training regimens to keep him busy. And he loved to spend that time lazing around and relaxing in this patch of green, his own special spot in the abundant Newara Forest.

The sunlight streamed in through the canopy above and fell on Bezaleel's eyelids and he forced them open. The leaves that greeted him shone like emeralds. He listened to the sounds of the forest: the rustling leaves, the sound of waterfalls, the chirping of birds. There was another sound, like soft wind chimes, in the mix that day. Such random sounds were no stranger to Newara, as it housed fae and creatures of all kinds.

A tiny leaf-like being flew around Bezaleel's shoulders, yellow in color and glowing. Four wings accompanied the body, and its tail was like the petals of a dandelion. Bezaleel gently raised his hand and the creature circled his fingers twice before flying away.

The Teiyyan's lips twitched into a small smile. He let his hand fall back down and his gaze went to his cloak. The emblem of the Raathri clan was sewn in striking red threads on the back.

Members of the Raathri clan were always proud of who they

were. They wore the clan's symbol with pride. The Raathri was known for prowess in battle, brute strength, and quick reflexes. When it came to fighting, the clans Endhra and Raathri were equals.

And perhaps it was for that reason that Marvak felt some spite toward Endhra. Both Endhra and Raathri were equally strong, with powerful leaders and skilled clan members. The only reason Endhra was a step above them was because their bloodline could produce a Teiyyan.

Other people hailed them for it, looked up to them for their renowned honesty, trusted them, and chose them to be the nation's leaders. The first Deva of Endhra knew it would benefit the nation if Endhra and Raathri worked together. He knew what the Raathris were capable of. And with a strong clan of warriors by their side, the military would be stronger than any other nation's, more than capable of protecting their land and keeping the peace.

But as time passed and the leaders of the Endhra clan changed after each generation, Raathri's strength was seen as a threat. Even without any Devas or any special powers, no clans could match them in battle. They were like a pack of wolves that could tear apart even the most dangerous beasts. And so, Endhra slowly pushed the Raathris back until they served them from the shadows. The equal stance that both Endhra and Raathri shared in the beginning was no more.

Bezaleel lifted his face, his eyes drifting between the four watchtowers that encircled the Newara Forest and overlooked the area that the Raathri clan resided in. To an outsider, it would seem like they were given special treatment with acres of land to their name, but the truth was that this was the best place for the eyes of Endhra to keep an eye on them.

Even so, Raathri and Endhra were like yin and yang, light and darkness. One can't exist without the other. If one was destroyed, then the balance would tip. Chaos would ensue.

And that was one thing Bezaleel absolutely didn't want.

———⋈———

The soft noise of grass crunching beneath feet snapped Bezaleel out of his nap. A red spark whizzed across his eyes as he activated his visual powers. He saw energy a few feet away: two people. No threat to him, but other Raathris wouldn't abide their trespassing into their territory. Bezaleel peered down from his branch, his eyes searching for whoever was brave enough—or stupid enough, depending on who you asked—to enter uninvited the land of assassins.

A girl came into view. She was carrying a basket covered by a white cloth.

"Adelyn!" a boy's voice called as a second figure joined the first one. Bezaleel released a breath when he recognized the siblings from before. "Are you crazy? Did you forget what the Raathris tried to do to us? If they find us here—"

"I didn't ask you to come along."

"And just let you walk into a trap? You don't even know if *he* was the one that left those flowers on our doorstep."

"There was a black feather. Who else could it be?"

"Well, it could have been—"

Bezaleel dove down from the tree, barreling toward the pair. The girl gasped when he stopped himself just before he crashed into her, his face hovering a few inches away from hers. His sweet breath brushed against her cheeks. His body stayed vertical, with his legs up in the air, his gently flapping wings keeping him suspended above them.

"What are you doing here?" Bezaleel asked in a tone that would make a brave man quiver.

Adelyn raised the basket. "F-for...thanks. Um...that is, thank you for the Night Flowers. Our mother is recovering thanks to you."

Bezaleel looked from the basket to the girl's face and back a few times, then righted himself and landed on the ground as gently as a fallen leaf. "You shouldn't be here. It's dangerous."

The girl didn't cower. "I just...wanted to say thank you."

"What if I wasn't in the forest? Were you planning to come all the way to the Raathri's estate after what they almost did to you?"

She opened her mouth to speak but stopped when he abruptly turned his head. His eyes had seen someone enter the other end of the forest. While he was distracted, the siblings started to bicker amongst themselves again about Adelyn's stupid idea.

"Quiet!" Bezaleel hissed.

"What's wrong?" the brother asked. Bezaleel didn't bother humoring him. He grabbed the girl and flung her over his shoulder like a sack of potatoes, then hooked his arm around the boy's waist. "Hey!"

"Keep your voices down," Bezaleel urged, holding the boy in one of his arms like he was carrying a load of laundry. Making sure that the siblings were held tightly in his grasp, he lifted them all into the air. The girl gave a startled yelp as he flew high above the trees. He carried the siblings without much effort, as if they were as light as the basket Adelyn held. When he reached the outskirts of Marim, where the siblings lived, he gently set them on the ground. "The forest is not safe," Bezaleel warned them again. They knew he wasn't talking about the animals.

He extended his hand toward Adelyn, who stood confused for a moment before she worked out the meaning behind his gesture and handed him the basket. Her cheeks were tinted red. "Thank you...for your help."

Bezaleel nodded and watched as they made their way home. He lifted the cloth to find a few hot buns resting in the basket. He reached for one and took a bite. Warmth and sweetness flooded his tongue and Bezaleel's lips twitched into a smile.

⟞◆⟝

Bezaleel picked up his forgotten cloak from the branch he had been resting on earlier. A fine object to forget. Nothing irked Marvak more than his warriors being seen not wearing the symbol of their clan.

With the cloak and basket in hand, he made his way down. As his feet touched the soft grass, a voice spoke from behind him. "Where have you been flying off to, Bezaleel?"

Bezaleel knew who it was. He had already felt his presence, had recognized the energy signature before he deactivated his powers. He turned his head and looked directly at the boy waiting beneath the tree. "What are you wandering around the forest for, Rahel?"

"I just wanted to take a breather from training. Aren't you doing the same?"

"Seems so."

"So? Where did you fly off to?" Rahel's eyes fell on Bezaleel's hand and the basket in his grasp.

"I was hungry."

Rahel was clever. Tricky. Cunning. In many ways, he resembled Marvak. Not much of a surprise there, considering he was his son and Raathri's next heir. But Bezaleel made a point to not indulge Rahel. The boy might be talented and reliable on a mission, but personal affairs were something he would rather not share with him. There was a darkness in his eyes that triggered a warning in Bezaleel's mind—a warning that told him to think twice about trusting Rahel.

Rahel shot him a toothy smirk. "You went to the marketplace because you were hungry?"

"There's a good baker on Nak-im Street." Bezaleel gave a quick, convincing answer, hoping to shake his peer with the mundane information.

Rahel reached into Bezaleel's basket and took a bun, biting into it and chewing slowly. "Introduce me next time...to the baker."

Bezaleel said nothing. He didn't want to walk right into whatever trap Rahel wanted to catch him in. It felt like Rahel was trying to read into his soul, trying to wrench out any secret he was hiding. "We should head back."

Instead of pushing him, Rahel nodded. "Let's."

Their walk back together was anything but silent, as Rahel kept asking Bezaleel questions about Marim and getting answers that weren't clear or satisfying, if the tension between them was anything to go by.

CHAPTER EIGHTEEN

THE SCROLL

The next three weeks after the incident with the stolen Scrolls were tranquil. Since the Raathris had dealt with it as soon as they got the news, no rumors had the chance or time to spark among other clans. Rasa had even commended Bezaleel for the way he dealt with the situation: carefully and cleanly. No traces left behind.

And so, all of Alayl was as peaceful as it ever was. The Raathris went on new and dangerous missions, and returned triumphant every time. Everything was as it always had been.

But Bezaleel could tell all was not as it seemed. The Raathri clan was quieting down. To an outsider, it wouldn't seem as though anything were out of the ordinary, but to Bezaleel—a Raathri himself, and someone who was always around them—could observe the difference. One part of the clan took fewer missions than usual. It was subtle, but still noticeable if one was paying attention. Rahel started training more vigorously than before, and then there was Marvak.

Marvak often disappeared into the library in the Ancestral Hall, and Bezaleel had to wonder why he would frequent it all of a sudden. Marvak was not someone who spent hours of the day flipping through old books. He was not passionate about reading and seldom did so in his spare time. So why now?

Bezaleel considered following him to the library and confronting him, but he would have to be a fool to go through with such a plan. Marvak was not a calm or understanding man. He had a temper that could be switched on quite easily, to the point that he wouldn't think twice about giving cruel punishments or sentencing someone to death for minor infractions. Bezaleel had no interest in exploring either of the two options.

So he did what he thought was best. He didn't pursue his suspicions. He let it be. If there was something brewing, time would tell. Until then, Bezaleel had to just take things one day at a time.

The waterfalls of the Newara Forest were said to be the most beautiful in all of Alayl. The pristine waters fell gently from above, curving around giant rocks and stones to gracefully splash into the aquamarine pool below. The surrounding emerald green forest added to its beauty and helped make the shining, white waters look like rainbow crystals as they fell.

Bezaleel took off his cloak and shirt and stepped into the pool wearing only his tunic pants. Wading in until he was waist deep, he then took some water in the palm of his hands and splashed it over his shoulders, his wings, and his long white hair. The falls were also known for its healing properties because of the various mineral rocks and stones it housed, so he made a point to visit them when he could.

"The Newara Forest never ceases to amaze me," a feminine voice said behind him.

Bezaleel turned his head and found none other than Rasa's daughter Eiwa standing nearby, wearing the clan's iconic white and blue colors. She flew around him and made herself comfortable on top of a rock that rose from the middle of the pool.

"Eiwa." Bezaleel resisted the urge to cover his exposed chest. "What are you doing here?"

"Do I need a reason to fly around Alayl?" Eiwa asked coolly. "Or to visit the future Deva?"

Bezaleel's face softened and the ends of his lips twitched into a half-smile. "Is that your way of saying you are keeping an eye on me?"

Eiwa pointedly looked up at the watchtowers looming over them. "I think my clan is doing enough of that."

"It's dangerous for you to be out here alone. Where is your bodyguard?" Bezaleel raised an eyebrow.

Eiwa waved her hand, dismissing his worries. "If I can't take care of myself, how am I going to help you take care of the people?"

"Does that bother you?"

"What?"

Bezaleel's eyes fell on his reflection in the clear waters, then shifted to Eiwa's reflection before tracing up to actually look up at her. "My possibly being the next Deva. If I wasn't born a Teiyyan, you would have been the next in line to rule Alayl without contest."

Eiwa raised her eyebrows. "Well, it is true that Ashkaar has never before seen two Teiyyan's born at the same time in one nation." She stood up on the rock, balancing on one foot. If it wasn't for her clan's robes, she would have looked like any other curious thirteen-year-old having fun, prancing about. "But fret not, Bezaleel. It doesn't matter to me who the Deva is as long as they keep Alayl and its people safe." She flapped her wings and flew across the water, stopping just inches away from him. She lowered herself into the pool until she stood waist deep. "Besides, it's not like I'm going anywhere." She laid a hand on his shoulder. "I will be by your side as the Deva's advisor, just as your mother was to my father. And that's all I need. You can take care of the headaches while I live a freer life." She put her hands on her hips, tilted her head, and gave him a sly smile. "Besides, I believe that you being the Deva will lessen the tension between the Endhra and the Raathri."

"You're aware of that, then."

"I'd be a fool not to be. I'm not like the rest."

That was obvious to him without her having to mention it.

"But to have an assassin as a Deva..." Bezaleel muttered.

"No Deva's hands are free of blood, Bezaleel. That's what it means to protect a nation. But the question is, *whose* blood is on your hands? To what or whom does your allegiance lie?"

To whom indeed. There was no doubt that he served Rasa and Alayl, but he also had a duty to his clan. The ones that raised him. The family that his parents belonged to.

Eiwa chuckled and it brought Bezaleel's attention back to her. "My father says that you are a lot like your mother."

"Am I? I don't remember my parents all that much," Bezaleel said. "I remember my mother's warmth and my father's voice, but they are like a distant memory." He gave her a tight smile. "They passed too soon."

"I'm sorry, Bezaleel. I didn't mean to remind you of such things," Eiwa apologized with a frown.

Bezaleel smiled, more genuinely this time. "There is nothing for you to apologize for. I was told that they both died on missions serving Alayl. It was honorable."

Eiwa reflected his smile. "And I'm sure they would be proud to know how their son is growing up." She flapped her wings and lifted up out of the pool. The bottom half of her robes was dripping wet, but she didn't seem to mind. "Well, I'd best be going. I've interrupted your bath for long enough."

Bezaleel blushed as red as cherries. Eiwa laughed and flew out of the forest, leaving Bezaleel to think about what they'd discussed. A Deva that could ease the tension between the Raathri and the Endhra? If that were true, he would do all that he could to see it come to fruition.

As day turned into night, Bezaleel was unexpectedly summoned to the meeting chamber in the Ancestral Hall. As he stood outside the door, an uneasy feeling rumbled in his gut. He knocked twice.

"Enter," Marvak answered. Bezaleel turned the doorknob, pushed it open, and was greeted by the clan's main heads, along with Rahel.

Bezaleel's eyes swept across them. He could feel the seriousness of their gazes and the heaviness of an unspeakable secret hanging in the air. His fingertips twitched nervously, but he refused to show even the tiniest amount of distress as he walked toward the table. Keeping his gaze on the rest of the people present, he dragged a chair out and sat down.

"What have I been summoned for?" he broke the silence.

Marvak placed a heavy scroll on the table and rolled it open. Bezaleel's stoic expression came undone like a loose knot. His eyes widened with shock as he saw the written incantations, spells, and a lot of squiggles and lines he couldn't make heads or tails of. "This... This is the Forbidden Scroll."

His mind was tumbling into a mess. He returned the scroll to Rasa with his own two hands. How could it possibly...?

"It's not the real one. This is a replica," Rahel answered as if he's heard Bezaleel's thoughts.

"How is this possible?" Bezaleel asked.

Marvak spoke up. "Bezaleel, that mission you were sent on to retrieve the Scroll was just a diversion. The one who stole the Scroll was a spy from our own clan—"

"You," Bezaleel interrupted, his tone flat. "You made me kill one of us?"

"It was his choice." Marvak's voice grew hard. "We placed him to work for Lord Rasa and his administration. He died with honor."

"You placed him under Rasa so he could find a way to steal the Scroll," Bezaleel corrected.

Marvak stood up from his seat and circled the table, his thin fingers running gently atop the paper. "By the time you got to him, he had already duplicated the Scroll. While you and your team fought them, another of our spies had already escaped with the replica and brought it here."

"I was sent on that mission so Rasa *wouldn't* suspect that the Raathri was behind the theft. And you didn't tell me what was going on to make it all the more believable. So we would still have Rasa's trust," Bezaleel surmised. "But why? Why steal this?"

Marvak came to a stop directly in front of him. "We are planning a coup."

Bezaleel sat there with wide eyes, unable to utter a word or shake off the weight of the information he had just received. Surely, the man was joking.

"The Endhra and the Raathri clan was all Alayl had when everything began," Marvak continued. "We're the two clans that hold the roots of this nation. Yet we're cast aside and thrown away, feared for being strong. Watched like animals in a cage. Even when a Deva is born into the clan, they don't plan to give us the right to be leaders. Eiwa is to watch over you and the Raathri once you become a Deva. We have no freedom. This can't go on."

Bezaleel couldn't diminish that fact. With the isolation of the Raathri clan from Alayl's affairs and how they'd so often been cast aside, this was bound to happen. "But even if we succeed in overthrowing the current administration, it will still start a war. The other Devas and clans will not sit idly by when they know we have used the Forbidden Scroll." Bezaleel's tongue finally moved, voicing all of his concerns. "Raathri is strong, but we're not strong enough to face everyone else at once."

"The Forbidden Scroll contains Nahms that have existed since the first Deva. Nahms that give various powers." Marvak's eyes twinkled with a sinister glint. "They can turn anyone into a Teiyyan."

For a moment Bezaleel forgot how to breathe. "Impossible."

"It's in the Scroll. It's possible," Feivel, the third head, interjected.

Bezaleel's gaze fell on the back of his hands where they rested atop his knees. Turn anyone into a Teiyyan? If that happened, it would be mayhem. Marvak was planning to turn the Raathris into an invincible powerhouse. Not even the four Devas together would be able to stop them.

"But we will need to prepare the other members," Marvak said, snapping Bezaleel back into the present.

"Prepare?" Bezaleel questioned.

"The Nahms are not something to be taken lightly. If your body can't handle their intensity, you will succumb and die."

Now the puzzle was coming together. This was why the Raathri clan had cut back on their missions. They were training their members physically and mentally so that, when the time came, they would be ready to gain the powers from the Scroll without breaking down and killing themselves.

"Why haven't you told me this before now?" Bezaleel asked in a tone that remained humble, yet strong and unwavering.

"You are the one that Rasa watches the most. We needed you to be unaware of it until the right time," Rahel answered.

"If we carry out this coup, hundreds of innocent people will be killed," Bezaleel said.

"Are you against us, then?" Marvak's question introduced a new level of tension in the air.

Bezaleel thought for a moment. The words of the spy echoed in his mind once again. *"You think you are serving the right people, but you are just being played, Bezaleel."* Then Eiwa's voice chimed in. *"To whom does your allegiance lie?"*

After a few long seconds, he stood up from his chair to meet Marvak's eyes directly, staring into the other man's face with an intensity that most his age lacked. "I'm not."

"Even though you were always against spilling unnecessary blood?" Marvak tested.

"I don't see this as unnecessary. I am a Raathri and I take pride in my clan. I will not let others bring us down, not even Endhra. I will follow your order and do what is needed."

Marvak nodded. Bezaleel knew where his duty was. His part of the plan was clear, and as Bezaleel didn't see anything further to discuss, he bowed to Marvak and the other superiors before exiting the room.

As he walked out of the hall, the expression on his face changed to something he'd never worn before. His lips turned into a frown and his eyes darkened with dangerous intent as he reconciled his mind with what he had to do. It was something terrible. Treacherous. Something he would never be forgiven for. Something that would turn the fates of both Raathri and Endhra upside down.

CHAPTER NINETEEN

THE COUP

The clan members were given two weeks. That was all the time the Raathris needed to finish training their minds and bodies to handle the Nahms.

Bezaleel had been visiting Feival in the library more often now. The third head was the most knowledgeable among all of them, the on who could decipher the Nahms in the Scroll, and Bezaleel wanted to know everything he could about the contents in the Scroll and how to read it.

That was how he got to know just why the Scroll was so forbidden. It contained all sorts of Nahms, from those that could turn anyone into a Teiyyan, to ones about retracting a Teiyyan's wings in order to make them look like a normal person. He was shocked to find that there were even spells to control a Teiyyan's core attributes. That was dangerous. That meant that if the Raathris learned all that was in there, then they could suppress Bezaleel's powers.

There were also Nahms that would let them gain all sorts of abilities. Conjuring weapons out of nowhere. Healing incantations. Magical shields. Nahms to control light and dark. It was no wonder that the Devas would go to great lengths to protect this Scroll. Overthrowing one or all of them was quite possible with something like this.

Sitting in his room, Bezaleel's mind wandered. His hand moved back and forth as he sharpened the blade of his sword with a small piece of whetstone. The sound rang out repeatedly in the otherwise silent room.

Within two days, the Raathris would learn to manifest the Nahms. Then they will make their move to attack Endhra. There would be bloodshed. If Bezaleel was going to carry out his plan, he needed to move now. Tonight. While everyone was asleep and oblivious.

He stood up from his bed, donned his armor, strapped his two swords to his waist, and made his way to the Ancestral Hall. Once inside, he turned to the door on the right that led to the twisting staircase and below, to the library. As he approached the huge wooden doors, he clenched his fists and took a deep breath to get rid of all the impossibilities raging in his mind and to steel himself and see his decision through.

Lamps dotted the walls and lit the room with a warm, orange glow. Tall shelves that touched the ceiling lined one after the other, each of them stacked at least a hundred books. The scent of leather permeated the air. It was a world of pages and one could easily spend hours there.

Bezaleel made his way past the shelves to the middle of the library, where a few tables and chairs were neatly arranged. And just as he had guessed, Feivel was there, standing behind a pile of papers on the table and deciphering the Nahms. The man never seemed to sleep. He was holed up in here day and night. He turned around when he heard footsteps making their way toward him.

"Bezaleel," the old man greeted. "What are you doing up this late?"

"I couldn't sleep, and you are always here," he said matter-of-factly as he circled the table. The Scroll lay atop the wooden surface, opened halfway. A candle was placed on one end, while the other dangled off the corner of the table. Bezaleel came to stand beside Feivel. "I have a question that I need an answer to."

"What is it, boy?" Feivel asked without taking his eyes of the papers.

"If you let the Raathri clan learn the Nahms, they will gain powers that they will then use to create war. Hundreds of innocent people will die."

"There is no choice. It needs to be done." the priest automatically replied.

"So you are not against it."

"I'm not." When the silence grew uncomfortable, Feivel turned to him. "Why are you asking me this, Bezaleel?"

Bezaleel looked him in the eye and hoped his features conveyed just how sorry he was that it had come to this. "Please forgive me."

There wasn't even a chance for Feivel to speak or take cover before Bezaleel drew one of his swords and ran the blade through Feivel's body. He covered Feivel's mouth with his palm, muffling the man's shocked cry. The white of Feivel's eyes turned bloodshot. Bezaleel waited till his last breath left his body before he carefully laid him on the ground.

He then rushed at the table, grabbed the scroll, cut a couple of pieces from different parts of the paper, and stuffed it inside his robe. He grabbed the rest of it and fed it to the flames of the candle. The fire roared through the middle of the ancient paper, spreading in all directions and consuming it in no time flat.

Bezaleel had no time to watch it burn to a crisp. He bolted out the door, up the stairs, and out of the hall. From there, he ran out of the estate and headed towards the town, sprinting across the grassy field as fast as he could. It would be morning by the time the Raathris found the dead priest and the burned scroll.

But at that moment, fate had already turned against him. He didn't know that Marvak had gone to the library soon after Bezaleel left. He had found Feivel lying on the floor, blood oozing out of his lifeless body. He had seen the burned Scroll and his fury burned even hotter.

It didn't take long for Marvak to figure out what Bezaleel had done.

❖

Bezaleel had calculated everything down to the last detail. He had learned what the scrolls had contained, even the plans for Marvak's coup—down to their time of attack. Because he knew everything, Bezaleel was able to act on his own. He knew the perfect time to act, to strike Feivel down while the entire Raathri clan slept. To burn the Scrolls and run. He was sure he had everything covered, but ran faster still. Just in case. It would be the biggest betrayal in Ashkaar's history.

As he ran through the field, his eyes picked up on life energy a few miles behind him—a life force with energy as strong as the entire Raathri clan. Bezaleel furrowed his eyebrows. Something had gone awfully wrong.

If he kept running like this, they would catch up to him in mere minutes. He wouldn't be able to outrun them, and the weight of his wings would only slow him down. If he tried to fly, they would spot him in an instant.

He thought of another option, one that would cost him time, but hopefully not his life. He took a momentary detour, changing his direction to veer to his right and the edge of the forest, where there were more trees and shrubs than plain grass. Plenty of places to hide there. He dove down between the massive roots of a tree. Flat on the ground with his wings drawn close to his body, he was camouflaged by the darkness, hidden between the tree roots and partially covered by shrubs. This way, the Raathris would probably miss him. They wouldn't think that he'd continue on his legs. They wouldn't look at the ground; their eyes would be too busy raking the sky.

Bezaleel focused on the cool earth beneath him as he waited: the smell of mud, the brush of grass. He could see the energies of the Raathri get closer and closer until they whizzed past him in a blur. A group of at least twenty assassins was as silent as the night and rushed past him without even rustling a leaf—as expected of the assassins of the Raathri clan.

When Bezaleel was sure that they were out of sight, he crawled out from his hiding place and started to sprint again.

A dozen questions swirled in his mind. Someone must have woken up in the night—probably Marvak. He must have gone searching for Feival, and it wouldn't have taken him long to figure out that it was Bezaleel who killed him, who turned his back on the clan that raised him. He was a traitor.

There was no doubt that they were searching for him now. Marvak wouldn't think twice about killing him. And to make it worse, they were running into town. They were carrying out the coup, but Bezaleel wondered how they were planning to do it without the Nahms. Perhaps they were hoping to catch Lord Rasa off guard.

Either way, they would probably reach the town before Bezaleel could. He needed to get there before they wreaked too much havoc, or at least in time to see his plans through. But as Bezaleel reached Marim's outskirts, he saw that he was already too late.

What awaited him was a burning town that was slowly but surely becoming a sea of fire.

Bezaleel's eyes widened, and something within him shook his entire frame. Was it fear? Distress? Outrage? He couldn't tell.

The buildings creaked and groaned as they fell apart. Bloodied bodies lay all over the place. Some faces he recognized—innocent people. No doubt it was the Raathri's doing. They had planned to set the town ablaze and rebel so Rasa would send out his troops to stop them. He would be left with only a handful of his soldiers to protect him, enough for the Raathris to easily overpower and then engage the real foe. One Deva against an entire clan of Raathri would be a tough fight.

Bezaleel clenched his teeth. Muddled thoughts made him lose focus for a moment and he wasn't paying attention to the two people running out from a narrow space in between two buildings.

They were running for their life and came crashing into Bezaleel.

He stumbled, but managed to maintain his balance. When he saw who had bumped into him, he was yet again left with no words.

The two siblings had somehow come across him again; this time their faces carried fear. But the boy's reaction changed at the sight of Bezaleel. His fear turned into seething anger. "You!" he pointed accusingly at Bezaleel. "Why the hell are you here? Are you here to murder like the rest of your damned clan?"

Bezaleel stared intensely at them and muttered, "Yes."

The boy's face fell. Perhaps he expected a different answer.

Bezaleel gripped the hilt of his sword and slowly removed it from its scabbard. His silver blade reflected the fiery hue of the chaos unfolding around them. His orange-red eyes shimmered with the same intensity and danger as the flames devouring the town. The girl clung to her brother's arm and hid her face in his sleeve. The fear the boy had overcome came rushing back to his face.

"This will be over soon. Please close your eyes." Bezaleel raised his sword and held it diagonally above his head.

The boy's eyes widened in horror just before Bezaleel swung his sword. The girl screamed, and blood splashed all over them. But it wasn't their blood. It belonged to one of the Raathri, who had tried to sneak up behind them to secure another kill. Bezaleel had cut down one of his own; the warrior's body lay behind the siblings in a heap.

"Come." Bezaleel sheathed his sword and grabbed their hands and yanked them along as he started running. "I came to kill, but not you."

"You... Why did you—"

"Later," Bezaleel cut off the boy's broken question, urging them to hurry. The siblings followed Bezaleel without another word. He knew he needed to get them to safety, along with the rest of the townspeople who had survived the fire, if he could.

He already saw a few of them up ahead: white silhouettes of energy running from all corners of the town, from behind broken houses and shops. They were trying to make their way out of the wreckage without attracting the Raathris' attention. Some were helping others who were trapped under debris, pulling them out and telling them to get to a specific location. That was the place he needed to take his two charges. From what he was seeing and hearing, the town's citizens had a hidden escape route, a final countermeasure in the event of an attack. Perfect.

But reaching it was going to be anything but easy. Using his enhanced vision, Bezaleel could see the Raathris that were following him from a distance. Five of them had sniffed out his trail. Bezaleel needed to stop them. If he didn't, they would catch up to him and the townspeople in no time.

Bezaleel briefly glanced back at the siblings. "Keep running."

"What?" the boy asked.

"Keep running." Bezaleel stopped them before they could argue. "You need to trust me."

With a determined look on his face, the boy nodded, signaling that he was ready to place their lives in Bezaleel's hands. The girl didn't question anything, either, so they both continued to run ahead.

Bezaleel twisted sharply on his heel and sprinted back in the opposite direction. He grabbed a bow and a few arrows that were lying around, strapped the quiver with the arrows to his back and flew up into the air. He flew above the clouds and stopped, observing the five Raathris in pursuit. They were two miles away, but moving faster than they should have been able to. Bezaleel narrowed his eyes. They were riding a Yongma, a horse-like creature that was distinguished by its smoky mane and equally smoky, black legs. They were fast on land, but even faster on water. There were two people on the Yongma in front and three following behind.

Bezaleel drew three arrows from the quiver, pulled them back on the string of his bow, pointed them at a slightly upward angle, and released. The arrows shot forward, slicing through the air until they bent toward the earth and came down at an angle to hit the three riding in the rear.

He drew another two arrows, pulled back on the bowstring, aimed, and released again. They followed the course of the previous arrows before coming down toward the remaining two. But they didn't hit them.

At the last second, they maneuvered their animal to the side, though not fast enough. Instead of hitting the two riders, the arrows hit the animal. There were only two people Bezaleel could think of who could evade an attack with that kind of skill: Marvak and Rahel.

But the arrows did slow them down, giving Bezaleel more time. But the Raathri assaults didn't end there. With his three-sixty-degree vision, Bezaleel was able to keep track of the two siblings' progress. And that helped him see the several Raathris that were waiting for them, swords ready.

The siblings kept running, just like Bezaleel told them to. They kept hastening toward the Raathri without the wherewithal to stop. They placed their trust in Bezaleel and counted on him to protect them. And Bezaleel did not let them down.

He dove down with the speed of falling rain. As he neared the ground, he reversed his position and landed on his feet. The impact splintered the cobblestones and sent dust flying everywhere.

In between all that dust, the Raathris caught a glimmer of silver, of Bezaleel drawing his two swords from their sheaths. They rushed at him and sword clanged against sword in a furious battle. One after the other, they attacked Bezaleel, sometimes together, but it wasn't enough to defeat him. Bezaleel's movements were a flurry of violence as he evaded all their strikes and cut them all down. He jumped, kicked and slashed in calculated motions that were too quick for anyone to follow. His white hair was dyed red with the blood of his enemies. Their bodies fell until only Bezaleel remained standing. Like a true demon of the dark.

"Come!" Bezaleel pulled the siblings along again, racing toward the people he had seen escaping earlier. He needed to get to them before more of the Raathris did. He needed to get them to safety, and then he could worry about his own. Despite being strong enough to be a Deva, Bezaleel could never overcome the strength of the entire Raathri clan all at once. They were too skilled, and they would kill him without mercy.

The townspeople had gathered before the hidden passageway. At the sight of Bezaleel, the people's eyes clouded with despair and he saw them visibly shiver. Tension choked the atmosphere. It was to be expected; it was his clan that bought about this hell.

But that fear was soon erased when a couple emerged and exclaimed, "Dan! Adelyn!"

The siblings rushed to their parents. The parents cried with joy and relief as they enveloped their children in a tight embrace. At that sight, the rest of the people looked at Bezaleel, clearly baffled by his actions.

"He saved us!" Adelyn exclaimed.

Her father looked at Bezaleel with eyes full of gratitude and muttered, "Thank you."

Bezaleel nodded and then walked over to the boy, Dan. "The Raathri clan has planned a coup. Lord Rasa is in danger." Shocked gasps and murmurs issued from the others. Bezaleel ignored them and handed Dan a piece of paper he had tucked in his robe. "This is information about the coup and the people involved. I need you to get to Rasa as quickly as you can and give it to him."

Dan nodded and took the paper from Bezaleel's hand without hesitation. "Aren't you coming with us?" he asked.

"I can't," Bezaleel replied. "Right now, I'm the biggest threat to the Raathri clan and they will be looking for me. You will be in more danger with me than without."

"But—" Bezaleel pushed Dan back before he could argue. He stumbled on his feet and bumped into his father's chest as Bezaleel took a few steps back and extended his hand out in front of him. He uttered a Nahm and a circle appeared in midair, followed by numerous other circles etched with runes, until they surrounded the group of people. A golden translucent light enveloped them like a bubble.

"Wait!" Adelyn rushed toward Bezaleel, but the circles stopped her from reaching him. The light had covered them, protecting them like a shield against any threats from the outside.

"This will keep you safe from the Raathris attacks if they find the hidden passage. The only one who can undo this spell is Rasa. You need to get to him."

"But, you will be in danger! They will kill you!"

Bezaleel smiled wholeheartedly, and it was akin to the beauty of stars. "It's alright."

He turned to run but stopped when Adelyn called out his name. He turned around for the last time. He'd never told her his name, but understood that she, along with everyone else, was aware of who he was.

"Please stay alive."

Bezaleel nodded, but it was weak. He wasn't sure he could. Adelyn sensed it and her eyes teared up. Bezaleel didn't wait a second longer and ran away from them as the people fled to the safety of the passageway.

Meanwhile, he ran as fast as he could to the Newara Forest. Some of the Raathris spotted him and tried to stop him, only for Bezaleel to cut them down like shrubs in his way. A few Alayl soldiers had also come to the aid of the town and tried to block Bezaleel's escape, but got knocked out by him as he raced by.

Bezaleel knew that the assassins were chasing after him. No matter. It would serve as a distraction for the others to escape. But this meant he had to be quick and get to Newara Forest before they could get to him. That was going to be a problem. Marvak was on his trail while Rahel followed the plan and went after Rasa. It wouldn't take much longer before Bezaleel was caught. So he risked it. He spread his wings and flew into the air.

It was faster than running, and he evaded arrows as much as he could. A few still managed to graze his skin, but he kept flying until the earth below changed from the wreckage of the town into the greenery of the forest.

Marvak was closing the distance, though he still had a lot of ground to cover. Bezaleel saw it with his eyes. He dove down to the darkest and most remote area of the forest and landed on the lush grass, then pulled out a piece of paper he had cut out from the Scroll earlier. As he did, he saw Marvak reach the forest edge, along with at least twenty-five other Raathris.

Rapidly glancing and reading the instructions on the paper, he plucked a feather from his wing, recited an incantation, and slapped the feather onto the middle of his back. The excruciating pain he felt as his wings folded and forced their way inside his body was almost too much, but Bezaleel inhaled sharply and bit his lips to stop himself from screaming. A drop of blood dribbled down his chin as his teeth dug hard into his bottom lip. After what felt like an eternity of pain, a black circle seal appeared on his back where his wings had once sprouted from.

Bezaleel fell to his hands and knees as his eyes watered from the pain. He panted and gasped, but there was no time to rest. Trembling and exhausted, Bezaleel pushed the piece of paper back into the pocket of his undershirt and took out another. By now, the clan had entered the forest and was making its way to Bezaleel. Only a couple of minutes and they would find him.

Bezaleel wiped the blood from his lips with his thumb. He used the blood to quickly draw a circle with runes, diagonals and swirls into the mud around him. He planted his palms on the ground on top the drawing and recited a different incantation.

"The Veyil that keeps the worlds of Jihan apart, I command you to lift and open your path to Yalim."

Small sparks of lightning emitted from the circle. Bezaleel flinched and drew his hand back as the sparks doubled in number and size.

He whipped his head from side to side as the sparks kept growing, connecting and interlacing until a dome of blinding blue light formed above his head. He felt energy swell up around him and braced himself.

His body felt heavy. Pain pricked him and his skin started to tear. Bezaleel couldn't contain his anguish anymore and let out a scream. Parts of his skin ripped like paper and blood seeped into his clothes. Bezaleel wondered if he was being dragged into hell rather than someplace safe.

The light around him got brighter and brighter until he couldn't see anything anymore. He felt the change in the atmosphere, in the sounds around him and on the ground on which he stood. More seconds passed before the light finally started to dim.

Finally, Bezaleel could make out his surroundings again—even if they were blurred from his hazy vision. Blood oozed out of his body and the pain he felt was so intense that it was starting to numb him. His energy was gone; his knees gave in and his body fell to the ground with a pitiful thump. It was hard and cold, not like the warm mud of the forest he was in a few moments ago.

The last thing he saw was a man and woman climb up a stair to where he was. The woman gasped and the pair rushed toward him.

Their voices were a dull echo in Bezaleel's ears, words that Bezaleel had no hope of comprehending. A warm finger touched the junction between his neck and shoulder. He had no energy to even recoil.

That was the last thing Bezaleel registered before he gave in and lost consciousness completely.

CHAPTER TWENTY

ANOTHER WORLD

When the light of day fell on his eyelids, Bezaleel forced them open. He was met with the intensity of bright morning light and resisted the urge to shut them again. Squiggles of light and dots danced across his vision before they started fading and he could make out where he was.

There was a ceiling above him. He lifted his head and his eyes rolled between all four corners of the beige room before he gave up trying to identify anything familiar about the place. There was hardly any furniture except for the white, fluffy mattress he was laying on. Someone must have brought him here, because he hadn't landed on it when he arrived.

He lay his head back down, calmed his nerves, and let his senses come back to him as he remembered how he got here in the first place.

He had turned his back on his clan to save Alayl and opened a portal to another world. The latter was a rule that, if broken, warranted no less than an execution. He wasn't allowed to lift the Veyil. No one was except the Devas. If they knew what he did, he would never get away with it. Had opening the portal alerted them somehow? He hoped not. Although, if it had, he was sure he wouldn't be here, resting comfortably right now.

The Raathris had probably already been captured. They would be busy fighting to save themselves rather than chasing him. If he was being honest with himself, he would say he had escaped by the skin of his teeth. If he'd delayed even a few seconds, they would have plucked his head from his neck.

Bezaleel slowly sat upright. His body felt heavy and sore. A soft wind caressed his long, white locks as if trying to soothe him. There was a floor-to-ceiling window to his right, so he could see the landscape outside: dark brown trees stood with empty branches. Green patches poked up at random spots between the mud on the ground. No snow, but the winds carried the cold air. It was the image of a thawing winter.

Where in Yalim did the portal take me?

Bezaleel felt a cold shiver run up his body. It was then he noticed that he wasn't wearing a shirt. He lifted the thin sheet that covered him and peeked underneath. He wasn't wearing any pants, either. He was stark naked and covered in bandages.

A long one rounded his torso multiple times and diagonally over his chest and his shoulder. One wrapped around his upper arm and another on his thigh. His body felt sluggish, which probably meant that he had been asleep for a while. But how long?

Next to his comfortable mattress, his clothes lay on the wooden floor. Bezaleel reached for them, but found they were still dirty with mud, sweat and blood. Whoever patched him up was wary of him, and for good reason. They probably thought that keeping his clothes as they were was the best insurance policy, if it came down to that.

But Bezaleel was relieved that his savior hadn't washed anything. He dug into the pocket of his undershirt, looking for the couple of things he'd brought from Alayl. He took out the four pieces of paper he had cut out from the Scroll. The papers were crumpled, but otherwise still intact. He could read the words clearly.

He had taken them for a reason. One of these four pieces of paper contained different sets of Nahms that could open the gateway between Ashkaar and Yalim. Another one was for creating shields like the one he used to help the people in Marim. And then there was the information to conceal a Teiyyan's attributes. Perhaps it could conceal the color of his eyes and hair so he could hide in the crowds here. But to suppress his powers, he needed a special plant: a sort of herb that could only be found in the Forest of Newara.

Bezaleel dug into his other pocket. His fingers brushed against soft leaves and stems and he gently took out the plant called Chiweu. He had cut some the night before he planned to save Alayl. It was pure luck that these grew in a place he frequented. The fruits from this plant would help him conceal the power in his eyes and make them look like regular ones, but he needed to plant this herb and let it grow first.

Bezaleel put it back into his pocket. This could wait; the Chiweu could go for five days without mud or water. Right now, he needed to find out where he was, and who his host was. He looked to his other side and found other clothes folded tidily: a white shirt and pants. They seemed two sizes too large for him when he unfolded them and held them up, but it was better than being naked.

He stood up on wobbly legs, and with shaky fingers, got dressed.

Once he had finished buttoning up his shirt, he looked at his trembling hands. They wouldn't stop shivering. He clenched them into tight fists, hoping it would help stop the tiny trembles.

Lifting the Veyil was no easy task. He had almost killed himself doing it, and his body was still suffering the aftereffects. He hoped there wouldn't come a time where he had to do that again. There was no use going back; all that awaited him in Ashkaar was either death by the Raathri clan or an execution by the Devas.

Bezaleel shook his head as if dismissing his thoughts. First things first. He had to figure out where he was. There was a door a few steps in front of him. He walked toward it and pushed, but it didn't open. Bezaleel furrowed his brow. Was he locked in?

He pushed it again, but it wouldn't budge. His mind started wandering in negative directions. Did he fall into the hands of the wrong people? Was he taken prisoner? Maybe they knew who he was. Maybe the Veyil didn't open to Yalim after all.

He placed both palms on the surface of the door. It felt light, like it would tear apart if he used enough strength, yet it still didn't open. He tried again to push and pull the door numerous times, but all it did was cause a loud racket. A few more seconds of Bezaleel fiddling with it passed, and then he heard footsteps coming from the other side, growing louder.

Thin sparks whizzed across his irises as he activated his eyes and saw a figure hurrying toward him. They slid the door open before he had a chance to think.

Bezaleel jumped back. Oh. He was supposed to slide the door sideways. It wasn't locked after all. How unusual. He couldn't help but wonder who in the world would build it to open sideways.

The woman who opened the door jumped back as well. She had a fair complexion and raven hair that fell past her shoulders; she wore a simple shirt over a knee-length skirt. Her half-moon eyes widened as she stared into his orange-crimson ones. This was the first time Bezaleel felt so uncomfortable having someone stare at him so intensely.

"*Reiko! Daijobu ka?*"

A man came running. He let out a loud gasp when he saw Bezaleel standing there, too. The man seemed just as young as the lady. His jet black hair was combed back and his brown eyes were kind. Shaken as he was at the sight of Bezaleel up and about, his face hinted at a mellow personality. From their reactions, Bezaleel figured that people like him must not be very common in this world. They were both left completely speechless by his appearance.

For the first time in his life, Bezaleel was out of ideas, utterly clueless about what to do next or how to ease the tension in such an uncomfortable situation. He wondered if he'd have to stand there like a fool until both of them got over their shock.

But the couple didn't dwell on their astonishment for long. The woman was the first one to snap out of her trance and took a step toward him. Bezaleel took a step back. The last thing he was going to do was let a stranger get too close to him.

The woman smiled and stopped as if she understood his train of thought. "*Karada itai ka?*"

That was definitely a question. But he had no idea what she was asking. Bezaleel looked at her and hoped he was conveying his puzzlement without words.

She pointed to his bandages, twisted her expression with exaggerated discomfort and repeated, "*Itai?*"

This time, Bezaleel was able to understand what she was hinting at; she was asking him if he was in pain. He shook his head. From the looks of their faces, their surroundings, and the way they were treating him, they appeared to be decent people who were genuinely just worried about a lost child they had found.

"*Nan nadake kimi?*" the man asked. Bezaleel wished he knew what in the world they wanted to know. "*Ore wa Shinichiro.*" The main pointed to himself and repeated, "*Shinichiro.*" Then he pointed to the woman and said, "*Reiko.*"

Oh. Their names.

"*Kimi?*" He pointed to Bezaleel, asking for his name again.

Bezaleel opened his mouth to tell them who he was, but decided against it. If they knew his name and someone came looking for him, these two would be in danger. The less they knew the better. So he decided to seal his lips. He could have given another name, but the names of this world sounded strange and unusual to Bezaleel, and he couldn't pick a name from a world he knew nothing about. The only ones he knew were from Ashkaar, and that wouldn't help mask his identity.

Silence stretched on, and the couple exchanged glances. It seemed they had felt Bezaleel's quiet distress and had decided not to ask again.

A heavy atmosphere surrounded them. Neither Bezaleel's appearance nor the mysteriousness around him helped break it, but the sudden, loud rumble of his stomach certainly did.

Reiko, as the woman was called, laughed. "*Harahetta?*"

Another loud grumble—Bezaleel's cheeks flushed. How embarrassing.

"*Oide, oide.*" Reiko gestured with her hand for him to follow her.

And so he did. Even though he was still out of his element and wary, he found himself trailing behind her without a second thought. Perhaps it was because they saved his life and they seemed harmless. Perhaps it was the gentle reassurance in the air around them. Whatever it was, he could do with a bit of food.

He followed her to their living room. A low table already laden with food awaited them. They must have been sitting down to eat when Bezaleel interrupted them with his loud examination of the door.

Shinichiro and Reiko sat themselves down on opposite sides from one another. Bezaleel stood there, gaping at them like an idiot while they sat on the floor. Reiko had to motion for him to sit before he snapped back to reality. Hesitantly, Bezaleel sat down next to Shinichiro.

"Tetsu!" Reiko yelled out. Bezaleel flinched. Out of one of the rooms, a kid came dashing out like there were wheels under his feet and fell right into Reiko's arms. The second he loosened his arms from around her neck his eyes fell on Bezaleel. His tiny mouth dropped open.

He waddled his way toward him. Bezaleel wanted to lean away, but felt that might be insulting after his parents had treated him so kindly. So he sat still: rigid and stiff. The kid, who was probably around six years of age, leaned closer to him. He raised his little hand and touched Bezaleel's cheek.

Bezaleel sucked in a breath. He was not at all used to physical contact. The last time he vaguely remembered such a warm touch was the embrace of his parents when he was a toddler.

The kid stared into Bezaleel's multicolored orbs, and, with eyes full of wonder whispered, "*Kirei!*"

The mother chuckled and pointed at the boy. "Tetsu."

Bezaleel might not have understood the words she spoke, but he definitely understood her affection for the child. This was their son. Bezaleel nodded and Reiko smiled.

Then the three of them clasped their hands and uttered a loud, "*Itadakimasu!*"

Bezaleel flinched again. What *was* that?

They started to dig into their food and Bezaleel cocked his head to the side like a confused puppy. Was that a signal for him to eat?

He glanced at the food on the table. White rice in a bowl, some kind of soup in another. Grilled meat and sliced vegetables. What intrigued him was the pair of long, really thin sticks next to the bowl. Was that a utensil to eat with? How in the world was he going to do that with a pair of sticks?

He reached for them anyway. One stick in each hand. He briefly looked at Reiko, who was picking at her rice and vegetables with such ease and grace. She held both in one hand, between her thumb and forefinger.

Bezaleel tried to mimic her actions. He held the sticks in one hand, but they were unsteady between his fingers. He took the bowl of rice from the tabletop and tried to pick at it with the sticks, but all he got was fumbling fingers, unsteady sticks, and falling food. Bezaleel furrowed his eyebrows in irritation. How was he supposed to eat this if he couldn't even get one grain of rice into his mouth?

Reiko eyed him for a couple of seconds and stood up from the table. She went to the kitchen and came back with a spoon. Bezaleel flushed for the second time. Ever since he woke up, all he had done was make a fool of himself. He had never felt so out of place before.

Bezaleel took the spoon from her, grateful that she was being so considerate but unable to say so in a way that she'd understand. He took the bowl, dug into the rice, and ate until he was full enough to overcome his fatigue.

CHAPTER TWENTY-ONE

NAME

It had been three weeks since Bezaleel lifted the Veyil and escaped to Yalim. He found this world strange. Strange customs, strange language, and a way of life he was absolutely not used to. The family he'd found himself was very cooperative, although they'd asked him to stay in the house.

With words and a lot of actions, in the best way they could, they conveyed to him how his appearance was "different," that people in this world did not have hair or eyes like his, and didn't talk the language that he did. That it would be dangerous for him to go out in public. So, it was safer for him to stay inside the house. He was fine with it, too, since he didn't want to deal with people until he adjusted to his surroundings.

It was also safer in the sense that if anyone from Ashkaar was looking for him, they wouldn't find him since no one other than this family knew he was here.

Even so, it was still difficult for him to adapt to his new home at first, especially since he had no idea what these three were saying. If he wanted to know more about the world he was in, he needed to understand the language.

And so he set out to try and learn. He started to pay close attention to the words they spoke, and, little by little, he began to catch on.

The first words he learned were "thank you." He had heard Tetsu mutter it a lot, and after watching him, he understood what it meant, or at least when to use it. So he tried it out.

Reiko was delighted when he muttered the phrase in their language for the first time as she passed some food to him during their lunch one afternoon. And when she realized that he wanted to try and communicate with them, she enthusiastically took the time to teach him. Shinichiro and Tetsu joined in later, too.

Two weeks later, he was able to speak to them in broken sentences, but his understanding of what they were saying was better than his actual spoken skills.

By learning to communicate with them, he had come to know a little more about this world. He was in a small town called Iwami, in the western part of a country called Japan. He didn't know why the portal had opened here specifically. Perhaps it had something to do with energy similar to the sort that resided in the Jihan also building up here. But that was information he didn't dwell on much.

Reiko and Shinichiro had found him close by in a shrine, which was a common place for worship in their religion. Reiko, being an experienced doctor, was able to patch him up by herself. It was obvious that, with his appearance and the state he was in, it would have caused unnecessary commotion if they had relied on the help of someone else.

Bezaleel started to learn other things as well. Mannerisms, greetings, and what was right and not according to the laws of Yalim. He began to understand the way of life there, but he still hadn't met anyone else other than the three of them. When people did come over, he stayed hidden in his room, knowing that his appearance was unusual and would cause trouble for him and the family if anyone saw him.

No one else had natural white hair or the dawn-colored eyes he did. Reiko and Shinichiro were intrigued by the "tattoo" on his back, but Bezaleel shrugged it off as a design he liked. He didn't bother to tell them about his wings, Nahms, or anything about Ashkaar.

Shinichiro had subtly tried to draw out the details from Bezaleel once—about him and where he came from—but he'd remained tight-lipped. The less the family knew about him, the safer they all were.

But Bezaleel didn't want to seem too shady after the great lengths the couple had gone to in order to help him, feed him, and give him shelter. Nor did he want to break their trust in him. So, he hinted at the possibility of another world, that maybe he'd run away from something dangerous. He gave them the notion that he was like a bug caught in a spiderweb, and he'd had no choice but to escape his previous circumstances.

After that, Shinichiro and Reiko felt that whatever Bezaleel wasn't saying was better left that way. They respected his decision to keep quiet, and never again prodded him about his former life, which made him wonder why the married couple was helping him at all. When he had asked, Shinichiro simply replied, "The shrine is a place for a kami: a god. The last thing we would find in there is a demon."

That didn't make much sense to Bezaleel, but it still made him feel elevated and relieved.

One thing he was sure about was that this family was genuine. He would never question their kindness, and wanted to show his gratitude in one way or another. He started by doing what he could, simple things like helping Reiko with household chores. But most of the time, she would decline his help on account of his still recovering wounds. But in Bezaleel's mind, this was the least he could do in return for their nursing a stranger like him. And in that manner, his passive days carried on into weeks.

The colors of the trees had changed from dark brown to livelier shades. Empty branches grew new leaves and started sprouting flower buds at their ends. Emerald green grass started to blanket the plain mud, and the chill winds were getting warmer.

Bezaleel sat on the steps of the porch as he mindlessly gazed at the scenery in front of him. A soft breeze rustled the still leaves and caressed his white tresses, which he had cut short. He could feel the wind tickle the back of his bare neck and rubbed his arms after a slight shudder traveled along them. Three weeks was hardly enough time to get used to the climate of another world, and Alayl never had such cold weather. It was always warm and green with fertile soil.

"Cold?" Reiko's asked from the yard just beyond the porch. She stood in her thick garden full of geraniums, jasmine and herbs. None of them had flowered yet, but they stood healthy and ready for spring.

Bezaleel nodded, then stood up, slipped on the garden sandals, walked over to Reiko, and crouched down beside her. She had been trimming a growing plant, snipping at leafless branches to let the new ones grow in healthy. Bezaleel gently took the garden scissors from her hand and snipped away at the rest of the unhealthy twigs.

"You don't have to," she said as she gently tweaked the strands of his hair.

"It's okay," Bezaleel replied politely in her language.

If there was one thing Bezaleel had learned from her, it was gardening. It gave him the chance to plant the Chiweu in the garden and cultivate it.

Bezaleel stood up and walked on to the other side of the garden, where he had planted the herb. It looked healthy, with evergreen leaves. His eyes twinkled with glee when he found ripe black berries hanging at the ends. Finally.

Bezaleel plucked and gathered all twelve berries in his hands. He knew exactly how much he needed for the Nahm to work; he had waited three weeks for this.

"What's that for?" Reiko gestured to the berries with her chin. "Eating?"

"No," Bezaleel answered. "Eating poisonous. Berries change eyes and hair."

Before Reiko could respond, he raced back into the house, leaving Reiko to call after him. Slipping off his sandals on the porch, he made his way into the kitchen first. He grabbed a mortar and pestle from the cabinet and dropped the berries in it.

Reiko had joined him by then and stood at the kitchen doorway, looking puzzled.

Without paying her much attention, Bezaleel used the pestle to crush the berries. They were soft and burst easily under the pressure. He kept grinding and crushing them until the berries were reduced to nothing but thick, black liquid.

He took the mortar bowl and rushed past Reiko to the bathroom in his room. He stood before the sink and stared at his reflection in the mirror, at his white hair and his otherworldly eyes. He glanced down at the mortar and took one last look at the black liquid. This was it. Bezaleel closed his eyes for a second, took a deep breath, and started pouring it onto his hair while reciting the incantation he found in the scroll in Zalek. "*Powers born of the night, you need not wake me again.*"

As he said this, the liquid glistened and changed into a lavender color before etching its way through his locks. The liquid stuck to every inch of his tresses, until his last white strand had turned raven black. Bezaleel kept his eyes on his reflection and watched his orange-red orbs fade to grey.

He took a step back from the mirror and stared at his new self. With black hair and grey eyes, he looked...normal. Like any other thirteen-year-old. It was strange, as if the reflection staring back at him was someone else. But he knew he would get used to this new appearance with time. In a peaceful world like this, he doubted he would ever need to use his powers.

Bezaleel walked out of the bathroom and into the living room, where Shinichiro and Tetsu were playing around. Reiko had also made her way to them, telling Shinichiro how the boy had plucked some berries and run to the bathroom for God knew what. But as he came into view, all three of them stopped and stared.

"Oh my," Reiko muttered.

"Well, look at that," Shinichiro said. They were more bewildered by Bezaleel's trick than his altered appearance.

Reiko stood up and walked towards him. She gently ran her hands through his hair. There were no traces of dye or any sort of liquid that she saw. It was like he was born with black hair. "Is this what the berries were for?" Bezaleel nodded. "I almost don't recognize you."

Tetsu let out a displeased cry, like something precious had been taken away from him. "What happened to your eyes?" the six-year-old whined.

"It's okay," Bezaleel said, trying to calm him down. "This is safe."

"I think Tetsu was fonder of your other eyes," Shinichiro explained as he pulled his son into his lap.

"Yes!" Tetsu replied. "I loved them! They were so pretty! Like sunrise!" Tetsu waved his hand around, trying to share the grandness of what he felt.

Bezaleel didn't know how to respond to that unexpected answer. No one has ever called his eyes beautiful before. They were all afraid of them, afraid that he could see things that they could not—as if he was always looking into their very soul. All anyone else saw in his eyes was death. It was the first time that anyone had looked at him without fear and saw something different in them. Something hopeful, like a sunrise.

He couldn't help the feeling that perhaps this family wouldn't think so fondly of him if they knew the things that he had done, but it was the first time that he felt it was okay to like his own multi-colored eyes.

He crouched down in front of Tetsu and ruffled his hair. "Thank you."

Tetsu grinned and giggled.

"Well now that you look normal, you can finally go out into the world. Don't you think it's time we give you a name?" Shinichiro said.

"Name?" Bezaleel echoed.

"Yes, what would you like to be called?"

Bezaleel remained silent. What would he like to be called? He didn't know. He had no knowledge of names in Yalim.

Seeing his puzzled face, Shinichiro laughed lightly. "I guess we will do the honors."

"That's right!" Reiko chirped. "Let's decide on a name for you." She put a finger to her chin, deep in thought. "How about Haru?"

Haru? Hell no. That didn't sound like him at all. Bezaleel shook his head.

"Okay, then how about Akatsuki?"

He shook his head again. Too hard to pronounce.

"Yuki?"

No way. Too soft.

This time, it was Shinichiro who offered a suggestion. "What about Mirai?"

That caught Bezaleel's attention. Mirai. That sounded nice. "What means Mirai?"

"It means 'future,'" Shinichiro replied. "Since you don't want to tell us who you *were*, maybe you can focus on who you want to become. How about it?"

"Mirai," Bezaleel repeated the word in a soft whisper, as if testing it on his tongue. It rolled quite nicely. Future. He liked that.

This time, Bezaleel nodded.

"That's decided then!" Shinichiro grinned. "Mirai, it is."

Bezaleel felt blessed to have ended up in the hands of this kind family, who had taken a stranger like him home, given him food, cared for him, and now gave him a new name. Maybe it wouldn't be so bad to stay with them as long as he could.

Maybe it wouldn't be so bad for him to be Mirai as long as he could.

CHAPTER TWENTY-TWO

MOMENT

Once Bezaleel had changed his appearance and was given the name Mirai, the first thing he did was step out of the house and explore this new world. At first, he just took short walks around. This humble home was surrounded by nature. Somehow, it reminded him of the Newara Forest. Not as magical, but the shining green leaves and the scent of fresh mud gave him the same kind peace the forest always had.

While exploring, he had tried his best to keep from interacting with the neighbors. He wasn't the socializing kind, and moreover, if they asked him questions, he doubted he would know what to say. But in time, he came to realize that in a small town like this, staying aloof was nearly impossible. With houses lined nearby, neighbors would often see him walking and would ask Reiko and Shinichiro about him.

In response the couple would say, "The boy? That's Mirai." Then, they would use a word that Bezaleel didn't yet know the meaning of. In return, the neighbors would show signs of delight.

Since Reiko was a respected doctor in their small town and Shinichiro was an honest restaurant owner, no one doubted them. In fact, probably as a result of whatever it was that the couple had said to them about him, the neighbors got used to seeing him around and began waving at him. At first, Bezaleel confined himself to a hesitant nod in return, but after numerous times of them repeating the act, he started to wave back.

When Shinichiro and Reiko realized that Bezaleel was curious about the town, they took the initiative to show him around. It was better than him sitting idle around the house. They would take him for walks, showing him the way to the nearby stores, all the important routes around town, and anything else that they thought would help the boy adjust to his new life better.

After that they, introduced him to the people they knew. They would use that same word that Bezaleel didn't know and then, like the rest, these people's faces would light up and they would do something like ruffle his hair. He had no idea just what the couple had said, but since it didn't do him any harm, he let it be. In all his thirteen years, he had never felt more like a child than among these people.

In Ashkaar, everyone saw him as a Teiyyan who would become the next Deva. As an assassin. As a Raathri. But here, he was just a teenager. No one knew who he was. All they saw was a child. It was the first time in his life he was being treated like one.

When they would ask his name, it would take him a second or two to respond with "Mirai" rather than "Bezaleel," but slowly he was getting used to being called that by both the family and the handful of people that regularly saw and spoke to him.

Tetsu was even more enthusiastic than the couple was about introducing Bezaleel to his world. He had shown Bezaleel the way to his school and back several times, then took him to the seaside, his favorite playground across the town, and even to his friends' houses—much to Bezaleel's reluctance. Slowly, he was getting used to it all.

It came to the point that some days he would go and pick up Tetsu from his school without the boy having to demand it of him. They would walk back together while Tetsu shared the details of his day and stories about his friends. But there was something else he began to notice during these walks.

Bezaleel sometimes saw a boy in the woods, on a path that was also a shortcut to the house. This boy looked to be around his age, and was always getting beaten up by three other boys.

Bezaleel had ignored it at first. He didn't like it, but he didn't know what the right reaction was in this world. If he was in Ashkaar, he would have challenged them and knocked them out.

The bullies wore a kind of dress he had never seen anyone in Yalim wear until then. It was more reason for him to not get involved. What if it was some kind of uniform that gave them authority? Interfering would just get him into trouble. He was still getting used to this world and the last thing he wanted was to draw unwanted attention to himself.

But the second time he saw the same scene in the same place, Bezaleel was irked. He silently curled his fist and chose to look the other way when Tetsu tugged at his clothes. They were probably beating this boy up in the woods because no one else used that route.

There was no doubt about it; the boy was getting bullied.

After the third time, he decided to ask Shinichiro about it indirectly. He wanted to know how someone in Yalim would handle such a situation and then act accordingly.

"What do we do if someone gets bullied?"

Shinichiro raised an eyebrow as Bezaleel helped tidy up the tables and chairs in the restaurant. The place was empty for the night. "Well, that depends on the type of person you are," Shinichiro said matter-of-factly as he flipped the sign on the door from "OPEN" to "CLOSED." "But if you ask me, I say you should always help the person who is getting bullied. If someone needs saving, save them."

"Can I beat bullies?" Bezaleel asked.

"Well, I wouldn't encourage you to be violent, but if they are violent and you feel unsafe, then kick their butts."

"Butts?"

Shinichiro playfully tapped his own to show him the literal

meaning. Then he walked over to Bezaleel with a serious expression and asked, "Is someone bullying you?"

"No." Bezaleel thought for a moment before continuing. "Dress. Bullies were wearing long pants. Loose." He motioned around his thighs to try and paint a more accurate picture than his still developing speech could. "Very loose. Black. Like skirt, but pants. White shirt."

Shinichiro tried to guess what he was hinting at before the light bulb in his head clicked. "Oh. You mean a hakama?"

"What's that?"

"It's for martial arts. Fighting. The bullies you saw are probably students in a dojo. They know how to fight."

Bezaleel thought back to what he saw. It didn't look like training. That was definitely a one-sided beating because the other boy wasn't wearing one of those hakamas. In a small town like this, they probably knew each other from the same school, or were neighbors. "Not fair," Bezaleel muttered.

Shinichiro let out a small sigh. "Don't get into trouble, okay?" He grabbed Bezaleel by the shoulders from behind and playfully pushed him out the restaurant's back door and stepped out along with him. He took out the keys and locked the door.

"Okay," Bezaleel agreed as he decided what he'd do if he saw those three again.

After asking Shinichiro, he didn't see those four boys for a while. It was as if fate knew his savage thoughts and decided not to leave anything to chance. Bezaleel came to the conclusion that perhaps the boy told his parents what was happening and the bullying had stopped.

But a few days after that, the boy was back in the woods, getting beat up yet again. This time, Bezaleel decided he wasn't going to ignore it. He decided to appease his boiling blood.

He stopped walking, told Tetsu to stay put, then let go of his hand and turned toward them. The bullied boy had fallen on the leafy ground. The side of his face was turning multiple shades of purple. The bigger bully lifted his hand and threw a punch at the fallen boy's face, but his fist met with Bezaleel's palm instead.

The bully was bigger than him, but as a Teiyyan, Bezaleel was much stronger than a human his age. He gave a light push and the bully stumbled back.

Bezaleel helped the fallen boy stand up. "Are you okay?" he asked and the boy nodded.

The bully's face turned red. More from embarrassment at being manhandled by a boy who was much thinner and shorter than he was than out of anger, Bezaleel assumed.

He let out a growl and charged at him. Bezaleel ducked and hooked him in the gut. The first bully's friend ran at Bezaleel at the same time, but the Teiyyan grabbed him by the collar and flung him into the first kid. They both went crashing down.

When they tried to get up and rush at him again, Bezaleel lifted a fallen tree trunk from off the ground. The bullies took a step forward, and Bezaleel flexed at them as if he was about to swing at them without restraint. They flinched and took two steps back. Bezaleel tightened his hold on the trunk and narrowed his eyes, arranging his face in such a way that he knew it clearly conveyed that if they came at him, he'd beat them into a pulp.

The bigger bully pointed at the boy behind Bezaleel. "You! You'll pay for this," he growled before he and his friend took off like scared rabbits being chased by a wolf.

Bezaleel hadn't even broken a sweat. For him, the whole thing was as easy as tossing a coin. He was sure that they wouldn't come running back or get the adults involved, seeing as how they'd beaten the boy black and blue.

"Iz *ayrik et tu orkanthe, vidi*," Bezaleel mumbled to himself in Zalek. *And I'll make you pay double, idiot.* He turned back to the boy and extended his hand. "Can you stand?"

"Yeah," the boy responded and grasped Bezaleel's palm so the other could heave him up. "Thanks."

"I'll keep watch," Bezaleel responded.

"On what?"

"You." Silence took over them until Bezaleel explained. "Walk home. I'll guard you. They hurt you, you tell me."

"And what do you plan to do about it?"

Bezaleel smirked. "Kick their butts," he said, quoting Shinichiro.

The boy burst out laughing and Bezaleel could somehow tell it was more from relief than mockery. "You're pretty cool," he said. "I'm Ren."

"Mirai."

"Thank you, Mirai."

"Onii-san! That was so cool!" Tetsu exclaimed as he threw both hands in the air when the boys met him where Bezaleel had told him to stay. Bezaleel smiled, took Tetsu by the arms and swung him onto his back. Tetsu giggled as he latched onto Mirai's neck. The latter supported him by hooking his hands under Tetsu's knees. Tetsu loved piggyback rides, and Bezaleel had no problem indulging him.

He kept his promise to guard Ren until he was safely at home. On the way, Bezaleel learned that Ren went to a school near Tetsu's. It was just an extra five minutes away, so Bezaleel decided to meet Ren whenever he would pick up Tetsu, and then the trio would walk together to their homes. Ren was one of their neighbors, much to Bezaleel's surprise. Then again, he never made an effort to meet people in the first place. He only knew the faces of those that waved at him, and most of those belonged to adults.

Ren had decided to meet Bezaleel more often than the walks from school. He would constantly be dragged out to "hang out," which was a phrase Bezaleel had never heard of before. He started dropping in at Reiko and Shinichiro's house, and the couple once even forced Bezaleel to return the gesture by doing the same at Ren's house. Bezaleel had never felt more awkward or fumbled about so much in his life.

He had come across Ren's bullies a couple more times, but they would only scurry off if Bezaleel so much as looked at them. Ren laughed about it with him later, and would often say he was grateful for it. As a result, he'd decided to call Bezaleel his "friend."

Ren taught and showed Bezaleel things that Reiko and Shinichiro couldn't: things that only friends knew like sleepovers, getting ice cream together, talking about everything and anything. It was a part of life that he wasn't aware of since he never got to live it in Ashkaar. He didn't have friends his age, and he definitely wasn't allowed the time to socialize when he was an assassin.

Ren took him to play a lot of field games, too. Most of the time it was something called "basketball" with other kids from his school. At first, Bezaleel didn't find it very interesting to throw a ball through a hoop, especially since he was faster than the others and could jump higher. But he started to like the teamwork involved in it, especially when he would "score" and the others would slap him on the back as a compliment. What he enjoyed even more were the so-called "video games" that Ren had at his home. It fascinated him that things could move on a tiny screen according to how he wanted with the push of a few buttons.

Being around someone his age and having fun together was starting to become something Bezaleel cherished, and he loved every moment of his time being Ren's friend.

CHAPTER TWENTY-THREE

BELONG

Days passed into weeks, weeks became months. The season was starting to take on all of the colors of spring, and Bezaleel was still freeloading at the house.

There might have been endless differences between Ashkaar and Yalim, but if there was one thing that was common in both of them it was using one's manners. And the universal language of manners and goodwill made Bezaleel feel that it was not okay to take someone's kindness for granted.

Sure, he didn't have anywhere to go and he had no idea what to do with his life now, but he decided to take it step by step. And the first step was repaying the family for looking after him. When he approached the couple about it, Shinichiro asked him if he wanted to help out at the restaurant since he'd dropped by a couple of times and the staff was already familiar with him.

Bezaleel agreed even though he was unsure how that would go, but being in a new world, living a life that he had never known before, he decided it wouldn't be too bad to try something else new. So he started helping Shinichiro at his restaurant. He did all he could, from helping customers to kitchen work.

At home, he helped Reiko with household chores, from cooking to gardening.

The couple kept insisting that he didn't have to do anything in return for them sharing their home, but Bezaleel insisted that he wanted to.

Their lunches and dinners were filled with conversation, laughter, and playful bickering. It was all starting to feel so natural, almost like he was part of the family from the very beginning.

But even as he was getting more involved in a "normal" life, he made sure his other skill sets stayed sharp. Sometimes he would wake up in the morning, earlier than everyone else, and head to the backyard to practice with his sword away from any prying eyes. He wanted to get used to the body that didn't have the power of his eyes or the shield of his wings.

In a town like this, he knew he'd never have to be as cautious as he used to, but his skill with a sword was something he was proud of and he didn't want to let that go. However, if given the choice to live as just Bezaleel or Mirai, he found himself thinking that he would probably choose the latter.

The spring season in Yalim was very different from that of Ashkaar. In Alayl, this was the time when most forest and water faes would awaken. They would dance among the trees, leaves, and grassy fields to change nature's colors, bring harvest, and put the whole world in splendor.

Here, the trees took on a different color on their own. There were no fae creatures, not even one. There were a lot of insects and animals similar to those of Ashkaar, like butterflies and fireflies, but Yalim had no magic. Still, it had its own charms.

Bezaleel loved the view of the pink trees that stood together, lined up in abundance. Then, in a flurry, the thousand petals would scatter, coloring the world around them in a hue of beautiful pink. It was a sight worth seeing.

"Sakura." Shinichiro joined Bezaleel on the porch facing their backyard on a lazy afternoon. He grunted as he sat down on the wooden floor. "They're called sakura trees," Shinichiro explained as he followed Bezaleel's gaze.

"It's beautiful," Bezaleel remarked.

"They're Mirai's favorite!" Tetsu announced as he came running out and latched onto Bezaleel's back, earning a smile and a ruffle of the head from the older boy.

"What do we have here? Are you three leaving me out?" Reiko teased as she joined them with a tray holding four cups: three filled with hot tea and one with sweet grape juice.

"Reiko-san," Bezaleel greeted her. She set the tray on the wooden floor between him and Shinichiro. They both picked a cup and Reiko straightened up, walked to the porch stairs, and picked up a sakura flower that had landed on there. She placed the perfect flower in Mirai's tresses behind his ear and chuckled when the boy looked puzzled.

"It suits you," she said as she gazed at him with the same tenderness she held for Tetsu. "You have such a pretty face." She lightly pinched his nose in affection.

Bezaleel couldn't help the red tint that spread across his cheeks. "Aren't flowers for girls?" he muttered under his breath as he removed it from his hair.

"There is no such thing when it comes to nature. You like them, don't you? You're always staring at them," Reiko replied. "And these flowers have a special meaning, you know."

"Meaning?" Bezaleel echoed.

"That's right," Shinichiro interjected. "They are a symbol for beauty and rebirth. They were also the symbol for warriors."

"And..." Reiko briefly glanced at Shinichiro before continuing, as if she was silently confirming something with him. "They're also used to welcome a new member to the family."

Bezaleel stared at them. He clearly understood what they said, but he wasn't sure if they were implying what he thought they were. When the silence dragged on, the couple decided to speak plainly.

"Mirai, we are planning to adopt you."

Adopt. That was the word Bezaleel had heard the couple tell other people before. When they would ask who he was, they would use this word and then the person would suddenly light up and ruffle his hair or say something kind.

"What is 'adopt?'"

Reiko turned to face Bezaleel completely. She smiled and combed back his hair affectionately. The gentle touch reminded him of his mother. "It means to accept someone into the family officially."

Shinichiro scooted closer to him. "Mirai, would you like to become our son?"

Bezaleel's eyes widened, taking in the pink-tinted world, and both Reiko and Shinichiro with it. Son? *Him?*

Reiko's lips turned into a slight frown when he failed to respond right away. "Is there somewhere else you need to go? Someone you know?"

Bezaleel shook his head almost immediately. There was *no one*. They were the first people he knew in this world. They'd given him food, shelter, and care that he didn't even know he'd needed.

Reiko and Shinichiro smiled. "Well, then, how about it?"

Bezaleel wanted to say a lot of things, to tell them he was ever so grateful and that this was the first time in a very long time that he was experiencing the warmth of a family. That nothing would make him happier, and he would thank the whole Jihan and God who created it for this. But his words, all of them, got stuck like a lump in his throat and all he could do was nod like a fool as he tried so hard to swallow around it.

The couple grinned at his response.

"Mirai is going to be my big brother?" Tetsu jumped up and down with excitement.

"Do you like that, Tetsu?" Reiko encouraged, although they knew what Tetsu's answer would be after seeing how attached he was to the boy from the very beginning.

"Yes!" Tetsu flung himself at Bezaleel, wrapping his small arms around him in a loving embrace. "Nii-san!"

"Welcome to the family," the couple said simultaneously as they enveloped both children in a hug.

Bezaleel couldn't help but crack a smile. His chest clenched. For the first time in his life he had something that he had always wanted. Something that he had lost before he could experience the warmth and happiness of it all. Something that he had imagined and dreamt of in his lonely room at the Raathri estate of Alayl—parents, a family.

Now, he had it all for real. There was nothing more he could ask for. He finally had a place to belong.

CHAPTER TWENTY-FOUR

YEARS

"Nii-san!" Tetsu called out for the third time at the lump of sheets curled atop the mattress like a croissant. He scrunched his eyebrows, planted his hands on his hips, and adopted an exasperated voice as he said, "Come on, nii-san. Wake up already! You need to go to work!" He whacked the blanket where he figured the head would be.

The covers shifted, and Mirai pulled down the sheet and squinted at Tetsu through his barely open eyelids. That hit was going to leave a mark. He wondered when Tetsu had gotten so strong and tall. His features had grown sharper, matured over time to turn him into a handsome young teen. His voice was like honey, sweet and gentle like his soul, which was reflected in his dark brown eyes.

But in terms of growing up well, Bezaleel was no different. He had grown taller, and his body stayed slim with lean, toned muscles. Although his hair was not as long as it was when he first arrived, it still cascaded in smooth, jet black waves to the nape of his neck. Mature and focused eyes set off his chiseled facial features.

Mirai leaned up towards Tetsu, hooked his arms around his neck and pulled him onto the bed. Tetsu fell on top of the soft mattress with a loud yelp. In a second, Mirai had pulled the covers over him and whispered, "Sleep."

Tetsu shot out his hands from under the sheet. "Like hell I can!" He flailed in a futile attempt to free himself from the cobra–like grip of his older brother. "I know you're tired but come on! Dad's going to yell at me for being late to school!"

"Being late to school one day won't hurt you," Mirai said in perfect Japanese, as if he had spoken it his entire life.

"I have archery practice today!"

"That's in the evening."

"Stop making excuses!" Tetsu pulled at Mirai's cheeks.

"Thaht hurtsh."

"Mirai! Tetsu! What's taking you both so long?" Reiko's annoyed voice carried up the stairs. The pair of brothers jolted.

Mirai sighed in defeat when his brother gave him a disgruntled look. "Alright, I'm getting up." He swung his legs over the side of his bed and stood, stretching. "I'll be down in ten minutes." He paused to ruffle Tetsu's hair before making his way to the washroom.

True to his word, he was down within minutes after freshening up. Even though ten years had passed since he came to Iwami, the teachings he had learned when he was Bezaleel of Alayl stayed with him. Punctuality and impeccable discipline were two of them.

As Mirai trotted into the kitchen, the clock on the wall ticked five past eight. Reiko was in the middle of preparing lunches for Tetsu, Shinichiro and Mirai to take with them. She turned when she heard the creek of the wooden floor as Mirai made his way towards her.

"Good morning," he greeted.

"Good morning!" Reiko chirped back. "How are you feeling? You worked until pretty late last night."

"I'm fine. Healthy enough to take on a new day."

Reiko offered him a loving smile. "You should rest and hang out with Ren from time to time. When I saw him a few days back, he complained that he doesn't get to see you much these days."

"Did he?"

"Yes. Now eat your breakfast." She pointed to the plate with two rice balls and rolled eggs. "Heat up the tea if you want some."

"For me, too, please!" Tetsu announced from where he sat behind the low table.

"Yes, yes," Mirai replied with mock annoyance, though his heart held none of it. He was used to these antics, and as Tetsu grew up, Mirai had spoiled him the most. Even so, he had grown into a fine sixteen-year-old.

"Isn't your tournament this week?" Mirai asked Tetsu as he poured hot green tea into two cups. The sound and smell added to the sizzling noise of oil in the frying pan and the aroma of delicious fried chicken filling the air.

"Yeah! We're competing against the district schools."

"And to think you were so nervous the first time you held that bow."

"You're never going to let me live that down!"

Mirai snickered as he placed the tea on the table for him. Reiko joined in with a chuckle of her own. "I'll come see your tournament." Mirai promised.

"You will?" Tetsu's eyes twinkled.

"Wouldn't miss it for the world." Mirai replied as he took a bite of a rolled egg.

Ten years. Mirai counted mentally as he glanced at Tetsu. It had been ten years since Reiko and Shinichiro found him in that shrine. Ten years had passed since he became Mirai.

He fit in with their family like he was born into it. His parents showed no bias toward either of their sons. Tetsu was proud to have a big brother that indulged and looked after him at every turn, and Bezaleel was more than happy to fill that role.

As years passed, he'd melted into the life of Mirai. Although he was reserved, the townspeople saw him as a kind, well-mannered young man who would help them if needed. He had proved himself to them on many occasions.

As the seasons shifted endlessly, one after another, Bezaleel began to fade away. Without the powers or the physical appearance to remind him of his previous life as an assassin, he started being simply Mirai, and he held no regrets about that. His life in Ashkaar became a fleeting memory, like a blurry reflection on running water.

He was content with that. As Mirai, he had a family. He helped Shinichiro run a business that was also now his. He had the loving, caring family that he had always wanted. And he would be damned if he let it go.

After relentless reminders from Tetsu about his archery competition and a lot of complaints from Ren about ignoring him, Mirai decided to drag him along when the day of the tournament came.

Mirai had left the restaurant earlier in hopes of arriving on time to see Tetsu pull the bowstring, or he knew he wouldn't hear the end of it. As Ren and Mirai sidled across a few empty seats, the stadium slowly started filling with parents, friends and classmates that had come to support the contestants and possibly witness their victory over the competing schools.

"Over there." Ren spoke over the growing noise and murmuring of the audience and tapped Mirai's shoulder, pointing toward three empty seats at the front row. "We can see Tetsu clearly from there."

Mirai and Ren squeezed their way through the crowd and sat down next to each other. Over the years, Ren had grown from just a friend to family; he was like another brother to Mirai.

He could call Ren at four in the morning for help and he would come running without a second thought. He could rely on Ren in tough times and happy ones, whether he was upset or overjoyed. With Ren he would laugh a little more and cry a little less, and any burden he carried would be reduced by half with his friend around.

They told each other anything and everything—except Mirai's past. He didn't want Ren to look at him as if he were a stranger, or worse, with fear. To Mirai, his life as Bezaleel was better kept secret even from the person he trusted most.

The audience quieted down when the contestants walked into the stadium. Mirai's eyes found the uniform colors of Tetsu's school and then spotted him standing on the fifth row, behind two other students from the same school wearing similar clothes.

"I heard that one of the schools Tetsu is competing with is pretty good in archery. They won the championship three times in a row," Ren informed him as he followed Mirai's gaze to his brother.

"Winning or losing doesn't always depend on a medal. Tetsu has been practicing day and night. I have faith in his skills. I just hope he does, too."

The presenter started announcing the contestants' names. They watched students from three schools give it their best before it was Tetsu and his team's turn came around.

Mirai watched tensely as Tetsu stood, got into position, and drew back his bowstring. The boy was rigid. His muscles were tense. He was nervous.

Tetsu let go off the arrow and it landed with a dull *thwack* beyond the target. He frowned and Mirai felt a slight nervousness growing in him as well. The other teammates took turns and almost all of them hit the target. It was evident that they had been trained well and Tetsu was no exception, but his nerves were getting to him.

When it was his turn again, he missed. And missed again. One of his arrows hit the outer ring, but that was the best that he had gotten that day. When his last arrow landed outside the ring again, his chance was over and he had lost. Even across the distance, Mirai could make out the frustration and disappointment marring Tetsu's usual bright face.

Mirai waited until the ceremony was done and the competition was over. Then he trotted over to Tetsu, with Ren following close behind. When he saw both of them, Tetsu's frustrated face turned glum.

"I was terrible," Tetsu whispered when his brother was close enough to hear him.

Mirai placed a comforting hand on Tetsu's shoulder. "First-time nerves happen to everyone. There is always a next time."

Tetsu sighed in defeat and hung his head. Mirai frowned at the sight of his brother's dejection. Tetsu's eyes remained downcast and Mirai took the opportunity to exchange a silent glance with Ren.

Ren, understanding Mirai's thoughts, spoke up. "Tell you what! Let's go to that ramen shop you love so much. Lunch is on me!"

At that, Tetsu raised his head and gave a weak smile. "Alright."

Ren gave Mirai a thumbs-up behind Tetsu while he gathered his gear.

⊰⊱

The walk to the ramen shop dispelled Tetsu's remaining gloominess. He doubled over in laughter after hearing Ren's comedic narrative about how a squirrel hunt with his father had turned into a disaster.

Mirai was grateful that a positive friend like Ren was present in moments like this. Mirai would never know how to handle such moments without his help.

Lunch breezed by with jokes, teasing, and encouraging comments. When the sun lowered in the sky, they walked back home. But after Ren left for the day, Tetsu's mood plummeted again.

"What's wrong?" Mirai asked as they walked side by side.

"Are you disappointed in me?" Tetsu's question caught Mirai off guard. It couldn't have been further away from how he actually felt. "I know you wanted to see me win."

Mirai halted, causing the boy to turn around and face him. "I want to see you happy. It doesn't matter whether you win or lose. Not everything is about victory. Sometimes it's about experience. Enjoy what you do, and the rest will follow."

"But I messed up so badly today, and that's after I practiced so hard. When I pulled the bowstring, I realized that I was doing something wrong but I couldn't tell what. How can I win next time if I don't know where I'm messing up?"

Mirai took a moment to think before his brain came up with

something that could uplift Tetsu's mood in the only way he knew how. It would mean letting him know more about his past than he wanted, but at that moment it didn't matter.

"Come with me." He grabbed Tetsu's arm and tugged him along, taking their usual shortcut through the woods. They stopped in a cluster of trees with heavy bark and thick trunks.

"Draw your arrow," Mirai told Tetsu as he pointed to a tree. "Try hitting the center of that trunk."

Tetsu took the arrow from his quiver and did as he was told. When he pulled back the arrow Mirai stepped closer to him and touched his fingers.

"You are too tense." The light tremble of Tetsu's hand would have gone unnoticed by a normal person, but a master archer's gaze easily caught it. "Ease up a bit so your fingers don't quiver from the tension. You'll be able to hold your bow more steady and hit whatever target you want. An archer's mind is the arrow. Don't concentrate on anything else," Mirai explained. He gently pushed Tetsu's arm to adjust it properly. "Widen your stance a bit more for better balance. Calm your mind, take a breath, aim, and release the arrow."

Tetsu's eyes held him, almost like he was looking at someone else. But the boy didn't ponder on it long. Still, Mirai felt that he had given a little too much away, but it was too late to take back now.

Tetsu followed Mirai's instructions and released the arrow. The arrow whizzed along its path and hit the center of the trunk. His jaw dropped and he turned to Mirai. "How did you know that?"

Mirai shrugged and tried to give a vague but convincing answer. "I...did archery when I was around five." A half-truth was better than a lie, right?

"No way. Why didn't you tell me?" There was awe in Tetsu's voice that Mirai felt he didn't deserve.

"It's not a good memory."

Tetsu must have picked up on the hesitation in Mirai's voice, because he didn't dwell on it any further. Instead, he eagerly asked, "Would you practice with me some more?"

"Of course."

"Right now!" Tetsu was too excited for Mirai to turn him down.

"Sure," he agreed.

The two of them spent hours practicing, with Mirai giving him tips to better his skills. They stayed in the woods until the last light of the day had sunk behind the horizon. The sky grew dark and the night's mist wafted through the air. The sun above them had been replaced with the full moon and numerous dazzling stars.

"We've been out here for a while. Let's head home now." Mirai told Tetsu, who was picking up the fallen arrows on the ground.

"Let's!" the boy chirped. All the gloominess he had carried with him that afternoon had vanished without leaving a single trace of it in his face. They walked back together, chattering softly and playfully bickering.

As they neared the path to their house, though, Mirai stopped talking. His ears picked up on faint, unusual sounds. He hushed an oblivious Tetsu and clamped his hand on his shoulder, keeping him from walking any further.

Mirai sniffed. There was the smell of smoke. Of burning wood and flesh.

He strained his ears again. Faint sounds, like something crackling...and distant screams.

Without another word, he grabbed Tetsu by the hand and rushed toward home.

"Nii-san?" the younger boy called out. "What's wrong?"

Tetsu didn't receive an answer. He was left with no other choice than to run ahead with his brother. Once they reached the edge of the woods, an orange glow came into view. Mirai skidded to a stop, and Tetsu bumped into his back. At the sight in front of him, Mirai's heart rate faster and he could feel every beat thumping in his ears. Every drop of blood drained from his face. As soon as he realized what they were staring at, Tetsu gasped from behind him.

The town was ablaze in a sea of fire. Houses burned and charred in the furious flames. Dead bodies lined the street.

Between the angry red of the fire and the unfolding chaos, Mirai saw the robes that he thought he would never have to see again. He recognized the symbol that etched on the back of them. No matter how many years passed, he would always recognize that symbol and the color of those robes. It was the one thing he would *never* forget. His mind railed against the reality that had come crashing back into his life.

The robes were those of the Raathri clan.

Mirai heard a loud growl as one of his neighbors ran at the Raathri member with a steel rod. The Raathri pulled out a sword and, with zero hesitation, slashed the man across his chest.

Tetsu opened his mouth, and Mirai covered his mouth just in time to muffle his scream. He pulled him behind a tree and hid them in its shadows.

The Raathri member turned around, as if he'd sensed them. He stalked to the edge of the trees and peered into the darkness of the forest. Mirai clamped his lips tightly shut and steadied his breathing so as not to let the faintest sound escape and give away their position. His heart thumped with every movement the Raathri made around them. If they were found, they were dead. Mirai hoped with each step the Raathri took that he and Tetsu would go unseen.

Tetsu was frozen still. After a dreadful twenty seconds or more, they were left unnoticed. The Raathri walked away.

Mirai forced Tetsu to look at him by tilting his head. He brought his forefinger to his lips, signaling him to stay silent. Tetsu nodded, but he was still in a daze. It was the sort of numbness one feels as the world around them collapses. Mirai knew it well.

Grabbing his wrist, Mirai guided him along in the shadows, away from the predatory eyes of anyone who was on the hunt for victims. There were more Raathri members walking around, setting more houses ablaze as if they were smoking out a rat.

Mirai hid behind trees and ducked beneath bushes with Tetsu to escape the Raathris' gazes. While he made his way to their home, his mind whirred with endless questions. How did the Raathri clan lift the Veyil? He had destroyed the scroll. Did they try the coup again and win this time? How did they find him? What was happening?

As his house came into view, Mirai let out a tiny breath of relief. The fire hadn't reached their home yet. Even so, he still felt a foreboding sense of danger. He silently crept around the backyard and made his way into the house through the back door.

The lights were off. The silence was deafening. No movement. No sign of anyone.

He wanted to yell Reiko and Shinichiro's names and hear their voices in return, but he tamped that temptation down. If there was an intruder in the house, he would only give them all away. So he quietly crept into the living room with Tetsu following behind him. It was dark. Pitch dark.

And then his nose picked up on the scent of blood, fresh as a new kill. Mirai became stiff as a stone when he saw the pool of blood on the floor and the two bodies that lay atop it.

Tetsu screamed in despair and pulled himself free from Mirai's grip, rushing to the lifeless bodies of his parents. He knelt by them, unable to utter a single world or do anything besides sob and whimper as he shook Reiko and Shinichiro's bodies one after the other. No movement. Not a sound.

After a few tries at reviving them, he rested his head on top of Reiko's back and wailed as tears streamed down his face endlessly. Mirai stood numb with shock, watching the scene before him as if he was hallucinating. He couldn't move. He couldn't think. His mind was blank and everything seemed to have come to a complete halt.

The only thing that snapped him back to reality was the silhouette moving behind Tetsu. When Mirai saw the flash of a silver blade, his eyes widened.

Tetsu felt the movement and turned around in time to see the edge of a sharp sword swinging directly toward his neck. He went rigid from fear, but Mirai moved at the speed of a lightning bolt. Before the blade could so much as graze Tetsu's skin, Mirai slid in between him and the attacker. He wrapped his arms around him and pulled him into his chest.

But the sharp edge of the sword didn't hit Mirai's back. Instead, it clashed against his wings. Diamond hard, black wings.

"Bezaleel." The attacker sounded completely baffled once he recognized the infamous black wings that belonged to only one person in the history of Ashkaar.

A thin red spark zapped across Mirai's eyes, turning his passive grey eyes into his original orange-red ones. All his rage at what had befallen his family, his friends, and his neighbors was enough to break the Nahm that kept the form of Bezaleel hidden.

As he cocooned himself and Tetsu inside his wings, he could see another three Raathri invade his house. They must have heard Tetsu's cries. Bezaleel took a deep breath. This was as far as they would go.

He opened his wings and the Raathri's swords collided with his impenetrable feathers. The Raathri that stood in front of him swung at Mirai, but Mirai was Bezaleel again, and Bezaleel was one of the best assassins Ashkaar had ever seen.

He easily dodged the strike while still protecting Tetsu. He grabbed the Raathri's hand, twisted the sword out of his grasp, grabbed it, and plunged it into the man for an instant kill. With the sword in Bezaleel 's hand, the rest of the Raathris only caught the blur of his movements as he struck all of them down, slashed until blood poured out of their bodies and they dropped lifelessly to the floor.

Tetsu stood there gaping as the last intruder fell. "Nii…san?"

"Come." Bezaleel pulled Tetsu up the stairs.

"Wh-what's happening?"

Bezaleel pursed his lips. What could he say to even begin to explain all of this? It was foolish of him to have believed that the Raathri would never find him, that he could live the rest of his life in peace.

Bezaleel raced into his bedroom, flung open his cupboard and pushed aside his clothes. He stared at the two swords resting in the bottom corner, the red symbol of the Raathri etched into both hilts. He grabbed his dual blades and turned to Tetsu, pointing at his armor that resided in the cupboard. "Burn it," he said as he strapped the swords to his hips.

Tetsu watched with wide eyes and an open mouth, unable to wrap his head around what was going on.

Bezaleel turned to him again. "Where are your arrows? The sharp ones."

"In-in my room," he muttered as Bezaleel pulled him by the wrist again.

He dashed across the hall to Tetsu's room, grabbed the bow and arrows resting at the foot of the boy's bed and pushed them against Tetsu's chest. "Use these on whoever attacks you. Don't think twice, don't hesitate." There was a commanding hint to his voice that Bezaleel knew Tetsu wouldn't be able to defy. It was a tone that warned Tetsu he couldn't make any mistakes. "Do you hear me?" Tetsu nodded and Bezaleel returned the gesture. "Good. Stay here. Stay hidden. Don't come out until every single one of these robed men is gone. Do you understand?"

Tetsu nodded again, with more assurance this time, but it was clear that he was still just as confused and upset. Bezaleel turned to leave through the window.

"Your real name...is Bezaleel?"

Mirai halted and turned around to face his brother for what he knew could possibly be the last time. He cupped Tetsu's face with his usual tenderness, even as his eyes dared Tetsu to question him. "You never heard that. You don't know who that is." Tetsu's eyes filled with tears as he understood the meaning behind those words. Mirai felt his own eyes pricking, but he continued and choked out what needed to be said. "You never knew me. You have never seen me before. There is no Mirai, and there never was."

Tetsu's expression twisted, as if someone had cut him with a blade and squeezed out his heart. "Please don't lea—"

"Tetsu!" Mirai cut him off, still holding his face in his palms. "I will make sure that you will be safe but you need to stay hidden. And you must *never* speak my name again."

Tetsu placed his hands above Mirai's warm ones. "Promise me." Tears fell from his half-moon eyes, sliding down his cheeks as he pleaded, "Promise me that you will come back."

"I can't do—"

"Promise me!"

Mirai felt that if he refused Tetsu now, the boy would disobey and do everything but what he had told him to. And because he never could resist giving his little brother what he wanted, he rested his forehead on Tetsu's and stared into his wet eyes as he whispered, "By daybreak... I promise."

CHAPTER TWENTY-FIVE

CARNAGE

Ren. He had to get to him. Bezaleel needed to know if he was alright, and if he was, then he needed to warn him and get him to safety. He rushed through the shadows at a speed he'd never reached before. The effort made his knees ache and his feet burn, but still he ran with all his might. He drew his wings back inside his body so he'd be more agile as he moved along the row of houses like a snake on the hunt.

After what seemed like hours, but had barely been five minutes, he reached the front yard of his friend's home. The door had been forced in.

Bezaleel's heart sank. He knew the Raathri and he knew the outcome of such an invasion. But still he hoped that he was wrong, that Ren was alright.

He hastened into Ren's house. What awaited him was the too-familiar image of dead bodies. Ren's parents and siblings. Reiko and Shinichiro's own bodies flashed before his eyes in a traumatizing flood of carnage and loss.

He tried to push it away as he hurried to the end of the hallway that ended in Ren's room.

As he stood in front of the door and reached for the doorknob, his hand shivered. It was a feeling that Bezaleel never knew. It was a feeling that shook his whole core with fear and uncertainty.

But despite his hesitation, despite wanting to turn tail and run away from all of this, he pushed open the door. And he saw. He saw Ren lying on his bed. A hole torn through his stomach. Blood stained the mattress.

There was a hot searing pain in Mirai's chest at the sight of it, as if someone was squeezing his heart from the inside. He was at Ren's side in a flash. Ren was breathing hard, taking every last pull of life he could as blood dripped down his chin.

At the sight of Mirai, he painstakingly lifted his hand. "Mi...rai," he gasped out.

Mirai grabbed his best friend's hand and placed the other on his forehead as if doing so would relax him somehow. His eyes raked across Ren's body trying to come up with a way—any way—to save him. "I'm here," he whispered to Ren. "It's okay."

"Mirai," Ren whispered again...and then stopped breathing. His fingers lost their grip and fell from Mirai's hand.

"Ren?" Mirai whispered his best friend's name even though he knew he couldn't hear him. He let out a defeated sigh and rested his forehead on Ren's silent, still chest. There was no heartbeat, no steady breath. After a few agonizing seconds, Mirai lifted himself up, kissed his friend's forehead, and gently ran his fingers over Ren's eyelids to close them.

"The fearsome Bezaleel finally shows his face," someone said in Zalek behind him. "But if the Raathri saw you like this, they wouldn't think you are one and the same."

Rage and fury flared inside Bezaleel, temporarily numbing his grief. He stood, turned around, and drew one of his swords from its sheath. He crossed the room so quickly that, by the time the man realized what was happening, Bezaleel's sharp sword was already pressed against the Raathri's throat, just barely breaking the skin. A drop of blood trailed along the shining metal blade.

The Raathri stared at the fiery hues of Bezaleel's eyes. Bezaleel didn't need to see his reflection to know that the color of them would resemble an angry, undying wildfire full of hate and revenge. "How the hell did you get through the Veyil?" Mirai seethed in Zalek.

The man remained silent. Ready to face death rather than spill the secrets of his clan.

Bezaleel clicked his tongue. Damn Raathri. Loyal to the very end, but for all the wrong reasons. "Who sent you after me?" Bezaleel pushed even though he knew it was futile.

The man smirked as if he'd heard his thoughts. "What good would it do you to know, Bezaleel? You are going to die here anyway, just like the rest of these dogs."

Bezaleel's restraint snapped. He slashed the sword across the man's throat.

His chest heaved with every breath he took. He gritted his teeth against the fury that wanted to burst out of him as he stared at the blood stains on the door from the Raathri he'd just killed.

"Please, let me go!" a woman cried outside.

Bezaleel ran to the window and peered out. A group of Raathri had dragged the remaining residents to kneel in the center of the road. A woman was shoved forward; she fell on her side and sobbed.

The Raathri were killing anyone they saw. It was like looking back at Alayl all those years ago, with dead bodies and burning houses strewn all over the town. The Raathri were not just looking for him—they were trying to break his very soul, make him experience the pain of his treason tenfold.

Bezaleel didn't think any longer. He tore the sleeve of his shirt and tied it around his face, across the bridge of his nose in a makeshift mask. The only features visible were his eyes and hair. In this form, the people of Iwami would never recognize him.

He let out his wings and flew from the window, into the skies and above the carnage. He raked his eyes through the hell that was unfolding, counting the number of Raathris that dared to do this to his town.

Four...six...ten. All it took were ten Raathris and a single night to turn this town, and his life, upside down.

Bezaleel's eyes fell on a man whose attire was slightly different from the rest of the clan, and who was probably responsible for this mayhem. The clan's symbol was etched onto the fabric of his cloak. That face: Bezaleel would never forget who that was.

Marvak.

Bezaleel gripped the blade he had taken from the Raathri he killed, raised his arm, aimed, and flung it. The blade rotated a dozen times in the air before it clattered to the ground, right in between Marvak's feet.

He looked up at the skies knowingly, expectantly. Without fear.

Bezaleel met his eyes. "Marvak." He hissed the name under his breath with unfathomable hatred. The rest of the clan gazed up as well. Bezaleel hovered in the skies like a grim reaper ready to drag them to hell. With just his gaze, he sent a deathly, foreboding shudder through the Raathris.

"Bezaleel," Marvak spat his name like a curse and sent him a glare that one reserved just for a traitor.

Bezaleel flew into the forest, disappearing into the darkness. He knew Marvak would take the bait and that the Raathris would follow. He was here for Bezaleel, and he would rather abandon the chance for more casualties than let a traitor go free.

Marvak was too prideful, and that would be his downfall.

Bezaleel heard their shouts echoing louder as the Raathris tried to close the distance between them.

"Don't lose sight of him!" Marvak shouted.

"Bring him back at all costs!" someone else followed.

"Keep your eyes open! He's a tough one!"

Tough one. The Raathri clan would know all about him. If they were warning the others about what he was capable of, that meant some of them who were wearing the clan's robes weren't actually part of the clan. Something must have happened in Ashkaar while he was away. But it didn't matter to him now.

Yes, keep your eyes wide open, so you can watch my blade take your life.

Bezaleel let the dark feelings spread until he was overcome with bloodlust. He wanted to gnaw on their bones, wrench out their guts and peel off their skins. He wanted to paint the forest red with their blood. He would never have mercy on them for torching his town and slaughtering his family, his friend.

Bezaleel flew further between the leaves and trunks, disappearing into the blackness of the forest that engulfed them.

"He's gone," one of them finally said. They came to halt in between the circle of trees.

Bezaleel watched them from the darkness as they removed their swords from their scabbards. A nerve-racking silence followed. The only sounds they could hear were the crickets, a bird flapping its wings.

In the haunting silence, Bezaleel listened to their labored breaths.

He could sense their fear. They knew he was toying with them. Ramping up their nerves until they were reduced to nothing but dread. He could see it already clouding their judgment. They had unknowingly walked right into his trap. And now it was time for Bezaleel to draw them out.

He quickly moved between the branches, rustling leaves on purpose as he whizzed past them, throwing off their concentration as he distracted them.

"There!" one of them cried out in unfamiliar, hesitant voice laden with false courage.

Yes, follow my shadow.

A few minutes of racing through the forest and Bezaleel stopped again. The assassins followed, not knowing where they were being led.

And that would be the final nail in their coffins. Bezaleel knew these woods. He'd wandered in and out of them for ten years. But the Raathris didn't. To them, these woods were as unexplored as the rest of Yalim.

As the Raathris stood still, trying to spot any sign of him, he swooped in like an eagle in the blink of an eye, grabbed one of them and pulled him high into the trees. The assassin wailed, but

Bezaleel grabbed him by the head and twisted his neck, silencing him for good. Bezaleel then pulled out the dagger that belonged to the man he'd killed and flung it at another Raathri. The man let out a short groan as the blade pierced his chest.

Seeing such unpredictable killing methods, which were so unlike the Bezaleel they'd known, the Raathris were stricken, frozen in shock. To make matters worse, they couldn't see as well as him in the dark. They couldn't fly.

Marvak motioned with his hands to point their arrows in the same direction from which the dagger had dropped. Without a word, the Raathris released a dozen arrows into the branches.

Bezaleel leapt away from that spot without being noticed. They were shooting at nothing.

Marvak motioned for them to stop, having sensed the futility of the attack. But Bezaleel was only getting started.

Taking his time, he snatched the Raathris one by one, pulling them into the shadows and killing them instantly. Their frightened, shrill cries of pain echoed through the forest.

It was the first time such a side of him had come out. Twisted. Manipulative. And unforgiving.

Bezaleel stuck to his silent vow and painted the forest red with their blood, until the only one standing was Marvak.

He knew this whole invasion was Marvak's plan, but he didn't know how they had found him, or how they had lifted the Veyil. And he knew damn well that Marvak would never reveal any of his secrets.

Bezaleel watched his former commander pacing slowly across the grass, straining to hear any sounds that would give him away. Marvak would put up a tough fight, and Bezaleel saw no point in putting off that battle.

He dropped down from the trees. His shoes crushed the leaves on the forest floor as his feet met the ground.

Marvak turned around at the noise. "I see you haven't forgotten your ways."

Bezaleel remained silent. His only response was to rotate his dual blades as he gripped them tightly in his palms before he rushed forward. Their swords clashed together. Marvak pushed him back and tried to hit him on the chest but Bezaleel brought his wing in front of him as a shield. He retaliated, but Marvak blocked his strike again.

Former master and student went against each other in a flurry of attacks. Marvak's blade caught on Bezaleel's shirt, tearing at the fabric across his abdomen, and Bezaleel drew back into the darkness again.

Marvak halted and looked all around him. Bezaleel zipped through the trees at lightning speed.

No more games.

Before Marvak could regroup, Bezaleel pinned him against a tree. He gripped Marvak by the throat and drove the blade deep into his gut as he leaned in.

"How did you open the gateway?" he growled lowly.

"I would rather die than tell you," Marvak spat back.

Bezaleel shoved his blade further into Marvak's flesh and the man gritted his teeth against the pain. "Tell me!"

"No."

Bezaleel knew he wasn't going to get the answer he needed. Marvak would never betray his own clan. "So be it." Bezaleel twisted his sword and drew it out of Marvak's body. Blood poured out from the wound and he glared into Bezaleel's eyes as his life slipped away.

He gritted his teeth as blood stained his lips and dripped down his chin. "Bezaleel...this isn't...over," he wheezed as his lungs gave out. "The clan...will...find you."

Bezaleel narrowed his eyes and leaned in before hissing back, "If they value their lives, they will not."

The clouds parted in the dark sky and the moonlight streaked through the branches, illuminating the otherwise pitch black forest. Bezaleel waited until Marvak's body went limp before letting go of him. The body slumped to the ground and Bezaleel sheathed his swords.

As he stared at Marvak's remains, his mind calmed and he remembered the one person he had left behind.

Tetsu.

Bezaleel flew back as fast as he could, but stopped himself from actually going into town. He dropped down on a branch on the edge of the forest just as the first light of day greeted the world.

He could see everything clearly. The fire had been put out. Most of the houses were reduced to nothing but burned debris and charcoaled wood. Bezaleel's house had burned down, but Tetsu was unscathed. Bezaleel let out a sigh of relief as he saw the teen standing safely amidst a few of the surviving townspeople in the middle of the road. His face was somber.

Bezaleel doubted he would ever see him smile again.

Tetsu's head hung low until one of the neighbors called out his name, rushed to him, and enveloped him in a hug. Bezaleel knew her; that was Reiko's best friend. Her shoulders trembled with sobs as she clutched Tetsu close to her.

Bezaleel's chest stung. There was no way he could go back. It was his fault that this had happened. If it weren't for him, Tetsu would still be happily laughing with his family, the parents he'd inadvertently wrenched away from the boy.

Tetsu could only hate him for being the reason that his family had been murdered. The reason his friends had been killed.

Bezaleel's eyes raked across the survivors. How would he ever be able to look them in the eyes again? As long as he was around them, if he ever got close to people, he would only bring more death.

There was only one thing to do. Leave. Leave this place and never come back.

Bezaleel had to do everything in his power to not call out Tetsu's name—just once. To tell him that he will watch over him and keep him safe. His forehead creased as morbid questions swirled around in his head. How many more corpses would he have to walk on while he lived?

The only way he could protect Tetsu, his only remaining family, was to leave.

He took one last look at the boy. "Goodbye, Tetsu," he whispered so softly that his voice wouldn't reach anyone before he turned around and vanished without a trace. Just like how he had appeared all those years ago.

But with his back turned, he failed to see Tetsu, who had turned his gaze toward the trees where Mirai perched only a few seconds before. The boy stared into the empty branches as if he had felt someone's stare on him. As if he had heard Mirai call his name one last time.

Bezaleel didn't know how long he had been walking. Had it been minutes? Hours? He didn't know and he didn't care. His legs kept carrying him forward without a specific direction in mind. Images of the night before played inside his head. Burning houses. People screaming. Blood and bodies.

"*Bezaleel.*" A feminine voice called his name like a whisper of wind.

Bezaleel gasped. His head snapped up and whipped around. The whisper he thought he heard calling out to him was as gentle as a mother. Could it be…?

But there was no one. Not a soul. Just his imagination.

That was when he took in his surroundings. He had walked farther than he would have guessed. He didn't recognize this place, but he was surrounded by cherry blossom trees that danced in the breeze. A lone flower broke from the end of a branch and gracefully floated down. Mirai mindlessly extended his hands and it fell right into his palms.

"*They are called sakura trees.*" Shinichiro's voice resounded in his head as clear as day.

"They're Mirai's favorite!"

"Welcome to the family."

"You're pretty cool! I'm Ren."

Droplets fell onto the flower, tears that rolled unchecked down Bezaleel's cheeks. He held the flower to his chest as his shoulders trembled with heavy sobs. For the first time in his life, he cried. In a single night, he had lost everything. The only people that loved and cared for him were no more.

He fell to his knees and cried as his heart broke over and over, until nothing remained but the bitter feelings of sadness, pain and regret.

CHAPTER TWENTY-SIX

SEARCH

Mafuyu listened to Mirai's story from beginning to end. He listened more than he ever did with anything else anyone had ever said in his entire life. He would never have imagined Mirai had gone through such torment or carried such guilt all this time.

"You're uncharacteristically silent," Zen commented after a few minutes.

"I mean, there isn't anything I can say."

Zen leaned back in his chair as if to give Mafuyu space to breathe and take it all in.

"What happened after that? I mean, how did you find him?" Mafuyu asked.

"Mirai had somehow made it to Tokyo after that," Zen continued. "We found him six months later...or, Nagisa found him."

"What?" Mafuyu thought that he had heard everything that could possibly baffle him, but he was proven wrong again. "She knows?"

Zen nodded. He'd expected Mafuyu to throw another fit once he was done, but the boy remained passive. He leaned forward, both elbows on his knees, like a child that was eager to hear more.

Earlier that day, Mafuyu would have yelled for being kept in the dark by the people he trusted the most, but now he couldn't bring himself to do so. He understood that they had their reasons for not revealing Mirai's identity before. If they had, they would have leaked top secret and sensitive information.

A secret that could change the fate of both worlds if word got out.

"It was on a mission four years ago. Nagisa wasn't captain then. Her team was trying to reel in three dangerous Second-Levels and one almost got the better of her when Mirai—or, Bezaleel jumped in front of her and saved her. It was as quick as a blinking light; all she saw was a blur of black and eyes that were like the colors of dawn. Luckily, the rest of the team was scattered and too busy fighting monsters to even notice.

"Bezaleel didn't wait. He bolted as soon as he had shown himself. Nagisa tried to chase after him, but he disappeared before she could. She told this to me when they came back. We had no idea how he had gotten there. All we did know was that he matched the description of the Rev'er that a few of the Iwami survivors had seen when we were called in to investigate the mass murder and fire. We labeled him as a First-Level, then Nagisa and I tried to look for him. We started with the place where she first saw him, but there wasn't a trace of him there. Which made me think that he could probably hide in a crowd without being noticed. Nagisa said that she saw wings, but that maybe he could conceal them. We searched for months, but we couldn't find a single clue. It wasn't something we could ask around about, either, and from the looks of it, he'd concealed himself well. Even in a densely populated place like this, no one was even aware he existed."

"How did you find him then?" Mafuyu probed.

"I didn't. He found us," Zen answered, "We kept searching for him high and low, especially where Rev'er activity was more frequent. We even went back to the place Nagisa first saw him several times. Perhaps all that 'nosy poking,' as Bezaleel termed it later, irked him enough to come out of hiding.

"We were rounding up another Rev'er in Tokyo when I got a glimpse of Bezaleel. He let me see him, and he knew I would chase after him. Stupidly, I did. Before I knew it, he'd cornered me. He held a blade to my gut and asked me why I was looking for him. I was stunned.

When I felt his blade on my skin, I knew he was serious about cutting me in half. That he wouldn't give a damn about taking my life. He was dangerous. The kind of dangerous that will get you killed if you so much as think of playing around with it.

"My mind was blank as I stared at him. He had black wings as dark as night and white flowing hair that glowed like the moon. But his eyes were what intrigued me the most. It was like he had the rising sun in his eyes. I had never seen eyes with as many shades as his: yellow, orange, red, and a golden line outlined his pupils. It was magnificent. And even though he looked like the darkness itself had spit him out, there was warmth in the depth of his eyes. There was light. And in that vein, I thought it was best to tell him who we were and why we were investigating the Iwami incident. I wanted to coax information out of him, but at that moment I felt like I was standing at the edge of a cliff and that, if I did question him, he would push me to my death.

"When Bezaleel was done listening, he flew off, but not before I placed a tracker on him.

A couple weeks later, using that tracker, I got hold of him again. When he found out what I'd done, he wasn't pleased at all. I found myself at the end of his blade again. He was about to sink his sword into my neck when Nagisa tried to talk to him and calm him down. She had come with me that time and she told him how we wanted his help to figure out First-Levels so we could prevent another incident like the one in Iwami from happening. Somehow, that convinced him to listen. He asked what was in it for us, and Nagisa told him it was our job to protect people from things that they can't defend against. That we needed to know what happened in Iwami to make sure that it never happened to anyone else again. Only he could give us that missing peace. Then she promised that whatever he said would be between the three of us.

"That seemed to crack the iron walls that Bezaleel had put up against himself. And we gave him a final push by saying if he helped us figure things out, he could work with us and he wouldn't have to worry about getting shelter and a decent meal. From the looks of his baggy eyes and disheveled clothes, we knew he was possibly homeless and living on scraps.

"He must have felt Nagisa's honesty, because he seemed like he was listening. Even so, it wasn't easy to get him to come to our side. He said he would consider helping us, if we brought him back an herb that was in one of the homes that had burned down—*if* we could find it. It was only later that we learned he was referring to the Chiweu he bought back from Ashkaar. Luckily Reiko's garden was only half burned. Bezaleel's herb was untouched.

"We brought it back to him and then... Well, things went from there. Bezaleel made a deal with us. He said he would tell us about what really happened in Iwami only after he felt that he could trust us and that he would only work for us because he had his own agenda. He wanted to make sure that no one else lifted the Veyil. He looked for signs of it on every single mission he went on. But in the end, there was no sign of any Teiyyan and he quit two years later." Zen finished as he walked towards Mafuyu with a cup of water. The boy really needed it from the looks of it. "The flower shop he owns now was from a dear friend of mine. I introduced Mirai to him after he quit the Corps. Before my friend passed away, he gave the shop to Mirai and everything else is as you know."

"No wonder," Mafuyu mumbled.

"What?"

"Mirai...he... Sometimes he looks at the plants with this bitter-sweet look. Now I know why. His adoptive mother had a garden and it reminds him of the family he lost. And taking care of those flowers is a way for him to fill that hole in his heart."

"Mafuyu," Zen said. "Other than me and Nagisa—and now you—not a soul knows about this and no one ever should."

Mafuyu nodded. He knew that without Zen having to mention it.

"I wanted to add the information about First-Levels to our database, but after knowing the truth, I decided it was best that no one knew. This kind of information in the wrong hands could be the end of two worlds." Zen walked back towards his desk.

"So, why did you tell me this here?" Mafuyu gestured to the space around him. "A little risky to do this at the office, don't you think?"

Zen looked at him as if Mafuyu was missing something that he should have known. "Didn't you know?"

Mafuyu shook his head.

"Are you telling me you didn't know, after all this time, that my office door and walls are soundproof?"

"Really?" Mafuyu shrugged and waved his hand in the air, indicating he didn't care about that one way or the other. "Anyway, the information about Ashkaar and Yalim *has* fallen into the wrong hands. Rahel knows about our world and he wants to destroy it. We've got to take care of that before he succeeds." This was so much more than he had signed up for. He stood up from the chair. "But I'm sure Mirai already told you that."

There were so many things he didn't know about the man he was assigned to protect. He had been walking, eating and living with *the* Bezaleel: a First-Level that had toppled an entire clan in one night. A Teiyyan who drew blood without a second thought and was skilled enough to kill in his sleep if he wanted.

"He did. I have already planned what to do next," Zen answered.

Mafuyu was determined. "I'm going after him. I know where he's heading."

Zen furrowed his brow and his lips took on a frown that only surfaced when he was completely opposed to something, especially if it sounded suicidal. "And just what do you expect to do? Do you have the power to fight Rahel? You're a Rev'er Hunter, not a Teiyyan."

"According to our database, Rahel is a Rev'er."

"You know how strong he is. We need you here, with your team, to defend our world against whatever it is he plans to unleash."

"Zen-san." Mafuyu's determined voice was enough for Zen to at least hear him out. "I will not leave Mirai alone. Like you said, I know... I've *felt* how powerful Rahel is. Mirai will die if he fights him alone."

At that, Zen sighed in defeat. "You both better come back alive." It came across as the sort of worry that only a parent would understand.

Mafuyu beamed at Zen's begrudging permission. He bowed from his waist at the man that had taught him everything he knew, and his voice couldn't have held more sincerity when he said, "Thank you, Zen-san."

Without waiting for Zen's reply, he rushed out of the office; Mirai would probably have left his apartment by now, and there was a plane that Mafuyu needed to catch.

CHAPTER TWENTY-SEVEN

ALONGSIDE

The streets of Iwami were different than those in Tokyo. Skyscrapers were cast aside for traditional, humble homes and buildings that lined the streets, giving the place a historical touch. It was as if the place was untainted by modernity. If Tokyo was a collage of silver and steel in daylight, then Iwami was earthy with brown wood and green trees. The whole place was painted in the colors of nature.

As Mafuyu walked through the town, he breathed in the scent of the sea and he could hear the waves crashing against the shore nearby. Through the winding pathways, bordered by wilderness on both sides, he walked to the one place he *knew* Mirai would want to visit.

The place where he first arrived in this world: the shrine.

As Mafuyu stood at the foot of the stairs leading up to it, he could see Mirai's shadow moving around inside of the shrine. Mafuyu stayed where he was and gulped. Doubts resurfaced and started to swirl in his head. What if Mirai really didn't want him around anymore? What if he actually hated him?

Maybe he shouldn't have come. He took an unconscious step back, but someone shoved him from behind—a gentle, yet strong push that sent him stumbling forward and made him climb a few steps before he regained his balance.

Mafuyu whirled around to see who on earth had done that, but all he saw was the forest, the trees and wild bushes surrounding the shrine. There was no one there.

He squinted. No, someone or something definitely pushed him. And the longer he looked, the better he could see the transparent outline of two people: a man and a woman. The spirits of a young couple.

His eyes widened when he realized who they had to be. His lips opened to speak, but he never got the chance.

"Mafuyu?" A familiar voice drifted down from the entrance of the shrine.

He turned around. The man he had been looking for stood on the top step.

"Mirai," Mafuyu greeted back, sounding a bit out of breath than he'd intended.

"What are you doing here?"

Mirai was surprised to find the boy he had so harshly told off standing on the steps of the shrine. But he refused to drop the cold and distant tone he'd adopted earlier to get him to leave. "How did you find this place?"

Mafuyu didn't back away. Instead, he climbed the stairs to reach him. Mirai's creased eyebrows flattened when he realized what must have given the kid the gumption to follow him.

"Zen told you." It was more of a statement than a question.

"Yes," Mafuyu said as he stopped on the stair below him.

Damn that old man. Mirai internally cursed, but it was half-hearted. He knew that Zen wouldn't have told Mafuyu his story if he felt that the boy was a threat. And above all that, Mirai knew personally how honest and straightforward Mafuyu was—when he wasn't pretending *not* to be his bodyguard, at least. "So why are you here?"

"Because you don't have to do this by yourself."

"Go home, Mafuyu." Mirai turned his back to the Hunter and walked back into the shrine. "I can do this alone."

"You know you can't!" Mafuyu followed him.

"That's not for you to decide."

"I know why you're pushing me away." Mafuyu's voice bounced off the shrine walls. Mirai's shoulders lifted up and fell back down as he breathed in and exhaled. "I know you are worried that something might happen to me if I help you. And I know that you didn't mean a single word of what you said back in your apartment."

Mirai whipped around. "Then why—"

"Because you can't decide for me whether I live or die! You can't just decide whether or not I try to help you! Are you saying that I'm so weak that I can't help you in a fight?"

"My family died just by being close to me!" Mirai raised his voice for the first time, and the small room only made it sound that much louder. "My friends were brutally murdered! I've had enough innocent blood on my hands!"

Mafuyu let Mirai release all his pent up anger. He understood all of his worry and his pain. Then he calmly replied, "Mirai, you've saved a lot of lives—back in Ashkaar and in this world. What happened four years ago was not your fault."

The scowl on Mirai's face faded into his usual relaxed expression. "This conversation is over. You're going back home."

Mafuyu crossed his arms over his chest. "No."

There were only a few moments in Mirai's life that had caught him off guard; he could literally count them on one hand. One was when Eiwa had given him a present on his tenth birthday. Another was when a seller in Ashkaar sweet-talked him into buying a magical amulet only to realize later that it was a fake. And the third was Mafuyu's reply. "What?"

"You heard me. I said no."

"Don't be stubborn. I can't put you in any more danger than you are already in."

"Well, if I'm already in danger then I don't see the point of not tagging along. Don't you think?"

Mirai clenched his jaw. *This* boy! "Why are you so obsessed with coming along?"

"Because I want to fight alongside you." The sincerity in Mafuyu's voice made Mirai bite back any argument he might have otherwise countered with. "I don't want you to take on this burden all by yourself. It's what you've been doing since you were a kid. This fight involves both our worlds now, but more than that, I want to fight by your side. Do I need any other reason?"

"What about you?" Mirai asked. "Can you promise you won't die?"

"Hell yeah, I can."

"How?"

"'Cause I trust that you've got my back." Mafuyu lightly smacked Mirai on his chest with the back of his palm. "Just like I have yours."

Mirai let a small smile spread his lips. He said nothing more and took Mafuyu by the wrist, leading him into a smaller room within the shrine where he had drawn a circle with Zalek letters and runes on the ground with his blood.

"Rahel wants a war," Mirai explained. "He had been planning it for years. Those Third-Levels going rogue are all Rahel's doing. He has a Nahm that can control them. He first did it to lure me out, but I think he is also planning to use them to fight the Hunters and take over Yalim." Mirai chose his words carefully, trying to make it sound less frightening. But to make something like war sound less terrifying was nearly impossible. "He wants a war in Ashkaar, too. The night I destroyed the scroll in my clan's library, I didn't see the job through. The entire scroll didn't burn like I wanted it to. A small piece of it remained intact." Mirai scoffed. "And that piece had a revival spell."

"So that means—"

"He used that revival Nahm to restore the scroll I burned." Mirai rubbed his temple. "Four years ago, when the Raathri invaded Iwami and Marvak refused to tell me how he lifted the Veyil, I knew that they couldn't have done it without the Nahms in the scroll. Which to me meant one of two things—either a few Raathris escaped and tried the coup again, or Marvak reasoned with his clan and made me out to be some kind of scapegoat. He might have painted it to look like the people I tried to save didn't make it, and that he was the one that appealed to the Deva to try to stop his own clan from killing Lord Rasa. He could have even made the coup seem like it was all part of *my* plan. And after proving his loyalty, the Devas could have sent them after me. But even that theory had a loophole. Lord Rasa wouldn't wait ten years to hunt me if he thought I was the reason for that town's destruction. He would have sent his spies after me right away. In the end, I was still left with no answers and more questions."

"That's why you wanted to join the Rev'er Hunter Corps—to see if the Raathri had lifted the Veyil again." When Mirai nodded, Mafuyu returned the gesture and continued. "So what's your plan now that we're going back to Ashkaar?"

"I need to get to the Devas. I broke a lot of rules in Ashkaar. There is no doubt I'll be in trouble, but I'm hoping for a miracle. That's why I want you to stay here to protect Yalim."

"That's the worst idea you've ever had, Mirai." A third voice interrupted their conversation. Mafuyu spun on his heels and Mirai's gaze fell on their unexpected guest over his shoulder.

"Nagisa!" they exclaimed in unison.

Nagisa leaned on the shrine's doorframe, her trademark half-smile lining her mouth. "Are you really leaving our world in the hands of this idiot? We'll all be dead in no time."

"Hey!"

"How long have you been standing here?" Mirai paced toward her.

"Long enough to hear all of that. Seriously, you guys sounded like a married couple." She took a few steps toward Mirai, meeting him halfway.

"Are you alright?"

Nagisa's expression softened. "I should be asking you that."

"You shouldn't be up and walking around."

Nagisa waved her hand, dismissing Mirai's worries. "It's nothing.

I was just walking around, gathering information on some Third-Levels." She was wearing her usual outfit of a casual button-up shirt and jeans rather than the Hunter's official uniform.

"How did you know we were here?"

"Zen gave me a call." She shrugged. "Thought I should drop by. So, what was that about protecting our world?"

Mirai smirked and played along. "Well, like you heard. I need someone for it. Think you can handle it?"

"You know it." Nagisa extended her hand and twirled the tip of her forefinger through the ends of Mirai's black locks. "You better take care of him for me," she whispered. "And yourself. Come back in one piece."

Mirai's fingers gently closed around her palms. "I will."

When they loosened their hands, Nagisa walked up to Mafuyu and unclasped the necklace around her neck. "For good luck," she said as she put it on Mafuyu instead. The cool pendant touched the skin on his chest. "And protection."

"I'll be fine. Don't worry," he reassured her.

Nagisa stepped away from the circle and Mirai walked back into it. "Stand close to me, Mafuyu."

The boy did as he was told and stood closer to Mirai, until their toes touched. Mirai's grey orbs once again reverted back to their original shades while his hair faded to white. It was unnerving for Mirai to do this in front of someone, but Mafuyu's unflinching self and his wholehearted acceptance of who Mirai really was put the man at ease.

"Um..." Mafuyu started and Mirai's gaze trailed up from the circle drawn on the floor to meet the boy's tense expression. "I heard that the first time you...opened the Veyil...that you were wounded pretty badly."

Mirai couldn't suppress a snicker and was rewarded with Mafuyu's disapproving look. "Relax, it was because I wasn't able to focus properly. I'll make sure that no harm comes to you. But—" Here, Mafuyu visibly gulped. "That doesn't mean it's going to be completely painless."

"What do you mean?" Mafuyu looked fairly green for someone who was so confident about this plan just moments earlier.

"Opening gateways to Jihan and crossing to another world requires a certain amount of energy from Ashkaar. That world is the focal point of the Jihan. Since you're not from that world, this might be painful to you." He took hold of Mafuyu's hand. "But the reason you can banish Third-Levels is because you have a bit of magical energy reserved in you."

"That's...reassuring." Mafuyu's voice cracked. He wasn't sure if that was something he should be particularly happy about or not.

"Last chance to back away."

"Not happening."

Mirai huffed like he was against this, but in all honesty he was glad that Mafuyu had followed him. He helped ease the torment that was raging inside Mirai's mind and heart for years. And for the first time in his life, he felt the weight of his burden had eased, at least somewhat. "Here we go," he warned before he whispered an incantation in Zalek.

"The Veyil that keeps the worlds of Jihan apart, I command you to lift and open your path to Ashkaar."

At Mirai's command, the circle beneath them glowed a pale blue. Mirai heard Mafuyu gasp and kept a firm hold on the boy. Wisps of light crackled around them and Mafuyu flinched. They grew in length, connecting together into a dome above their heads. The light grew brighter and brighter until it enveloped them whole. Mirai's grip on Mafuyu's wrist tightened as they locked eyes. There was no turning back.

CHAPTER TWENTY-EIGHT

ASHKAAR

It was nauseating, dizzying, and above all else, painful. Mafuyu never experienced so much pain in his entire life. Every cell in his body felt like it was being pierced by needles. Gravity seemed to be pulling him down, threatening to crush his body and seal his breath. He was choking.

The blue light around him was blinding him. His ears started humming. He fell to his knees and hands.

"Hang in there, Mafuyu." Mirai's voice sounded distant even though he was crouching down right beside him. "Just a few more seconds."

He could still feel the warmth of his fingers around his wrist. It was Mirai that was keeping Mafuyu from losing his mind.

The blinding blue light started to dim. The ground under his feet started to stabilize, the ringing in his ears ceased, and Mafuyu could breathe again. The hard floor of the shrine beneath him had become soft grass. Mafuyu gasped, filling his lungs with as much air as he could. It was as if he'd broken through the surface of a lake for oxygen.

"Are you alright?" Mirai extended his hand.

"Yeah." Mafuyu found it easy to speak despite what he had just been through.

"Can you stand up?"

Mafuyu nodded and took Mirai's hand so the other man could heave him up. His legs weren't shaking anymore, and all the terrible sensations he'd felt vanished as if they never occurred to begin with.

"Whoa," he breathed out in awe as he saw the scenery surrounding him.

Emerald green grass reflected the warm sunlight that streaked through puffs of pure white clouds in golden rays. Lavender, pink and purple trees lined up, one after the other, in abundance. Flowers carpeted the forest floor. Mafuyu bent down to take a closer look. Some of the buds were gemstones, reflecting the daylight.

"This... This is beautiful."

"You haven't seen anything yet." Mirai pulled the hood of the cloak he was wearing over his head. "Come. We shouldn't waste time."

"Are you sure you'll be fine going like that?"

"As long as no one sees me, yes. And if we stick to the town's back ways, we can avoid detection."

"Alright."

Mirai's long cloak swished as he turned around. Mafuyu fell into step behind him. "Hey, this is—"

"The Forest of Newara," Mirai said, confirming his guess.

Mafuyu's eyes wandered all around, taking every detail around him without a pause. He never wanted to forget this sight or this feeling: the feeling of discovering a fairy land that no one else from his world knew existed. For him, it was a privilege.

As he was gazing around, he bumped into Mirai, who had suddenly stopped walking.

The soft sound of something falling onto the grass reached Mafuyu's ears. He peeked over Mirai's shoulder to see what had stopped the man in his tracks. And to his surprise, it was a girl.

She carried a basket of fruit, which had tumbled to the forest floor. She looked at Mirai with shock, frozen and gaping. She appeared to be the same age as Mirai.

Oh no. Mafuyu remembered what Mirai said—that they shouldn't be seen by anyone.

Mirai's hair and eyes would alert anyone to who he was. Was she going to run and scream and tell everyone that the fearsome Bezaleel had returned?

He leaned close to Mirai's ear and whispered, "Should we knock her out?"

But Mirai didn't answer. Mafuyu wondered if he even heard him. He just kept staring at the girl in front of them, until finally he spoke. "Adelyn?"

The girl brought her hand up to cover her mouth. Her eyes couldn't have opened any wider.

"*Adelyn, tu enta urr ner—*" A man speaking Zalek came into view and stopped short when he, too, saw Bezaleel.

"Dan." Mirai had recognized them both. The man, Dan, had the same shocked reaction as the girl. But unlike her, his eyes narrowed into a glare, his nostrils flared, and he stalked toward Mirai, who stood still—as if he was welcoming the rage.

When Zen gave Mafuyu the book containing the Zalek language, he didn't think it would ever come in handy. Now, he was thankful he took the time to read and study it.

"You!" Dan grasped Mirai by the collar. "How could you?"

Mafuyu was about to step in and save his friend when Dan continued.

"Where have you been, you bastard? We thought... We thought you died."

The corners of Mirai's eyes crinkled. "I'm glad you're doing alright."

Dan's fierce expression faltered. He let go of Mirai's collar and brought his arms around the man in a tight embrace. The girl cried tears of joy as she enveloped the both of them in her arms. Mirai stiffened at the contact, but eventually relaxed as they held him.

Adelyn and Dan? Mafuyu racked his mind until the names rang a bell. They were the ones that Bezaleel had saved from the assassins and the coup. They were the two siblings.

⋙◆⋘

It would have been a lie if Mirai said that he didn't miss the sight of his hometown, his real hometown. The land where he was born and raised. He missed the familiar scent of sweet baked goods that wafted through the central marketplace, the daytime chatter of people as they crowded around the plaza, the sounds of hidden faes, and the visual proof of magic in the air.

"Try to act normal," Mirai whispered to Mafuyu, who was busy gaping at an inn keeper fixing his broken window with magic. The broken glass pieces reattached themselves, as if time had been reversed.

Mafuyu turned away quickly. It took everything in his power to not even glance sideways at that marvel. He stepped closer to Mirai, their shoulders brushing with every step. "Is this a common thing? People being able to use magic?"

"Yes. Ashkaar is home to people who can manipulate magic, and those who can't. Those with stronger magic that can be used in battle usually pursue a path like that: as in, the soldiers or knights working for the nation. You can climb up the ladder to become part of the elites if your magic is strong enough."

"And the Teiyyans are the strongest, then they eventually become Devas."

"Yes, they are the ones born with incredible magical energy. But Teiyyans also exist in the lower classes of the clans. They are powerful, too, but they aren't differentiated by virtue of having wings and weird-colored hair and eyes."

"Wow. I feel like I've traveled back in time to the age of dungeons and dragons."

"Dragons don't exist in Ashkaar."

"Really? That's a shame. I was hoping to see some."

Mirai snorted. They passed a small fountain where kids leaned across the concrete edge and splashed each other with water from its pool.

Mirai was internally thankful that Mafuyu chose to wear a simple, white button-up shirt, beige pants, and plain brown boots. It let him blend with the crowd and didn't make him stick out like a sore thumb.

He pulled the hood over his head, trying to cover as much as he could. He didn't want anyone to know that he had returned as he walked through the very town that was targeted for the coup fourteen years ago. Seeing it now, no one would believe it had gone through such devastating destruction.

All of the houses had been rebuilt. There were more inns to welcome travelers and customers. The marketplace was bustling with stalls of all kinds. The town had been rebuilt to its original state: perhaps even a better one.

"Son, son!" a seller called out to Mafuyu. "How about an amulet? It can foretell your future, or even the destiny of your love."

He was shaken out of the trance when Mirai grabbed his forearm. "Don't fall for it. Happened to me once. It's fake."

"*You* got tricked?" Mafuyu couldn't help but let the teasing tone bubble out of him.

"I didn't get tricked. I was just a kid."

"*Sure* you didn't."

Mirai rolled his eyes and picked up his pace to catch up to their guide. "Dan." The man hummed and tilted his head toward Mirai. "What happened after that night?" If there was one thing Mirai always wanted to know, but never had the courage to find out, it was what happened after he stopped the coup.

Looking around at the town and the happy faces of its residents, he knew that his plan had worked. But he wanted to know the missing pieces.

"I'll explain everything once we're home," Dan whispered back.

Mirai nodded and continued walking until they had passed through the bustling center of Marim.

———◆———

"This is where you live?" Mirai couldn't take his eyes off the house. It was built with a single floor, but in a space where two more houses could have fit. It was laid out in an L shape with ten windows that let in the midday sunlight. They passed through a large gate with intricate designs and into a vast, neat, green lawn.

"Thanks to you." Dan flashed a grin at Mirai. He didn't remember Dan being rich or influential enough to own something like this. They once lived in a small cottage on the outskirts of town. He came from an average family who lived each day by the hard-earned labor of his parents. Only someone of high status, who worked directly under the Deva, could afford such luxury.

Mirai and Mafuyu followed Dan into the house. He led them through a long hallway. Light streaked in through the spacious windows. They walked into a huge dining hall with a table that would comfortably seat eight people. Mirai and Mafuyu sat opposite the siblings.

An older lady walked in with a tray holding four cups. Mirai immediately recognized her. She was their mother. Her skin had grown older and her hair greyer, but unlike when he had seen her last time, there was more color to her face. Her lips were pinker and she was healthier.

She recognized Bezaleel and gave him a light bow. He nodded in return. After setting the tray on the table, she left the youngsters to themselves.

Mirai focused his attention back on Dan. "Who is ruling Alayl now?"

"It's Lady Eiwa. She took over a few years ago," Dan began. "After you saved us and we escaped through the tunnel, we were able to reach Lord Rasa. You distracting the Raathri gave us more time. By the time they found the tunnel, I had already delivered your note."

"What happened after that?" Mirai prompted.

"Lord Rasa readied troops with his most elite warriors and soldiers to take down the Raathri clan. They were able to capture and execute them for high treason, but a handful of them managed to escape: Marvak and Rahel among them. Rasa hunted them for months, almost a year. And then one day, his spies found all their remains—including Rahel and Marvak's. They had tried to escape to Jabilsa. They died on the border trying to cross the Shahn desert."

"That wasn't them."

"What do you mean?"

"I saw Rahel and the Raathri clan again after that. They were well and alive."

"That's not possible."

Mirai could tell that Dan wasn't lying. He was telling the truth. If there was even a hint of deception in his face, Mirai would have been able to tell. "Rahel is planning to attack Alayl again."

"What?" The instant disbelief that passed over Dan's eyes told Mirai that he definitely wasn't lying. "But the Devas' spies found their bodies. How could the Raathris be alive?"

"Because they faked it. They would have killed people who looked similar to them and used their bodies as cover. Rahel probably used some kind of Nahms to make them identical, too. He can outwit the Devas, and I know that he has. Ashkaar is in trouble."

"Lady Eiwa headed for the Four Deva Summit yesterday."

Mirai tapped his fingers on the table, never taking his eyes off Dan. "The Four Deva Summit happens once a year in irregular time. How do you know all this, Dan? No one but the Devas and their few chosen soldiers is supposed to be in on important information like that."

Dan grinned from ear to ear. "Because I'm the second-in-command of the Deva army. Other than me, only the head general, the most trusted advisor, and the most loyal guards know when the summit is taking place."

Mirai's eyes brightened and a smile made its way to his face. "You're second-in-command?" Dan nodded. That's why he knew so much. "My belated congratulations."

Dan shook his head as if to tell Mirai to drop the formalities. "You passing on that message helped me get where I am today." He stood up from his chair and circled over to Mirai, kneeling in front of him as one would before a Deva. "I'll help you in any way I can. You saved our lives years ago, and I could never ever repay that debt. I know you returning wasn't a coincidence, so please tell me what help you need."

Mirai lowered himself from the chair to bring himself eye-level with Dan. He placed a hand on his shoulder and looked the man in the eye. "I need to see the Devas."

Dan stood up and nodded. "If we leave tomorrow morning, we can interrupt the summit."

"Wait a second," Mafuyu cut in, speaking for the first time in Zalek. The language suited him, as if he had been speaking it his entire life. Mirai was impressed, to say the least. "Isn't that dangerous? Won't we be killed for doing that?"

The siblings exchanged looks and shrugged, as if the answer was an obvious one.

"We could if they don't listen to us. But it's worth a try," Mirai said.

"What exactly is the Four Deva Summit?" Mafuyu asked.

"The Devas meet once every year to discuss issues related to their nations or treaties, any threats from the outside, and the future of Ashkaar. It's held at random times so that none of the nations will be targeted when they are gone."

"That's why you said it was perfect timing. They'll already be together in one place, so we can explain what's happening and convince them to ally with you."

Mirai nodded.

"So we're going to interrupt an all-Devas party? Uninvited? And we might end up dead if they're not in the mood to listen?"

"Exactly."

Mafuyu rubbed his face with his palms and groaned. "Perfect."

CHAPTER TWENTY-NINE

DESERVE

Mafuyu fluffed the pillows on the bed in the guest room. He sat on the mattress, facing Mirai, and watched as the other man lay out his blanket on the mattress on the opposite side of the room.

"What's wrong?" Mirai asked without turning around.

The question snapped Mafuyu out of his temporary trance. "It's just... This all feels so surreal."

"That I can understand."

"And I still can't get used to your look."

Mirai's movements paused. He let go of the pillows he was fluffing and turned around.

Mafuyu tried not to give away too many of his emotions on his face. He wondered if he had said too much. Perhaps he'd hurt Mirai's feelings.

Mirai walked over to him, leaned one knee and a hand on his mattress, and leaned in close to Mafuyu's face. The younger man stayed still, determined not to flinch in the face of a real predator. "How about now?"

"Huh?"

"Are you getting used to me now?"

Mafuyu stayed stunned for a moment before laughing and pushing his face away. "You weirdo."

Mirai relaxed and sat beside him, resting his elbows on his knees. "I want to apologize for the things I said before. For what I said back in the apartment. Even though I didn't mean any of it, it was still a horrible thing to say. So, I'm sorry."

Mafuyu smiled. "Apology accepted."

A knock on the door interrupted them. Dan opened the door, holding clothes and a few berries. He threw some clothes to Mirai and handed him the Chiweu berries. "Here you go, Bezaleel. Just as you asked."

"Thanks, Dan."

"You're welcome." He handed the other clothes to Mafuyu. "For you."

Mirai turned towards the Hunter. "Let's go."

"I thought we were leaving in the morning," Mafuyu said as he turned over the shirt and inspected the pants.

"For the summit, yes."

Mafuyu paused, his pants dangling in front of him. "Then where are we going now?"

"Don't you want to see Alayl?"

His eyes twinkled. "Really? Is that okay for you?"

"Of course. You deserve to experience it."

Mafuyu didn't question anything further. He changed into the new clothes with more enthusiasm than anything he'd ever done in his entire life.

The nightlife in Alayl was nothing like Mafuyu had expected. His first impression was that this world was on a different timeline to his own, so he thought that the nights would be dark and dim with little to no people roaming around. He couldn't have been more wrong.

It was full of people and energy. Hundreds of lanterns hung on ropes and wires around the town, making the whole place flood in a bright orange glow. As they passed inns, they could hear loud chatter of men, the clanging of utensils in busy kitchens and plates, and glasses and bottles being served to the tables. Stalls with sizzling food surrounded them, and the aromatic scent of barbecued meat filled the air.

There was music and dancing on what Mirai called the Center Stage. A lady dressed in an elegant, fluttering green skirt and a silk top danced as men played music on lutes and flutes behind her. Her brown hair flowed as she engaged in a fun dance that left the people hooting and cheering for more.

"Is it always like this?" Mafuyu asked Mirai, who had used the Chiweu plant to turn his hair black and his eyes grey. No one would recognize him like this. He had grown from a boy to a man. If he did tell anyone that this was Bezaleel, they would only laugh in his face and call him insane.

"Well, this is thanks in part to the autumn festival."

"Autumn festival?"

"Yes. Alayl has two main festivals. One is the harvest festival during spring, then the autumn festival marks the start of a new sol. This one goes on for a week."

"Sol?"

"Year. But this isn't where I wanted to take you." Mirai led Mafuyu away from the crowd, away from the busy streets, and into the Forest of Newara.

When Mirai asked if he wanted to know what Alayl was like, he thought that the older man would take him to the streets, not into the wild. He wondered what was there to see among wild trees and grass, but as Mafuyu ventured into the forest, he felt ashamed for being so narrow-minded.

Thousands of tiny yellow lights floated in the air. He first mistook them for fireflies, but as one floated close to him, Mafuyu realized it was neither firefly nor flower bud. It was some kind of small creature. It tucked itself into a ball by holding its tiny legs, and it was fast asleep.

Mafuyu crept as silently as he could around the wilderness, fearing that the faintest sounds would rouse the forest and take all this beauty away before he could enjoy it. His shirt brushed against a plant, and its leaves lit up with a warm, red light. Amused, he touched some more and they lit up like dozens of colored bulbs in the dark.

Mirai stood a few steps away from him, put his forefinger and thumb into his mouth, and blew a soft, clear tune that blended with the sounds of the forest. Out of nowhere, a creature appeared. Mafuyu's eyes widened in wonder. It was a fae, the kind that he had only heard about in stories.

It was green, with eyes that shone like gold. It fluttered around Mirai, then made the same whistling sound as he had. Then, from beneath the grasses, behind the bushes, and between the flowers, hundreds more popped up and flew around them.

Mafuyu couldn't suppress the low, surprised laugh that bubbled out of him. He was always banishing Rev'ers and creatures that weren't from Yalim, so seeing them so open and harmless allowed him to experience another side of them—a side that was docile, magical, and simply wonderful.

For the remainder of the night, he was awed again and again as Mirai led him through the forest, showing him all there was to see. Especially the famed waterfalls that looked like they had shining crystals in their depths—the waters flowed as clear as glass and gathered in a pool that glowed with an equal shade of blue as the falls themselves. The water sirens that swam around the pool, and the two moons reflected on its surface added to its beauty.

Once they were out of the forest, Mirai showed him more of the town, where Dan and Adelyn later joined them. Mafuyu walked all around the stalls, tasting some of the delicious aromatic food and the drinks. Adelyn even pulled him into doing one of their dances in a crowd of people who were too busy enjoying themselves to mind the awkward dancing teen and the pretty girl on his arm.

Mirai laughed and clapped lightly with Dan by his side as he saw Mafuyu fumbling about. It was the first time he'd seen Mafuyu's most happy and heartfelt smile. He had never heard the boy laugh like nothing else in the world bothered him.

Mafuyu had never been happier in his entire life than he was in this moment, and he knew he would remember it until his last breath.

All the worries from his mind faded, if only for the moment. When they returned to Dan's house tired, giggling, and full of happiness, he internally thanked the heavens, all of life itself, and the universe for the chances it had created in order for him to meet Mirai.

MOVE

Rahel stood on the terrace of his home, a place hidden deep in the rocky mountains of Sie-bu. It was an abandoned land that bordered the outskirts of Alayl, with the other end stretching into the edges of the Shahn desert. A perfect place to get away from the eyes of the Devas, an area not on any maps.

He stared into the brown barren land below and flexed his huge grey wings to rid them of their stiffness as he listened to the information Zephyr had to offer.

"Are you sure it was him?" Rahel asked.

"Yes, my lord," Zephyr replied as he kneeled behind the Raathri leader. "It was him. There is no mistake. He had that boy with him, too."

So, Bezaleel was back, and carelessly walking around the streets of Marim with that boy to boot. The Bezaleel he knew wouldn't have done something so stupid. Then again, he wasn't the same Teiyyan of Terror that he once was. It was Rahel who broke the demonic Bezaleel that once struck fear in the hearts of all who knew him, and turned him into nothing but an empty shell.

And it was so easy. All Rahel had to do was target the heart: the one place Bezaleel's unbreakable wings couldn't protect. Once that was done, physically and mentally hurting him was easier than he had thought.

But even then, Bezaleel had enough guts to return to Ashkaar. It was because of that boy, the one trailing along with him.

Rahel narrowed his eyes. His silver irises held the same darkness that was in his heart: a bottomless pit of malevolence. He looked up to the two full moons above. He knew Bezaleel would do the most unexpected things known to man and get away with them, but he wouldn't have guessed that he would return to Alayl after fourteen years—even when he had the chance.

"He is planning to meet Eiwa," Rahel thought aloud.

"Impossible. If he goes to them now, they will execute him."

"Maybe," Rahel mused. "Maybe not. He did save Alayl and Rasa all those years ago. Perhaps the Devas will overlook his other crimes. To think he would take that chance and come back."

"But what does he hope to gain? He can't stop you now that you have all the Nahms."

"What if the Devas let him learn them?"

"Even then, it would take him years to meet half your strength. His body won't hold."

What Zephyr said was true. Even the Devas take years to cultivate the Nahms and use them without breaking themselves down. There is no way Bezaleel would be able to learn them overnight. So what was he there for?

"My lord." Zephyr's voice interrupted his thoughts. "This could mean trouble."

"Indeed."

Bezaleel was always trouble. Not only did he burn the scrolls that they'd worked so hard to get, but he turned his back on his own clan and killed half of their members in a single run—all while he was still a child.

Rahel thought back to the night of the attempted coup. Bezaleel had taken away the Raathri clan's hope of gaining power. He could still see it in his mind, as if it had happened yesterday. In the midst of the burning town, with his silver blades that reflected the flame around him, his white hair and robes were soaked red with blood and his orange eyes had shimmered with an intensity Rahel had never seen before. With a focus and mercilessness far beyond anything someone his age should have been capable of, he had looked like a true demon that had been spat out from the smoke and chaos around him.

Rahel had tried to capture him, but Bezaleel escaped to Yalim. And during the pursuit, Rasa had sent troops after the Raathris. They were caught, and almost all of them were executed without a second thought. Rahel and Marvak, along with twenty other members, managed to escape later.

But before they went their separate ways to steer clear of Rasa's elite spies, Rahel had made a brief stop at their estate. It was a risk, but one that he was definitely willing to take.

And it had paid out. As if fate was with him, he had found the part of the scroll that hadn't burned—the part that detailed a revival spell. He had to fight two of Rasa's soldiers to escape with the scroll, and then he went into hiding, along with the five members that had accompanied him.

To shake off Rasa's surveillance, he faked their deaths using the homeless and some refugees from the outskirts of Alayl. No one would know or care about a few nameless people that were nonexistent on paper. And it had worked. They threw off Rasa's spies and went into hiding.

It took them ten years to find one another, and it took him even more time to revive the rest of the scrolls and learn the Nahms.

Everything had been going according to plan from there, except his decision to send his father to Yalim to track down Bezaleel. He thought that Bezaleel would have grown weaker in that world, but it was the opposite. That night, he lost more of his clan members— his father—to Bezaleel, and that only fueled the flame within Rahel.

This was his payback for Alayl pushing the Raathris away. It was his chance to get back what they had lost, and not just from Alayl. He wanted the whole of Jihan. He wanted to crush everything that Bezaleel fought for, to punish him for being a traitor and a powerful warrior, but choosing to wag his tail for the Devas rather than help his own clan gain some influence in their world.

Rahel hated the Devas. They were liars who pretended to be justified rulers. In truth, they were just scared little Teiyyans that didn't have the courage to face and accept people that were just as strong as them. They used underhanded ways to beat them down.

Justified and noble? The Devas were anything but. And Rahel wanted to tear them apart for bringing about the demise of his clan, for pushing them away so callously. He wanted to return the favor tenfold.

"Zephyr, we move tomorrow."

"But my lord, we still don't know where the Four Deva Summit is being held."

"Not to the summit." He turned around. "To Alayl." He walked towards Zephyr, his eyes gleaming. He was the personification of terror and nightmares, of the chaos. "And you to Yalim."

CHAPTER THIRTY-ONE

MESAI-TOR

Night went by too quickly for one to feel fully satiated with sleep, and with the morning came a new sense of urgency. It was the day of the Four Deva Summit, in which all of Mirai's hope lay. There was only do or die, and he certainly hoped it wasn't the latter.

Mirai spent the night on his side, still like a log. He would have loved to think he was fast asleep, but the truth was that he was awake for most of the night. His mind had played numerous scenarios on how meeting the Devas would go, and it was hard for him to believe in any of those conclusions that ended well.

Mafuyu, on the other hand, peacefully snored on the opposite bed. It was a characteristic that Mirai found extremely annoying at first, listening to the boy making as much racket as an elephant roaring, but now, instead of glaring at the younger boy in anger, Mirai simply snorted when Mafuyu's snores ranged all over the place in both length and tone.

When daylight fell through the windows and it was time to get going, Mirai roused Mafuyu.

Mafuyu woke with ridiculous bedhead and bleary eyes. When Mirai reminded him where they were going and what they had to do, Mafuyu scrambled about, almost tripping on the sheets coiled around his ankle, before regaining himself and catching up with Mirai.

❖

"What is *that*?" Flabbergasted. Horrified. Dumbfounded. Confused. Every single word he could think of was an understatement of what Mafuyu was feeling as he stared at the animal that stood at least twelve feet tall. In all of the books on all the different Rev'ers he'd read, he had never come across a creature like this.

"Easy there." Mirai's voice was gentle like the chime of bells compared to the creature's groaning and chirping. Adelyn gently pulled on the reins tied to the bird's beak and tugged its head down. He patted it and smoothly ran his hands along its long, red beak. "They're called Tumwis," Mirai spoke with a sense of awe that Mafuyu never heard from him before.

Mafuyu looked the animal up and down, trying to make sense of what he was seeing. The majority of its body was the beautiful blue of a peacock, with its head and much of its body resembling the same shades. But the ends of its beak and talons were as sharp as an eagle's. Its body was long and its tail was split in two near the end, with orange feathers that highlighted them like fire. What Mafuyu couldn't lift his eyes from were the gigantic wings that stretched from its body. Those also had similar orange shades going up half of their length. The Tumwi looked like an elegant cross between a peacock and a phoenix, with the intimidating presence of a hawk. And to add to his discomfort, there were two of them.

Mirai turned towards Adelyn. "How did you manage to get them?"

"I'm their trainer." Adelyn smiled and Mirai had never looked more impressed.

"You have guts." His eyes twinkled. "But won't you get in trouble for having these two here without Eiwa's permission? It is their royal animal, after all."

Adelyn shrugged, "I can use a lot of excuses, like taking them for a flight exercise, pruning their feathers, or making sure they have no disease. Lots of reasons." She ruffled the feathers of the one she was holding by the reins. "Don't fret about it."

"Wait a minute." Mafuyu's voice was filled with anxiety as it broke through their conversation. "Why did you say she 'has guts' to train these…birds?" Mafuyu wasn't sure if that was the right word. Could they even be classified as birds?

"Because they are carnivorous…and generally ferocious." All blood drained from his face as Mirai continued to explain, adding to his terror. "They'll tear you to bits if you are not careful but if you train them and tame them," he rubbed the side of the Tumwi's head for effect as the bird purred under his warm hands, "they will be loyal to you until they die."

Mirai gently tugged on the reins of the bird and it bowed its neck toward the ground and then flopped down. He climbed on top of its body as easily as mounting a horse and extended his hand towards Mafuyu.

"Wait, am I supposed to climb onto this thing?" There was no way in both worlds he was mounting a creature that could attack him any minute if it wanted to.

"Don't worry. They are tamed," Adelyn assured him as she helped her brother climb onto the back of the bird she had already mounted. "And trained."

Mafuyu didn't voice the doubts; the last thing he wanted was to piss off the trainer who could command the bird to eat him anytime it wanted.

"We can't get there without the Tumwis," Mirai reasoned when he understood Mafuyu's silent distress.

"Why not?"

"Because the Four Deva Summit is held in a cave. For anyone other than a Deva, you need a Tumwi to get there *undetected*," Dan said, leaving Mafuyu without any further room for argument.

"Come on, Mafuyu. You banish Rev'ers," Mirai cajoled.

"Well, I didn't have to ride them!"

"Mafuyu." Mirai's tone grew serious even as his voice was

nearly drowned out by the impatient groaning and flapping of the Tumwis. He switched to Japanese and spoke for Mafuyu's ears only. "Ashkaar's animals are not like Yalim. No matter what...*transport* you want to take, you'll have to deal with a creature you've never seen before."

Mafuyu internally cursed. He couldn't afford to be stubborn in a land he didn't know a thing about. It was his decision to come here in the first place. What good would it do now if he couldn't even deal with an animal? He let out a deep breath and took Mirai's outstretched hand, warily climbing onto the back of the Tumwi and trying to fit himself comfortably on the saddle behind the man.

"Ready?" Mirai asked as he bunched up the reins in his fists.

"No," Mafuyu squeaked out just before Mirai pulled the reins and the Tumwi took flight. Mafuyu bit his lip to keep from letting out an embarrassed squeal as the bird flew vertically towards the sky like a bullet going upwards. The gravity worked against him and he felt he would slip and fall off his saddle any second if he didn't hold onto something.

The world was tilting beneath him. He tightened his legs, hoping it would keep him in the saddle, and wrapped his arms more securely around Mirai's torso, clinging to him for dear life. He shut his eyes as the wind whipped against his face, pulling his hair backwards. He heard Mirai chuckle at his reactions.

"Why don't these things come with seat belts?!" he yelled.

"Open your eyes. You're missing the view."

"Hell no! You're used to these kinds of things!"

"This is the first time I've flown on one."

"So? You're still used to flying with your own wings!"

The bird changed course and the winds died down to a calm breeze. Mafuyu felt gravity align once more as the bird tilted into a horizontal position. He reluctantly cracked open his eye and the scene before him caused him to ease his hold around Mirai. He was met with the magnificent view of golden light shimmering in the vastness of the sky, falling atop the fluffy white clouds. It made the world gleam in a manner that was so divine that Mafuyu forgot to even breathe.

His eyes traced the sky before they fell to the land below. Breathless, he said, "Whoa." The bird stretched its orange and blue wings as it glided across the air, and Mafuyu couldn't take his eyes off the passing clouds and the occasional sight of land beneath them.

Mirai kept his eyes on Adelyn, who flew in front of them. When the bird gently glided right, Mirai pulled on the reins of his bird, guiding it to follow the other.

"You know," Mafuyu said. "We did go around the town last night. Don't you think that was a bit dangerous? What if Rahel knows we are here now?"

"He would know we are here even if we didn't. He probably has eyes all over Marim, so it really doesn't make a difference what we did last night."

"Wow. Is this the same Mirai that wouldn't step out of the apartment without looking both ways twice?"

Mirai huffed, but didn't say anything otherwise.

"Do you think the Devas know about Rahel?"

"I'm sure they've noticed something, but we are not going there just to warn them of that." Mafuyu remained silent and Mirai continued. "Rahel has the knowledge of the Forbidden Scroll, which means it's almost impossible to stop him. If there is anyone who knows how to, it will be the Devas. We need their help to overcome his spells, protect both worlds, and end this once and for all."

Mafuyu's eyes fell on Mirai's back, where his wings once were. "What about your wings? Will they be able to—"

"I don't know." After the silence stretched on between them for a few long minutes, Mirai's voice broke it. "We're almost there."

The landscape changed; the clouds cleared out to reveal brown, rocky hills up ahead. The green plains became azure blue waters and the hills stood tall, protruding from the deep river below. Some were clustered together, while others stood alone like jagged rocks.

The Tumwis flew between them and tilted to pass between narrow openings between hills that towered over them on all sides.

Mafuyu looked around. A gushing waterfall broke through the rocks beside him. He turned his head to his right to see a giant statue of the top half of a person carved into the rock—an intricate work that probably took years to carve without destroying its surrounding environment. The waterfall fell around the statue's crowned head, dousing its shoulders before joining the river beneath them. It was well preserved, without the slightest of cracks destroying it. There was no doubt that the statue depicted someone of prominence.

"The First Deva. This place honors him," Mirai supplied when he noticed Mafuyu's gaze lingering on the monument.

"Where are we?"

"Mesai-Tor."

"What does that mean?"

"Howling Valley." As if on cue, a wind whistled past them, making a slight howling sound ring around the rocks. Adelyn slowed down her Tumwi and came up beside Mirai. Dan took out four cloaks from the brown sack he carried. They were made from feathers of the same colors as the Tumwi. He tossed two of them to Mirai, who caught them easily.

"Here." Mirai handed one to Mafuyu. "Put it on."

Mafuyu briefly watched the twins pull the cloaks over themselves, covering them entirely from head to toe. If it was for camouflage, it failed to do the trick. All it did was make them look like a disfigured part of the bird. Anybody would be suspicious if they saw something like this flying around. But Mafuyu kept his doubts to himself. He had decided to trust Mirai at each and every turn, so he followed suit and donned the cloak.

Once he was done, Adelyn's lips puckered and she whistled lowly. A second later, the Tumwis' colors started to fade until each of their feathers were transparent. Mafuyu gasped and grabbed Mirai's shoulders. If he hadn't still felt the flesh of the Tumwi beneath him, he would have believed that it had disappeared right from under him. And, like the birds, the cloaks they were wearing had reacted, rendering all of them invisible to any onlookers or guards. This was probably what Dan meant when he said that only the Tumwis could get them to the Devas undetected.

Mafuyu felt the heat of Mirai's skin through the cloak and let out a sigh of relief. He knew Mirai was there, but not being able to see him in a world that was completely new to him was a little nerve-racking. The only reason this plan was working was because Mirai could see past physical appearances. Right now, he could see all of them with his ability.

The Tumwis increased their speed again. Mafuyu couldn't see Adelyn or Dan, but he could feel their presence beside them. The birds dove closer to the waters, barely grazing the clear surface. They spread their wings and glided into a cave.

Darkness momentarily impaired Mafuyu's vision. He could hear another gushing waterfall, although this time it was stronger and louder, with what sounded like more than one rushing stream. When they ventured further, he could see a small arch, similar to the end of a tunnel. Once they reached the opening, the darkness that surrounded them brightened.

It wasn't an exit to the cave. Rather, it was an opening; the top of the cave had no roof and the sunlight filtered through the arch. A castle-like structure sat atop of what seemed like a small floating island. Several streams of the waterfall gushed from the island and fell freely into the pool of water below. From the walls of the cave, similar white rivulets of water fed into the azure blue river. The power of the numerous rushing falls made mist rise into the air. Trees and greenery made up the island, while bushes, algae and vines crept across the cave walls, painting the whole scene in bold colors of sky blues, greens, and white.

Mirai steered the Tumwi toward the white citadel. The fortress had at least several dozen glass windows on each floor. And with a structure as huge and complex as it was, it would be difficult to know where the Devas were...for normal people, that is.

Mafuyu leaned in and whispered, "Can you see them?"

"Yes. Fourth floor. There are guards stationed at the windows and doors on each floor except for the sixth one. The second window to the left: that's our way in."

"It isn't called The Hundred-Window Castle for nothing," Dan said from beside him. "Let's get as close as we can. Once you separate from the Tumwi, your cloaks will lose their transparency and they will go back to being visible."

"Understood," Mafuyu voiced since nodding wasn't going to help when they couldn't see each other.

"I hope everything goes well," Dan replied.

"Thank you, Dan...Adelyn," Mirai said. Mafuyu could feel Mirai shift in front of him. He was probably turning around to face him before he added, "Mafuyu, we will have to jump through the window. You can't afford to miss it."

"Is that all? I thought you were going to tell me to do something crazier."

Mafuyu heard the faint crack of Mirai flicking the reins, and the Tumwi flew ahead. As they got near the castle, Mirai steered the bird toward the windows on the sixth floor. Mafuyu was surprised at how discreet a giant bird could be.

Mafuyu felt Mirai shift again, along with what sounded like him letting go of the reins. "We need to stand up," Mirai instructed.

Despite not ever wanting to pull off a move that belonged in a circus show while hovering so far from the ground, Mafuyu didn't have much of a choice. He stood up on shaky legs. With the Tumwi being invisible, it felt as if he was standing in midair.

"Now!" Mirai signaled. Mafuyu didn't think twice and propelled through the open window. He somersaulted and landed on his feet. Mirai followed close behind, leaping as gracefully as a leopard and landing perfectly. Once they were off the Tumwi, their cloaks returned to their original colors. They took them off and discarded them right by the window they'd used as their entrance.

"Let's go." Mirai rushed ahead and Mafuyu followed as they made their way to the hall of the Devas.

CHAPTER THIRTY-TWO

THE FOUR DEVAS

The castle was quiet. Closed windows and dark curtains let in hardly any light. Just like Mirai had seen, there were fewer guards stationed on this floor. With a bit of quick thinking and by hiding behind decor pieces, clinging to the ceiling with Mafuyu latched onto him, ducking under stairways, and knocking some guards out cold, they made their way to the fourth floor, where the Devas meeting was being held. His eyes could see them, the incredible signs of four energies behind the door to the hall.

He motioned Mafuyu to follow close behind him, and the boy did exactly what he was told without questions. Mirai was about to take another step when he heard a voice from his right warn, "Stop!"

Mirai halted and took in the source of the voice from the corner of his eye. A guard. Damn it.

Mafuyu had followed instructions and froze right where he was. They could hear thudding footsteps and the noise of armor clanking as more guards headed toward them. In no time, they formed a circle around the pair.

"Who goes there?" one of the guards demanded. An emblem on his armor distinguished him as the unit's commander.

Mirai didn't say a word. Instead he slowly raised his hand and slipped off the hood, revealing his distinctive white hair hidden underneath. He lifted his face and stared at the guards. Gasps echoed around them followed by shocked murmurs of, "It can't be!"

"Bezaleel!"

Mirai lunged forward, grabbing one of the men by the end of the spear he held and pulling it toward him. The guard stumbled forward and Mirai elbowed him in the face. From there, Mirai used the spear to fight the other guards that attacked him, while Mafuyu helped him fend off the rest.

Mirai refused to draw his sword. He did not intend to kill any of them, so he resorted to knocking them out one by one, hitting them in the junctions between their necks and shoulders, and in the backs of the heads.

A guard yelled aggressively as he charged. He swung a fist and Mirai slid to the right. He threw a punch at his right and Mirai dodged to the left. Then Mirai ducked, stepped in closer, and brought his fist upwards in a bone-breaking uppercut to the man's jaw.

He turned around to see Mafuyu knock out a guard with a swift roundhouse kick, followed by a jab to another guard's neck. And the last one was down.

"Hurry! Before more arrive!" Mirai warned and sped off with Mafuyu following closely behind. There was no time to be discreet anymore. If those guards had found him then the others would have been alerted. It wouldn't be long before they were surrounded and captured.

They raced down the spacious hall and went straight for the door to the meeting room. As they did, they caught the attention of the guards that were stationed across the hallway. It was like raiding a battalion.

"Mafuyu!" Mirai called to the boy who was running by his side. "If we make it through the door, the guards can't follow. They are forbidden from going inside."

"Got it!"

Another guard raced toward them. Mirai leaped at him and rendered him unconscious with a flying kick.

"Stop!" guards bellowed from behind them, but to no avail. The guards closed the distance, causing Mafuyu and Mirai to hasten their footsteps.

"Stop, I say!" one of them shouted, his voice was much closer than Mirai would have liked. If they got caught then, they would be killed for sure, and all of this would have been in vain.

Mirai sped up, extended his hand, and pushed open the door. Mafuyu followed, running so fast that he ended up sliding across the marbled floor as he passed through the doorway. He stumbled, turned around, and helped Mirai shut the heavy door.

Mafuyu then drew his bo staff and slid it through the handles, locking the doors in place for the time being. There was a bang on the other side as the soldiers tried to pry them open, but the doors didn't budge.

Mirai nodded at Mafuyu. They stood in a huge entrance hall. Ornaments and weapons decorated the walls around them. Mirai glanced at the second door at the end of the space, and Mafuyu followed his gaze. Behind that was the room in which the Four Devas were meeting.

There was a loud clatter, followed by raucous banging against the doors and then shouts. It was too loud for them to ignore, even in the midst of an important discussion that didn't leave any room for distractions.

"What's that noise?" Leka stood up from his chair. He was the first one to respond to the unusual clamor outside their hall.

"Intruders?" Ismat questioned. Attacking the Devas was not unheard of among their enemies, but to do so in the middle of their summit was just absurd. No one knew when they held the yearly meetings. "Could someone have leaked when we would be in council?"

The disturbance grew in volume, jolting the rest of the Devas seated around the table. Pounding footsteps came closer. And closer.

The Devas stood up to meet the interlopers. Bless the poor soul who had the guts and the idiocy to barge into a meeting attended by four of the most powerful people in the entire world. Whoever it was better have a good reason if they wanted to get out of this alive.

They expected to see familiar faces of enemies from battles past, but once the door was flung open, they were at a loss for words. In came the one person they would not have imagined seeing for another dozen years, if ever.

"Bezaleel!" Mikael exclaimed in sheer disbelief. Bezaleel, the Raathri who escaped execution by opening a portal, rushed through their door. Time had matured him into a man—a man that had just as much as power as any one of the Devas. Years of toil and hiding had changed his once childlike eyes into something sharp and dangerous, something that burned as fiercely as his soul.

With him stood a boy who looked like he had seen a ghost. Or, four ghosts. Even so, there was a sign of bravery in him that couldn't be easily dismissed.

Bezaleel knelt on one knee, submitting himself to the Devas in a sign of peace and obedience.

"Why are you here?" Ismat was the first one to recover enough to speak.

"Please, I need to speak to you all," Bezaleel pleaded, his voice mellow and nonthreatening, yet still urgent.

"And why should we listen to a fugitive? And a Raathri member, no less," Leka spat.

"Leka," Mikael addressed his peer. "We mustn't forget that it was because of Bezaleel that Alayl was saved that night, and that Lord Rasa's life was spared. Without him, Alayl would have lost its Deva and the Raathris would have started a war across our nations."

"Yet he didn't warn Lord Rasa of the coup beforehand. Perhaps it was all part of another twisted plan of his." Leka's eyes scrutinized the man still kneeling before him. "Did you also forget that he stole parts of the scroll, lifted the Veyil, and ran away with it? A member of the Raathri clan cannot be trusted."

"Yet in the last fourteen years, he did nothing to harm us," Mikael said.

"Mikael is right," Ismat agreed. "We should listen to what he has to say."

"Lady Ismat," Leka chided. "I expected you to be more neutral, not to take the side of a Raathri."

"Don't be ridiculous. I'm not taking his side."

"Enough," a fourth voice broke in. At the other end of the table stood Eiwa, dressed in her clan's colors of white and blue. She didn't raise her voice, but the authority she had in every word dared anyone to speak further. "You are all bickering like children." She walked toward Bezaleel and motioned with her hand for him to stand up. "Why have you come here after all these years, Bezaleel?" Her voice was low, yet stern. There was neither anger nor gentleness; it just conveyed a simple question that needed an answer.

"Rahel is planning a war in both Ashkaar and Yalim. He has learned the spells in the Forbidden Scroll."

"Impossible," Leka intervened. "The Scroll they had was destroyed. You did that yourself."

Bezaleel pressed his lips together in a thin line. They might not choose to believe this but he still had to try. "It didn't burn completely. He found the revival spell."

The Devas remained silent, not because they doubted Bezaleel's words. Even if he was lying, he needn't have risked his life to inform them of what was going on. If what Bezaleel said was true, then they were in for a war that Ashkaar had never seen before. Moreover, if Bezaleel was actually there, it meant that the situation was worse than that of the coup.

"Follow me." Eiwa watched Bezaleel look at the boy next to him and nod, silently instructing him to stay put until he returned. The boy nodded back. "Lord Mikael, you know what to do."

With a smirk, Mikael turned toward the boy as Eiwa led Bezaleel out of the hall and into the next room.

CHAPTER THIRTY-THREE

DESCENDANT

If Mafuyu had told anyone back at headquarters about what he was seeing right now they would have one of two reactions—striking awe, or they would think that he'd gone bat-shit crazy. Probably the latter.

He was glad that he understood Zalek, but it did nothing to ease his wildly beating heart in the face of the four most powerful people to ever exist. And they were surrounding him like tigers around a Pomeranian.

"Why do you think Bezaleel brought this boy here?" a lady asked the others. Her arms crossed over her chest, and an iron glint shone in her magenta-colored eyes. She wasn't belittling him. Far from it, actually—she appeared to regard him with caution.

Her attire consisted of a high-collared, full-sleeved jade top that stretched all the way to her ankles, with slits in the sides from her waist to the hem. She wore white pants underneath, and combat boots. A magenta sash that matched the color of her eyes was secured around her hip with an emblem in the middle, probably that of her clan, etched in gold. Her whole outfit was made so she could move easily in a fight, yet showed her status as a ruler. There were beautiful golden patterns on the hems of her sleeves, the edges of her collar, and along the bottom of her long shirt. She had the emblem of the Devas stitched on the upper side of her right sleeve. Her long, emerald green hair was pulled up into a high ponytail.

"I wonder," Leka mused. Mafuyu only saw a blur before he drew a sword and rushed toward him at a blinding speed. Mafuyu didn't flinch; Leka's blade met with the edge of Mafuyu's dagger. The Deva smirked. "So you can handle yourself in a fight." He drew his blade back, but Mafuyu knew that Leka hadn't even used an ounce of his real strength.

"That must be the reason," Ismat commented.

Leka's outfit was more striking than the rest. He wore a peach-colored robe that fluttered around his legs, hiding the pants and boots underneath. He wore a thin red cloak embroidered with detailed golden designs. The Deva's symbol was stitched into the material in gold, just like the rest of them had. His long peach hair, the same color of his robe, was combed back and tied in a half ponytail. The rest of his tresses fell long and loose to his waist.

None of the Devas had their wings out. They hid them just like Mirai did.

"But that simple weapon is not enough for you to fight the Raathris, especially if they're using Nahms." Leka's purple eyes bore no sympathy as he asked the other Devas, "Why do you think he is with Bezaleel?"

Mafuyu stared back at the Deva who'd questioned his purpose and answered him, though the question wasn't really directed at him in the first place. "He is my friend. He saved humans like me many times, and I will do the same for him."

Mafuyu would have given his life to capture the expressions that crossed the Devas' faces so he could see them again and again. They were astounded, to say the least.

After a noticeable pause, it was Mikael who cried out in amazement, "Would you look at that! He speaks Zalek!"

"No doubt Bezaleel taught him," Ismat joined in.

"But the way he speaks it…" Mikael crossed the distance between them and touched Mafuyu's cheek. The boy went as stiff as stone and the hair on the back of his neck stood on end. He thought he was going to be killed for stepping out of line, but instead Mikael's lavender eyes sparkled and he laughed gleefully.

If Mafuyu had to describe it, he'd have said it was the same kind of reaction he saw on Nagisa's five-year-old niece when he took her to Disneyland for the first time. Mikael turned to Ismat with that look still intact.

Ismat raised an eyebrow in question before understanding Mikael's silent statement. "You must be joking."

"Are you saying that you do not see the resemblance?" Mikael pressed. Leka joined Ismat by her side and looked the most confused out of the three.

The lady Deva squinted at him. "None."

Mikael turned back to Mafuyu. "There is no such thing as coincidence. Even a chance acquaintance is predestined."

Mafuyu had no idea what was happening. He wondered if they were still talking about him because if so then he definitely didn't follow.

"Seems like it isn't a coincidence he was able to cross the portal," Leka said. "Bezaleel always had eyes for those who are strong."

"Look at you. Ever so admiring of him and yet you act like you distrust him with your entire being," Mikael teased.

Leka made a noise that sounded like he was being choked and had tried to snort at the same time. His face turned a shade of red and he scowled in embarrassment. "Says the one that joined in the act," he huffed.

Act? Mafuyu's eyebrows creased. So they weren't against him.

Mikael shrugged. "I was just voicing my honest thoughts. I did want to worry him a little for breaking the rules, but I'm not stupid enough to make an enemy of the person that saved a Deva and a nation. I just wanted to know if spending time in Yalim had corrupted him. I'm glad it didn't." Mikael regarded Mafuyu again. "Now, going back to my original point."

"Are you sure about this?" Ismat casually leaned on the table they'd been sitting around moments ago.

"There is only one way to find out. Do you disagree, Lady Ismat?"

Ismat's eyes narrowed like she was contemplating some idea. Eventually she shook her head. "The boy is here with Bezaleel. That means he is here to fight Rahel. I think he will need all the help he can get. And if your theory proves correct, all the more reason to give it to him."

Mikael pointed at Mafuyu. "You. Follow me."

Mafuyu still wasn't sure what they were talking about, but he decided to take a chance and follow Mikael. His feet carried him forward and fell in step behind the Deva as he led him out the door. There was a sense of ease around him. Mafuyu's eyes fell on Mikael's back. His robes were unlike the others—simpler, less tight. His shirt was the same lavender color as his eyes, the collar was white, and the upper part of the shirt had no buttons. It was loosely held together by a sapphire brooch shaped like a leaf, with a white teardrop stone. It pinned the shirt together at the abdomen, giving a glimpse of the Deva's toned muscles underneath. It fell around his knees and his pants were white, tucked into equally white boots. Like the rest of the Devas, his clothes had golden designs on the collar and hems. The Deva's symbol was tailored onto the back of his shirt. He also wore silver gauntlets over his long sleeves. His midnight blue hair was combed back, but free, framing his face and flowing over his broad shoulders and chest.

There was a different aura about him than there was around the others, a calm demeanor with just a hint of dormant danger. Every step he took was calculated, every movement was graceful.

"I know what you are thinking." His deep voice drew Mafuyu's attention back to the present. "You needn't be afraid. Allies of Ashkaar are always welcome."

"Why do you trust Bezaleel?" Mafuyu blurted out before assessing if it was the right question to ask.

Mikael didn't seem to mind. "To speak the truth, I would say that Bezaleel is the strongest among us due to sheer skill alone. We are only a step ahead of him because of our knowledge of the spells. If he'd wanted to, Bezaleel could have learned the Nahms, killed both Rasa and Eiwa, and taken their place. Or, he could have killed all of us one by one and taken over the whole of Ashkaar. He is certainly capable enough."

"But he would never do that." Mafuyu didn't miss a beat when it came to defending his friend.

"Indeed. Since you know of Bezaleel's origins and of us, I take it that you also know about the Forbidden Scroll?" Mafuyu nodded and Mikael continued. "Bezaleel had the opportunity to take the Scroll for himself, yet he took only what he needed to stop a coup from happening. He put himself at risk to save Alayl, protected the nation for the sake of peace, and never demanded any sort of reward." He turned right at the end of the hallway, with Mafuyu still on his heels. "But of course, the previous Devas were skeptical of him when he lifted the Veyil."

"They knew he did it?"

Mikael snickered. "Of course they did, boy. We are aware whenever the portal opens. The other Devas wanted to capture him and bring him back, but Lord Rasa suggested they observe him first. He sent a spy to watch Bezaleel for five years. The previous Devas and those of us who were next in line kept track of him to see what he planned to do after crossing over to Yalim. But as the days passed, and months turned into years, we realized that Bezaleel had only means to escape. He did no harm. He was even shedding his former self, living like a normal boy with a normal family." Mafuyu's heart constricted at the mention of Mirai's family. "We knew he did not want to return to Ashkaar or regain his life as Bezaleel. So Lord Rasa decided to let him be as long as he didn't disrupt the balance between our worlds. He always had a soft spot for Bezaleel."

"Then how did you not know when Rahel opened the portal?" Mafuyu's voice was more accusatory than he had intended, and Mikael had to have heard it.

But his reply let the young man know that he wasn't sour about it. "Rahel has found a way to lift the Veyil without our notice. He hid away from us for years, and we thought the clan had perished. Even now, if it weren't for Bezaleel we still wouldn't know." Silence fell over them again. Absorbed as he was in their conversation, Mafuyu hadn't paid much attention to where they were going until he stood in front of an intricately designed door. "The one who you should be more worried about is yourself."

"Me?"

"Not only did you, a mere mortal of Yalim, pass through the gateway into Ashkaar, but you have also seen the secret palace. Why should I let you free now?"

A determined expression hardened Mafuyu's face. "Because I'd rather die than spill the secrets of Ashkaar. That's my way of protecting Bezaleel."

"Then let me ask you another question."

"Y-yes?"

"What do you know about yourself?"

"Myself?" To his own dismay, Mafuyu didn't know how to answer such a broad question about who he was at his core. "What do you mean?"

"You work as a Hunter in Yalim, yet you don't know anything about your organization."

Mafuyu was stupefied. He did not expect the Devas to know about Hunters. "How do you know about us?"

"What do *you* know about them?"

He sifted through his memory, wondering if Mikael was toying with him. "I know that they were established hundreds of years ago and that we banish Rev'ers into the Jihan."

"You speak of the Jihan, yet you do not know that the inscriptions on your weapons are Nahms."

"What?" Mafuyu was baffled.

"You do not 'banish' the Rev'ers into the Jihan. You simply just return them to their world."

"I'm not following."

"The Jihan is what we call the parallel worlds. Like Ashkaar and

Yalim belongs to the Jihan, there are several other worlds, and all of them are separated and protected from one another by the Veyil."

"But we use bullets to banish—" Mafuyu paused to correct himself. "To *return* them to the Jihan."

"The Nahms on your weapons cancel out their lethal intent. In other words, you can use bullets or whatever you want, but it's not going to hurt them. But that only applies to them. Use those same weapons on us or any humans and that could still be the end of someone's life."

"So we return them to Jihan and make sure that the balance stays with the Devas," Mafuyu summarized.

"Correct." Mikael smiled, seemingly pleased that Mafuyu was catching on. "Four hundred years ago, the Devas noticed a weakening in the Veyil around some worlds. One of them was Yalim. Because of this, creatures from other worlds were able to pass into Yalim. But, once the creatures passed to your world they were unable to go back. The Devas couldn't leave Ashkaar every single time it happened, so they held a summit. It was decided that one person from each of the clans—one person from each nation to show that there was no ulterior motive or political corruption— who was capable of returning these creatures would head to Yalim.

"The inscriptions on the weapons allow you to lift the Veyil for a brief second when in contact with the creature in order to send it back to the world that it come from. But there was no finite solution to this, nothing we could do to stop the Veyil from weakening every now and then, so the members of the four clans stayed in Yalim. They concealed their true identities and blended in with the people there. As time passed, their children carried on their duties without knowing their origins. They 'banished' these creatures and created the Rev'er Hunter Corps. Their bloodline spread, and this is why people like you can see otherworldly creatures while others can't."

"So all the Hunters are descendants of the Deva's clans?"

"Somehow, yes. Of course, their bloodlines would have split off and differentiated with each generation, but some abilities stay. Yet, only a handful remember where their blood is from—like you. It is the reason that you learned Zalek so quickly as well. Your blood did not forget its origins, even if you weren't aware of them yourself."

Mafuyu couldn't believe what he was hearing. He was a descendant of one of the clans? Did that mean Nagisa was, too? She had a dagger with Zalek runes and she was able to fend off First-Levels by herself.

"But...my parents. They were very normal," Mafuyu finally said.

"Of course. It's just like any other variation in DNA." Mikael explained. "For example, your great-grandmother might have blue eyes, but your both parents have brown eyes. Then there is you, who was born with blue eyes that you inherited from your great-grandma."

"I understand."

"Good." He grabbed the golden knob on the door and turned it. "That'll make this easier."

Mikael opened the door and stood to the side, motioning for Mafuyu to enter first. The boy obeyed and stepped through, listening as Mikael followed and gently shut the door behind them.

Mafuyu didn't know what he expected to see, but he definitely didn't think that Mikael would lead him to a room with a pair of weapons in the middle. A sword stand rested atop a small table in the back of the room, with two gorgeous gold swords on display. They were sheathed in intricately designed bronze scabbards. A pattern that resembled a fierce Tumwi curved its way across the scabbards' surfaces, decorated with dazzling stones. The hilts of the swords had black grips.

Mafuyu took a few steps toward the stand, but then stopped. What if this was a trap? He glanced at Mikael over his shoulder. "You said I was a descendant of one of the four Deva clans. So...I mean..." He trailed off without knowing how to form the question.

"*Vaal.*"

"What?"

"Say it. It's a Nahm."

"*Vaal?*" Mafuyu repeated uncertainly. A swishing sound echoed through the room. Mafuyu turned his head in time to see the two swords race through the air to him on their own. He caught them, one in each hand, on pure reflex. "What?"

"Ismat," Mikael said. "That weapon only reacts to her bloodline."

"I'm...related to Lady Ismat?" Mafuyu couldn't believe what he was hearing.

"You definitely belong to her bloodline. Though, it's weaker than if you lived here."

"You know this because of your...powers?"

"Yes. I can tell a person's bloodline with just a touch."

Mafuyu glanced down at the swords. They looked powerful, unbreakable, and fit perfectly in his hands like they'd been made just for him.

"If you plan to fight Rahel alongside Bezaleel, you'll need those."

Mafuyu turned around to look at the Deva. "Why are you doing this for me?"

"Because you are here to fight Rahel, are you not? What good are you going to do us if you become a liability or end up dead?" Mikael pointed to the swords. "Those will help you in more ways than one."

"Thank you."

Mikael nodded as a smile brightened his features. "Is there something else you wish to ask?"

"Uh...no." Mafuyu felt that he was staring at the Deva too much and forced himself to look away.

But Mikael was captivating. His strong presence paired with his looks made it difficult to *not* stare. His features were carved and elegant. His dark hair was like the night sky and his lavender eyes shone like stars. There was a small blue mark on his forehead in the shape of a diamond that somehow made him even more attractive. His smile was enough to turn heads.

"That blade can withstand Nahms," Mikael offered without any prompting. "Or, to be specific, it cancels them. If Rahel aims a spell at you, you can cut right through it." He slowly made his way towards Mafuyu. "If you wish to help Ashkaar then you will need it." The gentleness in his eyes suddenly turned cold. "But if I see the smallest hint of betrayal from you, I will not think twice before cutting you where you stand."

Mafuyu had to hold back a shiver that threatened to make his hands tremble. "You can trust me. That won't ever happen." His voice betrayed his discomfort, but his words were firm.

"Good. Let's head back, shall we?"

CHAPTER THIRTY-FOUR

APOLOGY

The soldiers stood aside as Mirai and Lady Eiwa entered a private room. Mirai didn't fail to catch the glower one of the soldiers shot at him as they locked the door behind them.

It was a soldier that Mirai had punched earlier. He mentally apologized to the man; it wasn't like he had anything against any of them. He'd just been in the middle of a desperate attempt to get to the meeting hall.

"Bezaleel," Lady Eiwa said, drawing his attention back to her. Her face didn't drop the stern persona she wore, but a flicker of something softer flashed in her eyes as she spoke. "First, I want to apologize."

"Apologize?" That caught him off guard. He didn't see any reason for Eiwa to offer *him* an apology.

"If we—" She paused and corrected herself. "If my father had known about the Raathri clan's plans sooner, then you wouldn't have had to turn against your own kin all those years ago. Their blood wouldn't have been in your hands. That was a burden you shouldn't have had to bear. And I apologize on behalf of my father for putting you in that position, however inadvertently."

"Lady Eiwa, please." Mirai's voice was soft as his words. "I had to do that to save the people. It was not your fault. It was the Raathri clan's misdeeds."

"We still drove them into it. A hatred like theirs is not created in a day, Bezaleel." Her robe elegantly fluttered around her feet as she turned to the window. Her eyes were fixed on the distant white clouds that floated above them as she recalled things from before her time. "Their hatred piled up after years of isolation and restraints. Since the first Deva of Endhra, our leaders have feared the Raathri's strength. Instead of ruling Alayl together, making use of both our strengths to balance out the weaknesses, we forced your clan into a corner, cut them off from Alayl's affairs, and made them look like animals that needed to be watched. It was only a matter of time before they rose up against that role. Raathri and Endhra were the two clans that founded Alayl, yet one of them was unjustifiably diminished. My father tried to break that cycle, tried to fix the rift by affording you your position as a Deva, but the Raathris' hatred had already blinded them."

"You do not blame them?"

"Far from it. In fact, I think all of this could have been prevented if they were acknowledged in the way they should have been from the beginning."

"But Marvak's greed was not something that could have been quenched with mere acknowledgement or a peace treaty. He wanted something that neither you nor any Deva could have ever given him, and now Rahel is doing the same—if not worse. He wants to take over Ashkaar *and* Yalim. He wants to destroy them both."

Eiwa closed the distance between them and placed a hand on his shoulder. Mirai's vibrant orange-red eyes met her almost white ones as she said, "A Deva's job is to protect Ashkaar at any cost. It is no lie when I say that there is no truer Deva than you, Bezaleel. You are a true leader and my father believed it without a doubt. With his dying breath, your name was on his lips. He prayed that you were alright."

"Lord Rasa...he..."

"Passed away three years ago. Tuberculosis."

"I'm sorry." Mirai thought back to what he recalled of Rasa. "He was a good man."

"Thank you, Bezaleel." Eiwa resembled her father in many ways, from the polite manner in which she spoke, to her strong personality, her kind heart, and her even judgment as a ruler. Even her physical features resembled Lord Rasa's: the long blue hair and white eyes, and the robes she wore, even though it was more feminine. She stood tall and proud, and there was a strength to her that was unseen even in Lord Rasa. Her eyes were like steel, unwavering as her principles. "You are the perfect half of both your parents," she remarked. "Unyielding like your mother, with a sense of right and kindness like your father. They would be proud to know how you have grown."

Bezaleel smiled. "You as well, my lady. You are so much like Lord Rasa now. The last time I saw you was when you were a child."

"Likewise. It has been years." A flicker of nostalgia manifested in the form of a ghost of a smile on Eiwa's lips, but it disappeared as soon as it came. "What is the other reason you are here, Bezaleel? I'm sure you didn't risk your life to interrupt us only to say that Rahel is waging a war. Why else have you sought us out?"

Bezaleel paused for a moment before turning around. He shrugged the cloak off his shoulders and let it fall to the ground. He heard Eiwa draw in a breath at the sight.

"Your wings." The tips of her fingers caressed the skin in between the burned wounds. He subtly flinched at the unexpected touch.

"Rahel has learned all the Nahms that exist."

"Has he become so cruel?"

"I'm afraid 'cruel' is an understatement." Mirai put the cloak back on. "Lady Eiwa, do you have any countermeasure against someone who has learned the spells from the Forbidden Scroll?"

Eiwa stared at him, trying to read him. Scrutinizing him for asking a question that no one dared to even think, let alone voice. Her gaze was hard enough to make anyone kneel before her and apologize for asking something out of line. Yet Bezaleel held his ground. He wasn't backing out now, not after coming this far and facing everything he had.

After what seemed like painfully long hours, but were actually just mere seconds, Eiwa finally spoke. "I will tell you, but I'm afraid that after that—after this fight with Rahel is over—I will have to take away all your knowledge. What I'm about to tell you as well as the knowledge of the Scrolls that you already possess." Mirai nodded. He'd expected as much. "We do have Nahms that are the opposite of the ones in the Scroll and serve as countermeasures for each and every spell." She tapped her temple, "But they're memorized and not written, passed on from one Deva to another through generations. That way, if something like this happened, we'd have something that couldn't be stolen."

"So, you can stop him." Hope brimmed in his voice.

"Come with me." Eiwa paced across the vast room to lead him back to the other room, where the rest of the Devas stood waiting for them. Mafuyu was next to Mikael with a pair of swords strapped to his waist.

"Lord Mikael," Eiwa addressed the other Deva as they both made their way in.

Mikael bowed. "How shall I be of assistance?"

Eiwa turned her head toward Mirai, gesturing for him to explain the situation to the others. Mirai said exactly what he had earlier and dropped his cloak to show Mikael his burned wings as he explained how it happened. Mikael's face went sour. Burning off one's wings was the same as burning off one's hands.

"Can you do anything?" Eiwa asked.

Mikael leaned in close to inspect the burned wings. He pressed a finger to his chin as his eyes traced the wounds. "You're lucky you still have a little bit of them intact. If Rahel had burned all of them, it would be impossible to revive them," he said.

"Can you restore my wings back to what they were?"

Mikael shot him a lopsided grin. "You're talking to a Deva who specializes in medicine. There is nothing these hands can't revive." He wiggled his ten fingers as if to emphasize his point, "Except dead bodies of course." He stepped back and ordered him to kneel. Mirai did so without protest, giving the lavender-eyed man access to his back. Mikael reached around Mirai and unbuttoned his shirt as he added, "We need to get you a new robe."

Mirai stiffened when the shirt was peeled off of him. The two Devas would see the seal that he used on his back to hide his wings. It was forbidden to use Nahms without their permission and it was punishable by law.

But then again, he had done much worse.

Mikael raised his hand without a word. The tips of his fingers lit up with a lavender smoke that looked like a transparent, warm flame. It flickered as if it was swaying in a breeze. "Clench your teeth," was all the warning Mirai got before he felt a jab in the middle of his back followed by an unexpected, intense pain.

Mirai's breath caught in his throat. His stomach tightened as a blinding pain surged through his back and held him frozen in place. He tightened his fists and dug his fingernails into the flesh of his palms. He saw flashes of white when his vision blurred and sat there, wide-eyed and mouth agape, until he felt a different kind of warmth seep into his back: a tingle that enveloped his flesh from his shoulders to the bottom of his spine.

And then he could feel it—his wings growing back. He could feel the veins and tendons connect. The feathers grew, one top of the other, faster than anybody could count: like a hundred flower petals blooming at once. The weight of his wings returned and Mirai's hands twitched when he felt the familiar brush of his feathers on his forearms. He felt relieved. They were back to how they once were, as if they'd never been damaged in the first place. They might have looked even better.

Mikael took his hand away and the smoke-like substance faded from his fingertips. Mirai rose from his knees and turned to Mikael. He didn't utter a word but his doubt was obvious.

"Go on," Mikael encouraged. Seeing the assurance in the other man's eyes, Mirai let out a shaky breath before flexing his wings. On command, his feathers hardened, becoming as strong as diamonds. "I added a little something extra."

Mikael's words drew Mirai's attention back to him. "Extra?"

Mikael nodded. "Your wings were able to withstand blades and weapons, but now they can also withstand Nahms."

Mirai bowed from his waist. "Lord Mikael, I cannot thank you enough. I'm in your debt."

"Indeed."

"I have another favor to ask of all of you. I'm afraid this involves the fate of our nations." Eiwa was one that never asked for favors. For her to do so then, it was clear that what she was about to ask would be no easy feat.

Mirai braced himself. He had good instincts, and right now, his instincts told him that Eiwa was about to ask him something he would never have deemed possible—even if he was to be born with twice his strength in another ten lives.

CHAPTER THIRTY-FIVE

ATTACK

The last time Mirai stood in this room was fourteen years ago, when he bowed to Lord Rasa. Despite all the years that had passed, the room still remained the same. The same light curtains were drawn to block out the sunlight and the same decor adorned the walls. It hit him with a nostalgia that he could have done without.

After their miraculously successful meeting with the Devas, Lady Eiwa had asked all of them to return to Marim with her, which they had agreed to after she told them her plans to fight Rahel. A small argument broke out between the Devas about that, but with a little bit of persuasion, they eventually came to an agreement.

Mafuyu had kept mum while the whole ordeal was unfolding, but Mirai could see the dissent on his face after he heard what Mirai had to do in order to assure victory, and how it would play out. Despite his unwillingness, Mafuyu respected Mirai's wishes and flew back with him and the other Devas to Alayl's Deva's tower, which stood beside Marim's academy.

Mirai glanced at the door, knowing Mafuyu waited patiently on the other side.

"You better be right about this, Bezaleel," Ismat warned as she joined the other Devas who sat on the floor on top of a marking that

Eiwa drew. "I won't think twice about locking you in the dungeon."

"Trust me," Mirai answered. "Rahel won't attack your nations while you're here."

"And why is that?" Ismat asked, not because she didn't have an idea, but because she wanted to hear Bezaleel's theory.

"First, because your lands are your best defense. Seylon is an island nation and its mainland is a fjord. Ismat and her soldiers can use Nahms that manipulate the water to their advantage. It's the same with Jabilsa. Lord Mikael's main town is located in a mountain valley, so he'd know how to use the land around him. And more than all of that, all of you are what Rahel is after. He doesn't care about the spoils of a kingdom. If you aren't there, then there is no point in him attacking your nation. We must consider the fact that he somehow knows that the summit is happening right now and that I am back in Alayl. It's more likely that he'll attack here, and we'll need your help to defend against him."

"Well, in that case, we must hurry." Leka motioned for Mirai to sit down and he plopped down before them.

Eiwa looked at the other Devas seated in a semicircle around him. "Ready?" she asked.

They nodded and looked back at Mirai, who leaned forward in response. The Devas spread their wings, touching the ends of each other's. They rocked forward together, raised their right hands, and touched the tips of their index fingers to his forehead.

"*Kaim'ar an lae*," they whispered in harmony. The second the words left their mouths Bezaleel felt a violent electric current pass through him. His first reaction was to move his head away from their magic, but Eiwa was quicker. She leaned in further and held Mirai steady by the back of his head.

Her hold on him was strong. Stronger than anyone he had fought and even stronger than he was. It would have been detrimental to break out of her hold now; she was keeping him alive by holding him in place.

Moments after the numbing pain began, a different kind of

ripple vibrated through his body. He opened his eyes and his vision was filled with swirling numbers, ancient Zalek letters, alphabets, words, and diagrams floating in the air. But they weren't actually in the air. It was all surging through his mind, reforming into sequences that made sense.

He was gathering knowledge. His mind was learning and storing Nahms without him having to memorize them. This must be it: the ritual that let Devas pass down their knowledge from one generation to the next. The Devas were breaking their strictest rule for Mirai and entrusting him with their most coveted information.

A dot of blue light shone where the Devas' fingers touched his forehead and slithered over his body. It looked like his veins were luminescent, from the tips of his fingers to the ends of his wings. Almost as soon as it appeared, it also disappeared, leaving his skin looking exactly as it did before.

Eiwa released him, the Devas withdrew their hands, and the swirling numbers and alphabets faded from Mirai's vision. "Well done. You held out quite well," Eiwa said as she slowly rose to her feet. "I knew you wouldn't be ripped apart."

Mirai lifted his chin to raise his eyebrow at her. "What?"

"Did I not mention that?" she asked, feigning innocence. "Controlling Nahms requires a tremendous amount of magical energy in both your body and your mind. That's why it takes us years to learn to control it at our beck and call. But transferring Nahms is like forcing pressure into a small balloon. If you can't contain it, it will try to escape, sometimes by ripping its container to shreds. It's good that you didn't." He'd figured she was exaggerating when she mentioned it could kill him. He did, after all, hold enough magical energy to cast Nahms. She was probably scaring him a little for her own entertainment. Eiwa's lips twitched into a sly smile, amusement dancing in her eyes. "Did you think this was easy?"

"Certainly not." Mirai replied, not giving her the chance to get a reaction out of him the way she wanted. "I knew that not all could handle the transfer of the Nahms, but I believed that one would only get severely injured in the process. Not ripped to shreds."

Eiwa extended her hand towards him. He grabbed her palm and the sleeves of her silk robes brushed against his knuckles as she helped him up to his feet. "All valuable things come with a high price, Bezaleel. Nothing that is of worth is gained easily."

"Undoubtedly," he answered. "I'm glad you 'forgot' to mention that point, though. I probably wouldn't have concentrated so well if I knew all that."

"All in a good day's work, then."

The door banged open. Mafuyu stood there with a worried face, not knowing what to expect. When he saw Mirai hunched between the Devas, the boy forgot all protocols and was by his side in a heartbeat. "Mirai!" Mafuyu placed a cautious hand on Mirai's back. "Are you okay? You were taking too long and—"

Mirai placed a hand on Mafuyu's shoulder in return, effectively calming the other down. "I'm fine. Just a little light-headed." He gestured to the length of his body to illustrate his point. "Completely unhurt."

Mafuyu let out a breath and Mirai grinned. Eiwa raised her eyebrows in pleasant surprise. Who knew that Bezaleel, who hardly cracked a smile back when she knew him, could grin so brightly?

"What about you? Are you alright?" he asked the boy.

"Perfect," Mafuyu replied.

Before leaving Mesai-Tor, Mikael had advised that Mafuyu learn Nahms that could aid him in battle, along with his new weapons. Sharing Ismat's bloodline meant it wouldn't take much for him to learn an easy spell or two. Coupled with his photographic memory and his ability to read and speak Zalek, it only took a couple of hours for Mafuyu to learn two basic Nahms that would improve his speed and strength. Having the blood of a Teiyyan flowing in him, the magic felt natural to him, like it was made to fit him like a glove.

But Ismat had warned him that should Mafuyu try anything that seemed like a threat or a betrayal of their trust, she wouldn't think twice about taking his life. And she wouldn't give a damn if he was her blood or not. But Mafuyu assured he had no such dark intent.

"Bezaleel," Leka called, taking his attention off of Mafuyu. "It's because you have the blood of the Raathri that you were able to take on two strong attributes. That's the limit for the Devas as well."

"I understand," Mirai replied.

Mikael slapped Leka on the back with a resounding *thwack*. "Explain it clearly; leave nothing out."

"Did you just strike me?"

"I'm sure it didn't hurt."

Leka pulled back his sleeve as if to free up his hand and whipped around. "How about I show you?"

Mikael laughed nervously and took a step back. "Come now, Lord Leka. Violence is never the answer." He put both his hands up in surrender. "Don't be like Lady Ismat."

"Excuse me?" Ismat looked dangerously close to whacking both of them.

"You're right," Leka replied with a sinister grin. "Violence is a question. The answer is yes."

Eiwa rolled her eyes at their bickering, almost as if it was a regular occurrence by that point. "Bezaleel, what Leka meant was that since you are able to take on two attributes so easily, you must expect Rahel to have one that could be even more powerful. It wouldn't be surprising if he could control three attributes now."

The banter between Leka and Mikael continued to grow louder, dominating the conversation and bringing everyone else's attention to them.

"I didn't expect the Devas to be so...free around each other." Mafuyu picked his words carefully as he watched the two. "I thought there would be political tension or something."

"Well, it wasn't always like this," Eiwa replied. "The previous Devas weren't so cooperative. When Mikael became a Deva, he realized that Ashkaar would only suffer if the nations were always at each other's throats. He strengthened the relationship between Alayl and Jabilsa through trade and he made a peace treaty between all four nations. I supported that. It is because of that treaty that they are here for Alayl." Eiwa glanced at the lavender-eyed Deva. "He wasn't even born a Teiyyan. Unlike the rest of us, he worked hard and earned his position." Her eyes fell back on Mafuyu. "The three of them are good people, and exceptional Devas."

"You're not to be left out of that description, Lady Eiwa," Ismat gently added.

Eiwa parted her lips to reply, but stopped short when they heard a loud rumble.

There was a sudden vibration under them, like an earthquake rippling across the town that made everything in its path quiver. And then things went still once again.

It started with one woman's scream, but more terrified cries soon followed. Mirai and the Devas exchanged glances, then hastened to the arched window and peered out.

In the middle of Marim, dust the color of bricks had gathered. A couple of buildings on both sides of the street had collapsed. Mirai's eyes narrowed with anger as he caught sight of the figure standing amidst the rubble. Rahel.

In one hand, he held someone by the throat.

Rahel turned his head toward the high tower; his eyes almost immediately fell on Mirai and the Devas grouped together by the glassless window. His silver eyes gleamed. Mocking them, provoking them.

The man Rahel held thrashed around, desperately trying to free himself. In response, Rahel tightened his fingers around the man's throat. The innocent citizen grew limp in his death grip.

Mafuyu was the first one to react. He took a javelin from the wall, took an aim, and threw it. A normal person's throw wouldn't have gone more than a few feet ahead before plunging straight down to the ground below, but with Mafuyu's newfound Teiyyan strength, the javelin zipped through the air with the speed of a bullet and shot toward Rahel's wrist.

Rahel flung the unconscious man aside and drew his hand back just in time for the weapon to whiz past him and pierce the wall of a building.

Mafuyu straightened his spine. He had given Rahel a warning, but to him who held the power of the Scrolls in his hand, it was as harmless as a falling needle.

Rahel held their gazes as his lips moved and then there were eight shadows around him, shadows that turned into silhouettes and formed into people—into Teiyyans.

"Lady Ismat," Eiwa spoke. Calm and collected, Ismat stepped forward and uttered a Nahm under her breath. A green circle appeared underneath them and a translucent green light surrounded them. Ismat's Nahm had enveloped them until they could no longer see their surroundings.

When it faded, they were standing in the center of Marim, but there wasn't a trace of Rahel to be found. Mirai looked around. He knew Rahel didn't flee; he was too prideful for that. He had planned this to attract their attention and lure them out.

"I never thought you would come back, Bezaleel," a shadow Teiyyan taunted before disappearing with three of its comrades. Four enemy Teiyyans remained, having regained their corporeal forms.

"Is that Bezaleel?" one of the older citizens voiced nearby.

"I thought he died," a woman whispered in response.

"He's back? He has been gone for over thirteen years," another chipped in.

Their whispered chatter was interrupted when an explosion sounded from the other side of town. Distressed and pained cries punctuated the noise.

Eiwa turned to Leka. "Lord Leka, can you escort the people out of Marim?"

"Leave it to me, Lady Eiwa." He gave a quick bow before fiery red wings sprang out of his back and he rose into the air. "Follow me!"

The people rushed after him toward the gate, clearing the area in which the three enemies, the rest of the Devas and Mafuyu stood. As the citizens fled, another explosion sounded off in the distance, in the opposite direction, and was followed by another even further away.

Eiwa frowned, and in that moment there was nothing more intimidating than the storm that passed over her eyes. Her train of thought was clear; no one got out alive after messing with her nation, her town.

Mirai curled his fingers into a tight fist. This was definitely a trap. Rahel was creating havoc because he knew the Devas wouldn't stand by and let chaos ensue.

"I'll go after them," Ismat said as she watched smoke rising in the distance, dirtying the clear air with clouds of grey.

"Well, looks like I can't sit still either," Mikael responded, looking to where the third explosion had sounded.

"This is a trap. Rahel wants to divide you so he can take on each of you one by one," Mirai warned even though he knew that the Devas were aware and would go after the instigators anyway, no matter what he said.

"Do you doubt us, Bezaleel?" Ismat challenged.

"Not at all," Mirai was quick to reply, and he meant it entirely. He just understood Rahel's drive for vengeance all too well and knew that there were few lines he wouldn't cross to get it.

One of their enemies, watching all of this unfold, motioned to one of his men. "Kefir."

Eiwa and Mirai thought that Kefir would target the two of them, but instead he flexed his wings and flew off in Leka's direction.

Mirai was about to take flight and go after him when Eiwa grabbed his hand. "Bezaleel, Leka can handle himself. You and the boy go find Rahel. I'll take care of these three."

Mirai nodded. The two Devas went in opposite directions, while Mafuyu followed Mirai on another path.

The three Teiyyans surrounded Eiwa as she undid the cloak from her shoulders and flung it to the side. Four white wings jutted out of her back and her palms curled into tight fists. She stared the Teiyyans in the eyes like a wild beast ready to attack and tear apart its prey.

"Come." Her invitation was the beckoning call of death.

CHAPTER THIRTY-SIX

HUNTERS AND HUNTED

Nagisa walked along the line of Hunters, checking their weapons and making sure each and every one of them was present and accounted for. She stood before them, strong and disciplined like any general in front of her army should be.

Before she left for Iwami, she'd asked Zen to give her all the information he had acquired on the Third-Levels going haywire and where the next swarm could possibly spring up. Zen had refused at first, saying that she was still wounded and needed rest, but Nagisa was stubborn. She threatened to go whether he gave her the information or not.

Seeing no other point in arguing that, Zen succumbed to her demands. *"If you are going to go on your own, might as well do it the right way."*

Indeed, as Mirai had said before, the Third-Levels that went rogue were being controlled by Nahms, and Nahms had to be physically cast. Which meant it had been Rahel's doing all along.

Nagisa had decided to make her way to Iwami and the neighboring towns to see if there were any sudden surges in "strange activities" or something "supernatural," as normal people would likely call it out there. And to her surprise, there were none. That was strange in and of itself. Perhaps Rahel meant to misdirect them. Perhaps he was lying low until the perfect moment to strike presented itself. Whatever was going on, she knew it wasn't good.

The idea that someone was playing with the Hunters like toys and had them wrapped around their finger irked her.

After scouting around, she planned to return to Tokyo, but wanted to make a stop at the shrine where Mirai was first found. It seemed important, like something within her was pushing her to pay the place a visit. She didn't know why, nor did she expect to find anything there, but she was glad she made that choice.

She saw both Mirai and Mafuyu there, and before going back to Ashkaar, Mirai told her to gather as many Hunters as possible there because he was sure that Rahel would try to cause chaos in Yalim. First-Levels would undoubtedly show up and they would need all the help they could get. When she relayed the message to Zen, he sent three hundred Hunters to Iwami and stationed more in groups of five to ten in Tokyo and other areas where Rev'er activity was seen more often. No questions asked.

Nagisa stood before the hundreds of soldiers positioned in the forest near Mirai's town.

"I don't have any specific instructions for you right now." She held all their gazes as her voice rang loudly enough for all to hear. "But our task is simple. Don't let a single Rev'er leave this forest, and try your best not to die. Understand?"

"Yes, ma'am!" they shouted back in unison.

"Good."

As if on cue, a bright glow appeared in the midst of the forest. Nagisa turned around. The blue light appeared out of nowhere and radiated at a single spot, growing large enough for someone to step out of it.

An ominous feeling crept into the air, and Nagisa removed the gun from her hip holster.

There was a sudden gust of wind; the sound of the Hunters' clothes flapping added to its low whistle. Nagisa's hair danced wildly around her neck, but she didn't break her stance.

There was no doubt about it. This had to be the Veyil Mirai had talked about: the gateway to Ashkaar.

As the wind slashed and sped up around them, a figure stepped out from the gateway.

Nagisa knew right away that it was a First-Level. The portal closed and the light vanished; at the same time, the wind ceased. Standing in front of them, still a notable distance away, was Zephyr. His brown wings were spread wide, and his purple eyes shone maliciously in the dark.

In her job as a Hunter, Nagisa had seen a lot of ugly monsters and brutal deaths. Some still kept her awake for entire nights at a time. But none of that seemed as spine-chilling as the image of Zephyr standing there, his very being oozing endless bloodlust.

He took one slow step forward.

Hundreds of guns' safeties clicked off as the Hunters readied themselves.

Another step.

Nagisa could hear one of the Hunters mutter a frantic prayer in a shaky voice, asking God above for protection from death.

But Zephyr stopped.

"Why isn't he moving?" Azumi, who stood to the left and behind Nagisa, whispered.

Nagisa tore her eyes away from Zephyr and raked them all around her, observing the surrounding area and looking for any signs of an ambush. Perhaps this was a diversion, designed to make way for something bigger and more destructive.

But all Zephyr did was stand there.

It was strangely silent, like the stillness of the sea before a tsunami. And then Nagisa saw Zephyr mutter something. She couldn't hear it, but she had a few guesses as to what it was.

"Quick! Draw your arrows!" she shouted to the group of fifty archers behind her, and they moved in unison. There was a rhythmic sound of arrows being removed from their quivers and the stretch of the bowstrings as they were pulled and stretched, ready to release their projectiles at a moment's notice.

And as they waited for the captain's next command, the Hunters felt it. It started with the leaves on the trees wriggling wildly around them in the dark, followed by the tremor of a stampede on the ground. They heard the loud cracking of trees being uprooted. And then, a swarm of Third-Levels rushed out into the clearing toward them.

"Fire!" Nagisa commanded. Hundreds of arrows shot upward and rained down on the Third-Levels, banishing several dozen in an instant. But they weren't in the clear yet. "Fire!"

The Hunters drew their arrows again, faster than before. Another barrage of arrows flew out, banishing more Rev'ers than the first round did. When the remaining Third-Levels started closing the distance between them, the Hunters switched gears.

The first and second line of Hunters stepped back and the third and fourth line came forward in experienced synchronization. Arrows were switched for guns. Nagisa signaled for the third time and a rapid round of gunshots rang out in the woods, slowing down the Third-Levels with maximum capability.

In between the sound of gunshots, smoke, and banishing Rev'ers, Nagisa's eyes met Zephyr's. He had the audacity to shrug. The Hunters fighting back didn't bother him. He stretched his head from side to side, ridding his neck of its stiffness as he muttered to himself, "Time for the Hunters to become the hunted."

CHAPTER THIRTY-SEVEN

NAHMS

The townspeople followed Leka, flocking toward the gate of Marim in a desperate attempt to escape the impending death that awaited them at the hands of Rahel and his new Teiyyans.

"This way!" Dan stood at the tail end of the crowd, helping to the citizens out.

Thanks to the coup thirteen years ago, Rahel knew about the town's hidden exit through the tunnel, and the route had been sealed off. There was no way out other than the main gate.

Citizens poured out of it. Some shrieked and cried, more from fear than any physical pain or injury. Leka watched as the people flooded out of the gates like water being released from a dam's constraints.

"Lord Leka!" Dan called out. The Deva looked down at the soldier. Dan stood facing the opposite direction of the gates, his eyes fixed at some point off in the distance. Leka followed Dan's gaze and a deep frown of annoyance crossed his features. A Teiyyan with orange hair and beige wings was quickly making his way toward them. He whispered something to himself and then shot forward even faster.

"Soldier!" Leka hollered to Dan. "Get out! Now!"

Dan overcame his frozen body and nodded, returning to his previous occupation of getting the people out—this time, he hurried them along a bit more. The Teiyyan got closer to the people at the back of the crowd. A nasty grin spread across his face as he eyed them and extended his hand, swooping in on them like a hawk over a bunch of mice.

The people screamed as he got close, but a golden ripple suddenly formed between them and the Teiyyan. It was like transparent water had been lifted in the air from the ground before it took shape as an equally transparent golden dome, engulfing the whole city while forcing the people out in a blast of air. Some citizens were hurled onto the vast grassy plain, while some fell even further away.

Leka knew they would only suffer minor injuries that they would be thankful for later.

The Teiyyan wasn't so lucky, and banged against the inside of the dome walls. He kicked it and punched it, but it wouldn't let him out. It wouldn't break—not even a crack. All his attacks only resulted in ripples, one after the other, like he'd thrown pebbles into a lake.

"That's futile. You won't get out of here." Leka's melodic voice halted the Teiyyan's aggressive attempts at escaping his new prison.

He turned to face Leka and gritted his teeth in frustration. A moment later, he smirked. "That's very cheeky of you, Lord Leka," the Teiyyan said as they both hovered in midair. "You think you can fight me while maintaining such a large Nahm. This is too heavy a burden, even for a Deva."

Leka's expression remained unaffected. "We'll see if you are still breathing at the end of this fight."

The impatient Teiyyan didn't waste time exchanging any more words. He raced toward Leka so quickly that is was hard to keep track of him. But Leka extended his hand and made a fist. A circle of runes appeared before him. From within, tens of thin, sharp, blade-like threads shot forth at the Teiyyan in a speed that matched his.

Mikael looked up as the golden wave swished over the town. The sun's rays reflected on the dome, making it shimmer like gold. "Leka," he muttered under his breath as he flew over the rows of buildings. Leka often used this kind of dome to keep charges or his prisoners in, and he was the only one who would be able to undo the Nahm.

To trap himself and the Devas in the dome meant he ran into something or someone dangerous.

Mikael might have stared at the dome for a bit too long, because when he took his eyes away from it, the first thing he saw was a silver dagger whizzing toward his forehead.

In the span of a breath he closed in his wings and rotated in midair. The dagger caught the sleeve on his shoulder and nipped his skin before going past him. Sensing that it could be dangerous to stay in the air, Mikael dropped down and landed gracefully on the concrete below.

He spoke a Nahm and the ends of his fingers glowed in a lavender-white color. He brought it to his shoulder and touched the wound on his flesh. The blood that had been flowing from the cut stopped in an instant. The skin that had torn apart reattached itself, like threads coming together to create a flawless fabric. In a matter of seconds, Mikael's wound had closed completely. His skin was as good as new. Once he took his hand away, there was no sign of a gash, no evidence of a cut except for the tear in his sleeve and the tiny droplets of blood around it.

A Teiyyan with gradient pastel hair glided down to the ground and stood a good twenty feet away. "As expected of a Deva. Even at the last moment, you manage to evade attack," the Teiyyan said. "But it's dangerous to take your eyes off of your enemy, Lord Mikael."

"And who might you be?" Mikael's voice was low and calm, like the soft wind and still air before the start of a raging tornado.

"Azazel of the Raathri Clan."

"Well, Azazel, I don't see anyone that poses a threat here," Mikael replied. Although he had made it seem like he thought the Teiyyan could be defeated as easily as plucking a leaf, the Deva knew better. To fling a dagger at him without first being noticed meant Azazel had used a Nahm to mask both his and the weapon's presence.

Mikael needed to be cautious. From what he had heard, Raathris were already powerful enough without Nahms. There was no telling what they could do now that they could wield more power.

"That's not very nice." The Teiyyan's voice grew somber.

"I hope you are aware of what you are getting into."

"Oh, I'm aware." The Teiyyan pushed his sleeves up to his elbows. "Mikael the Healer. Deva of Jabilsa. No matter how hurt you are, you can heal your wounds in an instant." Mikael's lavender orbs followed the Teiyyan's every step as he started to circle the Deva. "In the end, I would be the one ending up wounded and defeated against a Deva with an attribute like yours."

And then he stopped.

Mikael's eyes widened. He lifted his arms to block the rapid kicks that came simultaneously from both sides, above, and even below. He jumped back to bring space between him and his four unexpected attackers. It was only then that he noticed it wasn't four different people. They were all the same.

Clones. Azazel had cloned himself.

"You look a little surprised, Lord Mikael," Azazel said as he stood far from Mikael's range of motion. "But this was the best plan of attack, don't you think? Instead of having four different people that you can easily defeat, my clones are tougher. I can keep cloning myself as many times as I want. You won't have a chance to heal yourself in this fight. Soon, you will run out of energy."

Mikael darted his eyes from the four clones to the Teiyyan who'd conjured them. The enemy had thought this through, and thoroughly planned who would attack who. They researched the attributes of the Devas and studied Nahms that would most effectively work against them.

Mikael's preferred fighting styles were close-range, where he could target vital parts of the body and hit them hard from the outside. They would burst on impact. One hit was all it took to subdue his enemies. But Azazel knew that and was keeping his distance so as not to get caught in Mikael's range.

This was direr than he had thought. Rahel seemed to be one step ahead of them. Like Bezaleel had warned them earlier, they had walked into a trap.

"Fine, you have my attention," Mikael said. He snapped the hem of his robe back and it bellowed behind him. "Bring it on."

Ismat stood with her arms folded over her chest. Long knives she'd summoned hovered over her head, pointed at her opponents. At her command, they flew through the air toward their targets. Three Teiyyans drew up circles to shield themselves and deflected her weapons.

"Come now, Lady Ismat," one of the Teiyyan taunted. Ismat felt something was awfully familiar about him, but couldn't put her finger on it. "You must think very little of us if you are using one of your weakest Nahms against us."

That was it. That was the reason he seemed so familiar to her. There were only a few people outside her clan that knew about the Nahms she used, and they were from smaller royal clans appointed directly under her as advisors and generals. She could count them all of on her fingers.

"Barna," Ismat said.

"At your service." Barna gave a bow that would have warranted applause if he were on a stage. Of course it was him. She couldn't recognize him at first because his appearance had changed once he became a Teiyyan. He had served as one of her generals before he betrayed her.

"So, now you're helping the Raathri clan wage war."

"Indeed."

"If I knew you would turn out like this I would have killed rather than banished you." Ismat's voice remained indifferent despite the disbelief she felt.

"Your mistake," Barna retaliated.

The female Teiyyan that had been standing on Barna's side disappeared, but Ismat had sensed her magical energy and where she would show up next. She appeared behind Ismat and swung a skull-splitting kick to the back of the Deva's head.

Or, she would have, had Ismat not tilted her head and, without turning around, grabbed the Teiyyan's ankle tightly. Her grip was strong as steel. The Teiyyan didn't have time to counter before Ismat pulled her down and smashed her to the ground.

The female Teiyyan fell with an impact strong enough to leave a crater in the concrete. Before she could stand up again, Ismat drew the sword at her hip. Gripping the hilt, she spoke a Nahm and swung her sword horizontally as if cutting the air. A wave of emerald green light rushed out at the female Teiyyan. When it grazed the ground, the concrete sprung up in spikes, impaling the female Teiyyan. It happened in a matter of seconds, so fast that the two remaining Teiyyans had only managed to release a breath.

Ismat sheathed her sword as Barna snarled. The Deva let a provokingly sly smile tug her lips and knew he'd hear her scoff at him.

Unable to keep his calm any longer, he rushed at her. The Teiyyan who stood next to him let out a warning, but Barna was beyond listening. He whispered a Nahm that imitated Ismat's moving daggers.

The lady Deva extended her hands and a shield appeared in front of her. Barna's daggers crashed against it with a dull *thwack*. But he didn't let that deter him. He rushed at her with a speed that rivaled her own and threw a punch that could have broken a boulder in half.

Ismat dodged it.

At that instant, the Teiyyan felt something wrap around his legs. He looked down to see a metal chain coil around his ankle like a snake wrapping around its prey, then glanced back up to meet Ismat's merciless eyes. She tightened her fist and motioned her hand upward; Barna rose with it.

Ismat swung her hand from side to side like she was holding a whip. Barna was thrown from left to right as if he was tied at the other end of it. He bashed against building sides and the unforgiving ground. She swung her hand and let him go. Barna crashed into another building and it collapsed into a heap of rubble. The last thing they heard was Barna's scream as the building tumbled down on top of him.

The remaining Teiyyan sighed dejectedly. "Barna was never good at keeping his cool. That must have been how he got found out by you, Lady Ismat."

"Who are you?"

"I am Ilir of the Raathri clan." He looked around at the spikes impaling the other Teiyyan and then back at the rubble that Barna was under. "I should have known it would take more than two Teiyyans to get rid of a Deva."

"Oh?" Ismat asked. She realized that he hadn't lifted a finger all this time. He must have been observing her attacks, learning more about how she moved so he'd stand a chance when his turn came. This fight was far from over.

"Looks like I'll have to kill you myself," Ilir concluded as he steadied his wings.

Magenta wings popped out of Ismat's back. They were as large as she was and swept the ground when she flexed them. "You can die trying," Ismat allowed.

Ilir rushed towards her and their blades met with a loud clash.

CHAPTER THIRTY-EIGHT

HUMANS VS. ZEPHYR

The Hunters fired bullet after bullet at the horde of Third-Levels, switching empty magazines for full ones as fast as they could. The clicks and bangs of gun mechanisms were deafening. Despite what the Hunters would have liked, the bullets weren't giving them any edge over their enemy.

While they were occupied in taking down the Rev'ers, Zephyr decided it was his time to attack and rushed into the fray.

The Hunters didn't waste time waiting to pull their triggers, but Zephyr avoided the bullets as if they were simply too slow to catch him. If they did reach him, they only managed to graze his clothes before he was out of their range again.

Nagisa clicked her tongue. If this kept up, none of them would be standing by the end of all this. Zephyr had kept more than half of her Hunters busy with attacks from Second- and Third-Levels. And he was using that division to his advantage. Guns weren't helping.

"Switch out your weapons!" Nagisa shouted. She stashed her guns in her hip holsters and pulled out a long saber from the sheath on her back. The rest of the Hunters followed her order, and the synchronized *shwing* of them removing their swords from their scabbards echoed around them.

Zephyr got closer...

The Hunters raised their swords and issued a battle cry as one.

...Closer.

The humans rushed forward and clashed with him like ants against a tidal wave. They swung their blades at him as he dodged, jumped, and blocked all of it with his bare hands. All the while, he kicked, punched and threw the Hunters on every side. It was like he had eight hands and ten feet, moving more quickly than they could even lift their weapons against.

Nagisa swung her sword at him, her strikes relentless against his formidable defenses.

"You are very brave," Zephyr said in between Nagisa's ferocious blows. "But your mistake was thinking a bunch of humans could take me down."

Nagisa ignored his discouraging ramble and brought her sword down on him again.

Zephyr ducked and moved in closer to her, just as she had predicted. Nagisa removed a second, shorter blade she kept hidden on her and slashed at him with it before he could see it coming.

Zephyr was caught off guard, but not nearly enough. The sharp end of her shorter sword clashed against his arm, but he remained unhurt. The skin on his arm had turned hard, imitating the toughness of stone—a mere sword couldn't cut it. He pushed her back and Nagisa reeled back.

This time it was Zephyr who attacked, swinging his rock-like fists at her. Nagisa ducked, jumped, and used her sword to try and stop his momentum. It was attack after attack, blow after blow. Nagisa was left only defending, barely even finding a chance to switch gear, let alone go on the offensive.

"Give up," Zephyr snarled as they clashed.

"Never," Nagisa shot back.

"Look around you," Zephyr scoffed as his arms pushed against her blade again. Nagisa's hands quivered with all the strength she had to muster to stop him from bashing in her face. "Your hubris is getting them massacred."

Nagisa knew that Zephyr was speaking the truth, but she tried not to hear it: the screams of the Hunters being killed. Their rushing footsteps. The sound of occasional gunfire. The swishes of blades swinging and slashing. It was the sound of war and chaos.

"Even so!" Nagisa said through gritted teeth. "We will die trying rather than surrender Yalim to you!"

"Then die." Zephyr easily pushed against Nagisa's blade with a strength that he had kept hidden. The blade inched toward her face, and even when she used both hands, her strength was no match against a First-Level. The blade jerked closer and closer to splitting her face in half while Zephyr smirked down at her. His pearly white canines peaked out from behind thin lips.

But the pressure was gone as soon as it came when he saw movement behind Nagisa. A girl jumped forward, her sword raised and coming at Zephyr's head quicker than a falling stone.

Zephyr drew one hand back in time to block the girl's attack. "Nice try," he grunted. He had thought that was all the opposition he'd meet until a third Hunter slashed at him from behind, ripping the skin across his shoulder wide open. Zephyr let out a loud growl and turned his head to see the man that had attacked him. Before he could strike again, Zephyr reeled back, keeping a safe distance from the three Hunters.

He straightened, reached around and touched the wound on his back. Red coated the tips of his index and middle finger. Zephyr's irises turned dark as his eyes darted from the blood on his fingers to Nagisa and her teammates.

The Hunter that had managed to wound him joined the other two. "Sorry! I didn't quite get his wings," Hiro panted.

"It's alright," Nagisa assured him, never once taking her eyes off their foe.

Zephyr frowned, his dark gaze still fixed on them. He flexed his brown wings as rage pulsed in his veins. He muttered a Nahm, and brown circles with runes formed all around him in the air.

The Hunters had managed to graze the tip of the iceberg.

CHAPTER THIRTY-NINE

THOUSAND PETALS

Eiwa jumped back in zigzag motions to avoid several dozens of sharp steel spikes raining down on her. She was getting attacked from all sides one after another. They were being thorough by making sure she had no chance to strike back.

The ground shook underneath her. She straightened her broad white wings, preparing to take flight and get away from whatever attack was coming next, but she was a second too late. Two halves of a giant metal sphere sprang up from the ground on both her sides, then clamped shut around her like a giant round cocoon, crushing Eiwa in it.

The male Teiyyan laughed. "Your attribute is useless against those sharp blades inside the sphere, Lady Eiwa. Although I doubt you are alive to hear me now."

The female Teiyyan next to him snorted. "I guess when over-powered by three Raathri, even a Deva doesn't stand a chance."

A noise like a stone being grinded interrupted their merriment.

"What's that noise, Eben?" one of the Teiyyans asked.

Eben looked all around him, trying to figure out where the faint sound was coming from. His sensitive ears traced it until his gaze fell to the sphere. "Impossible," he muttered just before beams of light shot out of it like there were cracks running all over its surface. Unable to contain the energy much longer, the sphere exploded into smithereens.

The Teiyyans shielded their eyes with their arms and turned their heads to avoid the gust of pebble-sized shards of metal flying their way.

"Overpowered?" Eiwa's voice was loud and clear over the sound of debris crashing to the ground. She extended one hand towards them. "You're a hundred years too early for that."

Another beam of light shot forth from the magic circle she summoned.

"Move!" Eben warned and pushed the female Teiyyan on her side and out of the way. The light licked the edge of her sleeve and disintegrated the material there. Eben gestured to the other two Teiyyans and they disappeared from view only to reappear before her a second later. They muttered Nahms and raised their hands to trap her in their spell.

"Know your place," Eiwa warned menacingly. The ends of her fingers glowed with a bright white light. She spun on her heel just as the two Teiyyans got close to her and evaded their attack. In return, struck them in their chests with her palms. A blinding beam of light burst out of their backs, and the whites of their eyes widened. They went still, coughed up dark mouthfuls of blood, and dropped to the ground.

Eiwa turned to Eben and said, "Next." It was an order with an underlying challenge for him to try and attack her with his best.

Eben stared at her without faltering or cowering. Seeing his two teammates dead didn't bother him. He rose from the ground and flew toward Eiwa. The Deva did the same and the Nahms they muttered along the way clashed together.

Eiwa shot at Eben with a wave of light, and it was then that Eben decided that he had dragged this out too long. He whispered a Nahm too low for Eiwa to hear. A black, shapeless mass appeared in front of him. Eiwa's light collided with it and got sucked into the darkness completely. Not a glimmer was left behind.

The Deva stood motionless as she watched her magic get snuffed out without doing even the slightest of damage.

"I can tell you're surprised, even if you're too proud to show it." Eben closed his palm into a fist and the black mass disappeared. "It's only natural I would need to take such measures when facing the strongest Deva Alayl has ever seen. Your use of light magic is versatile and powerful."

"I will give you credit for being able to control Varo's third Deva's attribute, Eben." Eiwa's voice held more amusement than unease.

"So you do remember me." Eben smirked. "It wasn't polite to act like you forgot."

"I wouldn't forget the faces of the Raathri clan that tried to kill my father." Eiwa flapped her white wings to keep herself in the air and looked down her nose at her opponent.

"Somehow that infuriates me even more."

Without dignifying that with a response, Eiwa used her light Nahms to attack Eben, only for them to get sucked into a black hole again, one after the other. She clicked her tongue, irritated. Gravity Nahms. They were the only ones that could make her attribute useless.

The Nahms Eben used could suck anything into it, just like a true black hole did. If it hit her, she would perish as well. He could separate her upper body from its lower half with just the touch of the Nahm.

It was the perfect attribute to defeat her.

Eiwa gestured with her hand like she was throwing something forward; a wave of light slashed at the air. Eben returned the same gesture and an equal wave of black clashed with hers, absorbing her light whole yet again.

And on it went: dark against light, Nahms thrown at each other as if in a frenzy. Their magic clashed, breaking buildings, absorbing objects into the black Nahm, and destroying anything in its wake.

Eiwa gritted her teeth. Eben was strong.

"Give it up, Eiwa," he sang as he flew close to her.

Her response was a Nahm that summoned an enormous white-blue circle with runes that appeared high above the city. It was as wide as the area they were in. There was nowhere to run or hide from whatever oncoming spell Eiwa was about to cast.

She made a motion with her hand as if pulling something down from above and a rain of needle-like bolts of light as sharp as shard of glass shot forth. They sliced anything and everything in their path—the hanging clothes of the townspeople, canopies, wooden crates, and even cement bricks—as they fell from the sky in the thousands.

Eben acted quickly, making circles of black masses around him. They absorbed the light shards that came his way and protected him from getting torn apart. "So, this is Lady Eiwa's strength. Truly terrifying. You can't escape this kind of attack. If I didn't have the black attribute, I would have ended up in pieces." Eben spoke with genuine respect in his tone before he mocked her. "But that attribute of yours is useless against someone who is more powerful than you."

He thought that was all she had up her sleeve, until he realized that Eiwa wasn't fazed in the slightest. This wasn't her last attack. This wasn't the Nahm that made her enemies retreat on the spot. It wasn't the Nahm that no one could escape from.

Eiwa clasped her hands together and whispered, "*Thousand petals.*" As soon as she spoke the Nahm, her rain of needles seized. She pulled her palms apart, and from in between them a thousand tiny lights burst forth, floating gently through the air like fireflies in the wind.

"What is this?" Eben was bewildered by the unusual petals of light floating around.

"Rise," Eiwa commanded. The sharp needles of light that had rained down earlier and pierced into the ground rose into the air all around Eben. Each of them widened just enough to reflect a sliver of the world around them.

"Mirrors?" Eben guessed.

Eiwa motioned with her hand and the thousand petals she had summoned suddenly shot forth at the speed of light. They bounced off the mirrors and aimed themselves right at Eben.

Eben brought his hands together to create the black mass and erase Eiwa's magic, but a petal whizzed at him before he had time to speak and slashed his wrist open. Eben grunted at the sudden stinging pain, but tried to conjure the Nahm again before several dozen light petals were slicing at him from all sides, rendering him unable to concentrate enough to counterattack. The light petals hit the mirrors and darted at Eben endlessly, marring his skin in every possible way.

"Eben," Eiwa called out over the sound of ripping flesh. "You said before that I would have trouble fighting someone who is more powerful than me." She watched as he struggled to escape her Nahm. "Well, I haven't met that someone yet."

The Deva's light petals were as hot as the sun and the reflection of the mirrors only intensified it. The Teiyyan grunted as the petals seared his broken and bleeding body.

Eiwa gestured at her magic and all the flower petals flowed together in a blinding flurry, enveloping him whole in its light.

"Burn," Eiwa whispered and the light intensified, burning bright as daylight. It bleached the surrounding area a spotless white.

Eben growled and then screamed under the onslaught. When he stopped, Eiwa waved her hand and the light faded.

Eben fell to the ground as his last breath wheezed past his lips.

She took one last look at his lifeless body and flew east to find Bezaleel.

CHAPTER FORTY

STRINGS OF SOUND

Leka drew up a circle to shield him, just in time for his enemy's fists to bang against it. The punch was strong enough for Leka to feel the ripple of his strength even behind the defense. Another circle of runes joined the first one, and dozens of fine nylon-like strings shot out, curving and bending their way to the target.

At Leka's command, the strings snaked around the Teiyyan's wrist quicker than the latter could avoid. The Deva motioned with his hand and the Teiyyan was jerked forward with a wild tug.

It was an attribute that Leka was known for: agile strings that could slither to any object undetected. They were almost invisible, light as a feather, and as sharp as Ismat's blades, allowing him to attack his enemies before they could even notice what was coming for them.

The Deva turned his palm upwards and the strings erupted into flames. The thin line of ferocious fire smoldered its way toward the still hovering Teiyyan. No blades could cut these strings. They were as unbreakable as Bezaleel's wings. This fight should have been over that instant.

Except he heard something that sounded an awful lot like strings being snapped in half.

The Teiyyan's fingernails turned into talons that sliced right through Leka's strings as easily as a knife passing through a block of melted butter.

But Leka regained his composure before the enemy could notice his discomposure.

The Teiyyan landed on the ground. Leka motioned with his fingers and the strings drew back as he glided down and his boots touched the mud.

"Just as I heard. Your strings are dangerous indeed, Lord Leka," the Teiyyan huffed. "They can hardly be seen in daylight and, worse still, you can make them change attributes." He placed his hands on his hips and his shoulders trembled as tremulous laughter bubbled out of him. "But you didn't think that I would be able to *cut* them." Suddenly, his laughter stopped and his eyes narrowed into a furious glare. "Did you?"

Leka made a face. He was more disturbed by the rapid change in the Teiyyan's mood than him being able to cut the strings. The Deva couldn't help but think his opponent was on the verge of insanity—if he wasn't in the thick of it already.

But with this exchange, Leka finally realized why the Endhra—no, why *the world* had always been wary of the Raathri clan. They were powerful enough to easily merge their energy with Nahms and embody them as if they were their own from the very beginning.

"What's your name?" Leka asked in a tone that was neither submissive nor threatening, hoping to distract his opponent and gain some more information in the process.

The Teiyyan gave an honorable bow, his arms stretching sideways to showcase sharp six-inch talons, and Leka got a peek at the runes inscribed on them. The runes could cut Leka's strings and undo his magic.

"I'm called Kefir."

"Why are you here, Kefir?"

Kefir snorted loudly, as if he couldn't believe Leka would ask that. "This is why!" He gestured to Leka and everything going on around them. "You Devas are unjust! The world needs undoing, and it starts with the ones ruling it: the hierarchy where the chosen Devas get to rule. The new era should carry the name of the Raathri clan."

"And so, you foolishly sought out this path."

"If you Devas were so 'righteous,' then this war would have never come to be."

"I cannot answer for Alayl."

"Yet you are here fighting for them."

"I fight for peace. If I turn a blind eye, tomorrow it will be my nation that you attack."

"Attack your nation?" Kefir shook his head. "We won't 'attack' your nation. We will tear it to pieces after I do the same with you today. And then we will rebuild this world the way it should be, without the Devas and your pathetic justifications."

Leka's fingers curled into tight fists of rage. If he were his younger self, he would have attacked Kefir without a second thought. But he was a Deva. He couldn't lose his head over a fool's provocation.

Rahel knew the Devas would come to Alayl's aid. And when they did, the Raathri planned to take them all out at once so they could conquer every nation afterward, without any remaining Devas to defend them. The Raathri clan would be too powerful for anyone to stand in its way.

So Leka didn't chide Kefir for his words. He extended his hand in front of him and dozens of threads shot forth quicker than one could blink.

Kefir was taken off guard when the strings wrapped around his wings and arms, and then bound themselves to his body. This time, instead of flames, it was bolts of lightning that whizzed across the strings. As the bolts jolted him, Kefir's wings turned as sharp as blades and cut right through the threads, loosening the strings and freeing himself.

Relying on the strength in his legs and, using his wings, Kefir shot right at Leka like a cannonball. He was moving at the speed of sound, and Leka failed to see him coming or react in time.

Kefir's long, sharp talons reached for Leka only to slam against the shield the Deva summoned at the last second. The edge of the shield cracked under Kefir's pressure, and Leka crinkled his eyes in concentration. It was going to be tough to fight against Kefir's speed. His strings weren't as quick. They were flexible and agile, but the exact opposite to Kefir's brute force.

Kefir whistled. "It's just as they say, one would rather run than fight you. Leka the Silent Deva: the only Deva who has found a way to activate Nahms without speaking their names."

Leka tried to grab and bind Kefir with his strings, but the Teiyyan kept dodging them. In return, Kefir's attacks were stopped with the Deva's strong shields that popped up everywhere.

He shot up at the Deva again, and Leka brought up another shield. But this time, the Teiyyan vanished.

The Deva realized it was misdirection when Kefir appeared behind him. He extended both his claws. Leka didn't have time to draw up a shield to defend himself; instead, he motioned at his strings and used them to practically catapult out of harm's way. Kefir's claws pierced the ground while Leka landed on top of a nearby building.

Kefir chased after him, landing on the other side of the same roof. The building quivered under his hard landing, and Leka frowned. Not only did he have to fight against a Teiyyan that was the worst match against his attribute, but he had to make sure the shield dome stayed intact to keep the townspeople out and safe.

He couldn't drag this fight on any longer.

Kefir lunged forward with extended claws towards Leka's chest. This time, Leka stood his ground. Instead of trying to evade his attacker, he twisted his body slightly, so that Kefir's talons caught on Leka's ribs and tore the fabric of his robes.

Leka winced, but took that chance to take hold of Kefir's arm and lock him in place. His strings snaked out again. Realizing that it had been a trap, Kefir used both his legs to push the Deva away before the strings could ensnare him. The force sent them both reeling to opposite sides again. Leka's strings only managed to graze the skin on his hip. Kefir looked at the shallow cut; a thin trail of blood dripped from the wound. But a tiny paper cut like that posed no danger.

"Some suicidal tendencies you have," Kefir said as his eyes, full of fury, shifted from the cut to the Deva. "If I had noticed your plan a little later I would have had my upper half chopped off."

He smirked as Leka touched the wound on his side. His fingers twitched as the pain passed through his thorax. Kefir's claws had dug deep into his flesh, his muscles had torn, and it hurt to even make the slightest movement with his arm.

The nicked part of his peach robe was stained with blood.

Kefir pointed at Leka's wound. "It's going to be tough for you to pull out those strings now huh?" He crouched like a panther about to leap. "Time to end your reign, Lord Leka."

Kefir rushed at him at a speed that Leka wouldn't be able to retaliate against with just one fully functional hand. The fate of this fight had been decided.

As Kefir raised his talons and bought them down toward Leka's face, the Deva stood still. But the claws stopped inches away from Leka's forehead: frozen, unable to move an inch more.

"What?" Kefir growled out between stiff lips. It wasn't just his hand; his whole body was paralyzed. Even his eyes wouldn't blink. His hands trembled as he tried to force them to move, but he couldn't. His eyes dropped to Leka's injured hand. He had runes on his fingers with strings, red strings, extended toward Kefir.

The Teiyyan followed the lines of the red strings and found them connected to his shallow wound. Kefir inhaled sharply through his bared teeth.

Leka moved his hand to the side and flung Kefir's body halfway across the space. His body was completely under the Deva's control. Leka parted his lips and vocalized a Nahm for the first time since they began the fight. "*Blood binding technique: strings of sound.*" As he said the words, a golden circle of runes appeared above his strings and flitted about like stardust, eventually disappearing into the air.

"You," Kefir snarled. "You let me attack you so you could draw my blood."

Leka's lips lifted in a ghost of a smile. "Correct."

"You did not have this Nahm!" Kefir yelled at the top of his lungs.

"I did. But no one knows about it. Do you know why?" Kefir pressed his lips together, but Leka didn't actually expect him to try and answer the question. "Because no one lives to tell the tale."

Despite knowing he was fully trapped, Kefir's insolence didn't let up. "So you can control me using my blood and paralyze me. And? Are you going to keep me here until your Deva friends come to your aid?"

"What makes you think I need their help?" Leka raised his other hand above the red strings and ran his fingers across them the same way one would strum a zither. A single, sharp note reverberated along the strings, a deep sound that was as elegant and ethereal as the Deva himself. Kefir trembled and dropped to his knees. He tried to bring both his hands up to cover his ears, but the binding wouldn't let him. His eyes turned bloodshot as Leka spoke in a voice that was as melodious as the note he played. "You were truly formidable for making me speak this Nahm. I only wish that you were on the right side."

Kefir's face twisted into an angry scowl. The sound of another strum had him trembling more violently this time, and his head hung low as he spat, "I hope...you...die!"

Leka sighed the same way one would in response to a stubborn child. He played the strings a few more times and the sound built into a strange, yet beautiful melody. It caused hundreds of strings to erupt out of the air and form around Kefir like a giant ball of yarn.

While playing his tune, Leka whispered, "Alight."

The ball caught fire, burning everything that was caught within it. He gave the blood strings one hard strum to make sure that Kefir passed quickly and without the pain he would have felt in the fire. He watched as the sphere burned, until it turned into a blob of melted black tar with bits falling to the ground.

Once the fire had stopped and the strings had faded on Leka's command with a final musical note, Kefir lay in plain sight; his body had turned grey like ash. Leka bowed, offering his respect to the dead, and flew to find his fellow Devas.

He didn't linger long enough to see Kefir wiggle about like he had been given a second life. He wasn't around to see a strange symbol form on Kefir's forehead, or how the Teiyyan stood up, still unconscious—as if he'd risen from death.

CHAPTER FORTY-ONE

HUNTERS VS. ZEPHYR

The ends of Nagisa's fingers turned white as she clutched the hilt of her sword tighter. Sweat dribbled down her back. She couldn't tell if it was from physical strain or the worry that was currently building up inside her as she realized that Zephyr hadn't been fighting them at full strength. He had underestimated them.

Now, when he realized that the Hunters were stronger than he gave them credit for, he was pissed.

Seeing Nagisa's temple crease and her eyes grow more focused than ever before, her teammates braced themselves. When the captain had that look on her face, it usually meant their situation wasn't a good one and she was concocting a plan.

"Azumi. Hiro," Nagisa said, speaking barely above a whisper. "You know what to do."

"Leave it to us, Captain," Hiro assured her.

Zephyr motioned with his wings and brown beams of light shot out from the circles of runes he had summoned.

"Watch out!" Nagisa warned and pushed Hiro out of the way. The thick brown rays came gushing toward her, but she swiped her sword against it and the spell was broken.

The runes on Nagisa's sword glowed lavender.

⟢❖⟢

Zephyr's eyes fell on the runes etched into Nagisa's blade. Those were Zalek runes. There was no way a human like her would know how to read them, much less possess their power. She wasn't a Teiyyan. Bezaleel couldn't have stolen it either, since the Raathri had no weapons like that when he left the clan.

Nagisa's mouth stretched into a feral grin. Zephyr clenched his jaws as irritation boiled up inside him. *This* woman. He didn't think she would be so difficult. A mere human giving him a hard time—ridiculous.

He aimed more of his magic at her, but she canceled all of it out with her blade. And then she was running at him, swinging her blade in all sorts of precise and practiced movements.

She was fast, strong, and quick to retaliate. Zephyr struck at her in turn, but she managed to dodge or avoid most of his advances. Some of his attacks caught her off guard, cutting her skin or knocking the wind out of her, but she always managed to stand up, each time with a more determined look on her face than she'd worn before.

This time, Zephyr spoke a different Nahm and a powerful wind ripped through the place, throwing Nagisa back and onto her side in the mud. She had to have twisted something, or perhaps even broken a bone with the force of that fall.

Enough was enough. He'd had it with this female and the rest of the Hunters. He lifted himself into the air and spoke another Nahm; the wind whipped and slashed down like a tornado, taking out half the hunters in one go.

"Let's see how you can fight in the air," he growled. More brown circles with runes appeared all around him, until he was surrounded by magic runes that made it look as if he was summoning hell itself.

The runes turned brighter and brighter. Now, he saw the woman frown as worry flashed in her eyes. Zephyr grinned and opened his mouth to speak a Nahm that would end it all.

Except the only sound that escaped him was a short gasp as pain pierced through his lower abdomen. He shakily gazed down to see a tiny hole had opened in his middle. He couldn't tell what had caused it, but the pain he felt was immense enough to render him motionless.

He felt two more hits, like something heavy had been plunged into his chest and then his wings. Blood started pouring out of the wounds and he quickly lost his strength, flopping to the ground in a twisted heap.

Nagisa turned her head and looked to the top of the trees. Silver glinted in the dark shadows of the branches and within the black silhouettes of thick leaves. She signaled and the Hunters positioned there signaled back.

They were the Rev'er Hunter Corps' best snipers. They could hit targets from over two thousand meters away. But she needed Zephyr to remain still before they could take their shot, and Nagisa's guesses had been right.

Zephyr took to the skies once he found the Hunters difficult to handle on land. There was no way they could fight a First-Level in the sky. But the snipers could...*if* they remained unseen for long enough.

She stalked over to Zephyr. Blood was starting to pool under him. "You...won't...win this," he wheezed.

"Yes, we will." Nagisa's voice was as unforgiving as her stare. "We won't let you take over our world."

Zephyr's fingers twitched. He said nothing further, but the captain felt something was off. Something unusual weighed on the atmosphere, and the wind was blowing in the opposite direction than it had been before. She turned her head to the side, taking in the darkness of the forest with her piercing gaze. She felt a bad omen stirring in her gut.

She took a couple of steps in the direction the wind blew in from. She stared into the darkness until shadows began to take shape, forming strange, smoky silhouettes. And then, there were the eyes glowing red in the night. Dozens of them. Hundreds of them. Thousands of them.

"Oh no," she muttered.

"What?" Azumi asked beside her.

Nagisa hurried back to Zephyr without answering the girl. Her eyes examined him closely until she found that his hand had moved. Her eyes inspected the mud and saw runes scribbled into it by his side. Nagisa frantically scrambled over and dragged her feet through the markings, jumbling the mud and erasing the runes. Her head snapped back to peer into the shadows. The eyes were still there.

"What are they?" another Hunter whispered.

"Second-Levels," Nagisa said. "This is not good." She turned to Zephyr, whose life was leaving him by the second. "You summoned them."

"A Forbidden Nahm. Gathering souls...of the dead. You...can't... kill them. You are...finished."

Zephyr wheezed. Every breath was painful. His legs and arms were starting to feel numb. His lungs were failing him and he could feel his heartbeat slowing...and slowing. He closed his eyes and the image of Rahel after the failed coup flashed behind his lids.

"I'm sorry I failed you." Rahel apologized again. He'd broken out the remaining handful of the Raathri members from Endhra's prison.

"It's not your fault, Rahel," one of them said.

"It was Bezaleel. He was the reason we failed."

"We will find a way to take back what we lost, and I will bring you Bezaleel's head," Rahel promised them.

"Then lead the way, my lord." Zephyr bowed to his leader.

Zephyr grunted in pain as he forced himself to turn onto his back and opened his eyes one last time to look at the sky. It was sprinkled with stars.

Rahel had given him another Nahm the day before they prepared for the attack on Yalim to use on the Hunters if they gave him any trouble. He'd placed so much trust in him, and Zephyr was determined to prove that it was not in vain.

"I will not fail you...Rahel," he muttered without a soul to hear as he took his last breath.

Nagisa heard Zephyr mutter something before he went still. She looked back at the silhouettes that were starting to look very much like an army. This was it—a situation where they might not come back alive. The kind of situation she feared most.

The other Hunters gathered behind her. Nagisa gave Hiro a look of uncertainty, an apologetic look that she hoped convey how sorry she was for not ensuring their survival.

Hiro returned it with a smile, understanding her inner turmoil and silently telling her that it was alright, that he was honored to fight beside her. He raised his sword and yelled, "Till death!"

The other Hunters reflected his action, erupting with howls of equal intensity.

Nagisa clutched her sword with both hands as she saw the shadows move toward them like demons emerging from hell, scurrying between the dark trees like animals.

Her calm breathing quickened; her heartbeat sounded like drums in her ears. And even though the Hunters showed bravery, she knew they were feeling the same way as her, perhaps even worse. For the first time in her life, Nagisa felt uncontrollable fear ripping through her entire being as she stared death in the face.

CHAPTER FORTY-TWO

BLADE OF ENLIL

Ismat kicked Ilir square in the stomach and sent him flying backwards. He fell into the side of the building and the concrete collapsed around him. That kind of impact would normally have killed him—if not break him in two—but Ilir was a Teiyyan, stronger than Barna, and perhaps even stronger than Ismat.

A large, heavy piece of brick hurtled toward Ismat's face. That trajectory was too accurate to be just flying debris, but she avoided it by tilting her head to the side.

Ilir walked out of the rubble, dusting off his clothes and hands. The only visible damage was a few scratch marks on his face. "You're really violent, Lady Ismat. I expected more composure from the person known as the youngest Deva in history," he remarked as he stepped over the rubble. "How old were you when you became the Deva of Seylon? Sixteen? Ten years ago, right? And you only become a Deva once you prove you are powerful enough to handle the responsibility."

Ismat dropped lower in the sky to get a proper view of Ilir standing amidst the chaos. She didn't give a damn about his chitchat. He was hiding a bigger trick up his sleeve. This was too easy for him to be using the full extent of his abilities.

"I think I've warmed up enough to take on someone that strong." Ilir lifted his hands, palms facing upward. "Time to give you a rest, Lady Ismat." He released a cloud of purplish smoke in her direction; it traveled as fast as a rushing waterfall, yet remained silent as the wind.

A pungent scent filled the air before the smoke got near her. Ismat quickly covered her nose with the crook of her elbow and flew higher into the clouds.

This was trouble.

She knew what that Nahm was. It was Jabilsa's seventh Deva's attribute. That smoke was poisonous. She couldn't cut through something like that.

Ismat muttered a Nahm and a green circle of magic formed above Ilir and his poison. Several dozen long, sharp needles rained down but didn't even get within an inch of him before melting in the acid. Just as she thought they would.

Ilir gestured toward her and the smoke obediently rushed at the Deva. Ismat flew away from the substance, trying to put as much distance between her and the poison as she could. She looked back to see the smoke had gotten close enough to lick at the hem of her robe and it disintegrated the fabric.

Not good. If she didn't escape that soon, she would melt into a puddle of flesh.

She whispered a Nahm, and a portal opened up in front of her. Ismat passed through, and it closed before the smoke could follow.

The portal opened above the tallest building of Marim, and Ismat found herself tumbling toward the roof. Her boots screeched as her wings stretched sideways to regain her balance. She slid across the concrete before coming to a full stop. She straightened up, walked to the opposite edge, and peered below.

The ground was covered in purple smoke, and it was rising by the minute. It crept into each and every corner, leaving no space. If there was any living creature in there, it would have, no doubt, been reduced to bones.

Ismat couldn't drag this out further. The fumes were dangerous, too. The more she breathed it in, the greater the danger.

This attribute was a problem for Ismat in more ways than one. Her attribute was weapons, portals and metal. Smoke was something neither weapons nor metal had any effect on. And to make matters worse, Ilir hid his presence in the smoke completely. She couldn't see or feel where he was. And if she couldn't find him, she couldn't attack him. It had been a while since she faced someone this difficult. She didn't know where to aim her weapons or where to open a portal to suck him out of his hiding place. And she couldn't dive completely into the fray unless she wanted to burn herself alive.

And then it hit her. Ismat let a smirk stretch her lips. She always loved a good brawl, and wouldn't expect any less from one of the Raathri clan.

But this...

She shook her head, as if already disagreeing with herself. At this rate, it would only be a matter of time before the entire town was filled with the poison and the Devas drowned in it. Only Mikael would be immune to it, and she doubted he could get to all of them to heal them in time. She had to put a stop to this before it got any worse.

She spoke a Nahm and summoned a bow and arrows. She aimed in one direction and released the bowstring. When the arrows whizzed off, she gestured with her fingers so that they'd curve in different directions, leaving trails of green in their wake.

To her left, far away, a sudden cloud of purple smoke burst up.

"Found you." There was only one way to take down Ilir, and that was to travel through the smoke and get near enough to run a blade through him. But it would probably cost Ismat her life, and that was one thing she very much wanted to hold onto, if at all possible.

She muttered another Nahm and a metal suit of armor appeared above her robes. A dark black mask covered her face from the bridge of her nose down. That would be enough to at least keep the acid from burning her too much, and the fumes from getting into her lungs. She stretched her right hand to her side and commanded, "Come, Blade of Enlil!"

Green runes appeared before her palm, whirring around in circles until they stood still and the hilt of a blade emerged from within them. Ismat grabbed the hilt and pulled out a giant sword that was half as long as she was tall. The surface of the blade was wide and flat, and looked as if it was made to deflect objects. She rested it vertically on the ground with a sharp *tang*, its weight making cracks appear on the surface of the roof.

She eyed Ilir's smoke and steeled herself to jump into the hands of death. She closed her eyes, took a deep breath, and flew toward the smoke with the Blade of Enlil in her hand.

It was like diving into an ocean of purple. The closer she got, purple warped and obscured her vision, filling it with smoke and the pungent smell of acid.

When she neared the thicker part of the smoke, she swung her sword using both hands and the smoke recoiled like it had been fanned by a gust of air.

Ismat felt a smile tug at her lips and swung again. The smoke parted, giving her space to inch further ahead.

She kept repeating this action until she was deep within the thickest part of the cloud and she could make out the silhouette of Ilir. But her armor was bearing the brunt of her mission. Though made of indestructible metal, parts from her leg, the small of her back, and upper right arm had started to burn and melt. Feeling the hot acid creeping into her clothes where the armor was melting off completely, she opened her portal and teleported out into the sky above to take a breath of pure air and reattach her armor before diving back down into the purple sea.

Ilir wasn't expecting it when Ismat met him in the thickest part of the poison cloud, the part others could barely stand, let alone have enough endurance to attack him. But Ismat swung her sword around, pushing the smoke aside and giving her a clearer view of Ilir.

The Teiyyan was taken aback. "You're mad," he claimed before thickening the fog and sending a blast of it right to Ismat.

The Deva brought her sword in front of her. It acted as a shield and pushed the smoke to the sides. But the smoke was a Nahm, and, like any controlled magic, it stayed the course and curved around, then came rushing at her again, trying to swallow her whole. The arms of Ismat's armor melted, and the sleeves of her robes burned until what was left began charring her skin. The Deva tried not to wince or show any hint of pain.

"You can't fight me, Ismat!" Ilir yelled in hysteric delight. "You're just getting yourself killed!"

Ismat's mask crunched as her lips moved into a grin underneath it. Before the skin and flesh of her hands could burn off her bones, Ismat extended her hand and whispered a Nahm. A green circle appeared beneath Ilir's feet, and soon he was thrust up into the air, high above the mist of poison. Ismat rose to the sky with him.

Ilir used his wings to regain control of his body and somersaulted to a stop. As he did, a javelin pierced him right in the chest. A wall of black and green rose up from the ground and pinned him. As soon as his back made contact with the wall, iron bars sprang up from it, securing his wrists, legs, waist and neck. Green runes glowed on the rods and Ilir felt his energy drain rapidly.

He croaked, and the purple smoke disappeared like fog clearing in sunlight. When not even the faintest of puffs was left, Ismat pulled down her mask. "Quit struggling. It's useless. My iron binds lock your attribute. You can't cast a Nahm now."

Ilir laughed as if it was he who had won. "Splendidly done, Ismat. Even poison couldn't stop the Iron Deva. But you breathed in all that smoke. Your death is imminent. You might have captured me, but your lungs are now filled with poison and you only have minutes before you die."

He was right. She did her best not to show it, but her lungs burned like fire. She was actively suppressing the cough that tried to erupt from her throat. She could taste the blood that was threatening to pool in her mouth, and sweat was breaking out on her neck.

"Well, that makes two of us." Ismat's canines showed as she gave him a smirk. She curled her hands into fists, and the iron binds tightened around Ilir's neck, immediately killing him.

That was the last straw. She fell to her knees as that racking cough burst out of her. Blood dripped from her lips. She wiped her mouth and her palm came back coated in red. Her lungs were already failing.

With all the energy she had left, Ismat flew to find Mikael. He was the only one who could take out the poison and save her.

Unbeknownst to her, Ilir's body wriggled the same way Kefir's had when he died. The same symbol appeared on his forehead, and the iron binds broke. He landed on his feet.

TRAP

The buildings passed by in a blur as Mafuyu and Mirai raced across town. Mirai covered the sky while Mafuyu matched his progress on land, running through alleyways, jumping over short walls, and tearing through shortcuts to where Mirai believed he saw Rahel.

Something strange was going on. Mirai didn't know what it was, but he knew that Rahel had found a way to mess with his vision. One moment he could see Rahel's energy, and the next it would disappear and turn back up in a completely different area.

Mirai stopped and landed on the cobblestones underfoot. Endlessly chasing him around like this wasn't going to get them anywhere.

Mafuyu ran up to him. "What's wrong?"

"I lost him."

Mafuyu looked into Mirai's eyes, checking his irises to see if something had gone awry with them. But nothing seemed amiss. His eyes looked normal, with gradient hues of gold, red and orange.

Mafuyu had felt something was off, too, but he'd waved it off as his nerves acting up. But now that Mirai had confirmed his suspicion, he realized he had been right all along. "I don't think you lost him," Mafuyu said.

"What do you mean?"

"I've been feeling a little off, too." Mafuyu gazed around the buildings, taking in every crack and crevice that marred them. "We've been here before."

"What are you talking about?"

Mafuyu pointed to a basket of apples by the side of a building. One had fallen off the top and lay on the ground. "We've passed this about three times now."

Mirai would have said it was impossible, that they hadn't been running in circles. For one, they didn't take any unknown path or race through a maze that continually landed them on square one. Sure, he hadn't seen Marim for thirteen years, but that didn't mean the geography had changed. He had flown over this city countless times, knew every nook and cranny of it.

It must have been something else.

"It's a trap," Mirai said as he looked around him. "If what you say is right, then Rahel has cast a Nahm to trap us in—probably one of illusion—and another one to mess with my vision. That's why his energy signature keeps bouncing all over the place."

"How do we get out of it?"

"He must have set the Nahm in an area where it would be activated as soon as we passed it by. We just need to cancel it out." When Mafuyu didn't take his eyes off Mirai, he asked, "What?"

"Can't you?" Mafuyu asked nonchalantly.

Mirai looked at him as if the boy had lost half his brain; he wondered how Mafuyu could be smart one minute and totally stupid the next. There was no middle ground with this boy. "I don't know that many Nahms. I'm not a Deva."

Mafuyu tapped his lips. His eyes wandered all around to the skies, the space between the clouds and the land. "You said that he might have activated a trap when we walked by, right?"

"Yes?" Mirai answered more in doubt than assurance at whatever idea was forming in Mafuyu's head.

"So that means the Nahm could be surrounding us right now. Either on the ground," he pointed down and up, "or in the sky." Mafuyu unsheathed one of his blades from its scabbard. He flipped it in his palms as if offering up a quick prayer for success. He looked at Mirai, his eyebrow cocked.

Mirai nodded, giving his permission.
Mafuyu threw the blade toward the clouds.

CHAPTER FORTY-FOUR

DISPERSE

From being born without any sort of powers, to turning into a Teiyyan and using the Forbidden Scroll to then become a Deva was a first in his clan. One might think that Mikael would be the weakest of all the Devas, but Rahel was not that ignorant. He knew what Mikael of the medicinal clan was capable of. After all, Mikael had to prove to the former Deva, his clan, and to the people of his nation that he was worthy enough for that title through wits, bouts and battles.

And the Teiyyan who currently fought against Mikael was also aware of who he was up against.

So it didn't come as a surprise when the Deva held his ground and beat up the enemy's clones, reducing them to smoke left and right as soon as they appeared. His strength was not surprising—just how strong he was remained a mystery.

Mikael was a Deva in times of peace, so he hadn't shown the world what he could do. His attribute was something only his clan members knew, and they would rather die than betray their Deva.

"Getting tired, Lord Mikael?" his enemy questioned.

The five clones met their ends as Mikael hit each of them square in the chest, right where their hearts were beating. He was quick as lightning, and his movements were easy and fluid, yet packed with a power that could smash bones into dust and break veins.

Mikael wrung his hands as if flicking water from his palms. "What does it look like?" he teased as he stood up straight. His demeanor remained as fresh and tireless since they began this fight. But the truth was that Mikael was indeed starting to feel the tiniest bit of strain. He already had a few scars on him though his enemy had not even broken a sweat. The frustration was slowly starting to creep into him when he realized that he hadn't even begun to close the distance between him and Azazel.

It didn't help when Azazel's clones would spring up with heavy weapons that could slice the Deva into all sorts of ugly pieces if he wasn't careful. It was like his enemy had an unlimited reservoir of clones and energy.

Mikael internally cursed. It was no wonder that the previous Devas of the Endhra clan feared the Raathri. With Nahms, they were powerful enough to go head to head with Devas, and all that after only a few years of learning how to handle those Nahms, compared to Devas that were born with powers and trained since the moment they could walk.

"It seems to me, Lord Mikael, that you are the weakest of the Devas," Azazel taunted. "It isn't surprising, since you weren't born a Teiyyan. You must have gone through a lot of trouble to prove that you were worthy." Mikael's silence only tempted him to keep needling him. "Does it take a toll on you to churn out magical energy that isn't even yours?"

Six more clones appeared and attacked Mikael. The Deva ducked, kicked and hit vital parts of the clones until they disappeared as quickly as they had come.

A remark like that would have gotten under any Deva's skin. Any person would be shaken by its truth, but as Mikael destroyed all the clones that kept springing up, his expression was the complete opposite of disdain. It was calm and tranquil. A smile even dared to lift the corner of his lips.

Azazel narrowed his eyes at the Deva's unshaken appearance.

A muffled clap of thunder echoed from the skies. Azazel looked up to see the blue sky had gotten dark. The white clouds were grey and heavy, ready to burst. Another clap of thunder followed, this one louder than the last.

The Teiyyan scrunched up his eyebrows. There weren't any rain clouds mere moments before. There wasn't a chance of rain in the atmosphere.

As if on cue, a water droplet trickled onto his face, followed by a few more drops. Then it turned into a shower that drenched everything in its path and soaked up the dry ground and settled the dust around them.

Azazel sniffed. There wasn't even any scent of rain in the atmosphere. This wasn't natural. He looked back at Mikael, who was still fending off the clones. That's when he saw it.

The Deva's lips moved as he muttered a Nahm.

A flash lit up the sky, followed by loud, bellowing thunder and then several streaks of lightning streaked to the earth, zapping all of the clones once and making them disappear in the span of a breath.

There was a perfect stillness after that lightning strike, even though rain kept falling from the skies. It was as if time had ceased.

He looked at Mikael. In the dull, grey atmosphere, the Deva was a striking color of lavender and dark blue. His eyes were like blooming wisteria petals.

Before Azazel could blink, the Deva disappeared right before his eyes. Azazel had no time to conjure up his clones when Mikael appeared behind him as quietly as a single raindrop.

Azazel's eyes widened as he realized that the Deva was using the raindrops to move around. He hadn't been overwhelmed by the clones—far from it. He was just waiting to summon the clouds and unleash the rain at the right moment.

"Weak, you say?" Mikael's voice wasn't like the thunder that bellowed above them. It was more like the raindrops pelting the asphalt. "You couldn't be further off the mark." Azazel sucked in a sharp breath as Mikael laid a hand on the Raathri's shoulder. He whispered the Nahm, "*Disperse.*"

Azazel's organs seized without giving him a moment to even tremble. Cracks formed on his skin as every cell within his body died. The color of his skin grew grey, and he turned into dust.

For the Deva who wasn't born a Teiyyan, all it took was a touch of his fingertips to end it all.

Mikael sighed and looked up at the sky. With all the clones he had to fight against, it took more time than usual to concentrate and activate the rain Nahm.

Mikael hated to be violent. He lived for peace. Yet, his attribute was anything but. He looked at his palms and clenched his fists. It couldn't be helped. For a Deva of the famed medicinal clan, this attribute was only fitting. He looked up at the sky. Once he activated the rain Nahm, there was no stopping it. Nature is impossible to stop, after all.

"Mikael," a familiar voice called out to him. Mikael turned around as Eiwa landed in front of him, soaked from the sudden downpour. Her white clothes stuck to her like a second skin and Mikael knew the layers of inner robes she was wearing had to be hard to move around in. It was the opposite of Mikael's situation, whose thin shirt simply molded around and shifted with his toned muscles. "I knew this rain was your doing. Went a little far didn't you? I bet all of Alayl is pouring." Even though her words sounded like she was berating him, her tone held no bite. There was even some laughter in her voice.

"Apologies, my lady. I was a little irked." He gave a small bow "I suppose I did go a—"

Mikael's words were cut off when a body dropped between them from above. It was Ismat.

She fell on her stomach, her trembling hands barely keeping her up. She tried to sit up, but only managed to get into a crouching position on her hands and knees, wheezing. A racking cough burst out of her throat, sending blood dripping from her mouth and down her chin.

"Ismat!" Eiwa bent down to lift her up, looping her arm around her shoulders from behind to support her.

Ismat grabbed Mikael's arm. "Poison," she gasped out. "Jabilsa's... Deva's attribute."

"Say no more," Mikael interrupted, signaling that she didn't have to suffer more by speaking; he understood what she meant. He placed his palm on her abdomen and spoke a Nahm. The tips of his fingers lit up with a smoky lavender color that seeped into Ismat's skin. "It hasn't gotten into your vital systems yet." He looked her in the eye and gave a comforting smile. "That's some strength you have there, Lady Ismat, to withstand the seventh Deva's poison like that. I'm impressed."

"Of course," Ismat replied back. Her hacking coughs lessened as Mikael's magic mended her and she found it easier to breathe again. "I, too, am a Deva after all."

"Undoubtedly," Leka chirped as he lowered himself to the ground and joined the other three.

"Lord Leka, I'm glad you could join us." Mikael then pointed out, "You're wounded."

"Yes, a little tiff with one called Kefir. Fret not, I'm alright." Leka tried to brush it off despite the ghastly wound he was sporting.

But Mikael was having none of it. "Always putting up a tough front." He grabbed the Deva by the arm and yanked him closer. Leka let himself be pulled along and crouched beside Ismat despite his initial protest. Mikael used his free hand to heal Leka's wound as he did for Ismat.

By now, Ismat's color was coming back and her burgundy irises were livelier.

Leka watched as the wound on his side closed, muscles and skin reattaching and flesh forming quickly over the bloody mess. He couldn't take his eyes off the magic that Mikael had created. "This never ceases to amaze me."

"Why, thank you."

"That wasn't a compliment."

"It certainly sounded like one. You don't have to be shy, Lord Leka," Mikael teased.

"If it wasn't for your peace treaty, I would have strangled you by now." Although it might have sounded like a threat from anyone else, the emptiness in Leka's voice and the gentleness in his eyes said that it was anything but.

"Well, if it wasn't for my peace treaty, you would have certainly found a way to strengthen the relationship between Varos and Seylon by marrying Lady Ismat."

Leka's face erupted into a shade of red that was as dark as his cloak. "You *what*?" he sputtered like a teenager trying to hide how he felt about a girl he liked.

Mikael laughed and Eiwa thought that this time Ismat wouldn't hold back from jabbing Mikael in the stomach. But the expression on her face was far from anger. In fact, she chuckled and Leka's face turned even redder.

"But, back to a more serious matter." Mikael's playful look vanished and his eyes took on all the seriousness of a Deva as he said, "Right now, we cannot afford weaknesses. If you're injured, I'll do whatever it takes to heal you. We don't know what we will be facing ag—" His words halted when his eyes refocused behind the three of them.

"What is it?" Leka questioned. When Mikael failed to respond, the three Devas turned their heads to see what he was looking at.

"What in all of Ashkaar…?" Leka's breathy voice held all the shock and disbelief that the other Devas felt.

"I thought I killed him." Eiwa's voice was just above a whisper.

"So, did I," Ismat said as she made an effort to stand up. Her trembling had stopped and she was back on strong and steady legs. The Devas stood next to each other and stared at the Teiyyans they thought they had defeated.

They walked towards them, slowly and steadily. Their skin was a dead ashen color and their eyes had gone completely red, without an inch of white. They dragged their feet as if their bodies were forcing the movements.

"The Revival Nahm," Eiwa whispered as she kept her eyes fixed on the Teiyyans. "To think Rahel has gone as far as to learn them."

"You bet I have," a deep voice said behind them.

The four Devas whipped around and found Rahel standing in midair. His grey wings were almost camouflaged against the dark gloomy sky. His silver eyes glinted with a sadistic satisfaction as he watched the world around him crumble.

"Rahel," Eiwa hissed

"Don't let your focus wander, Lady Eiwa," Rahel challenged.

Azazel, who had become dust only moments ago, was back together in one piece. He'd become feral and lunged at Eiwa.

"Watch out!" Ismat pushed her out of the way and turned her back to Azazel. She flexed her wings and they hardened, standing on end like spikes. The sharp ends went right through his chest. But the Teiyyan didn't die. He pushed himself off from the wings, and blood slid down from his open wound.

He snarled and hurled himself at them again. The rest of the Teiyyans followed suit as if they'd gone mad, engaging the Devas once more in battle—one that would be almost impossible for the Devas to win.

"Damn it," Eiwa cursed. Revival magic meant that the Teiyyans couldn't be killed or restrained. They would become as fast and strong as the person who cast it. And to be able to cast such a Nahm took a ton of energy. Only a Deva or someone powerful enough could do it. In this case...Rahel.

The Revival Nahm was created by the fifth Deva of Jabilsa, but it was deemed too dangerous and all were forbidden from casting it. It hadn't been used even once in Ashkaar's history, yet Rahel had tapped into it and even managed to make it work on multiple subjects at once.

The Devas clashed with the Teiyyans again. Each time they attacked, it was more ferocious than the last. Nahms were spoken over Nahms, and circles with runes appeared and disappeared in the air as magic clashed against magic. The Devas found themselves being pushed back.

"That's right. Keep them occupied," Rahel whispered. He murmured a Nahm and black smoke rolled up in his palms. It grew in size, enough to cover all the Devas. It was a Nahm that could destroy the Devas and turn them into nothing but dust—he just needed to release it at the right moment.

Even Leka's shields wouldn't be able to stop it. It was a powerful Nahm, the real reason the Forbidden Scroll was hidden away. It couldn't be stopped, and nothing could fight against it. It was a Nahm that could end all Nahms and render magic useless.

Rahel raised his hand and aimed the Nahm at the Devas and the Teiyyans. "Time to end the era of the Devas."

Black thick mist crawled toward them. The Devas only had time to widen their eyes as they saw it pick up speed and hurtle their way like the strong currents of a river.

Rahel smirked in triumph.

A black blur swooped in, faster than Rahel's Nahm, and landed between the Devas and the oncoming mist. A pair of black wings spread out like a wall, and the black mist disappeared as soon as it hit the feathers—as if Rahel's Nahm had never existed.

Rahel's eyes grew impossibly darker from anger and irritation.

Eiwa let a grin of relief tug at her lips.

"About time, Bezaleel," Mikael remarked.

"Apologies," Bezaleel replied. "I lost my way."

He turned toward Rahel, drew his dual swords from his scabbards, and charged at him.

CHAPTER FORTY-FIVE

MIRAI VS. RAHEL

The sounds of sword meeting sword rang across the rooftop. Mirai and Rahel exchanged blows that sent waves of wind gusting all around them.

It was a fight between two strong enemies that wouldn't go down easily. Each new strike was more aggressive than the last. They were too fast to see, too fast to follow. They moved around in ways that were equivalent to those seen in a fight between two Devas.

Rahel threw a sword at Mirai that split itself into three and sailed toward him. Mirai closed his wings and rotated around the oncoming weapons before shooting forward toward Rahel. When Mirai was close enough, Rahel threw a punch and Mirai reflected it. Their fists struck each other's faces and threw them in opposite directions.

Mirai crashed into the middle of a building, leaving a large hole behind.

Rahel was thrown toward a roof, but managed to stop the momentum and regain his balance by kicking off the edge. He somersaulted to the edge of the roof.

Mirai pushed away the rubble that had fallen on his legs. He picked up the swords that had fallen by his side. As he scrambled to his feet, Eben and Kefir sprang up to his level on the collapsed building and lunged at him before he even realized they were attacking him.

Mirai barely had the time to defend himself, but it didn't matter. Several nylon-like strings shot up and wrapped themselves around the Teiyyans's legs and wings, then yanked them down. "You stay here with me!" Leka growled from below as he pulled them in.

Mirai's eyes followed the action for a moment before turning to Rahel again. He let out a low growl of irritation.

Rahel's control over the Nahms was strong. It was to be expected, since he had been cultivating that control for thirteen years while Mirai only learned them just hours before. Still, it was no less frustrating.

Rahel muttered a Nahm and conjured up a copy of Ismat's daggers, shooting them toward his enemy. Mirai used both his swords to deflect the weapons but a third and fourth one that he didn't see came hurtling at him. Again. Rahel was masking his vision again.

At the last moment, he was able to see the daggers shooting directly at his eyes.

He could have done a number of things in that moment. He could have used his wings, his swords, or if nothing else, he could have just moved out of the way. But he found himself unable to do any of those as the weapons honed in on his irises.

He wasn't frozen from fear or shock. No, it was something else: the work of a Nahm, a binding that rendered him paralyzed on the spot. His whole body was still as a stone. He couldn't even twitch his fingers.

Mirai stood in horror as the sharp tips of the daggers closed in on his eyes. Without his eyes, he couldn't win this battle.

He thought it was over until both weapons were knocked to the side by a sai sword. Only unbelievably accurate aim and impeccably good timing could have pulled off such a feat.

Rahel raised his eyebrow as another weapon appeared at his side, as if from thin air. He didn't have a chance to process what had happened before Mafuyu flickered into view by the blade, clutched it in his fist, and aimed a kick at Rahel's head.

Rahel blocked it in time, but the force sent him flying to the ground from the edge of the building he was standing on. The concrete cracked upon impact, shooting dust and stone into the air.

Freed from Rahel's Nahm, Mirai could move himself again.

In a flash, Mafuyu appeared next to where the sai had deflected the daggers and picked his weapon up from the ground. "You okay?" The boy walked toward him.

"A little late, aren't you?" Mirai retorted.

"Hey! After my sword broke that wall of illusion or whatever, you just took off! I had to run all the way here!"

"Sorry."

"Yeah, you better be. Now, you'll think twice about leaving on your own like that," he huffed.

A violent cracking, like bricks being blown apart, jolted them. The floor beneath them shook and then caved in.

"Shit!" Mafuyu cursed. The air in his lungs was forced out of him when he fell from the side of the high tower. Then he covered his face with the crook of his elbows to avoid getting bashed in the mug with falling bricks and rubble.

He tried to scream, but his body had gone into shock. He could hear the wind howl past his ears as gravity forced him down, down. He was falling to his death and there was nothing he could do to stop it.

And then something snatched him out of the air. A pair of arms wrapped around his lower back and behind his knees, holding him securely. He wasn't falling anymore. He was flying.

"You okay?" Mirai's voice broke the deafening silence ringing in Mafuyu's ears.

"Yeah," he said as soon as he found his voice.

Mirai snorted. "We're even now."

He glided them gently to the ground and released Mafuyu as soon as their feet touched the cobblestones.

"How pathetic." Rahel walked out of the smoky dust that had

gathered up around him. "To think the fearless and invincible Bezaleel would seek help from the likes of you."

Mirai opened his mouth to speak, but was cut off when Mafuyu stepped out in front him and pointed his sword at Rahel. "I don't give a damn about what you think and I *will* help Bezaleel. Why don't you try to take us down? If you can, that is."

At Mafuyu's provocation, Rahel grimaced. Nothing seemed more vicious at that moment than the downward tug of his lips. "As you wish." Rahel let loose a surge of hideous black smoke their way—just like the substance that burned Mirai's wings into a charred nothing. A sizzling sound emitted from it, and the cobblestones it touched were charred.

Mirai pushed Mafuyu out of the way. A golden colored circle the size of the two of them put together appeared in midair. Rahel's Nahm crashed against Mirai's shield of runes. It momentarily halted, but didn't stop. The edges of his golden circle cracked when the shield was unable to withstand the pressure of Rahel's black Nahm.

With Mirai's other hand, he pointed toward Mafuyu's legs and whispered a Nahm. An orange rune tattooed itself around Mafuyu's legs, sticking above his pants like a set of rings and glowing brightly like the tail of a firefly. "What's this?"

"Nahm to break your fall. Come on."

Mirai's shield broke and Mafuyu didn't have time for further questions. He grabbed him again and flew up as the black mist flowed around their feet.

As they neared Rahel, he let go off the boy.

Mirai figured that casting the black Nahm took a lot of concentration; Rahel needed to gather a tremendous amount of magical energy before he could use it, which is why he couldn't deploy it as often as he could the other Nahms. That meant that there was a time gap before he could send another wave of it their way. That delay was where their best chances at attacking him lay.

Mafuyu dropped and fell on top of Rahel.

Rahel leaped away from him. Mirai rushed towards his enemy and the three of them engaged in a power battle.

Mafuyu matched their pace by throwing his weapons into the air and appearing where they were set to fall. The runes on Mafuyu's legs helped him move around faster, jump higher, kick harder and with better accuracy. And even after dropping from about thirty feet, he could land perfectly fine on the balls of his feet, ready to dive back into the fray.

They fought toe-to-toe, but even two weren't enough against Rahel's strength.

Rahel blocked both of their attacks with speed that Mafuyu never would have thought any living creature capable of. And then there were the heart-stopping blows that he delivered, slingshotting them to the other side of the town, into the ground to create more craters and enormous cracks in the town's landscape, and toward already broken and jagged buildings.

But they would get up, time and time again. Except, after another kick to the gut sent Mafuyu flying again, and he felt his stomach tighten as if it were about to explode. For a few minutes, he couldn't move a muscle.

Rahel summoned a sword and swung it at Mirai, who used both his swords and all of the strength in his arms to block Rahel's attack. They pushed against each other's blades, and the swords quivered; neither was willing to give in.

"Come on, Bezaleel!" Rahel snarled, trying to get his blade closer to Mirai's flesh only for the other man to push back with equal strength. "I know you can use those Nahms. Do it! You stole them once, just as I did. You have the blood of the Raathri in you and you can never get rid of it no matter how much you want to!"

An axe came flying towards Rahel's legs from the ground. He

pulled back from Mirai to avoid getting halved by it, and the weapon whizzed past him. A mere inch of space was all that prevented his face getting sliced by it. It flew up and boomeranged back into Mafuyu's hand. The boy smirked as he caught it.

Rahel stared at him for a few long seconds. His fingers twitched, ready to cast another Nahm at the boy, when Mirai's voice distracted him.

"Enough of this, Rahel." As soon as Rahel's eyes slowly and grudgingly trailed away from his target, Mirai continued, "A war is not the answer. This will only make the nation hate the Raathri clan more than they ever have."

Mirai might not have always agreed with the Raathri clan's philosophies, but he never wanted the bloodline to fade away as if it never existed. He was still part of the clan. If he had a choice, he would never have betrayed or killed them. If he knew what was going through their heads thirteen years ago, he would have tried to change their minds instead of letting them act on Marvak and Rahel's hatred.

"More than they have?" Rahel's voice was condescending. "The Raathri clan was served unjustly, and you led them to their deaths, Bezaleel. I will not rest until I take over all of Ashkaar and Yalim. Everything you tried to protect will be gone. The Raathri clan will rule the Jihan. Endhra doesn't have the right to rule. The Devas are nothing but a joke."

"Bloodshed will only result in *more* bloodshed."

"Personally?" Rahel's hand made a motion as if he was throwing something away. "I don't care." His face turned from a scowl to delight as he added, "Say, Bezaleel. Do you remember the feeling of finding the dead bodies of your foster parents? When you helplessly watched your friend bleed to death?"

Those words snuffed out what was left of Mirai's tolerance. His patience broke like a twig, and he let out a snarl unlike himself as he rushed at the enemy.

Rahel sneered and conjured a portal.

"No!" Mirai reached out to grab him, but Rahel had slipped into the portal before Mirai could lay a finger on him. The portal closed with a note of finality.

Mirai glanced down at Mafuyu. It was exactly what he feared. His nightmares, his past— it was happening all over again.

When Mafuyu caught his breath again, he pushed himself up. The fight was far from over, and he couldn't waste a single moment. He had assured Mirai that he wasn't afraid, that he wouldn't die, and that he was brave enough to stand beside him and fight Rahel even though he was unbelievably strong. And yet, he couldn't help the cold sweat breaking out on the back of his neck.

He tried not to shiver at the sight of Rahel stepping out of the silver, swirling portal he'd conjured just a few feet away.

Mafuyu's legs glowed with the runes that Mirai had cast on him earlier. Rahel's eyes flitted to them before trailing back to his face.

"Say, do you know how Bezaleel's family was killed?" Rahel didn't wait for an answer. "I bet you do. You are here, so he must think highly enough of you." Mafuyu gripped his weapons tighter. "Looks like Bezaleel will lose someone important to him...again."

With that, Rahel lunged at him. Mafuyu whispered a Nahm that changed his weapon from an axe to a sword and lobbed it at him.

The Teiyyan leaped out of the way. He would have thought that was all Mafuyu had up his sleeve, until the boy's wrist glowed green with runes circled around it. He clenched his hand into a fist and made a pulling motion.

The weapon came hurtling back to Rahel. If he hadn't seen what Mafuyu had done, he would have been done for. But he knew those runes; he had the knowledge of the Scroll.

He turned around in time to see the blade whizzing back at his face and used his own sword to knock it off course. Mafuyu's sword spiraled off and pierced the floor several feet away

Rahel spun around, spoke a Nahm and waved his black mist at Mafuyu. The Hunter vanished, avoiding the toxic cloud, and appeared next to his sword.

"Rahel!" Mafuyu called out. Rahel turned around to face him. "I'm not like those people you ordered to kill in Yalim. I'm a Hunter. I take down monsters like you."

Rahel looked up just in time to see Mirai plummeting toward him, his double blades pointed straight for Rahel's head.

Rahel pressed his lips together. At the speed Mirai was diving in, it would be impossible to stop him. Rahel muttered a Nahm as Mirai got close, then waved his hand. There was a small ripple in the air, like a gentle wave in a river. It passed through Mirai like the caress of a wind and pushed him back—not enough to send him flying, but enough to delay his attack, giving Rahel time to counter.

Despite the temporary setback, Mirai pressed forward and landed where Rahel had stood, but his enemy had already teleported himself away. If he hadn't, he would have been crushed under Mirai in that landing.

And then Mirai felt it: the same quiver rippling through his weapons. His double swords, the extensions of his own arms, vibrated just before the blades broke into a thousand pieces.

CHAPTER FORTY-SIX

DAYBREAK

The Devas tilted their heads when they heard the sound of blades splintering.

Eiwa whipped around. "Bezaleel!" She extended her hand and a beam of light blazed towards Rahel.

Rahel muttered and then stomped his foot. A silver circle appeared on the ground around him and walls of light shot upward. Eiwa's magic hit the shield and vanished.

"Don't worry, Eiwa." Rahel locked eyes with the Deva, each glaring at the other. "Your turn will come after I'm finished with him."

Eiwa had no time to react before Ilir shot his poisonous smoke her way, but it was doused just as quickly with Mikael's torrent of rain.

The cursed Teiyyans attacked without strategy or consciousness. Trying to tear apart whoever it was in their way.

Kefir clawed at Mikael, and seeing the Deva in trouble, Leka used his strings to hurl Eben into Kefir. The Teiyyans crashed into each other, tumbling and rolling across the broken cobblestone ground. When they lay in tangled heaps on the floor, Ismat used her Nahms. Iron cuffs popped out of the upturned ground and gripped their bodies tightly, securing them to the broken stones and mud.

"This isn't going to keep them for long," Ismat said as she lowered her hand.

Leka raced to Mikael's side as the latter healed the side of his face, where three scratch marks had made a ghastly tear in his skin.

And like his Nahms before, the flesh reattached itself so that there was not even the lightest hint of a scar left behind.

"Are you alright?" Leka asked Mikael as the peach-haired Deva scanned his face.

Mikael nodded. "Thanks for that." His attention turned to Azazel and Ilir growling on the sidelines. "Bezaleel better finish this quickly or we are all in deep trouble. If we fail here, Rahel will target each of our nations next. And then he will attack Yalim. That world will not survive."

"Let's hope he can finish this before that happens," Eiwa replied.

"Let's hope we can stay alive until then," Ismat murmured.

A low growl and then a snarl snapped the Devas out of their short conversation. Eben was trying to break out of his chains.

"Ugh. How many times must we kill them?" Leka's forehead creased in annoyance.

"Getting tired, are you?" Ismat sidled up next to him.

"Barely."

"Quickly! We must hold them down," Eiwa ordered as she rushed towards Azazel. The other Devas were on her heels, and Eiwa shot a backward glance at Bezaleel. While others hoped that he could put an end to all this, Eiwa *knew* he could.

Mirai calculated in his mind. A Deva could use up to two main attributes, not counting the smaller Nahms they could summon.

Eiwa had said that the Raathri clan was capable enough to use up to three. So far, Rahel could use dark magic and Ismat's teleportation and weapons attributes. That had to be the end of his reserve. His three attributes were out in the open, and now Mirai knew what Nahms to use to fight against him.

He tossed his broken swords to the side. Between the both of them, Mirai was stronger in swordsmanship and hand-to-hand combat, but Rahel was more skilled in casting Nahms. He'd had years to work on it, while Mirai didn't. Rahel knew this and had planned to defeat him by forcing Bezaleel to fight with Nahms.

Mirai was left without a choice. "Mafuyu—"

"You got it," Mafuyu replied before Mirai even needed to explain. The boy was strong, stronger than he had given him credit for. Mirai just hoped he could hold out till the end.

"What's the matter? Running out of energy?" Rahel provoked.

"Enough." Bezaleel spoke a Nahm and motioned at a boulder that had broken apart earlier. It rose into the air and flung itself at Rahel.

Rahel threw a punch that smashed the boulder into smithereens before muttering a Nahm in return. A barrage of daggers zeroed in on Mirai and Mafuyu, but Mirai retaliated with a different Nahm and put both of his arms forward. A wave of runes appeared like the ocean crashing on land. It reached the daggers, and the weapons disappeared completely. Rahel's smug expression slipped as he watched his Nahm disappear. "What did you do?"

Mirai allowed himself a rare smirk. "I canceled out your spell."

"That's impossible. There were no Nahms that could cancel out the other."

"You're right. Not in the Scroll."

Realization crossed Rahel's eyes. "You came back to the Devas for this."

"Wrong. There's no way I would know that there were spells outside of the Forbidden Scroll if that were the case."

"Then how?"

Mirai shrugged in a way that was less like Bezaleel and more like Mirai. "I was just hoping they had a counterattack against you."

"Nonsense!" Rahel growled before opening up a portal. He disappeared into the blackness only to reappear right behind Mirai.

Mirai whipped around and brought his arms up in the shape of an X to block a kick from Rahel. The force sent him reeling in the other direction. Mirai cursed. The muscles on his forearms stung from Rahel's kick, like he had been whipped ten times with a flesh-tearing lash.

That kick could have broken his skull if he hadn't blocked and moved back in time.

Rahel had used more strength than he had during his earlier advances. And to top it off, he was using a Nahm to hide himself from Bezaleel's eyes. He couldn't tell where Rahel would pop up next, and that was a problem.

Mirai whispered a Nahm and flashes of blinding light blinked all over the place. Rahel, who was suspended in midair, grunted and was forced to shut his eyes. Mirai took that opportunity to fly at him and land a hit, but Rahel was more formidable than he had ever been.

A battle of Nahms ensued. Waves of strong magic appeared and crashed down everywhere. From light to dark, from blades to shields, attacks and parries were thrown at each other only to clash against one another at every turn. Mirai's Nahm of canceling magic did quite a number on an irate Rahel, forcing him to use more power. But, that was a problem for Mirai. Taking so much magic energy to keep Nahms coming was a first for him, and he found his body aching from the abuse. His fingertips were starting to feel numb and his arms were throbbing as the exhaustion began to set in. Weakness crept into each of his limbs as his body started to give in.

In that moment, Mirai realized that Rahel had been holding back all this time. Perhaps it was for the thrill of it, or to taunt him and prove just how powerless he was compared to a Raathri that trained with Nahms for years. But perhaps it was his way of testing the waters to see just how much Mirai was capable of, how much he was hiding.

Rahel rotated and landed a kick, followed by a series of black bullet-like drops. Mirai used his wings to block them, but a few grazed his leg and outer thighs. Blood seeped into his clothes almost immediately.

He turned around and let loose a wave of light magic against Rahel.

Rahel let out his own dark magic to counter and extinguish Mirai's.

Using his faithful wings, Mirai tried to cover himself, but the force of the magic sent him crashing into the ground. He fell on the jagged concrete floor and let out a painful groan as his back smacked against the unforgiving surface. His rib cracked on impact, and he could taste blood at the back of his throat.

With Mirai down, Rahel raised his hands above his head and spoke a Nahm. A giant, silver magical circle appeared under the sky, overshadowing the entire town.

Mirai didn't recognize the runes, but he knew that this was bad. Whatever was going to come from this particular spell would be their undoing.

Rahel sneered at Mafuyu just as the daggers made from his dark magic started to rain down on them. He had combined attributes of both dark magic and Ismat's weapon magic: a feat that even the Devas found hard to pull off.

Mafuyu tilted his head and looked up just as thousands of black, long blades fell from the sky. Mirai was by his side in a flash. He rose up five feet into the air, turned to face Mafuyu, and stretched his wings to shield the boy. He reached his hand out at the same time and roared out a Nahm. A golden circle of rune appeared over the two of them and above the Devas that were fighting the cursed Teiyyans.

Mirai could feel the tremors of Rahel's attribute as it hit his runes and disappeared, but some still managed to slip through. The Nahms were as powerful as the caster, and Rahel's was powerful.

The noise of concrete breaking and large pieces of debris falling drowned out all other sounds. As several dozen blades sliced through Mirai's runes, they also tried to pierce his formidable wings; they failed.

If Mikael hadn't made Mirai's wings strong enough to withstand any Nahms, then he and Mafuyu would have already been dead.

⬥

Leka raised his hand, almost mimicking the movement Rahel had made moments earlier. "Ismat!" he yelled. Ismat responded by opening her portals where the other Devas stood and transporting all of them, as well as herself, next to Leka. Golden circles with runes appeared all around them.

"Will this work?" Eiwa asked.

"We will have to try," Leka responded.

As the black smoky daggers neared the shield, the Devas gritted their teeth, tightened their fingers, and tensed their bodies. They knew Leka's shield wouldn't hold against the dark attribute.

The daggers inched closer, but suddenly, another set of runes appeared and shone above Leka's shield, glowing bright and whirring in circles around them. The dark weapons were erased as they met the magical barrier.

The Devas released a collective breath of relief. Leka whispered shakily, "Bezaleel."

"Wonderful, now we owe that jester." Anyone listening to Ismat would have misunderstood her words as being irritable, but the flat tone of her voice and the lopsided grin that stretched her lips said otherwise.

Mikael looked around them. "Rahel is hitting his own men," he remarked as he saw the revived Teiyyans getting impaled and pinned to the ground by their leader's own magic. Even then, they didn't perish. They were wiggling around like earthworms trying to escape the needle that held them to the mud.

"That's not it," Eiwa said as soon as she realized that something was off. "He is aiming for Bezaleel and that boy." She turned to Leka. "Drop this shield."

Leka furrowed his eyebrows and a frown pulled at his lips. "I cannot. It will put all of us in danger." His voice was stern as he wordlessly berated Eiwa for jumping into a decision that could harm all of them.

Eiwa tightened her fists and gritted her teeth. She knew it was unbecoming of a Deva to act without concern of her fellows, but she couldn't watch Bezaleel and the human meet their demise. Bezaleel would not have enough magical energy after using such a heavy Nahm to protect them all.

The tremors quieted down. The sounds of structures cracking and breaking all around them faded. Mirai's eyes darted around, raking across the space for signs of life. Within the blue and white world of his eyes, where he could see everything around him, he couldn't spot Rahel's energy.

"What's wrong?" Mafuyu asked as he regained his footing.

"I don't see him," Mirai whispered.

Without needing to explain, Mafuyu understood what he meant. It wasn't that he *didn't* see him. It was more that he *couldn't*. "You can't detect him at all?"

"No, he's using some kind of Nahm to—aagh!"

The sharp blade of a sword pierced through Mirai's shoulder and all the way through to his front. Mafuyu stood there, eyes wide and stunned into silence. Beads of red slowly dripped down from the sword and onto his cheek.

Drip. Drip.

The silver tip of the blade that jutted out from Mirai's shoulder was coated with blood.

"After using up all that magic energy, it would be impossible for you to cast another Nahm now, wouldn't it?" Rahel's voice echoed from behind Mirai.

With trembling hands, Mirai gripped the edge of the blade to keep Rahel from moving away. His head tilted to look toward his enemy and Mirai's gaze turned dark.

"You!" Mafuyu snarled. He signaled with his hand and his weapon flew at Rahel's head.

Rahel tilted his face and caught the weapon with his left hand. "That wasn't very wise."

Mafuyu signaled again and the weapon forced Rahel to lean forward. Mirai used the opportunity to reach behind Rahel and grab him so Mafuyu could drive that blade through him.

But Rahel jumped back, letting go off the sword he used to pierce Mirai in the process. "How very sneaky of you, Bezaleel."

Mirai tried to stay up, but his wings quivered and he fell; Mafuyu caught him before he could hit the ground. "What did you do to him?" The boy's voice was low, yet filled with more rage than he had ever felt in his nineteen years of life.

Rahel sighed dramatically and rolled his eyes at the pair. "You see, if there is one thing I've figured out about Bezaleel, it's the weakness in his wings." A knife appeared in Rahel's hand and he flipped it around in his palm for effect. He disappeared and popped back up an inch behind Mafuyu like a blinking light. "The part where his wings meet the skin on his back is his weakest spot." He lightly traced the fabric on Mafuyu's back with the tip of his blade and stopped just below his shoulder.

Mafuyu whipped around as Rahel disappeared and reappeared a short distance away from them. "You were always making sure no one ever snuck up behind you," Rahel addressed Mirai, who was clutching his shoulder with an expression of pain and anger while trying to stand up. "At first I couldn't understand why you were so afraid of that. You had your eyes to see everything around you, after all. But I remembered an incident when we were children. We were sparring; I had gotten behind you, yet your reaction was as if I had almost killed you. When I thought back on it I realized it was because your wings weren't so indestructible. They had a weak spot that you always tried to protect. If I hurt you there, you feel pain that is ten times worse than anywhere else on your body. You would find it hard to stand, let alone fight. Right, Bezaleel?"

Rahel laughed—a wicked chuckle that echoed around the stillness following the mayhem that he created. A line of blood trailed from Mirai's lips to his chin.

"Well, you'll find it even more difficult now since I poisoned that sword." Rahel spoke a Nahm and conjured black smoke that crept toward Mirai.

Mafuyu scowled and then bared his teeth like an angry wolf at the enemy that tried to harm its pack. In a way, that was exactly what Rahel had done, and the boy wasn't about to let him get away with it.

Mafuyu rushed forward, forming a plan of attack against Rahel as he went. The enemy turned as the boy ran toward him, intent on avenging Bezaleel.

But when Mafuyu got close, Rahel flew into the air. He threw his weapons at Rahel, who dodged them as easily as if someone had flung a pillow at him.

Quick as blinking, Mafuyu appeared next to the sword and attacked Rahel from behind, who still managed to block it with his hand. Mafuyu didn't have wings to fight in the air like Mirai did, but he used what he had to achieve the next best thing. By throwing them all around Rahel, then appearing at just the right second to try and do some damage to the Teiyyan, Mafuyu used unpredictable, almost reckless advances to make it that much harder for Rahel to predict what he'd do next.

This time, however, Rahel caught the weapon and Mafuyu appeared, clutching it. He swung his other blade, only for Rahel to grab Mafuyu by the wrist and stop him before he could make contact. Mafuyu used his legs to kick Rahel in the stomach and push them away from one another.

While Rahel gained his balance in the air, Mafuyu fell to the ground. Normally, that would have been the end of his life, but the runes on his legs helped him to land smoothly, rather than crash into the broken bricks and debris.

"Weak," Rahel muttered as he appeared next to him and grabbed him by the neck. The boy choked and clutched at Rahel's arm with both hands, clawing at his flesh to try and get him to release his iron grip. But Rahel's fingers clamped down like steel links, and Mafuyu's face grew bluer by the second. "Why did you even think you stood a chance when Bezaleel didn't?"

He tossed Mafuyu like a ball high into the clouds. The air rushed out of his lungs as he was flung up and then suddenly started dropping down again. Rahel appeared above him and went to punch him right in the face, but Mafuyu tilted his head to the side and Rahel's fist swiped through the air.

He grabbed Rahel's wrist and locked him in place by circling his legs around his waist, dragging him down with him. Rahel stretched his wings in response, catching the wind to break the fall.

"You're becoming a nuisance." Rahel snarled.

"Thank you. It's one of my strong suits," Mafuyu croaked before dropping his sword to the ground. Then both of them vanished from the sky like a flicker of candlelight.

The next thing Rahel felt was the impact of his back hitting the hard hilt of a sword. All that left him was a gasp of pain as his spine cracked with a sickening *crunch*.

In the very last second of their fall, Mafuyu had flipped his position so he would be safe while Rahel absorbed the impact all by himself. It was risky, to say the least, and if he'd been even half a second too late then he would have lost both the battle and his life.

"You think I was just trying to take on you by myself? You're wrong," Mafuyu said as the weapon beneath Rahel disappeared and Mafuyu pinned him to the ground. "I am just the distraction."

Rahel tried to throw him off, but he couldn't move his hands. "What?" he muttered as he whipped his head to the side to see his hands and legs had been restrained with chains.

His gaze fell on Mirai crouched a few feet away. His finger touched the broken ground and he was muttering a Nahm. Mirai should not have had enough energy for another Nahm after the last one, but somehow he had one last drop of strength to give.

Circles with runes shone under Rahel, and more chains sprang from the ground and locked him down even tighter. Rahel tried to release his black mist, but he was unable to do so. These chains with Nahms that he hasn't seen before was preventing it.

He whipped his head back around to Mirai as the latter raised his hand and spoke the next Nahm that would end it all. This Nahm wasn't in the Forbidden Scroll, or any of the scrolls in all of Ashkaar. This was a Nahm that only the Devas knew and passed down from generation to generation.

This was a Nahm that would undo all others.

"*Daybreak*," Mirai whispered and slammed both his palms on the ground.

A single wave of golden, green, lavender and blue light rippled through the air, carrying a sound like the chiming of bells as it went.

CHAPTER FORTY-SEVEN

CONDITION

Rahel widened his eyes in shock and tried to break himself out of the chains when he saw the wave of runes rippling across the space toward him. Several ropes of yellow light sprung from the ground, pinning him even tighter than before.

And then he felt the force of the spell like someone was forcing his head underwater, but it faded away as soon as it had arrived. Rahel tried to speak a Nahm to free himself from the chains, but nothing came to his mind. Not even one. He couldn't remember any of the Nahms he had used before or what he had seen in the Forbidden Scroll. He turned to Bezaleel with bloodshot eyes. "What have you done?"

Bezaleel stood up on trembling legs, pain still evident on his face as poison crept under his skin. "I erased your knowledge of the Nahms and the attributes you gained." He shook his head slowly. "And you'll never get it back, Rahel."

He turned his head toward the boy who had pinned him to the ground. He was affected as well. The runes on his hands and legs had disappeared. Golden ropes had snaked around his limbs, too. Rahel bared his teeth. Everything he had worked for had been taken away because of that mongrel!

He let out an angry snarl and tried to wriggle his way out from under the chains. But he couldn't. He was tightly bound. Everything—his clan, his father, all of it—was gone.

Mirai felt it: the knowledge of the Nahms disappearing from his memory. The Nahms he had used to lift the Veyil, to hide the power of his eyes, to keep himself looking human: all of it. Everything he knew was vanishing, and he felt his back loosen as the seal to hide his wings vanished. He recalled Eiwa's words from before, back at the summit, when she told him what he'd need to know to defeat Rahel.

"Only you can do this, Bezaleel. This Nahm takes away all knowledge and attributes of those who know and cast it. Everyone who stands on the ground when Daybreak is activated will be affected, including the caster."

"I understand," Bezaleel had replied. "The Devas can't cast it because you will lose the knowledge of the Nahms and the powers you gained with it. That can't happen. I'll do it."

Bezaleel knew he was the only one capable of pulling off a massive spell like this one, and even though he knew the Nahm would affect him as well, it was a sacrifice he had to make in order to defeat Rahel and save Ashkaar. He was never allowed to use Nahms in the first place, not without a Deva's permission. From the Devas' standpoint, it was a win-win situation.

And compared to killing and standing in the blood of his own people, this was a thousand times better.

But with this, he couldn't go back to Yalim.

<hr />

"That's our signal!" Mikael warned. The rest of the Devas flew up before the golden wave could hit them. If they had been even a second late, they, too, would have been caught in the undoing Nahm of Daybreak. Ismat made sure that the Teiyyans were pinned to the ground, and Eiwa blinded the enemy with her light to make sure they wouldn't try to fly off before the spell could work.

The Nahm rustled past the enemies, causing the cursed Teiyyans to stay still as stone before they turned into dust.

"May you find peace in the next life," Mikael whispered from his place above the town's wreckage.

When all was done, Leka gestured as if wiping something away in the air and the dome that had covered the entire town faded away like settling mist. The shield Rahel had put up also faded.

The chains holding Rahel to the ground came undone. He tried to stand up, but his energy was depleted and he fell to his knees. Mafuyu held a blade to this throat, silently communicating that if he made the slightest offensive move, Mafuyu wouldn't think twice before detaching his head from his neck.

He held Rahel there until he heard the Devas flying toward them.

Mirai limped to a furious and seething Rahel.

"You ungrateful bastard," Rahel hissed. "The Raathri raised you when your parents were dead, and in return, you slaughtered them like animals. Even now, you didn't even think twice before turning your back on us again. You are a traitor, Bezaleel, and you will always be known as one till the day you die."

Mirai parted his lips to speak for himself when another voice intervened.

"Bezaleel remained loyal to his nation," Eiwa said as her feet gently grazed the ground and she landed beside Mirai. "To his duty. He valued innocent lives above his own pride and emotions. You were starting a needless war, and Bezaleel stopped it. He saved the people as any Deva would have."

Mikael joined Mirai and placed a hand on his back, quickly healing him from the poison hidden in the blade, which might have otherwise been his undoing.

Rahel chuckled grimly. "Saved the people? He brought death upon the people that loved him. Didn't you, Bezaleel?"

Eiwa remained silent, feeling that it wasn't her place to speak about an incident that lay so close to Mirai's heart and beyond her realm. Mafuyu watched Mirai from the corner of his eyes, ready to defend him if need be.

But there was none when Mirai spoke. "No, you did."

"That's right." Rahel's voice dripped with venom. "And I enjoyed every moment of it."

Darkness passed over Mirai's eyes. The calm demeanor he always exuded came undone; the mercy in his nature vanished. Without giving Rahel the pleasure of seeing his despair, he swiped the sword from Mafuyu's hand before the boy could so much as protest and drove it through Rahel's chest.

Mirai had always resisted the bloodlust that ran through his Raathri veins, but for this moment, he gave in.

Rahel parted his lips in a silent, pained gasp as the blade pierced his heart and he coughed out blood. But even as his life left him, he remained fearless. There was only scorn in his eyes as he stared at Mirai. Slowly, the shaken concrete beneath him pooled with blood. Rahel narrowed his eyes at Mirai one last time before his muscles relaxed and he went limp.

Mirai's shoulders eased. *Finally*, it was all over. The threat that had tormented him for years was no more.

He turned to the Devas as Eiwa took a step forward to stand in front of him. There was no doubt that the Devas were worn out. Their bright clothes were dull with mud and dirt, and torn in places. Their skin was marred from fresh cuts and bruises, and they had probably come close to depleting their energy after using so much of it to cast the Nahms needed to fight the cursed Teiyyans and keep the people safe.

Roughly two-thirds of the town was in ruins. Buildings had collapsed or were in shambles. The cobblestone ground was overturned in some places and had cracks and craters deep enough to be a shallow well in others. Dust and mud had flown everywhere, and Mirai could still hear bricks and debris falling from one or two buildings that couldn't stand upright any longer from the damage they had taken.

Eiwa was going to have a tough time building Marim up again.

But even so, her face did not reveal even the slightest hint of exhaustion. The Devas stood upright as if they had enough strength and energy to repeat this fight all over again, though Mirai knew better.

"Bezaleel," Eiwa started. "You have saved us again." Despite her words, Mirai tensed. He knew what came next would not be words of apology or praise. "Even so, we cannot overlook the laws you have broken in the last thirteen years."

In any other situation, Mafuyu would have intervened if someone put down his friend. But this was a world of laws that he had no knowledge of, and seeing Mirai accept it without a single protest made Mafuyu feel it was better to remain quiet.

"You stole parts of the Forbidden Scroll, opened the gates to Yalim, flew into Messai-Tor without permission, injured the Devas' most trusted soldiers, and interrupted our summit."

At that, though, Mafuyu had to say something in Mirai's defense. "He did that because there was no other choice! He did it to save Ashkaar! To save you!"

Eiwa raised her hand and Mafuyu instantly bit his tongue. "Your more serious crimes lie in the fact that you used the stolen Nahms in Yalim, made their people aware of the existence of Ashkaar, Teiyyans, and the Devas. You even brought back a human from that world. You upset the balance of the Jihan, which the Devas have protected for centuries."

"I understand." Mirai did not put up a fight and Mafuyu felt more bothered by that than anything.

"Then you know I cannot let either of you leave Alayl after this. Normally, you would be executed or at least banished for what you've done. But for helping the Devas, you will be imprisoned and serve your time for the thirteen years that you went rogue." Eiwa turned to Mafuyu. "You, on the other hand, will be watched by one of my spies at all times, and I'm afraid I cannot let you return to Yalim."

Mirai and Mafuyu exchanged glances. Mirai knew the moment he decided to come back to Ashkaar that he would be met with his punishment, and he had already made peace with that. Mafuyu looked heartbroken. Angry. Ready to burst into tears from both anger and sadness at the thought of Mirai's imprisonment—less so at the idea of him not being able to return to his own world.

After all of this, it just seemed cruel.

Mafuyu glared at the Devas. "This is unjustified! Bezaleel sacrificed everything to save you Devas and your nations! You can't—"

"But," Eiwa said, cutting him off for the second time. "For everything you have done for us, from saving Alayl from a coup to protecting the Devas and Ashkaar itself not once, but twice, I'll consider your crimes negated and I will let you both return to Yalim under one condition."

Mafuyu and Mirai looked at each other, both wearing the same astounded expression.

The Devas glanced at each other as well, and in their gazes Mirai realized that they had already planned this before they had even decided to come back to Alayl. But he wouldn't have guessed in a thousand years what that one condition would be.

CHAPTER FORTY-EIGHT

RETURN

Nagisa relentlessly cut down one First-Level after another. Her shoulders and chest heaved up and down as she tried to take gulps of air in between the swings of her sword. Her feet burned and the skin on her fingertips had torn some time ago, but still she fought.

Her eyes quickly ran around the group of Hunters. Their numbers had gone down by more than half since this fight began. Her teammates were still standing, but if this carried on any longer there wouldn't be a single Hunter left by the end of the night.

"Ayumi!" Nagisa yelled out when a ghostly Second-Level reached for her from behind.

In a rush, and not having enough time to push her away, Nagisa stepped between them.

"Captain!" Ayumi shrieked.

A biting gust of wind cut off anything else she might have said.

Nagisa turned around and covered her eyes with the crook of her elbow. It was so brief that she barely even felt the wind when it blew past them. All the Hunters were enveloped in a cloud of flowing black dust before it scattered into nothing.

What followed was perfect, absolute stillness. No sounds of weapons clashing against another. No growling Second-Levels. No Hunters screaming. No sounds of a battlefield. Just the forest at night: a hundred crickets and an owl hooting somewhere in the distance.

The Hunters hesitantly uncovered their eyes. Nagisa looked around in bewilderment. All of the Second-Levels had vanished. Except for Zephyr's lifeless body on the ground, only the Hunters remained.

A lopsided grin made its way to Nagisa's lips. *Those two. They did it.*

She turned toward the other Hunters.

A second of silence, and then a triumphant yell erupted from them. They raised their swords in unison and cried out in victory, thrilled to be alive to see another day.

"You'll be fine. Rest right now and try not to move a lot," Nagisa said to one of the Hunters as she helped tend to their injuries.

"Captain, you need rest, too." Hiro chided as he walked up to her. "You've been going about nonstop."

"I'll get around to it," she replied. "How many did we lose?"

"One hundred and sixty-eight. I've already informed Zen. He will send in more medics for the rest."

"Good work, Hiro." When all Nagisa got was pointed silence as a response, she pressed, "What is it?"

"The First-Level. Who was he? He seemed like he knew you," Hiro replied. "He said something about Yalim. What are we missing here, Captain?"

If Nagisa could, she would have cursed out loud. She didn't have a proper excuse to give. She couldn't tell them about Ashkaar and Teiyyans, but she couldn't lie and lose the trust of her teammates either.

When all of the Hunters came around, they would definitely have questions that demanded answers. Answers that neither Nagisa nor Zen could give without raising even more questions or revealing crucial information. She knew fighting this war would come with a price, but she was hoping to have some time to prepare for what that meant.

Nagisa had come up with a quick excuse, but she didn't have the chance to give it before Hiro's eyes focused on something else behind her. In his irises she saw the reflection of a blue light.

She whipped around. A circle had appeared on the ground and from it the blue light rose up in a long, cylindrical shape. It was the same as what Zephyr had stepped out of before.

Some of the Hunters who had enough energy to at least move stood up, and Nagisa wondered if more enemies were coming. If they were, there was no way the battered Hunters would last.

A leg popped out of the Veyil, followed by another pair. Two figures then stepped out and Nagisa released a slow breath of relief when Mafuyu walked out with Mirai, who looked like his human self. No wings. No white hair. Normal eyes.

One of Mirai's arms was thrown over Mafuyu's shoulder as the younger man supported half his weight. They both looked worn out, Mirai especially.

Even though Nagisa couldn't be happier to see them alive, they couldn't have picked a more terrible time to portal home. Seeing Mafuyu and Mirai step out of the same light that the First-Level did just hours ago? Now there was no chance that the Hunters would be satisfied with half-baked answers.

Mirai could hardly take another step. Once his mind relaxed, weariness hit him like a bus. The last Nahm he used had zapped all his energy, not to mention the poison that had infiltrated his system before Mikael took it out.

His head felt light and his body was swaying. His legs couldn't handle his weight any longer and he dipped toward the floor. Mafuyu stumbled as Mirai started to fall, then lost his balance as the older man's weight pulled Mafuyu along with him. But Mirai didn't hit the cold ground. Instead, he felt a warm hand take his other arm while another snaked across his waist to hold him steady.

"I've got you," Nagisa whispered.

Mirai said nothing; his full smile and the light squeeze he gave her shoulder spoke more than anything words could have conveyed. Yes, she'd had his back from the very beginning, and that was something Mirai always relied on.

"Well, well." Mikael's soothing voice preceded him as he, too, stepped out of the portal. "So, this is Yalim." His lavender eyes traveled across the field and the Hunters who looked at him with jaws dropped and eyes full of disbelief. Some of them even reached for their weapons.

But this didn't seem to faze the Deva. "I must say, it is rather lackluster compared to Ashkaar." He spoke in Zalek. "I don't see why you like it so much, Bezaleel. A bit of a wrong place for you, is it not?"

"It is where I found the right people," he replied in the same tongue. In saying so, he pulled Mafuyu and Nagisa a tad bit closer to his sides.

"In that case." Mikael came to a stop beside Mafuyu. He muttered a Nahm, placed his thumb and middle finger together, and snapped. A light drizzle fell from the sky.

"What—?" Nagisa looked up at the sky, which was clear only seconds ago, but then suddenly covered with rain clouds. Her view was blocked when Mikael raised his dark blue wing over her and her two companions.

Nagisa looked at the Deva curiously, and Mikael nodded with a small smile of acknowledgement. For reasons unknown, Nagisa felt a sense of familiarity and found herself nodding back.

"It's for their memory," Mikael spoke in a hushed tone. "Anyone standing under this rain of mine won't remember anything that I don't want them to remember."

Sure enough, the rest of the Hunters seemed to be in a daze.

Their eyes were heavily lidded and they stood in a trance. Some of them mindlessly sat back down, as if they were hypnotized.

Mikael looked at Zephyr's body and whispered another Nahm. The Teiyyan vanished into thin air and the three under his wing turned to look at him. "Getting rid of evidence." Mikael winked at Mirai. "Well, I'd best be going." The rain stopped and he pulled back his wing. "Be well, Bezaleel."

Mirai felt Mikael slip something into his pocket as he brushed past him. "You as well, my lord," he replied and pretended not to notice the feeling of the paper he'd pushed inside his pocket.

Mikael nodded and walked into the Veyil. As soon as he did, the light vanished and the portal closed.

"Captain?" Hiro called out. Nagisa looked at him, searching his face for any traces of doubt or suspicion. "Quick, we need to treat Mirai!"

Nagisa glanced at the two by her side before walking Mirai toward Hiro and the medics. She sat him down with his back against a tree, and Mafuyu followed suit, dropping down beside him as fast as a falling raindrop.

<hr>

The medics inspected the two for any major injuries, but only found minor scars.

Everyone behaved in their usual manner, as if no one had seen a magical portal open before their eyes, or a First-Level step out of it with Mirai and Mafuyu. In fact, they believed both men had been fighting alongside the Hunters this whole time.

"Hiro," Nagisa called out.

Hiro had been sitting on a log, wrapping a bandage around a Hunter's arm. He stood up when his captain neared him. "Has anything strange happened after the fight?" Nagisa spoke in a voice barely above a whisper and stood close to him.

Hiro raised his eyebrow in question and his lips twitched into a confused smile. "Captain, you've got to define 'strange.' If you haven't noticed, we don't work with anything normal."

"Have you noticed anything else after the fight?" She searched for the right words to say without sparking any suspicion if there wasn't any. "Did any other First-Levels show up?"

Hiro shook his head. "Just the one we fought and the Second- and Third-Levels. And we pretty much had to kill him to save our own, so I don't think we'll be getting any answers from him. His body even disappeared right after. But I wonder why there was such a sudden attack in the first place. It's going to be real hard to investigate."

So, he didn't remember the portal that Zephyr stepped out from or the other First-Level appearing alongside Mafuyu and Mirai. Or rather, Mikael had altered his memory, the memories of everyone who stood under the rain. Good.

Hiro let out a small smile when he realized Nagisa's thoughts had run up to the clouds. "Don't worry, Captain. I'm sure there isn't any more danger. We fought the Rev'ers and we survived. We can figure out the why and how later."

Nagisa relaxed her shoulders. "Yes, I suppose you're right."

Hiro nodded and she dragged her tired, aching legs back to Mirai.

"You look like you've seen hell," Mirai commented as she flopped down beside him.

"I think hell wouldn't be so bad," Nagisa replied as she clutched her stomach. A pain that she hadn't noticed before surged through her when her body relaxed. She leaned in closer to Mirai and whispered, "The Hunters don't remember anything about the Veyil or the other First-Level. He successfully altered their memories. Now all I have to do is give them a believable story about this fight later." She tilted her face to look at Mirai directly. As close as they were, Nagisa realized that Mirai smelled of pine trees and the forest. It was comforting. "Who was that First-Level?"

"Mikael, Deva of Jabilsa." he whispered back.

Nagisa smiled. "So, that was a Deva."

"Magnificent, aren't they?"

Nagisa gave a nonchalant shrug. "Not as much as you." She grinned and Mirai returned it.

Mafuyu's whisper cut in. "You would change your mind if you saw Eiwa."

"Then maybe next time I should go instead of you."

"Ha! Keep wishing, Captain."

Mirai laughed and Nagisa caught herself thinking that she had never seen him so wholeheartedly happy before.

CHAPTER FORTY-NINE

SEARCHING

The day following the war, and after returning back to headquarters, Nagisa fed the Hunters a story about what caused the fight between them and the Rev'ers, before anyone could raise any questions.

She gave a convincing explanation of how the Jihan had weakened, causing Rev'ers to break out like a swarm of bees. Without giving away much about Teiyyans and Ashkaar, she had also admitted the possibility of First-Levels in the Jihan, said that they weren't related to humans despite how they look, and that, once they discovered that they could cross over to this world, had tried to take over it for reasons unknown. And they tried to do it by controlling the Second- and Third-Levels. They were able to cut the plot off at the knees because Mirai was in Iwami and had detected more Rev'er activity than ever before.

But because Zephyr had died, the organization wasn't completely sure what the First-Levels wanted or where they were coming from. They were stuck with a dead end, and the only way they could carry on an investigation was if another one showed up. She could tell from their reactions that the Hunters hoped to God that wouldn't happen again. They had gone to hell and back, and could all do without any First-Levels giving them a run for their lives. And if that meant never knowing more about them, then so be it.

Nagisa and Mirai later realized that that was probably the reason why Mikael kept their memory of Zephyr intact, so that they would know the pain and horror of fighting a First-Level, and in return, they would be reluctant to pursue them.

And though it seemed like the Hunters would continue the investigation on First-Levels if they got the chance, in all truth, Zen had closed the case record. There was no need to pursue it. They had to keep the secrets of Ashkaar from the Hunters to protect the balance of both worlds. But Nagisa knew if a time ever came when she had to spill the secrets to her teammates, they would give their lives to protect it.

Zen made a speech for the ones that lost their lives during the funeral. Their names were later carved into the wall of the building's main hallway, honoring them for giving their lives, and saving others in turn.

The following days passed in peace and rest for the Hunters. Those severely wounded in the fight remained at headquarters to be treated. Nagisa was forced into bed rest since she had a habit of being too impatient for medical treatments to actually have any effect. Zen strictly told her to rest and took her off the job until she made a full recovery.

Some requested time off, while others weren't fazed as much. With that, things returned back to normal. Or, as normal as the life of a Hunter could get.

Two weeks had gone by. Mirai was back to working in his flower shop, and Mafuyu still stayed with him in his apartment. Mirai hadn't said anything to Mafuyu about his continuing to stay there, or about him leaving. They carried on as usual, but Mafuyu knew that Mirai was just being mindful of his injuries and letting him stay until he fully recovered.

But he was all healed up by now, and the time for him to leave was drawing near. He didn't want to impose on the man any longer, but he had one last thing to do before he bid his friend farewell.

Mafuyu pushed open the door to Hanamatsuri Flower Shop. The bell above tinkled, filling Mafuyu with a sense of nostalgia.

Mirai was tending to one of his blooms and turned around when he heard the bell. Upon seeing Mafuyu, he smiled.

He had been doing more of that lately. Unlike the before, when his smile was just an empty tug of his lips, these were genuine. They shone in his eyes.

Mirai had also become much more at ease, and it only made Mafuyu realize how heavy a burden the man had been carrying all this time.

"Do you need help with that?" Mafuyu asked as he walked up to the man.

"Oh? And to think that the first time I asked you, you threw such a fit."

"Hey, I didn't even know you back then and the first thing you asked me was to haul a heavy bag of fertilizer."

Mirai laughed at the memory. Mafuyu chuckled along, but it faded quickly when he remembered why he was there. "Um... There is something I need to tell you."

"What is it?"

Mafuyu's eyes traced Mirai's face while he searched for the right words to say. He didn't know how to break it to him, how to put it mildly enough that Mirai wouldn't overreact. But he had to tell him. He had gone back and forth to Zen countless times to find what he was looking for. He had done that for Mirai.

Mafuyu stared into the depths of Mirai's grey eyes and finally said, "Your brother. Tetsu. He is here in Tokyo looking for you."

The only answer Mafuyu got was the loud clatter of the scissors hitting the floor as they slipped from Mirai's fingers.

"What?" Mirai's voice was just above a whisper, weighed down by confusion and doubt. Other than the movement of his lips, he was perfectly still.

Had he heard Mafuyu correctly?

"Tetsu is in Tokyo," Mafuyu repeated. "He has been for the past six months." He bent to pick the scissors up off the floor and motioned for Mirai to sit on the chair by the counter. "After the incident in Iwami, Tetsu started living with his aunt and uncle." Mafuyu placed the scissors on the countertop and moved to stand in front of Mirai. "He moved to Tokyo six months back to attend an arts college. Those students that went missing in Aokigahara were from his school. He came across the Rev'er Hunter Corps after that. He met with Zen and begged him to find you. He didn't know that you were one of us."

"Did Zen...?"

Mafuyu shook his head. "No, he didn't say anything. He told me it was up to you to decide." Mafuyu dug into the pocket of his jeans and took out his phone. After a few taps across the screen he showed it to Mirai. "That's his address."

Mirai stared at the words and numbers. "I can't." He shook his head and repeated, "I can't. Because of me his parents...his life... He would never forgive me for all of that."

"If that was the case, he wouldn't keep searching for you. He came to Tokyo because he thought there would be a better chance of finding you."

"I don't know how to face him."

"I think this is something that you need to do. It's time you free yourself."

"I don't know how."

"You start by forgiving yourself. If it's hard for you to do it alone, I'll come with you."

Mirai's shoulders lost some of their stiffness with his reassurance. "Alright. I'll close up."

Mafuyu nodded. Mirai seemed fine as he went about closing, but the slight tremble of his fingers as he closed the shop and the silent worried sighs that left his lips didn't go unnoticed.

CHAPTER FIFTY

BROTHERS

The pair stood in front of the wicket gate to the house that Tetsu currently lived in. Mirai stared at it for a good long moment, almost boring holes into it with the intensity of his gaze. He'd never been so unsure about anything in his life. Even turning his back against his clan and springing at the Devas was a much easier decision.

Mafuyu nudged him with his shoulder, snapping the man back to the present. Mirai let out a deep breath and mustered courage before pushing the gate open. He took a couple of steps into the yard, with Mafuyu following closely behind, but stopped when the door to the house opened.

The person who stepped out was none other than Tetsu himself. He held a watering can in his hand and had his back turned to the pair as he closed the door behind him. Then he turned around.

When his eyes fell on Mirai, the boy went rigid, as if an icy wind had swept over him and left him frozen. His fingers loosened around the handle of the can and it fell to the ground, splashing water over his feet and onto the marble tiles.

Mirai was just as still. Neither knew what to do or what to say.

The first one to break the silence was Tetsu. "Nii...san?"

"Tetsu." Mirai found his voice, assuring the other that it was indeed him.

The next thing he knew, Tetsu hurtled toward him and his arms had enveloped him in a tight embrace. His face was buried in Mirai's shoulder and his back heaved as he broke into heavy sobs.

"Where have you been? I've been looking everywhere for you!" Tetsu lifted his face, fresh tears streaming from his tired eyes. "I thought you'd died."

Mirai's guilt made it difficult to keep his gaze on Tetsu, so his eyes drooped to the path below his feet. "I'm sorry. I'm so sorry."

"Why are you apologizing?"

"Because of me, your parents...our friends...your home..."

"How is any of that because of you?"

"That night, those people came looking for me. But I would never have thought in a million years that they would follow me there, that something like that would ever happen. You and your family gave me a home. If I could turn back time, I would—"

Mirai's apologies were cut off as warm hands gently cupped his cheeks and forced him to meet Tetsu's eyes.

Mirai had thought of this moment more times than he could count, replayed it in his head on a continuous loop during the nights he lay awake. But his vision always ended terribly, with Tetsu calling him a monster, a cold-blooded killer. He should hate him for destroying his life, blame him for the death of his parents.

But when it was finally a reality, he was instead met with a kind smile.

Tetsu's eyes held the same sincerity and kindness that Mirai had seen in him as a child. He had a heart of gold and a pure soul: the rarest of traits. His words were sincere as he said, "Because of you, I was saved. Half our town was saved. I was able to live my life with people that cared about me. People that are alive because of you. How could I ever hate you for that?" He let his hands fall from Mirai's face. "I was always waiting for you to come back."

Mirai had no words. He hadn't truly prepared for this moment. The only way he could respond was with the tears that poured out of his eyes in a continuous, uncontrollable stream.

Every drop held the emotions he had locked up inside for years. He wiped his eyes, but they wouldn't stop. They fell as freely and easily as raindrops in monsoon season.

Tetsu wrapped him in his warmth until Mirai was able to get ahold of his emotions again.

Mafuyu watched the two brothers, glad that he was able to reunite them. Mirai deserved all the happiness this life could offer him.

He was finally with his brother again. Mafuyu's job here was done. As he watched them for a few moments more, he felt a wind caress his face—like the loving hand of a mother.

In the passing breeze, the air took the shape of two human figures. Mafuyu let his eyes follow them as they stood on either side of Mirai.

And then he recognized them: two silhouettes, transparent as water and almost shimmering like the reflection of the moon on a blue lake. These were the same figures he glimpsed back in the shrine. Now he could see them clearly. Mother and father, adorned in clothes that were not of this world but resembled the ones he'd seen in Ashkaar. They circled their arms around Mirai and pressed their faces against his tresses.

Mafuyu could easily guess who they were. They were Mirai's birth parents: Bezaleel's mom and dad.

They had always been watching over him, always guiding others around him to make sure their son was safe. Mafuyu felt like they were staring right at him, so he whispered, "Don't worry. I'll protect him."

The wind blew again and he could have sworn he saw a smile on both of their faces. They fluttered and then faded like mist. "Rest in peace," Mafuyu mouthed silently.

Mirai and Tetsu were smiling at each other, happy to get back the only family the two had left, to have found one another again.

This was no place for Mafuyu to linger, although that thought brought a prickling to his heart. He would have liked to belong.

A family so caring was something Mafuyu had never had.

Trying not to disturb them, Mafuyu turned around and headed for the gate.

"Mafuyu?" Mirai's voice stopped him in his tracks. Mafuyu turned around more quickly than he had intended and nearly stumbled. "Where are you going?" Mirai asked as if he'd never expected him to just leave.

"I...was..." He couldn't think of an explanation. Then again, what was he supposed to say?

"Is there anywhere else you'd rather be?" Mirai pressed.

Mafuyu shrugged casually, hands in the pockets of his trench coat. His lips stretched into a wide smile. "No. There is nowhere else I'd rather be." He trotted back over to Mirai and bowed to Tetsu in greeting. The other returned it.

"This is Mafuyu. He is my best friend. He's family, really," Mirai said.

Mafuyu tried his best to keep a straight face and not split his face with his grin.

"Would you like to come in for some tea?" Tetsu offered.

"I'd love to," Mafuyu replied. He jokingly added, "But only if you promise to tell me embarrassing stories about Mirai from when he was younger."

Tetsu laughed. "I've got plenty. But only if you promise to tell me some from his time with you."

"Oh, just wait. I've got tons from his boss."

"Deal."

"Is this what you call 'digging your own gave?'" Mirai mused.

The boys laughed, as did Mirai. He was finally free from all the torment that he had been carrying for years. He had his brother with him again, and his best friend was there to fight by his side.

They walked into the house, happiness echoing around them.

It was the start of a new beginning.

EPILOGUE

The Four Devas sat around the table, waiting patiently for the fifth to arrive. The winds of Messai-Tor howled, bringing with it the warm air of summer.

"Where is he? He's late." Ismat folded her arms across her chest and kept tapping her feet impatiently.

"Patience, Lady Ismat," Mikael's calm voice encouraged. He propped one leg on top of the other. "It's not easy as traveling from one nation to the other. He has to lift the Veyil. Give him some time."

Leka snorted. Mikael would have thought it was aimed at him, but the Deva's faraway gaze hinted that he'd reacted whilst thinking of something else.

"But honestly, I didn't think you would have made such a decision back then. To imprison him would have been the obvious choice, but to give him the position of the fifth Deva was unexpected."

"Yes, not much of a punishment I would say." Ismat raised an eyebrow, but her expression held no ill will.

Eiwa's lips turned into a half-smile as she thought about the reasons why she made said decision. "In a way, I would say it is. He wanted to be free of the chains that bound him to Ashkaar. And I had been thinking about this long before, even when my father was ruling; we need someone to watch over Yalim as well. Four hundred years ago, there was a disturbance in Yalim when the Veyil that held the worlds of Jihan apart weakened. Even though our ancestors came up with a solution, it wasn't a completely defined one. And then Rahel tried to take over; we weren't even aware until we were warned. I'm sure, as you all are, that this won't be the end of it. When one evil dies, another rises. We need a Deva in Yalim to help us keep the balance." Eiwa leaned forward and placed her elbows on the table. "Besides, he has saved Ashkaar twice and he doesn't deserve to be punished for that. His assistance in ending the war was enough to make up for the laws he broke. So that was the condition I gave him; he could return back to Yalim if he agreed to be its Deva and to come back whenever Ashkaar needed him. Whether it's to attend the Devas summit or for any other reason." Eiwa looked around at the others. "That is fair, do you not agree?"

"I agree," Leka replied and the other Devas nodded in kind.

They heard the sound of boots thudding and the creak of the heavy oak doors to their meeting chamber as they opened.

The Four Devas turned their heads as the fifth one walked toward them. "Finally," Ismat muttered.

"You're late," Leka joined in.

"Apologies. I'll make it in time for the next summit."

The fifth was dressed in a Deva's attire. His long black robes reached all the way down to his ankles. He wore grey pants beneath that tucked into his raven black boots. Beautiful and intricate works of golden designs lined his sleeves, collar and hem of his robe. A red belt was tied around his waist, and the symbol of the Deva was etched in red onto the back of his shirt.

Eiwa formally greeted him as he made his way to his seat at the table.

"Welcome back, Lord Bezaleel."

PRONUNCIATION GUIDE

Adelyn – Ad-el-in
Abel – Ah-bel
Alayl – Al-lay-il
Ashkaar – Ah-sh-kaar
Azumi – Aa-zu-mi
Bezaleel – Beh-za-lel
Barna – Bar-na
Eiwa – Ei-wa (Guardian)
Eben – Eh-ben
Ilir – E-leer
Ismat – Is-mah-th
Jabilsa – Jah-bil-za
Kefir – Keh-feer
Leka – Lek-ka
Mirai – Mee-rai
Mafuyu – Ma-fu-you
Mikael – Mee-ka-el
Marvak – Mar-Vek
Mesai-Tor – Meh-sai-tor
Nagisa – Nag-ee-sah
Rasa – Rah-sah
Rahel – Rah-hel (Death/he who is on a journey)
Reiko – Ray-ko
Shinichiro – Shin-ee-chee-ro
Seylon – Say-lon
Tetsu – Tet-su

Tumwi – *Toom-vee*
Varos – *Vah-ros*
Zephyr – *Zeh-feer*

ABOUT THE AUTHOR

Ameena Juveiria Navab (AJ Navab) writes action-packed fantasy fiction stories. Born in 1996, she is the only child of her loving parents and currently lives in the United Arab Emirates.

She first began penning her stories at the age of seven. After earning a degree in journalism at Manipal University Dubai, she worked in the industry as a writer and sub-editor before deciding she'd rather write her own stories and share her imagination with the world. When she isn't furiously scribbling out a new adventure, she spends her time watching anime, painting and traveling.

What does an author stand to gain by asking for reader feedback? A lot. In fact, what we can gain is so important in the publishing world, that they've coined a catchy name for it.

It's called "social proof." And in this age of social media sharing, without social proof, an author may as well be invisible.

So if you've enjoyed *Daybreak*, please consider giving it some visibility by reviewing it on Amazon or Goodreads. A review doesn't have to be a long critical essay. Just a few words expressing your thoughts, which could help potential readers decide whether they would enjoy it, too.

www.ingramcontent.com/pod-product-compliance
Lightning Source LLC
Chambersburg PA
CBHW051159190726
48288CB00006B/1718